THE AMERICAN GUN MYSTERY

ELLERY QUEEN was a pen name created and shared by two cousins, Frederic Dannay (1905-1982) and Manfred B. Lee (1905-1971), as well as the name of their most famous detective. Born in Brooklyn, they spent forty-two years writing the greatest puzzle mysteries of their time, gaining the duo a reputation as the foremost American authors of the Golden Age "fair play" mystery.

Besides co-writing the Queen novels, Dannay founded *Ellery Queen's Mystery Magazine*, one of the most influential crime publications of all time. Although Dannay outlived his cousin by nine years, he retired the fictional Queen upon Lee's death.

OTTO PENZLER, the creator of American Mystery Classics, is also the founder of the Mysterious Press (1975), a literary crime imprint; MysteriousPress.com (2011), an electronic-book publishing company; Penzler Publishers (2018); and New York City's Mysterious Bookshop (1979). He has won a Raven, the Ellery Queen Award, two Edgars (for the *Encyclopedia of Mystery and Detection*, 1977, and *The Lineup*, 2010), and lifetime achievement awards from NoirCon and *The Strand Magazine*. He has edited more than 70 anthologies and written extensively about mystery fiction. To learn more, visit his website at MysteriousBookshop.com

THE AMERICAN GUN MYSTERY

ELLERY QUEEN

Introduction by
OTTO PENZLER

AMERICAN MYSTERY CLASSICS

Penzler Publishers
New York

Published in 2021 by Penzler Publishers
58 Warren Street, New York, NY 10007
penzlerpublishers.com

Distributed by W. W. Norton

Cover image: Andy Ross
Cover design: Mauricio Diaz

Paperback ISBN 9781613162521
Hardcover ISBN 9781613162514

Library of Congress Control Number: 2021914487

Printed in the United States of America

9 8 7 6 5 4 3 2 1

INTRODUCTION

ALTHOUGH IT is fair to say that he was not the equal of John Dickson Carr in the arena of locked room mysteries (but, then, no one is), Ellery Queen nonetheless had the other-worldly ability to create some of the most baffling conundrums in the history of the mystery category.

In *The American Gun Mystery*, the sixth episode in the career of Ellery Queen, the author, and Ellery Queen, the detective, the background is a rodeo, set—not in Wyoming or the Dakotas—but in New York City at the Collosseum, the newest and largest indoor sports facility in the city. The headliner in Wild Bill Grant's rodeo is Buck Horne, the once enormously popular silent film cowboy whose career has fallen on hard times after the talkies pushed aside the silents and tastes changed. Still, though now regarded as an old-timer, his charisma and nostalgic presence has helped fill the seats with 20,000 viewers, including a great many celebrities, among whom are Ellery and Richard Queen, the gifted amateur detective and the high-ranking police officer.

The show is scheduled to open with a bang, and it did, though not quite as planned. Buck leads a charge of forty whooping and hollering cowboys around the arena until they pull their guns out of their holsters and, as a synchronized cadre, simultaneously fire into the air. Buck falls to the ground and is trampled by the racing horses. Quickly examined, he is discovered to have been shot with a .25 caliber bullet. The police instantly lock the doors so that no one can leave until they have been thoroughly searched.

The offending weapon has completely vanished.

This is, of course, standard for Queen novels, as an opening situation in which a murder is committed appears so confounding that it may be insoluble. If it weren't, the police would handle it and not have to bring Ellery to the scene to help them figure out what happened, how it was achieved, and who did it.

The tantalizing puzzles created by the Ellery Queen writing team are irresistible to anyone who enjoys fair-play detective stories, no matter how bizarre or impossible they may seem—the hallmark of what is often called the Golden Age of the detective novel, the years between the two World Wars that produced some of the most iconic names in the history of mystery. In England, the names Agatha Christie and Dorothy L. Sayers continue to resonate to the present day. In America, there is one name that towers above the rest, and that is Ellery Queen.

That famous name was the brainchild of two Brooklyn-born cousins, Frederic Dannay (born Daniel Nathan, he changed his name to Frederic as a tribute to Chopin, with Dannay merely a combination of the first two syllables of his birth name) and Manfred B. Lee (born Manford Lepofsky). They wanted a simple nom de plume and had the brilliant stroke of inspiration to employ Ellery Queen as both their byline and as the name of their protagonist, reckoning that readers might forget one or the other but not both.

Dannay was a copywriter and art director for an advertising agency while Lee was writing publicity and advertising material for a motion picture company when they were attracted by a $7,500 prize offered by *McClure's* magazine in 1928; they were twenty-three years old.

They were informed that their submission, *The Roman Hat Mystery*, had won the contest but, before the book could be published or the prize money handed over, *McClure's* went bankrupt. Its assets were assumed by *Smart Set* magazine, which gave the prize to a different novel that it thought would have greater appeal to women. Frederick A. Stokes decided to publish *The Roman Hat Mystery* anyway, thus beginning one of the most successful mystery series in the history of the genre. Since the contest had required that books be submitted under pseudonyms, the simple but memorable Ellery Queen name, born out of necessity, became an icon.

The success of the novels got them Hollywood offers and they went to write for Columbia, Paramount, and MGM, though they never received any screen credits. The popular medium of radio also called to them and they wrote all the scripts for the successful *Ellery Queen* radio series for nine years from 1939 to 1948. In an innovative approach, they interrupted the narration so that Ellery could ask his guests—well-known personalities— to solve the case as they now had all the necessary clues. The theories almost invariably in vain, the program would then proceed, revealing the correct solution. The Queen character was also translated into a comic strip character and several television series starring Richard Hart, Lee Bowman, Hugh Marlowe, George Nader, Lee Philips, and, finally, Jim Hutton.

While Lee had no particular affection for mystery fiction, always hoping to become the Shakespeare of the twentieth century, Dannay had been interested in detective stories since his boyhood. He wanted to produce a magazine of quality mystery stories in all sub-genres and founded *Mystery* in 1933 but it failed after four issues when the publisher went bankrupt. However, after Dannay's long convalescence from a 1940 automobile accident that nearly took his life, he created *Ellery Queen's Mystery Magazine*; the first issue appeared in 1941 and remains the leading mystery fiction magazine in the world to the present day.

Although Dannay and Lee were lifelong collaborators on their novels and short stories, they had very different personalities and frequently disagreed, often vehemently, in what Lee once described as "a marriage made in hell." Dannay was a quiet, scholarly introvert, noted as a perfectionist. Lee was impulsive and assertive, given to explosiveness and earthy language. They remained steadfast in their refusal to divulge their working methodology, claiming that over their many years together they had tried every possible combination of their skills and talent to produce the best work they could. However, upon close examination of their letters and conversations with their friends and family, it eventually became clear that, in almost all instances, it was Dannay who created the extraordinary plots and Lee who brought them to life.

Each resented the other's ability, with Dannay once writing that he was aware that Lee regarded him as nothing more than "a clever contriver." Dannay's ingenious plots, fiendishly detailed with strict adherence to the notion of playing fair with readers, remain unrivalled by any American mystery author. Yet he did not have the literary skill to make characters plausible, settings visual, or dialogue resonant. Lee, on the other hand, with his dreams of writing important fiction, had no ability to invent stories, although he could improve his cousin's creations to make the characters come to life and the plots suspenseful and compelling.

The combined skills of the collaborators produced the memorable Ellery Queen figure, though in the early books he was clearly based on the best-selling Philo Vance character created by S.S. Van Dine. The Vance books had taken the country by storm in the 1920s so it was no great leap of imagination for Dannay and Lee to model their detective after him. In all candor, both Vance and the early Queen character were insufferable, showing off their supercilious attitude and pedantry at every possible opportunity.

When Queen made his debut in *The Roman Hat Mystery*, he was ostensibly an author but spends precious little time working at his career. He appears to have unlimited time to collect books and help his father, Inspector Richard Queen, solve cases. Although close to his father, the arrogant young man is often condescending to him as he loves to show off his erudition. As the series progresses (and as the appetite for Philo Vance diminished), Ellery becomes a far more realistic and likable character.

"Ellery Queen *is* the American detective story," as Anthony Boucher, the mystery reviewer for the *New York Times*, wrote, and it would be impossible for any reasonable person to disagree.

—OTTO PENZLER

THE AMERICAN
GUN MYSTERY

To C. RAYMOND EVERITT
for one reason

and

ALBERT FOSTER, Jr. *for another*

FOREWORD

FOR THE half-dozenth time in a quartet of years I find myself confronted with the formidable task of introducing a new work from the pen of my friend, Ellery Queen. It seems only yesterday that I sat down to write a preface to *The Roman Hat Mystery*, that historic case which I bullied Ellery into fictionizing—the first Queen adventure to be put between covers; and yet that was over four years ago!

Now, so contagious is recognition of authentic genius, whether it is in the creation of a new *ocracy* or a new crime-story *métier*, Ellery Queen has become a symbol of the unusual in detective fiction in America. In England he had been hailed by no less distinguished a critic than the *London Times* as "the logical successor to Sherlock Holmes"; and on the Continent, where (as Vivoudiére says in his florid but earnest tribute) "*M. Queen a pris d'assaut les remparts des cyniques de lettres,*" he has been translated into a polyglot of tongues (yea, even unto the Scandinavian), so that his bookshelves bristle with unfamiliar-sounding titles and his correspondence alone provides his son and her with a steady supply of foreign stamps which would delight the soul of even a less enthusiastic minor philatelist. In the light of such recognition, therefore—I am tempted to say "fame," but that would probably cost me my friend—there is little I can offer which would not be sheer repetition. On the other hand, it should prove of interest to Ellery Queen's readers to get his personal view on the case which forms the basis of the present volume. I quote verbatim a letter dated some months ago:

> My long-suffering J.J.:
>
> Now that the pestiferous Egyptian is safely tucked into his sarcophagus and the lid clamped down, perhaps I shall have time to work on a problem whose actual inception and solution you no doubt recall from history and some conversations of importance between us. For some time I've been yearning to do the Horne case. What an affair it was that centered about that salty old character, Buck Horne, and that agitated these rapacious brains some years ago!
>
> It isn't so much because I am endeared to my own cleverness in that fantastic brush with criminality that I propose to write my next opus around it. Oh, yes, the reasoning was interesting enough, and the investigation was not without its moments, I grant all that. But it's not these things. Rather it's the odd nature of the background.
>
> I am, as you know, essentially a creature of cities; even in matters of practicality I must have my feet on the asphalt rather than the turfy ground. Well, sir, the dramatic *débâcle* at our w.k. bowl which precipitated me into that improbable adventure also succeeded in wrenching me from the familiar gasoline atmosphere of our fair city and thrusting me into a strongly scented atmosphere indeed!—of stables, horses, alkali, cattle, branding-irons, ranchos. . . .
>
> In a word, J.J., your correspondent found himself conducting an inquiry into a murder which might have been committed a hundred years ago in—in, well, old Texas, suh, or Wyoming itself, from which so many of the principals came. At any moment I expected a yelling Piute—or is it Siwash?—to materialize out of the arena's horsy air and come galloping at me with uplifted, thirsty tomahawk. . . .
>
> At any rate, J.J., this florid explanation is to announce that my forthcoming *chef-d'oeuvre* will deal with cowpunchers, six-shooters,

lariats, hosses, alfalfa, chaps—and, lest you think I have gone West of the Great Divide on you, let me hasten to add that this epic of the plains takes place—as it did—in the heart of New York City, with that fair metropolis's not unpleasing *ha-cha* as a sort of Greek chorus to the rattle of musketry.

Faithfully, etc., etc.

I have myself read the manuscript of *The American Gun Mystery* with my unfailing avidity; and in my opinion the Ellery Queen 'scutcheon remains gloriously untarnished, if indeed a new gloss has not been imparted to that brave *relique*. This latest episode from the intellectual exploits of my friend is every bit as stimulating to the connoisseur as *The Greek Coffin Mystery, The Dutch Shoe Mystery,* or any of the others in the Queen cycle; and possesses besides a tangy flavor pleasantly and peculiarly its own.

J.J. McC

NEW YORK

February, 1933

" . . . now bend thy mind to feel
The first sharp motions of the forming wheel."

PREPARATORY: SPECTRUM

"To ME," said Ellery Queen, "a wheel is not a wheel unless it turns."

"That sounds suspiciously like pragmatism," I said.

"Call it what you like." He took off his *pince-nez* and began to scrub its shining lenses vigorously, as he always does when he is thoughtful. "I don't mean to say that I cannot recognize it as a material object *per se;* it's simply that it has no meaning for me until it begins to *function* as a wheel. That's why I always try to visualize a crime in motion. I'm not like Father Brown, who is intuitional; the good padre—bless his heart!—has only to squint dully at a single spoke. . . . You see what I'm driving at, J.J.?"

"No," I said truthfully.

"Let me make it clearer by example. You take the case of this preposterous and charming creature, Buck Horne. Well, certain things happened before the crime itself. I found out about them later. But my point is that, even had I—by some miraculous chance—been an invisible spectator to those little preambulatory events, they should have had no significance for me. The driving force, the crime, was lacking. The wheel was at rest."

"Still obscure," I said, "although I begin to grasp your meaning dimly."

He knit his straight brows, then relaxed with a chuckle, stretching his long lean limbs nearer the fire. He lighted a cigaret and puckered smoke at the ceiling. "Permit me to indulge that rotten vice of mine and play the metaphor out. . . . There was the case, the Horne case, our wheel. Imbedded in each spoke there was a cup; and in each cup there was a blob of color.

"Now here was the blob of black—Buck Horne himself. There the blob of gold—Kit Horne. Ah, Kit Horne." He sighed. "The blob of flinty gray—old Wild Bill, Wild Bill Grant. The blob of healthy brown—his son Curly. The blob of poisonous lavender—Mara Gay, that . . . what did the tabs call her? The Orchid of Hollywood. My God! . . . And Julian Hunter, her husband, the dragon-green of our spectroscope. And Tony Mars—white? And the prizefighter Tommy Black—good strong red. And One-Arm Woody—snake-yellow for him. All those others." He grinned at the ceiling. "What a galaxy of colors! Now observe those little blobs of color, each an element, each a quantity, each a miniscule to be weighed and measured; each distinct in itself. At rest, inanimate, each by itself—what did they mean to me? Precisely nothing."

"And then, I suppose," I suggested, "the wheel began to spin?"

"Something of the sort. A tiny explosion, a puff of the cosmic effluvium—something applied the motive-power, the primal urge of motion; and the wheel turned. Fast, very fast. But observe what happened." He smoked lazily and, I thought, not without satisfaction. "A miracle! For where are those little blobs of color, each a quantity, an element, a miniscule to be weighed and measured—each distinct in itself, as distinct as the component suns of a fixed universe? They've merged; they've lost their prismatic quality and become a coruscating whole; no longer distinct, you will observe, but a flowing symmetrical pattern which tells the whole story of the Horne case."

"How you go on," I said, holding my aching head. "You mean that they all had something to do with the death of—"

"I mean," he replied, and his fine features sharpened, "that the non-essential colors vanished. I often wonder," he murmured, "what Father Brown or old Sherlock would have done with that case. Eh, J.J.?"

1: WORK IN PROGRESS

A LARGE subterranean chamber strongly acrid with the smell of horseflesh, loud and resonant with the snorting and stamping of horses. In one corner an alcove hewn out of solid concrete, and in the alcove a smithy. Its forge was violently red, and fireflies of sparks darted about. A half-naked pigmy with oily black skin and preposterous biceps hammered like Thor's little brother on metal which curved sullenly under his rhythmic blows. The low flat ceiling, the naked walls, framed the chamber in stone. . . . This might be Pegasus, this arch-necked stallion champing in his stall, naked and sleek as the day he was foaled. His harem of mares whinnied and nickered about him; and occasionally his scarlet eyes flashed as he pawed the strawed floor with the dainty arrogance of his Arabian ancestors.

Horses, dozens of them, scores of them; tame horses, trick horses, wild horses; saddle horses, raw horses. The sharp effluvium of dung and sweat and breath hung, an opalescent mist, in the strong atmosphere. Gear gleamed before the stalls; brass glittering on oily leather; saddles like brown satin; stirrups like shining platinum; halters like ovals of ebony. And there were coiled lariats on the posts, and Indian blankets. . . .

For this was the stable of a king. His crown was a flaring

Stetson, his sceptre a long-barreled Colt pistol, his domain the wide and dusty plains of the American West. His praetorian guard were bow-legged men who rode like centaurs, drawled in a quaint soft speech, rolled cigarets deftly, and whose brown wrinkled eyes held the calm immensities of those who scan the stars under an unadulterated vault of heaven. And his palace was a sprawling rancho—thousands of miles from this place.

For this stable of a king with his odd crown and his strange sceptre and his extraordinary guard was not set in its proper place on the plains of a rolling country. It was not in Texas, or in Arizona, or in New Mexico, or in any of the curious lands where such kings rule. It lay under the feet of a structure endemically American; but not the America of mountains and hills and valleys and trees and sage-brush and plains; rather the America of skyscrapers, subways, rouged chorines, hotels, theatres, bread-lines, night-clubs, slums, speakeasies, radio towers, *literati,* and tabloids. It was as remote from its native habitat as the cots of England or the rice-fields of Japan. A stone's-throw away that equally curious domain, Broadway, speared through the humor-less laughter of New York. Thirty feet above and fifty feet to the south and east roared the metropolis. Past the portals of the architectural Colossus in whose cellars it lay flew a thousand automobiles a minute.

The *Colosseum,* New York's new and hugest temple of sport. . . .

Horses, the warp and woof of the outdoors, crated like rabbits over immense distances so that West and East might meet. . . .

It could not happen in England, where institutions take root in their proper soil and, uprooted, die. The fountains of sacred rivers flow upwards only in America. Long ago the brawny men of the West occasionally gathered from far places in a holiday mood to show off their prowess with horses and lariats and steers. It was an amusement of the West, for the West. Today it was ripped up from its alkaline soil and transplanted bodily—horses, lariats, steers, cowboys and all—to the stony soil of the East. Its name—rodeo—was retained. Its purpose—ingenuous amusement—was debased. Spectators filed through iron aisles and paid admissions to sagacious promoters. And this was the largest fruit, the horticultural apotheosis, of the West-to-East transplantation—Wild Bill Grant's Rodeo.

. . . .

Now in the stable, near the stall of the princely stallion, stood two men. The shorter of the two was an odd creature with a muscular right arm; the left was a stump above the elbow swinging in a gaudy knotted sleeve. His face was lean, his expression was saturnine; whether it had been painted by the black brush of the burning sun or was a splash of something hot in the caldron of his own nature was not easily determined. In his bearing there was something of the stallion's arrogance; on his thin lips something of the stallion's sneer. This was that bitter man, One-Arm Woody—odd nomenclature for nobility!—who in the lingo of his caste was known as the "top-rider" of the outfit; which is to say, Wild Bill Grant's featured performer. Woody, whose amber eyes were murderous, possessed the sinewy agelessness of a myth.

The other was quite different, and in his difference equally extraordinary. He was a tall buckaroo, lean as a pine and ever so slightly stooped, as a pine stoops in the high wind. He seemed old and enduring as the Nevada hills; shaggy white on top, dark-brown underneath, and over all the glaze of sharp fresh air and time-buffeted strength. In his face one saw no outstanding feature; it was one with his strong old body, and the whole made an epic figure, like an ancient statue dimly perceived through the mists of ages. His eyelids were strong and brown, and habitually they dropped to cover all but the merest slits, through which frigid colorless chips of eyes stared unblinkingly. This creature of another world was dressed, strangely enough, in the most ordinary of Eastern clothes.

Old Buck Horne! Product of the acrid plains and Hollywood—yes, Hollywood, which like Moloch engulfs all; as dear to the hearts of modern American boys as that legendary buckaroo, Buffalo Bill, had been to the boys of a bygone generation. This was the man who had reanimated the old West. Not the West of Fords and tractors and gasoline-pumps, but the West of the '70's, of heavy six-shooters, of the James Boys and Billy the Kid, of horse-thieves and drunken Indians, of cattle-rustlers, saloons, false-fronts and board-walks and fighting sheriffs and range-wars. Buck Horne had accomplished this miracle of resurrection by the instrument of motion pictures; himself an authentic figure out of the past, he had been romantic enough to employ the silver screen to bring the past to life; and there was not a red-blooded young man alive who had not as a boy thrilled to Buck Horne's dashing exploits with horse and rope and gun in the flickering pictures which raced across a thousand screens the country over.

· · · · · · ·

Two blobs of color. One-Arm Woody, old Buck Horne.
And the wheel stood still.

· · · · · · ·

One-Arm Woody shifted his curved legs, and thrust his hatchety face an inch nearer the brown face of Horne.

"Buck, ya mangy ole breed, y'oughta go back to the flickers with the rest o' the dudes," he drawled.

Buck Horne said nothing.

"Pore ole Buck," said Woody, and his stump of a left arm jerked a little. "Cain't scarcely drag yore laigs aroun'."

And Buck said coldly: "Meaning?"

The one-armed man's eyes flashed, and his right hand forked the brass-studded end of his belt. "Damn you, yo're hornin' in!"

A horse nickered, and neither man turned his head. Then from the lips of the tall old fellow came a soft stream of words. Woody's five fingers twitched, and his mouth twisted wryly. The muscular right arm darted up, and the old man crouched. . . .

"Buck!"

They straightened up on the instant, like puppets at the pull of a finger, and they turned their heads with the same jerky motion. Woody's arm fell to his side.

Kit Horne stood in the door of the stable regarding them with level eyes. Buck's girl! Left an orphan, she was not of his dusty blood, but he had brought her up, and his own wife had suckled her at rich breasts. The wife was gone, but Kit remained.

She was tall, almost as tall as Buck, and sun-tanned, and as wiry as a wild mare. Her eyes were grayest blue, and her little nostrils quivered slightly. She was dressed *a la mode;* her gown was smart New York, and her jaunty turban latest Fifth Avenue. "Buck, you ought to feel ashamed of yourself. Quarreling with Woody!"

Woody scowled, and then smiled, and then scowled again as he flicked the brim of his Stetson. He strode off on his absurdly bowed legs; and though his lips moved no sound came from them. He disappeared behind the smithy.

"He says I'm old," muttered old Buck Horne.

She took his hard brown hands in hers. "Never mind, Buck."

"Damn him, Kit, he ain't goin' to tell me—"

"Never mind, Buck."

He smiled suddenly and put his arm about her waist.

.   .   .   .

Kit Horne was as well-known to the younger generation as her famous foster-father was to those who had been the younger generation ten and fifteen years before. Bred on a ranch, reared on a horse, with cowboys for playmates, a Bowie knife as a teething-ring, limitless rolling acres of range as a playground, and her foster-father a motion-picture star—around her a Hollywood press-agent contrived to drape a tinsel legend. Buck's producer had had an idea. Buck was growing old. Kit, who was more man than woman and more woman than Circe, should take his place in the films. That had been nine years before, when she was a straight-backed tomboy of sixteen. . . . The children went wild over her. She could ride, shoot, rope, swear; and, since there must always be a hero, she could kiss and cuddle too. So she became Kit Horne, the great cowgirl star, and her pictures sold at a premium while old Buck slid quietly into oblivion.

They walked out of the stable, up a ramp, and through narrow concrete corridors to a vast wing which held dressing rooms. Over one of the doors there was a metal star; Buck kicked the door open.

"Star!" he bellowed. "Come in, Kit, come in, an' shut the door behin' you. . . . An' I've got to take that horse-thief's lip! Sit down, I tell you."

He flung himself into a chair like a sulky boy, frowning, his brown hands clenching and unclenching. Kit ruffled his white hair fondly and smiled; and in the depths of her gray-blue eyes there was anxiety.

"Whoa!" she said softly. "You're off your feed, Buck, upset. Get a grip on yourself. Isn't this—don't snarl, you old catamount!—all this excitement just a little too much for you?"

"Stop talking like a prime fool, you, Kit."

"You're sure—?"

"Shut up, Kit! I'm all right."

"Did the rodeo doctor look you over, you old heller?"

"T'day. Says I'm fit."

She took a long match out of his vest pocket, struck it expertly against the back of the chair, and held it to the tip of a slender cigaret he had been rolling. "You're sixty-five, Buck."

He squinted humorously up at her through the fragrant smoke. "You mean I'm through. Listen, Kit, though I been out o' pictures for three years—"

"Nine," said Kit gently.

"Three," said Buck. "I made a come-back for National, didn't I? Well, I'm as frisky now as I was then. Feel that muscle!" He doubled his big right arm and obediently she tapped his biceps. They were hard as rock. "What the hell, Kit—this is soft pickin's. A little ridin', a little shootin', some fancy ropin'—you know how I been keepin' in trim at the ranch these nine-ten years. This racket here with Wild Bill is easy as brandin' a roped steer. Bill'll build me up, I'll get a nice fat movie contract. . . ."

She kissed his forehead. "All right, Buck. Just be—be careful, won't you?"

At the door she looked back. Buck had propped his long legs on his dressing table, and he was frowning thoughtfully at his reflection in the mirror through a screen of pearly smoke.

·   ·   ·   ·   ·   ·   ·

Kit sighed a woman's sigh as she closed the door; and then, drawing her tall figure up, she strode with a man's strides through the corridors and down another ramp.

Little *pops!* came faintly to her ears. Some excitement livened her pleasant face, and she hurried purposefully in the direction of the sounds. People passed her—the old familiar people: cowboys in chaps and sombreros, girls in buckskins and short flaring halved skirts. There was the smell of leather, the soft sound of drawling talk, the haze of home-made cigarets. . . .

"Curly! Now, isn't that remarkable!"

She stood in the doorway to the armory—rack upon rack of long Winchester rifles, blue-steel revolvers, targets—and smiled dreamily. Curly, son of Wild Bill Grant—a young man in dusty corduroys with wide shoulders and no hips at all—lowered the muzzle of a smoking revolver, stared at her, and then whooped.

"Kit! You ole son-of-a-gun! Shore glad to see you!"

She smiled again, more dreamily. Curly was as out of place in the *Colosseum* and Broadway as Kit herself. He *was,* she assured herself for the thousandth time, good to look at. As he dashed to her, seized her hands, and grinned into her face she wondered if this new atmosphere—with its reek of gin and gimcracks— would spoil him. There was nothing romantically heroic about him; he was not remotely good-looking, and his nose was far too hawk-like for the conventional hero; but there were interesting glints in his curly brown hair which sat his head like a mat, and his eyes were sure and honest.

"Watch this," he cried, and dashed back.

She watched, faintly smiling still.

He stepped on the pedal of a queer little apparatus with his right foot; it was a catapult. He tested it with the ball of his foot as his hands broke open the long-barreled revolver and swiftly reloaded the chambers with big fat glinting cartridges. Then he snapped the cylinder back, filled the alley of the catapult with small round objects, braced himself, and trod quickly on the pedal. The air became filled with little glass balls. And as fast as they skimmed into the air he made them disappear in a puff of smoke and tiny fragments, shooting at them with supple wrist and careless flips of his weapon.

She applauded gleefully, and he thrust his revolver into a holster and then bowed and doffed his wide-brimmed hat.

"Pretty neat, hey? Every time I pull this little stunt I think o' Buffalo Bill. Pop's tole me about him many a time. Used to shoot little glass balls, too, when he was with the Wild West Show. Only he was a rotten shot, an' used buckshot, so he *never* missed. . . . Another legend busted!"

"You're almost as good as Buck," smiled Kit.

He seized her hands again and stared earnestly into her eyes. "Kit darlin'—"

"Buck," she said hastily, coloring a little. "Poor Buck. I'm worried about him."

He put her hands gently away from him. "That ole bull?" He laughed. "He'll be *mucho* all right, Kit. These old-timers are built out o' rawhide an' steel. Like pop. You just tell Wild Bill he ain't the man he used to be—"

"*Isn't* the man he used to be, Curly."

"Isn't the man he use to be," said Curly, meekly. "Anyway, don't fret, Kit. I saw him go through the last dress rehearsal a while back."

"Any slips?" she asked swiftly.

"Nary a one. You'd never think the ole hellion was in his sixties! Rode like a red Injun. He'll be swell tonight, Kit, an' the publicity—"

"Damn the publicity," she said in a soft voice. "Did he have a run-in with Woody?"

Curly stared. "Woody? Why—"

There was a light step behind them, and they turned. A woman was standing in the armory doorway, smiling inscrutably at them.

No buckskins here. All silks and furs and scents. This beautiful creature with the lynx eyes, the incredible enamel complexion, the subtle curves of thigh and breasts, was Mara Gay. Darling of Hollywood, star of innumerable successful sex-pictures, three times divorced . . . the envy of a million shop-girls and the sweet painful dream of a million men.

Mara Gay ruled a kingdom which had no geographical boundaries and whose subjects were abject slaves. She was the incarnation in painted-rose flesh of a forbidden dream. And yet, at this close range, there was something cheap about her. Or was it the result of the usual disillusionment of adjusted focus? . . . She was in the East, resting between pictures. An impossible, insatiable woman with the appetites of a nature-myth and the lure of Cabellian Anaitis. Just now she was obsessed with a hunger for the society of overwhelmingly masculine men. Behind her loomed three of them, faultlessly dressed, carefully shaved; one of them held a yelping Pomeranian in his arms.

There was a little silence as Mara Gay drifted over the stone floor and meltingly looked at Curly, at his big frame, his flat hips, his broad shoulders, his curly hair and dusty clothes. Kit's small chin hardened; she lost her smile and took a little, cautious, noiseless, backward step.

"Uh—hello, Mara," said Curly with a feeble grin. "Uh—Kit, ya know Mara? Mara Gay? Hangs out in Hollywood, too. Haw, haw!"

The lynx eyes met the gray-blue expressionlessly. "Yes, I know Miss Gay," said Kit steadily. "We've bumped into each other in Hollywood on several occasions. But I didn't know *you* knew Miss Gay, Curly. So I'll be going."

And she calmly left the armory.

.   .   .   .

There was an uncomfortable interlude. The three large men in faultless clothes behind the actress stood quite still, blinking. The Pomeranian, his civilized nostrils scandalized by the vulgar odors drifting up from the stables, yelped and yelped.

"Cat," said Mara Gay. "High-hatting *me!* She and her small-time horse operas." She tossed her extraordinary head and smiled bewitchingly at Curly. "Curly, my love, you're *beautiful!* Where *did* you get that mop of hair?"

Curly scowled. His eyes were still on the door through which Kit Horne had vanished. Then Mara's words took meaning in his brain. "For the love of Pete, Mara," he grumbled, "can that kind o' mush, will ya?" His hair was the bane of his life; it lay in cunning ringlets which he had vainly attempted for years to straighten.

The actress rubbed herself gently against his arm. Her eyes went innocently wide. "This is *so* thrilling! All these awful re-volvers and things. . . . Can you shoot 'em, Curly darling?"

He brightened and moved away from her with alacrity. "Can I shoot 'em! Gal, yo're talkin' to Dead-eye Dick himself!" Re-loading quickly, he flipped his revolver and once more manip-ulated the catapult. Balls popped into nothingness. The actress squealed with delight, moving closer.

Outside, Kit Horne paused and her eyes were very cold-ly blue. She heard the *pops!,* the tinkle of breaking glass, Mara

Gay's little squeals of admiration. She bit her lip and dashed off, striding along blindly.

The actress in the armory was saying: "Now, Curly, don't be so bashful. . . ." Something predacious came into her lynx eyes; she turned sharply and said to the three men behind her: "Wait outside for me." They went obediently. She turned back to Curly and smiled a smile famous over the length and breadth of a romantic land, whispering: "Kiss me, Curly dear, oh, kiss me. . . ."

Curly took a backward step, very noiseless and cautious, like Kit's, and he lost his grin as his eyes narrowed. She stood very still. "Look here, Mara, aren't you forgettin' yourself? I don't aim to rustle other men's wives."

She stepped close to him; she was very close to him now, and her scent filled his nostrils. "You mean Julian?" she said softly. "Oh, we've a perfect understanding, Curly. Modern marriage! Curly, don't look so mad. There are five million men who'd leave their happy homes to have me look at them this way—"

"Well, I ain't one of 'em," said Curly coldly. "Where's yore husband now?"

"Oh, upstairs somewhere with Tony Mars. Curly, please. . . ."

.   .   .   .

If the *Colosseum* was the Colossus of sport arenas, its creator Tony Mars was the Colossus of sport promoters. Like Buck Horne, Mars was a living legend; but a legend of quite a different sort. He was the man who had put prize-fighting in the million-dollar class. He was the man who had scrubbed wrestling until it shone—not for ethical reasons but purely as a matter of big business—restoring it to favor with the sportsmen who financed him and the sportsmen who patronized him. He was the man who had punished the Boxing Commission by taking the largest heavyweight prizefight attraction in fistic history out of New York State and staging it in Pennsylvania. He was the man who had popularized ice-hockey, indoor tennis matches, and six-day bicycle races. The *Colosseum* was the culmination of his life's dream, which had been to build the largest sports arena in the world.

His office was at the peak of that vast structure, and it was made accessible by four elevators—an opportunity for approach not neglected by the hordes of parasites for whom Broadway is peculiarly notorious. And there he sat, far in the reaches of his citadel—Tony Mars; old, wily, swarthy, hook-nosed, a New Yorker born and a New Yorker bred. He was a "sport," in the most completely praiseworthy sense of the word. He was reputed the easiest man on Broadway for a "touch" and the hardest to put something over on. His derby rested on the bridge of his long nose, his unshined shoes scratched the veneer of his fabled walnut desk, and his two-dollar cigar smouldered between his brown jaws. He regarded his visitor thoughtfully.

The visitor was not unknown to these precincts. Suavely attired, boutonniéred, Julian Hunter was the husband of Mara Gay, but he was not historic for this feat alone; he owned a dozen night-clubs, he was the original playboy of the Main Stem, he was a sportsman with a string of polo ponies and a racing yacht, and above all he was a millionaire. Society opened its doors to him, for he came from society originally. But even society recognized him as something apart from the blue-ribboned herd. He had the pouchy eyes and pink cheeks of the well-massaged but always fatigued man-about-town; but there the resemblance stopped. It was only in the lower—or higher?—strata of the social structure that men acquired the peculiarity which was Julian Hunter's own: the expressionless face of a wooden Indian. It was the face of the inveterate gambler. In this, at least, he and the man behind the desk were blood-brothers.

Tony Mars said in a throaty bass: "I'll give it to you straight, Hunter, and you listen to me. As far as Buck is concerned—" He stopped abruptly. His feet crashed to the Chinese rug on the floor. His mouth curved in a disarming smile.

Julian Hunter turned lazily.

A man stood in the doorway—a man all chest and arms and legs. He was a tall man, a very tall man, a very young tall man. Set like strips of fur above his high-cheeked face were blue-black brows; his closely shaved cheeks were blue-black, as were his small bright eyes. This giant smiled, and showed white teeth.

"Come in, Tommy, come in!" said Tony Mars heartily. "Alone? Where's that nickel-nursing manager of yours?"

Tommy Black, new heavyweight sensation of the pugilistic world, shut the door softly and stood still, smiling. Behind the smile lurked a killer's savagery; such an expression, it was said, as Jack Dempsey had worn when he had battered Jess Willard to bleeding pulp in Toledo. The experts deemed this assassin's instinct, it appeared, essential for the successful pugilist. Tommy Black possessed it with savagery to spare.

He slid, almost slithered, over the rug. He was like a cat on his feet. And then he was in a chair, still smiling, his incredible bulk quiescent as poured steel. "'Lo, Tony, how's tricks?" His voice was charming. "In town for a day. Doc says I'm getting fine. Knocked off."

"Tommy, you know Julian Hunter? Hunter, shake hands with the best damned bruiser since the Manassa Mauler."

Hunter, the dandy, and Black, the man-killer, shook hands; Hunter indolently, Black with the crushing grip of an anaconda. Their eyes touched briefly; then Tommy Black rested quietly in the chair again. Tony Mars said nothing, seeming to be absorbed in the tip of his cigar.

"If you're busy, Tony, I'll scram," said the prizefighter softly.

Mars smiled. "Stick around, kid. Hunter, you too. Mickey!" he bellowed. A burly ruffian stuck his bullet-head into the room. "I'm in conf'rence—can't see anybody. Get me?" The door clicked shut. Black and Hunter sat without moving or looking at each other. "Now listen, Tommy, about the fight with the champ. That's why I wired you to come up from training camp if you could." Mars puffed thoughtfully at his cigar, and Hunter looked bored. "How you feelin'?"

"Who—me?" The fighter grinned and swelled his magnificent chest. "In the pink, Tony, in the pink. I could lick that stumble-bum with one mitt!"

"He used to be pretty good, I hear," said Mars dryly. "How's the trainin' going?"

"Swell. Doc's got me comin' around in great shape."

"Fine. Fine."

"Got a little trouble gettin' sparring partners. Busted Big Joe Pedersen's jaw last week, and it sort of brought out the yellow in the boys." Black grinned again.

"Yeah. Borchard of the *Journal* was telling me." Mars watched the long white ash; suddenly he leaned forward and carefully deposited it in a silver tray on his desk. "Tommy, I think you're gonna win that fight. You'll be the new champ if you keep your head."

"Thanks, Tony, thanks!"

Mars slowly said: "I mean, you *ought* to win that fight, Tommy."

There was a windy, stormy silence. Hunter sat very still, and Mars smiled a little.

Then Black raised himself from the chair, scowling fiercely. "What the hell do you mean by that, Tony?"

"Keep you shirt on, kid, keep it on." Black relaxed. Mars went on in a mild voice. "I've heard things around. You know how it is in this racket. They're always smellin' frame-ups. Now I'll talk to you like a Dutch uncle—or maybe like a father because, boy, you need one! That lousy manager of yours would just as soon give you a bum steer and the old double-cross as not. Kid, you're in the big time. Many a good boy hit the big time, and then the big time hit him because he wasn't a wise guy. See? You know my rep, Tommy—square. That's my way. You work my way and we'll make plenty simoleons together. You don't work my way—" He stopped as if he had come to the end of his sentence. There was a ringing inevitability about his words that was not entirely absorbed by the Chinese rug and the thick wall-hangings.

He puffed placidly at his cigar.

"Well," said Black.

"So that's how it is, Tommy," said Mars. "There's a lot of heavy sugar bein' laid down on you to win. It's straight sugar—nothin' crooked about it. On form, strength, youth, record—you're the comin' champ. See that you get there. Or if you stop one in the whiskers—an' don't kid yourself that the champ's a pushover— see that you stop it clean. See?"

Black rose. "Hell, I don't known what's eatin' you, Tony," he said in an injured tone. "You don't have to go back on me, too! I know what side my bread's buttered on, believe me! . . . Well, glad to've met you, Mr. Hunter." Hunter raised his eyebrows in acknowledgment. "So long, Tony, See you in a couple of weeks."

"You bet."

The door closed with a little snick.

"You think," drawled Hunter, "that the scrap isn't on the up-and-up, Tony?"

"What I think, Hunter," said Mars genially, "is nobody's business but mine. But I'll tell you one thing: nobody's stealin' the gold outa *my* bridgework." He stared at Hunter, and Hunter shrugged. "Now," continued the promoter in quite a different tone, as he replaced his feet on the shining walnut, "to get back to Bucko the Horne, God's gift to the kids. I'm tellin' you, Hunter, you'd be passin' up a swell chance—"

"I can keep my mouth shut, too, Tony," murmured the sportsman with a smile. "By the way, where does Grant come in on this?"

"Wild Bill?" Mars squinted at his cigar. "What the hell would you expect? Him an' Buck have been pals ever since Sittin' Bull took Custer for a ride. Sort of Da-mon and Py-thias business." Hunter grunted. "Wild Bill's entitled to his, and I for one aint' cuttin' him out of his gravy. . . ."

.   .   .   .

Wild Bill Grant sat at his desk in the elaborate office placed at his disposal by Tony Mars. It was from this fane that the Delphic words came which moved the whole complex machinery of the rodeo. The desk was littered: cigaret stubs, cigar butts, all dead and cold, were sprawled like fallen soldiers on the edge of the desk's side, where Grant had deposited them in an unconscious thrift which dated from less prosperous days. The ashtrays, of which there were a half-dozen, were quite clean.

Grant sat his swivel-chair as if it were a horse. His left buttock hung over empty space, and his left leg was stiffly outstretched, so that the whole effect was one of a man riding side-saddle. He was a square, chunky, grizzled old-timer with a walrus mustache and faded gray eyes; the skin of his rough face was brick-red, tough, and seamed and pitted as porous rock. That he was hard as nails was evident from the powerful muscles of his bare forearms and the complete lack of superfluous flesh on his torso. He wore a clumsy bow-tie, and an astonishingly ancient Stetson lay far back on his iron-gray head. This was the Wild Bill Grant who in his youth had been a fighting United States Marshal in the Indian Territory. He was as out of place in the midst of Tony Mars's shiny office appointments as an Esquimau in a tea-shoppe.

There was a confused mass of papers before him—contracts, bills, orders. He rustled them impatiently, chafing, and reached for a gnawed butt.

A girl came in—pert, trim, artistically cosmetized; genus, New York stenographer. "There's a gentlem'n wants to see you, Mr. Grant."

"Waddy?"

"Beg pardon?"

"Puncher—want a job?"

"Yes'r. He says he has a letter for you from Mr. Horne."

"Oh! Send 'em in, sister."

She departed with a neat wiggle of her slim hips, and a moment later held the door open for a tall spare poorly dressed Westerner. The visitor stumped in on high cowboy's heels; they clattered on the border of the floor. His shabby sombrero was in his hand. He wore a tattered, rainwashed old mackinaw, and his boots were down at the heel.

"Come in!" said Grant heartily; he surveyed his visitor with appraising eyes. "What's this about a letter from Buck?"

There was something the matter with the man's cleanshaven face, something horribly the matter. The entire left side was brownish purple in color, and puckered and drawn. The purple patch began below the jaw-line and extended to a half-inch above the left eyebrow. A very small spot of purple on the right cheek put a period to what seemed to be the ravages of fire, or acid. He had bad teeth, stained molasses-brown. . . . With a little twitch of his shoulders, Wild Bill Grant looked away.

"Yes'r." The man's voice was husky, hoarse. "Buck an' me, we're old bunkies, Mr. Grant. Punched long-horns down Texas way twenty year' ago. Buck, he don't forget his pals." He fumbled in a pocket of the mackinaw and brought out a rather crushed envelope; this he handed to Grant, and then stared at the showman anxiously.

Grant began to read: "'Dear Bill: This is Benjy Miller, an old friend. Needs a job. . . .'" There was more; Grant read the note through. Then he tossed it on his desk and said: "Have a seat, Miller."

"Shore nice of you, Mr. Grant." Miller sat down on the edge of a leather chair, cautiously.

"Cigar?" There was pity in Grant's eyes; the man made a pitiable figure. Although his hair was sandy in color, untouched by gray, he was undoubtedly past middle age.

Miller's mouth opened in a brown grin. "Now, that's shore friendly, Mr. Grant. Don't mind if I do."

Grant tossed a cigar across the desk; Miller sniffed it and put it in the breast pocket of his mackinaw. Grant pressed a button on the side of his desk; the stenographer came in again. "Get Dan'l Boone in here, youngster. Hank Boone."

She looked blank. "Who?"

"Boone, Boone. Sawed-off waddy who's always drunk. You'll find him jawin' around somewhere."

The girl went out, wiggling her hips; Grant stared after her appreciatively.

He chewed his frayed cigar. "Ever play the rodeo circuit, Miller?"

Miller's shoulders shuddered. "No, sir! I been on the range all my life. Never did nothin' fancy."

"Bulldog?"

"Some. I used to be purty good in my young days, Mr. Grant."

Wild Bill grunted. "Can you ride?"

The man flushed. "Listen here, Mr. Grant—"

"No offense meant," drawled Grant. "Well, we're full up, Miller, an' this ain't no *remuda;* don't need no cattlepunchers. . . ."

Miller said slowly: "So you ain't got a job fer me?"

"Didn't say that," snapped Grant. "If yo're Buck Horne's friend, I'll take you on. You can trail along with the posse aroun' Buck t'night. Got any gear? Got yore hull?"

"Nos'r. I—I hocked most ev'rything in Tucson."

"Uh-huh." Grant squinted at his crumbling cigar; the door opened and a weazened little cowboy rolled in, his bowlegs wobbly and his bandana knot set at a rakish angle. "Oh, Dan'l, you loco son of a cross-eyed maverick! Come on in here."

The little cowboy was very drunk. He cocked his Stetson forward and lurched to the desk. "Wil' Bill—Wil' Bill, I'm here at yore command. . . . What the hell you want, Bill?"

"Yo're tanked again, Dan'l." Grant fixed him with a disapproving eye. "Dan'l, this is Benjy Miller—friend o' Buck's. Joinin' the outfit. Show him the ropes—the stable, where he bunks, the arena. . . ."

Boone's bleared eyes took in the shabby visitor. "Friend o'

Buck's? Pleased t'meet ya, Miller! Shome—some outfit we got here, feller. We—"

They passed out of Grant's office. Grant grunted and, after a moment, put Buck Horne's note in one of his pockets.

. . . .

As they tramped down a long runway leading to the heart of the *Colosseum,* Boone tottering along, the man Miller said: "How come he calls you Dan'l? Thought I heard 'm say Hank to the girl."

Boone guffawed. "Shmart—smart filly, ain't she? Fresher'n new fodder! Well, I'll tell ya, Miller. I wash—was born Hank, but the ole man, he says: 'Maw, you kin call 'im Hank after yore mother's secon' husband's brother, but by hell! I'm callin' him Dan'l after the best damn Boone that ever drawed a bead on a red Injun!' An' Dan'l I been ever since. Haw, haw!"

"You sound like you come from the Northwest some'eres."

The little cowboy nodded gravely. "Do I? Fact ish—is, my paw he punched cows in Wyoming. Ole Sam Hooker, he used to say: 'Dan'l,' he says, 'don't you never disgrace the fair name of yore native state,' he says, 'or me an' yore paw we'll come a-ha'ntin' ya.' I been trailed by ghoshts—ghosts ever since. . . . Well, Miller ole hoss, here we are. Some range, hey?"

It was a huge amphitheatre, illuminated by thousands of harshly shedding bulbs. Its twenty thousand seats, arranged in an oval, were unoccupied. The arena, a long ellipse, was almost three times as long as it was wide, separated from the amphitheatre proper by a concrete wall, on the inner side of which ran the track, a fifteen-foot runner of tanbark. Inside this oval track lay the core of the arena, a bare expanse. It was here that steers were roped from running horses, wild broncos were "busted" by expert horsemen, and other rodeo events were staged. At each end of the oval—on east and west—a huge doorway led to the backstage of the arena, in one of which Miller and Boone stood. Other exits, many rigged with special chute gates for the equine events, dotted the concrete wall. High above—and yet not so high as that immensely distant roof of steel girders—the tiny figures of workmen crept along the tiers, manicuring the stadium for the evening's performance, which would officially open the New York stand of Wild Bill Grant's Rodeo.

In the hard-packed earth of the arena core a number of men in Western regalia lounged, smoking and talking.

Boone staggered forward into the arena, turning his woeful little eyes on his companion. "Reg'lar rodeo man, Miller?"

"Nope."

"Down on yore luck, hey?"

"It's hard times, cowboy."

"Shore is! Well, you gladhand the gang an' you'll perk up. Got boys here come all the way from the Rio."

Boone and his charge were greeted hilariously by the chapped and sombreroed men in the group. The ugly little fellow seemed a favorite with them; he was instantly the butt of friendly jeers and jibes. In the hubbub Miller was forgotten; he stood silently by, waiting.

"Uh—damn if I ain't gone an' fergot my manners!" cried Boone, after a moment. "Waddies, meet an ole bunkie o' Buck Horne's. Benjy Miller is his handle, an' he's joinin' up with the outfit."

Dozens of steady eyes took in the newcomer, and the talk and laughter died away. They surveyed his shabby clothes, his crooked heels, his frightfully mutilated face.

"Jock Ramsey," said Boone soberly, introducing a tall dour cowboy with a cleft upper lip.

"Meetya." They shook hands.

"Texas Joe Halliwell." Halliwell nodded briefly and began to roll a cigaret. "Tex is God's gift to the workin' gals, Miller. Here's Slim Hawes." Hawes was a dumpy, jolly-faced cowboy with unsmiling eyes. "Lafe Brown. Shorty Downs." Boone went on and on. Famous rodeo names, these; of men who followed the big circle with their well-worn gear, hopping from rodeo to rodeo, working for prize-money, paying their own expenses, most of them penniless, many scarred by the hazards of their profession.

There was an interval of silence. Then Lafe Brown, a powerful man in colorful costume, smiled and dipped his fingers into his pocket. "Roll yore own, Miller?" He proffered a little sack of tobacco.

Miller flushed. "Recken I will." He accepted the "makin's" and slowly, with unconscious facility, rolled a cigaret.

At once they broke into speech; Miller was accepted. Someone scratched a match on the thigh of his trousers and held it to Miller's cigaret; he lit up and puffed silently away. They closed in about him and he merged with them, disappearing into the group.

"Now you take this here c'yote," said Shorty Downs, a vast stalwart, as he crooked a horny finger at Boone. "You want to cinch tight when he's bellyin' aroun'. Steal the pants offen you, Dan'l will. His ole man was a horsethief."

Miller smiled rather tremulously; they were trying to make him feel at home.

"How," said Slim Hawes gravely, "how d'ya stand on the plumb earth-shakin' question of the hackamore versus the snaffle-bit, Miller? Gotta know that first off. Hey?"

"Always used the hackamore in bustin' raw broncs," grinned Miller.

"He ain't no pilgrim!" someone guffawed.

"Totes his weepens low, too, I bet!"

"Gittin' down to cases," began a third voice, when Downs held up his hand.

"Pull up," he drawled. "Somethin's wrong with Dan'l. Look sorta down in the mouth, Dan'l. Off yore feed?"

"Do I?" sighed the little cowboy. "Ain't no wonder, Shorty. Busted my Injun arrowhead this mornin'." Silent fell at once; smiles faded; like children's their eyes grew round. "Damn squealin' palomino stepped on 'er. Bad med'cine, boys. Somethin's primed to happen powerful quick!"

"My Gawd," breathed three of them in unison; and Downs with a swift look of concern fumbled for something beneath his shirt. Other hands dipped into the pockets of their jeans. Each one, in his superstitious way, furtively fingered his charm. This was serious; they regarded Boone with troubled eyes.

"Tough," muttered Halliwell. "Shore is tough. Better play 'possum t'night, Dan'l. Hell, I wouldn't even fork a circus cayuse with a busted lucky piece in my jeans!"

Ramsey reached into his back pocket and produced a flask, which he tendered to Boone in grave sympathy.

Benjy Miller's purple cheek twitched. He stared across the arena at a platform built on wooden trestles, upon which a number of conventionally clad city men were busy in a clutter of peculiar apparatus.

. . . .

They were obviously motion picture photographers. Tripods, cameras, sound-boxes, electrical equipment, boxes of many sizes lay scattered on the platform, which stood ten feet above the floor of the arena. Several were unreeling thick smooth cables sheathed in rubber, which snaked from a large and complicated machine on the floor. On each piece of equipment was lettered in bold white paint the name of a famous motion picture newsreel company.

A small slight man in dark gray stood in the dirt of the arena and directed operations; he wore a sleek black military mustache, very carefully trimmed and brushed. He paid no attention whatever to the group of picturesquely garbed Westerners some distance away across the oval.

"All set for the long shots, Major Kirby," yelled a man on the platform.

The small man below said: "How are you fixed for sound, Jack?" to a man with earphones clamped about his head.

"So-so," grunted this man. "Going to be a picnic, Major. Listen to the damn echo!"

"Do the best you can. It will be better when the place is full of people. . . . I want plenty of action, boys, and all the crazy sounds that go with this rodeo racket. There's a special on it from the Chief's office."

"Oke."

Major Kirby cast his very bright little eyes over the field of empty seats and naked concrete, and lit a cigar.

.   .   .   .

"And that," said Ellery Queen as he thoughtfully blew smoke at the ceiling, "was the wheel at rest. Now see what happened when the wheel began to whirl."

2: THE MAN ON HORSEBACK

NOT THE least piquant feature of the Queen *ménage* was its major-domo. Now this inestimable word, which with our Nordic genius for plagiarism we have appropriated from the Spanish, invariably evokes visions of regal splendor, solemnity, and above all pomposity. The true major-domo must have (besides the crushing dignity of years) a paunch, flat feet, the vivacity of dead codfish, an emperor's stare, and a waddle which is a cross between a papal procession and the triumphal march of returning Pompey. Moreover he must possess the burnished knavishness of a Mississippi gambler, the haggling instinct of a Parisian *marchandeur,* and the loyalty of a hound.

The piquancy of the Queens' major-domo lay in that, except for loyalty, he resembled no major-domo that ever lived. Far from evoking visions of splendor, solemnity, and pomposity, sight of him called forth nothing so much as a composite picture of all the gamins that ever prowled the gutters of Metropolis. Where a paunch should have been there was a flat and muscular patch of tight little belly; his feet were as small and agile as a dancer's; his eyes were bright twin moons; and his mode of locomotion can only be described as a light fantastic tripping in the best pixy-on-the-greens-ward manner.

And as for his years, he was "between a man and a boy, a hobble-de-hoy, a fat, little, punchy concern of sixteen." Except, alas for Barham! he was neither fat nor little; but on the contrary was lanky as a spider and as lean as adolescent Cassius.

This, then, was Djuna—Djuna the Magnificent, as Ellery Queen sometimes called him; the young major-domo of the Queen household, who had early evinced a genius for cookery and a flair for new gastronomic creations which had for all time settled the domestic problem for the Queens. An orphan, picked up by Inspector Queen during the lonely years when Ellery was at college, Djuna came to the Queens a beaten little creature with no surname, a swarthy skin, and a fluid cunning which was undoubtedly a heritage from Romany ancestors.

In time he ruled the household, and with no light hand.

Now, so strange is fate, had there been no Djuna there might have been no mystery—at least insofar as Ellery Queen was concerned. It was Djuna's gypsy hand which innocently moved the pieces that brought Ellery to the *Colosseum*. To understand how this came about it is necessary to reflect on the universal character of youth. Djuna at sixteen was all boy. Under Ellery's subtle guidance he had pushed his dark heritage into a locked closet of his brain and expanded; he became a refined gamin, which is paradoxically the essence of all so-called "well-bred" boyhood; he belonged to clubs, and played baseball, and handball, and basketball, and he patronized the movies with an enthusiastic passion which more often than not taxed his generous allowance. Had he lived a generation earlier he should have appeased his rabid appetite for adventure by devouring Nick Carter, Horatio Alger, and Altsheler. As it was, he made his gods out of living people—the heroes of the silver screen; and particularly those heroes who dressed in chaps and Stetsons, rode horses, flung lassos, and were "fast on the draw, pardner!"

The connection is surely apparent. When the press-agent of Wild Bill Grant's Rodeo caused the New York newspapers to erupt with a rash of hot red stories about its history, purpose, aims, attractions, stars, *ad nauseam,* he was playing directly to that wide unseen audience which makes its appearance in public only when the circus comes to town, and then fills the big tent with treble screams, the crackle of peanut-shells, and the gusty wonder of childhood. From the moment Djuna's burning black eyes alighted on the advertisement of the opening, the Queens knew no peace. He must see with his own eyes this fabulous creature, this (reverently whispered) Buck Horne. He must see the cowboys. He must see the "buckin' broncs." He must see the stars. He must see everything.

And so, with no premonition of what was to come, Inspector Richard Queen—that little bird of a man who had guided the Homicide Squad for more years than he cared to recall—telephoned Tony Mars, with whom he had a speaking acquaintance; and it was arranged without Djuna's foreknowledge that the Queens should survey the gladiatorial ruckus from Mars's own box at the *Colosseum* on opening night.

·   ·   ·   ·   ·   ·   ·

Tugging on the leash of Djuna's impatience, Inspector Queen and Ellery were constrained to "go early; come *on!*" Consequently, they were the first of the Mars party to arrive for the performance. Mars's box was on the south side of the arena near the eastern curve of the oval. The *Colosseum* was already half full; and hundreds were streaming without cessation into the building. The Queens sat back in plush-covered chairs; but Djuna's sharp chin was thrust over the rail, and his eyes smoked as they hungrily engulfed the broad terrain below, where workmen were still packing the hard earth of the arena's core, and the cameramen on Major Kirby's platform were still busy with their apparatus. He barely noticed the entrance of the great Tony Mars, a fresh derby on his poll and a fresh cigar clenched by his brown teeth.

"Glad to see you again, Inspector. Oh, Mr. Queen!" He sat down, his small eyes roving about the vast scene as if he felt the necessity of keeping a vigilant eye on all details at once. "Well, it's a new thrill for old Broadway, hey?"

The Inspector took snuff. "I'd say," he remarked benevolently, "for Brooklyn, the Bronx, Staten Island, Westchester, and every place *but* Broadway."

"Judging by the provincial manners of your audience, Mr. Mars," grinned Ellery. For the vendors were already busy hawking, and the characteristic sound of cracking peanut-shells filled the amphitheatre.

"You'll get plenty of Broadway wisenheimers here tonight," said Mars. "I know my crowds. Broadway's filled with a hard-boiled bunch, an' all that; but they're all saps an' suckers at heart, and they'll come an' chew goobers an' raise hell just for the kick they'll get out of actin' like hicks. Ever watch a morning crowd of hard guys at the State when they put on an old-time Western? They whistle an' stamp their feet an' all that, and they love it so much they'd cry if you took it away from 'em. Old Buck Horne'll get a good hand tonight."

At the magic name Djuna's prominent ears twitched, and he turned and slowly surveyed Tony Mars with a kindling respect.

"Buck Horne," said the Inspector with a dreamy smile. "The

old galoot! Thought he was dead and buried long ago. Good stunt getting him here, all right."

"Ain't a stunt, Inspector. It's a build-up."

"Eh?"

"Well, y'see," said Mars reflectively, "Buck's been out of pictures for nine-ten years. Did a movie three years ago, but it didn't pan out so well. But now with the talkies goin' full blast. . . . He an' Wild Bill Grant are buddies. Grant's a good business man to boot. Now the pay-off is this: if Buck goes over in the big time here, if his appearance makes a splash in New York, it's—well, rumored that he'll make a screen come-back next season."

"With Grant, I suppose, backin' him?"

The promoter looked at his house. "Well I ain't sayin' I'm not interested in the proposition myself."

The Inspector settled more comfortably in his seat. "How's the big fight coming along?"

"Fight? Oh, the fight! Swell, Inspector, swell. Advance sales are way beyond my expectations. I think—"

There was a little flurry at the rear of the box. They all turned, and then rose. A very lovely and feminine creature in a black evening gown and ermine wrap stood smiling there. A press of young men with hard eyes and cocked snap-brims were behind her, talking fast; some of them held cameras. She entered the box, and Tony Mars gallantly handed her to a front seat. There were introductions. Djuna, who had turned back to devour the arena once more after a single brief look at the newcomer, suddenly shuddered.

"Miss Horne—Inspector Queen, Mr. Ellery Queen. . . ."

Djuna kicked his chair aside, his lean face working. "You," he gasped to the astonished young woman, "you *Kit* Horne?"

"Why—yes, of course."

"Oh," said Djuna in a trembling voice, and retreated until his back pressed against the rail. "Oh," he said again, and his eyes grew enormous. Then he licked his lips and croaked: "But where—where's your six-shooter, ma'am, an' your—your bronc, ma'am?"

"Djuna," said the Inspector weakly; but Kit Horne smiled and then said in a very serious tone: "I'm frightfully sorry, but I had to leave them home. They wouldn't have let me in, you see."

"Gee," said Djuna, and spent five minutes staring at her radiant profile in fierce concentration. Poor Djuna! It was almost too much, this proximity to an idol. The great Kit Horne had spoken to him, to Djuna the Magnificent, by—by Buffalo Bill! That lovely wraith who had flitted over an impersonal screen, riding like a Valkyrie, shooting like a man, roping the dastardly villain. . . . And then he blinked and slowly, reluctantly, turned his head toward the rear of the box.

It was Tommy Black.

There were two others with him—another radiant vision, to whom all the males instantly deferred, Mara Gay; and Julian Hunter, impeccably dressed—but Djuna forgot everything, even the great Kit Horne, as he gulped the bubbling, incredible elixir so casually offered to him. *Tommy Black!* Tommy Black the fighter! Cripes! He retreated to his feet, overwhelmed by shyness; but from that moment no one in Tony Mars's box existed for him but the beetle-browed giant who shook hands all around and then, with easy possessiveness, slipped into the chair next to Mara Gay's and began to talk softly to her.

To Ellery it was faintly amusing. The reporters buzzing about; Djuna's speechless worship; the cool self-possession of Kit Horne and Mara Gay's supercilious condescension toward her; Julian Hunter's smiling silence and tight lips; Mars's nervous watch on the jammed bowl; Black's fluid movements and snaky gestures—as usual when a group of personalities gathered, Ellery reflected, there were undercurrents and crosscurrents; and he wondered what made Hunter smile so tightly and what made Kit Horne so suddenly silent. But most of all he wondered what was the matter with Mara Gay. This darling of Hollywood, one of the most highly paid screen personalities in the world, was something less than the pure and glamorous beauty she appeared on the magic screen. Yes, she was daringly dressed, as usual, and her eyes were also as extraordinarily bright as they always seemed in her films; but there was a thinness, an emaciation about her features that he had never been conscious of before; and her large eyes did not seem quite so large. Besides, here—where her gestures where unschooled by a watchful director—she was vividly nervous, almost quicksilver-ish. A thought came to him, and he studied her without seeming to do so.

There was polite conversation.

And Djuna, his heart big in his throat, jerked his head from side to side as the celebrities gathered in surrounding boxes. And then, of course, things began to happen in the arena; and from that instant he was insensible to the coarser realities and devoted his whole earnest attention to the spectacle below.

The bowl was packed with a boisterous, good-natured crowd. Society was out *en masse,* rimming the rail above the arena with an oval panel studded with glittering jewels. In the arena there was flashing activity; from the smaller entrances horsemen had appeared, each a whirling smear of color—red bandanas, leathery chaps, fancy vests, dun sombreros, checkered shirts, silvery spurs. There was roping and thunderous riding, and the steady crackle of pistol-shots. The cameramen were busy on their platform. The whole bowl was filled with a prodigious drumming of horses' hooves on the tanbark. . . . A tall slender young man gayly caparisoned in cowboy regalia stood in the center of the arena. The overhead arcs gleamed on his curly hair. Little puffs of smoke surrounded him. He operated a catapult with his foot and with nonchalant skill caused little glass balls to disappear as he twirled his long-barreled revolver. A shout went up. "That's Curly Grant!" He bowed, doffed his Stetson, caught a brown horse, vaulted lightly into the saddle, and began to trot across the arena toward the Mars box.

Ellery had moved his chair closer to Kit Horne, leaving Mara Gay with Tommy Black, while Hunter sat quietly by himself in the rear of the box. Mars had vanished.

"You're fond of your father, I take it," murmured Ellery as he noted her eyes roving about the arena.

"He's so darned—Oh, it's hard to explain those things." She smiled, and her straight brows came together in a solemn way. "My affection for him is—well, perhaps greater because he's not really my father, you know; he adopted me when I was a kid-orphan. He's been everything the best father could be to me—"

"Oh! I beg your pardon. I didn't know—"

"You needn't be apologetic, Mr. Queen. You've committed no social error. I'm really very proud. Perhaps," she sighed, "I haven't been the best daughter in the world. I see Buck so very seldom these days. The rodeo is bringing us together for the first time in more than a year—closely, I mean."

"Naturally, with you in Hollywood and Mr. Horne on his ranch—"

"It's not easy. I've been busy on location in California almost without let-up, and with Buck secluded up in Wyoming. . . . I haven't been able to visit him for more than a day or so every few months. He's been a lonely man."

"But why," asked Ellery, "doesn't he move to California?"

Kit's brown little hands tightened. "Oh, I've tried to make him. But three years ago he tried a screen comeback and—well, they just don't come back, it seems, in the movies any more than the prize-fighting game. He took it rather hard and insisted on shutting himself up on his ranch, like a hermit."

"And you," said Ellery softly, "the apple of his eye, to be more than slightly horticultural."

"Yes. He has no family or relatives at all. He leads a horribly lonely life. Except for his yellow cook-boy and a few old-timers who punch the small herd he's got, he's alone. Really, his only visitors are myself and Mr. Grant."

"Ah, the colorful Wild Bill," murmured Ellery.

She regarded him rather queerly. "Yes, the colorful Wild Bill. Occasionally he stops over at the ranch to spend a few days between rodeo shows. I *have* been remiss in my duty to Buck! He's not been well for years now—nothing really wrong with him. I guess it's just old age. But he's been losing weight, and—"

"Hi, Kit!"

She flushed, and leaned forward with eagerness. Ellery through half-closed eyes saw Mara Gay's lips tighten, and her voice faltered the merest trifle as she saw what was happening. The curly head of the glass-ball exterminator was grinning at them from below the rail. Curly Grant had with an easy leap left the saddle, caught the rail, and now hung suspended over the arena. The horse waited philosophically below.

"Why, Curly," said Kit, "you'll—Get down this instant!"

"And you a lady acrobat," grinned Curly. "No, ma'am. Kit, I want to explain—"

Ellery mercifully turned his attention elsewhere.

There was another diversion. The short military figure of Major Kirby appeared at the entrance to the box by the side of Tony Mars, who now seemed in the ultimate heaven of nervousness. He greeted Curly's disembodied face with a smile, and bowed with a precise little click of his heels to the ladies, shaking hands quietly with the men.

"You know young Grant?" asked the Inspector, as the curly head disappeared below the box and Kit sat back with a flushed smile.

"Yes, indeed," replied the Major. "He's one of those fortunate young devils who makes friends everywhere. I met him on the other side."

"In service, eh?"

"Yes. He was attached to my command." Major Kirby sighed, and smoothed his little black mustache with an immaculate fingernail. "Ah, the War. . . . A peculiarly rotten brand of delicatessen, if I may say so," he added. "But Curly—well, he was sixteen, I believe, at the time the great war to end wars called; enlisted under false colors, and very nearly lost his damn fool life at St. Mihiel when he tried to break up a machine-gun nest single-handed. These youngsters were—rash."

"But heroes," said Kit softly.

The Major shrugged, and Ellery suppressed a smile. It was evident that Major Kirby, who had probably acquitted himself with distinction in the War, had very few illusions about the glories of battle and the privilege of laying down one's life for the doubtful importance of wresting two yards more of torn earth from the enemy. "I'm in a bigger war right now," he said grimly. "You don't know what competition is until you try to score a scoop on some photographic story. I'm in charge of the newsreel unit here tonight, you know. We've got an exclusive."

"I—" began Ellery with some eagerness.

"But I must be getting back to my men," continued Major Kirby evenly. "See you later, Tony." He bowed again, and quickly left the box.

"Great little guy," muttered Tony Mars. "You wouldn't believe it to look at him, but he's one of the crack pistol-shots of the U.S. Army. Used to be, I mean. In the Infantry during the big scrap. Some kind of expert, he's turned out to be. Newsreels!" He sniffed, and nervously eyed the arena as he fumbled for his watch. Then a vast intensity came over his rather blurred features, and he sat down with the suddenness of a dog coming to point. They all turned their attention to the arena.

· · · · · · ·

It was emptying. Cowboys, cowgirls were riding briskly toward the exits. In a short time there was nothing left to see but the deserted track, the hoof-pocked dirt core of the oval, and the men on the newsreel platform. Major Kirby's erect little figure appeared, half-running, from one of the side doors; it closed behind him; he bounded across the arena, clambered like a monkey up the wooden ladder, and took his place on the platform among the sound and cameramen.

The crowd hushed.

Djuna drew a curiously musical breath.

Then from the big western gate came small sounds, and a uniformed man swung back the large leaves of the gate, and a lone man on horseback rode forth. He was a squat powerful man dressed in tattered old corduroys and a rather aged Stetson. At his right side hung a holstered revolver. He galloped recklessly across the track to the very center of the dirt oval, brought his horse to a sliding stop in a cloud of flying clods, stood erect in his stirrups, took off his hat with his left hand, waved it once, put it back on his head, and stood there that way, smiling.

Thunderous applause! Stamping feet! One Djuna's feet particularly.

"Wild Bill," whispered Tony Mars. His face was pale.

"What the devil you so nervous about, Tony?" asked Tommy Black with a deep chuckle.

"I'm always twitchy as a snow-bird at these damn openings," growled the promoter. "Shh!"

The man on horseback shifted his grip on the reins to his left hand, with his right jerking the revolver out of his holster. It had a long dulled-blue barrel which winked wickedly under the arcs. He flung his arm roofward and the gun kicked back, exploding with a roar. And he opened his heavy old mouth and screamed: *"Yooooowwww!"* with such a sustained wolfish quality that the echoes slithered off the rafters and startled the crowd into silence.

The revolver was hammered back into the holster. And Wild Bill, sinking down into his saddle, put one hand affectionately on his saddle-horn and opened his mouth again.

"La-dees and Gentle-men," he bellowed, and the words carried far distances, so that those in the topmost tiers heard clearly: "Per-mit me to wel-come you to the Grrrand Open-ing of Wild Bill Grrrant's Rrro-deo! (Applause) The Larrrgest Ag-grega-shun of Cow-boys an' Cow-girrrls in the Worrrld! (Cheers) Frrrom the sun-baked plains of Tex-ahs to the Rrrroll-in' Rrr-ranges of Wy-oming, frrrom the Grrreat State of Arrrizo-nah to the Mount-ins of Montanah, these Darrre-devils have come for Yore Enter-tain-ment! (Wild Stamping of Feet) To risk Life an' Limb in Dange-rrrous Con-tests of Skill in Rrrropin', Rrrridin', Bull-doggin', Shootin'—all the stunts that go to make the Grrreat-est Sport in the Worrrld—the Good Ole-Fashion'

Rrrrodeo! An' T'night, La-dees and Gentlemen, in ad-di-shun to my reg'lar show, I have the Grrreat Hon-or to pre-sent to the Grrreat Cit-y of Noo Yawk A SPECIAL EXTRAH ADD-ED AT-TRACTION!"

He stopped with something like triumph, and the echoes rolled forth majestically, to be drowned in a cataract of approval.

Wild Bill raised a meaty hand. "An', folks, he ain't no Drr-rug-store Cow-boy neither! (Laughter) Folks, I know you're rr-rar-in' to see 'im, so I won't take up no more of yore time. La-dees and Gentle-men, I take Grrreat Pleas-ure in intro-ducin' the Grrreat-est Cowboy in the Worrrld, the hombre who put the Rrrrroarin' Ole West on the Silv-ah Screen! . . . A-merri-cah's Grrrand Ole Man of the Mo-vies—THE ONE AN' ON-LY BUCK HORNE! *Let 'er rip!*"

They tore the roof down. And, of course, leading the cho-rus of assorted bellows, roars, thunders, screams, and shrieks was one Djuna Queen, yelling himself a lovely olive-green in the face.

Ellery grinned and glanced at Kit Horne. She was sitting tensely forward, an anxious expression on her soft brown fea-tures, watching the eastern gate of the arena with eyes of trou-bled gray-blue.

A uniformed attendant, very small and puny at this distance, manipulated the doors, they swung back, and out into the glare of the amphitheatre galloped a magnificent horse, a powerful animal with shining tight flanks and proudly tossing head. On his back sat a man.

"Buck!"

"Buck Horne!"

"Ride 'im, cowboy!"

Horne leaned forward in his saddle, riding with fluent ease, the gallant old buckaroo. In a roped-off section of the box-tier a band struck up. There was an unearthly din. It was like opening night of the circus in Kankakee, or West Tannerville, Ohio. Djuna was banging his palms together madly. Kit had sunk back with a smile.

Ellery leaned forward and tapped her knee. She turned, startled. "Nice animal he's riding!" shouted Ellery.

She threw back her head and laughed from a full throat. "He certainly ought to be, Mr. Queen! He cost five thousand dollars."

"Phew! A horse?"

"A horse. That's *Rawhide,* my favorite, my gorgeous pet. Buck wanted most especially to ride *Rawhide* tonight. Said it would bring him luck."

Ellery sat back, smiling vaguely. The man on horseback had doffed his splendid black ten-gallon hat, bowing right and left, and had urged his animal forward with his knees until they pulled up near the eastern turn of the oval after almost a complete circuit of the track, below and a little to the right of the guest-box in which the Mars party sat. He sat astride like an old god, with perfect ease; the brilliant lights caught the metal and leather glints on his rich Western regalia, the glints on his white hair where it blanketed his neck below his hat-brim. The horse posed like a model, proudly, his sleek right forefoot delicately extended before him.

Kit rose, a smartly gowned young woman, filled her deep chest with air, opened her red mouth, and gave vent to a long ululating cry which raised the short hair on Ellery's nape and brought him, blinking, to his feet. The Inspector grasped the arms of his chair. Djuna jumped a foot. Then Kit quietly sat down, grinning. In the din the man on horseback half-turned his head as if searching for someone.

Someone behind Ellery said venomously: "Slut!"

Ellery said hastily to Kit: "The call of the wild, eh?"

Her grin had vanished. She nodded pleasantly, but her little brown jaw tightened and her back was soldier-stiff.

Ellery turned casually. Big Tommy Black was sitting forward, elbows resting on his knees. He was whispering to Mara Gay. Julian Hunter smoked a cigar silently in the background. Tony Mars was staring as if hypnotized at the arena.

Wild Bill was roaring frantically against the surge of noise. The band played: "*Ta-ra!*" several times, *fortissimo,* its uniformed conductor waving his baton desperately. Then Horne himself held up his hand for silence, and it came with a gradual subsidence of sound after the lapse of mere seconds, like a thunderous sea receding swiftly from a deck.

"La-dees and Gentle-men," shouted Wild Bill. "I want to thank ya, an' Buck wants to thank ya, one an' all, for this Wonder-ful Rrrrecep-shun! Now the first e-vent will be a Rrrrip-Snortin' Ride aroun' the A-re-nah, with Buck leadin' Forrrty Rrrri-ders in a Hell-Bent-fer-Leather Chase! Just the way he used to lead th' posses after the Dirrrt-y Vill-'ins in his movin' pitchers! That's just a starter, an' then Buck'll get down to bus'-ness, per-formin' In-div-id-u-al Feats of Horrrse-man-ship an' Sharrrp-shoot-in'!"

Buck Horne pulled his hat firmly down on his forehead. Wild Bill hefted his revolver from the holster, pointed it at the roof, and once more pulled the trigger. At the signal the eastern gate swung open again and a large cloud of riders, men and women on wiry Western horses, charged out on the track, whooping and waving their hats. At their head rode Curly Grant, his head bare and his hair gleaming; and One-Arm Woody, upon whom for the moment all eyes centered; for his mastery with one arm of the dappled brute he was riding was amazing. Then the chapped and throat-swathed cavalry swept on around the farther, northern length of the track, racing toward the west. . . .

Ellery twisted his neck and said to the Inspector: "Our friend Wild Bill may be heaven's own gift to the great outdoors, but he really should brush up on his arithmetic."

"Huh?"

"How many riders did Grant bellow would follow Buck Horne on this epic-making charge around the arena?"

"Oh! Forty, wasn't it? Say, what in time's got into you?"

Ellery sighed. "In my unreasonable way—probably because Grant was so specific about the number—I've been counting 'em."

"Well?"

"There are forty-one!"

The Inspector dropped back with a snort, and his gray mustaches quivered with indignation. "You—you. . . . Oh, shut up! By God, El, sometimes you get my goat. What the devil if there are forty-one, or a hundred and ninety-seven!"

Ellery said placidly: "Your blood-pressure, Inspector. At the same time—"

Djuna whispered with ferocity: "Oh, *shush!*"

Ellery shushed.

The milling riders came beautifully still on the southern length of the oval, and once more silence fell. They were lined up in twos, a long string of them; Curly Grant and the one-armed Woody at their head were still some thirty feet behind the lone figure of Buck Horne.

From the center of the arena, where he sat his horse like an elevated ringmaster, Wild Bill rose in his stirrups and bawled: "Ready, Buck?"

Behind him on the trestled platform Major Kirby had disposed all his cameras; the photographers were taut, motionless, awaiting the word.

The single rider on the track swung his body a little, drew a big old-fashioned gun from his right holster, poised it muzzle roofwards, pulled the trigger, and out of the explosion came his voice: *"Shoot!"*

Forty-one arms dipped into forty-one holsters behind him, forty-one guns leaped into view. . . . Wild Bill from his commanding position shot straight up in the air, once. Then Buck Horne's broad shoulders hunched, he leaned slightly forward, and his right arm still pointing the gun at the roof, hurled his horse ahead on the tanbark track. At the same instant the entire cavalcade swirled into a roaring motion picture of sound, uttering piercing cowboy yells. In an incredible flirt of time's tail the horses had sped along the track to almost directly below the Mars box, led by that gallant figure on *Rawhide* some forty feet ahead now, just rounding the farther side of the eastern turn.

And as the troop followed, their big revolvers, uniformly pointed upward, came alive as one, belching toward the roof, enveloping horses, men, and women in a momentary explosion of gun-smoke. That single fusillade in answer to the one shot from the gun of the man riding swiftly before them. . . .

Twenty thousand pairs of eyes were fixed on the man riding ahead. Twenty thousand pairs of eyes saw what followed, and did not believe what they saw.

At the instant the fusillade cracked out, Buck Horne had been leaning sideways out of his saddle to the south, his revolver raised high above his head in his right hand, his left hand high above the pommel as he clutched the reins. *Raw-*

hide was finding his huge stride and had now advanced around the turn to a position directly in line with the troupe of riders and the Mars box.

And at that very instant the body of the man on *Rawhide's* broad back jerked, sagged, slipped from the saddle, and crashed to the tanbark . . . to be trampled upon all in a moment by the cruel hooves of the forty-one horses behind.

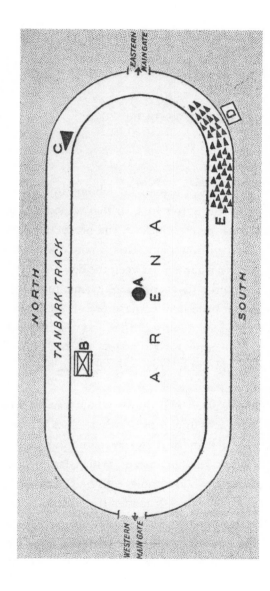

DIAGRAM OF ARENA AT MOMENT OF MURDER

A—WILD BILL GRANT'S POSITION   B—NEWSREEL PLATFORM
C—BUCK HORNE'S POSITION   D—MARS' GUEST BOX
E—POSITION OF RIDERS FOLLOWING BUCK HORNE

3: REQUIESCAT

THERE IS a story somewhere of a man for whom time stood still; or perhaps for whom time stretched, so that what was the blink of an eye to a normal being, a beat of the heart, the flick of a finger, was to him a full slow hour. This is not so fantastic as it sounds. There is indeed a garden between the dawn and the sunrise; and it may be found only at such rare cosmic moments when the normal activity of the real universe ceases. In human crowds, for example, such a moment solidifies and reigns to the exclusion of all coarser phenomena; it is a time when a molecular instant becomes an infinite interval—the interval between mass realization and mass panic.

It was such a manifestation of infinity which caught the densely peopled *Colosseum* at the instant when Buck Horne tumbled to the tanbark track and was swallowed up in a tangle of snorting, rearing horses. In that instant, which lasted only a second and yet endured for hours, no breath was drawn, no muscle twitched, no tiniest sound was made. The tableau below stiffened into phantasmagoric stone; and the tableau above was eternal. Had there been an observer perched at the apex of the vast ceiling, looking down upon the petrified thousands below, he might have thought himself the lone spectator of some gi-

54

gantic museum-group in complex marble, fixed to the sides and bottom of a titanic well.

Then the real world pushed through and the instant flashed on into eternity. There came a wordless noise, a plutonic sound, a rising groan of pure horror which rumbled from the *basso* of the gamut up the scale until it keened off beyond the perception of human ears into an eerie vibration sensed rather than heard. And the screams of the fighting riders broke through, and the terrified cries of the horses as they made spasmodic efforts to avoid trampling upon that invisible figure on the spot where the man on horseback had plunged to the ground.

As one, twenty thousand people sprang to their feet, shaking the *Colosseum* to its foundations.

As in a dream, the dream passed.

What followed was normal for what should follow. There were cries, thin shrill questions, restless movements toward the exits—movements instantly halted by the jack-in-the-box appearance of attendants at the gates and runways. In the arena some semblance of order was crystalizing. The horses were drawing off, apart. Out of the eastern gate ran a bareheaded man carrying a black bag, and under his arm a hurriedly snatched Indian blanket. Simultaneously in the center of the arena Wild Bill Grant—whose horse, whose hat, whose hand, whose very eyes had not moved—came to life and kicked his animal toward the nucleus of the confusion.

The occupants of the Mars box had been tiny members of the large tableau of silence—all of them, without exception. But there were four persons there who, for significant reasons, came out of their trance before the others, whose nerves were more sharply attuned to the exigencies of the moment. These were the Queens, father and son—the one a policeman to his neat shoe-tops, trained to respond to emergencies; the other a mental machine whom no amazement could paralyze long; Tony Mars, the sensitive creator of this monument to sport which of an instant had changed into a mausoleum to a sportsman; and Kit Horne, who more than all the others was to feel the full anguish of reaction. These four, in pairs, vaulted the rail of the box to thud onto the tanbark ten feet below, badly jarred but unmindful of the shock—leaving their fellow-occupants of the box behind, too stunned to move. Julian Hunter's cigar had dropped quite out of his mouth, and his mouth remained open; Mara Gay's thin body was quivering, and the blood had drained out of her cheeks; Djuna sat utterly bewildered; and Tommy Black stood rocking on his toes like a dazed pugilist warding off a rain of blows.

The riders had dismounted now; some were busy soothing their horses.

.   .   .   .

Kit and Ellery were in the van, leading the Inspector and Tony Mars by a dozen feet. The girl sped on wings of fear toward the scene of the accident, closely pursued by Ellery, whose brow was furrowed and whose eyes were still blinking at the suddenness of the tragedy. They dashed into the group surrounding the still crumpled figure on the tanbark, and stopped dead. The man with the black bag, who had been kneeling by the side of the figure, rose hastily at sight of Kit Horne and flung the blanket over the thing on the floor.

"Uh Miss Horne," he said in a hoarse voice. "Miss Horne. I'm so very, very sorry. He's . . . dead."

"Doctor, no."

She said it very quietly, as if by remaining calmly sane she might alter the physician's verdict. The rodeo doctor, a shabby rugged old man, shook his head slightly and backed away, keeping his earnest eyes on her white face.

Ellery stood thoughtfully by her side, watching her.

She dropped to her knees in the dust with a choked cry, and touched the edge of the blanket. Curly Grant, his face dead, and Wild Bill Grant, stupefied, made instinctive movements to intercept her. She waved them back, scarcely looking at them; and they stopped in their tracks. Then she lifted the blanket the merest bit; something remarkably pale here and remarkably red there that had been a living face was starkly uncovered. The features, drawn, bluish, distorted in death, spattered with thick blood and dirt, looked sightlessly up at her, as it were in uncrushed but pitiful dignity. She dropped the blanket as if it were a malignant thing, and knelt there in silence.

Ellery dug his knuckles into the muscular ribs of Curly Grant. "Come alive, you fool," he said softly. "Get her away from here." Curly started, flushed, dropped to his knees beside her. . . .

Ellery turned to come face to face with his father. The Inspector was puffing like Boreas.

"What the—what's happened to him?" he gasped.

Ellery said: "Murder."

The old man's eyes goggled. "Murder! But how the devil—"

They stared at each other for an instant, and then something cloudy suffused Ellery's eyes. He began slowly to look about. A cigaret which he had from habit stuck between his lips drooped toward the sandy blooded tanbark. As he took it from between his lips and crushed it between his fingers, he panted: "Oh, God, what an idiot I am! Dad. . . ." He dropped the fragments into his pocket. "There's no question about the murder part of this. He was drilled in the side; must have gone through the heart. I saw the wound myself as the doctor dropped the blanket over him. This is—"

The Inspector's color returned to his gray cheeks; his bird-like eyes snapped; and he darted forward into the group.

The group parted, engulfed him.

Curly's wide shoulders hid the bowed shining head of Kit Horne.

Wild Bill Grant stared and stared at the blanket as if he could not see enough of it.

Ellery squared his shoulders, drew a long breath, and started off at a lope toward the northwestern part of the arena.

4: THE THREADS

As HE charged across the hard-packed dirt Ellery was able to assimilate in flashes something of the activity around him. Behind him stood a silent ring of men and women, aliens in a strange land, surrounding the dead man and the sobbing girl. In the frenzied tiers above people scurried about like demented ants; there were thin screams from women's throats, and hoarse masculine voices, and the muffled thunder of shuffling feet. At the exits dotting the distant walls minute figures in blue with brass buttons catching vagrant spears of light, had sprung up— police summoned hastily from the recesses of the building to defend the bulwarks. They were pushing people back toward the seats, allowing no one to leave the amphitheatre; an excellent notion, to Ellery's mind, and he smiled a little as he ran on.

He scrambled faster, and then came to a stop at the trestles of the high platform on which stood the small figures of Major Kirby—pale but unruffled, quietly directing his group of wild-eyed, crouching-over-camera men.

"Major!" cried Ellery, striving to make himself heard above the din.

Major Kirby peered over the edge of the platform. "Yes? Oh—yes, Mr. Queen?"

"Don't leave that platform!"

The Major permitted himself to smile, briefly. "Don't bother yourself about *that*. God, what a break! By the way, what the devil did happen over there? Did the old chap have a fainting spell?"

"The old chap," said Ellery grimly, "had a bullet spell, that's what he had. He was murdered, Major—through the heart."

"Lord!"

Ellery stared gravely upward. "Come a little closer, Major." The newsreel man stooped, his little black eyes snapping. "Were your cameras grinding through *everything?*"

Something sparkled in the black eyes. "Good Lord! Good Lord!" a slight flush tinted his slick cheeks. "What a miracle, Mr. Queen, what a miracle . . . yes, every second!"

Ellery said rapidly: "Pluperfect, Major, simply pluperfect. An exquisite gift from the god who watches over detectives. Now listen: keep grinding, get every shot you can—I want a complete photographic record of what happens from now on until I tell you to stop. Do you understand?"

"Oh, perfectly." The Major paused, and then said: "But how long will I have—"

"You're worried about the film?" Ellery smiled. "I don't think you've need to, Major. Your company has a really exceptional opportunity to serve the police, and considering how motion picture companies throw their money around, I think the cost of the extra film is money well spent. Well spent."

The Major looked reflective, then touched the end of his little mustache, nodded, rose, and spoke brusquely to his men. One camera kept focused on the group surrounding the body. Another swept its eye, like a mechanical Cyclops, in a steady circle of the audience-tiers. A third picked up details in other parts of the arena. The technicians in the sound booth were working madly.

Ellery fingered his bow-tie, flicked a speck of dust off his alabaster bosom, and sped back across the arena.

.   .   .   .

Inspector Queen, that admirable executive, was surrounded by the grim halo of Work. He was the only person in New York who might be called, without intent to malign, an Ultra-crepidarian critic. It was of the very nature of his job to find fault with small and insignificant details. He was the scientist of trifles, a passionate devotee of minutiae. And yet his old nose was never so closely pressed to the ground that he could not keep in perspective the broadest view of the terrain. . . . The present task was worthy of his mettle. A murder had been committed in an auditorium peopled with twenty thousand souls. Two hundred hundred persons, any one of whom might be the murderer of Buck Horne! His bird-like gray little head was cocked fiercely forward, his fingers dipped unceasingly into his old brown snuff-box, his mouth rattled very good orders indeed, and all the while his bright little eyes were wandering about the auditorium as if disembodied, keeping in sight every intricate movement of the forces he had disposed. It was fortunate, perhaps, that while he awaited reinforce-ments from Headquarters—members of his own squad—he nevertheless had a large army of officers to place strategically about the spacious premises. The ushers and special officers of the *Colosseum* had been pressed into service, and those of the police who had been within the building at the time of the murder. All exits were grimly guarded. It was already estab-lished from relayed reports that not even a pigmy had slipped through the cordon. It was his calm intention not to permit one of the twenty thousand persons in the building to escape until the most searching investigation had been made.

Detectives from the nearby precincts had already responded to the alarm; they ringed the arena, keeping it clear as a base of operations. Hundreds of staring heads popped over the box-tier rail. The group of horsemen and horsewomen had been segregated, sent in a group to the other side of the arena; they were dismounted, and their horses, serene now, were pawing the earth and snorting quite peacefully. Their coats shone with the heat of their bodies after the short but strenuous gallop. The two special officers who had been stationed at each of the two main gates in the arena—at east and west—were on duty still, backed up by detectives. All the arena exits were fast closed, and guarded. No one was permitted either to enter or leave the arena.

As Ellery ran up, he saw his father sternly eying a diminutive cowboy with bleared eyes and convex little legs.

"Grant tells me you generally take charge of the horses," snapped the Inspector. "What's your name?"

The little cowboy licked his dry lips. "Dan'l—Hank Boone. I don't savvy this shootin' a-tall, Inspector. Honest, I—"

"Do you or don't you take charge of the horses?"

"Yess'r, reckon I do!"

The Inspector measured him. "Were you one of that crazy yelling bunch riding behind Horne tonight?"

"Nos'ree!" cried Boone.

"Where were you when Horne fell off his horse?"

"Down yonder, behin' that west chute gate," mumbled Boone. "When I see ole Buck passin' in his chips, I got ole Baldy—special at the gate—to pass me through."

"Anybody else come through with you?"

"Nos'r. Baldy, he an' me—"

"All right, Boone." The Inspector jerked his head at a detective. "Take this man across the arena and let him get those horses together. We don't want a stampede here."

Boone grinned rather feebly, and trotted off toward the horses in company with a detective. There was a temporary row of watering-troughs set up in the dirt across the arena, and he became busy leading the horses to water. The cowboys and cowgirls near by watched him stonily.

Ellery stood quite still. This part of the job was his father's.

He looked around. Kit Horne was a statue with dusty knees, as pale as the dying moon, staring without expression at the crumpled heap covered by the gaudy Indian blanket on the tanbark. To each side stood protection—poor protection, one would say, for Curly Grant was grotesquely like a man whose ears have been suddenly pierced and who finds himself in a frenzied soundless world; and his father, stocky marble, might be in the grip of a paralysis which had attacked him without warning and frozen him in an attitude of dazed pain where he stood. And both men, also, looked at the gaudy blanket.

Ellery, a not insensitive soul, looked at the blanket, too—anywhere but at those staring feminine eyeballs.

The Inspector was saying: "Here, you—precinct man?—take, a couple of the boys and collect every goldarned gun in the joint. Yes, every *one!* Rustle some cards or something and tag every weapon with its owner's name. Or bearer's name, if he doesn't own it. And don't just *ask* for 'em; I want every man-jack and woman on this floor *searched*. These people are accustomed to going heeled, remember."

"Yes, sir."

"And," added the Inspector thoughtfully, turning his bright little eyes on the silent trio staring at the covered body, "you might start with these folks here. The old feller, the curly-headed lad—yes, and the lady too."

Struck by a sudden thought, Ellery turned sharply and searched for someone. The man was not in this group about the body. The man with the single arm who had handled his horse so masterfully. . . . He caught sight of the one-armed rider far across the arena, sitting stolidly on the floor and flipping a Bowie knife up and down, up and down. . . . He turned back in time to *see* Wild Bill Grant raise his arms stiffly and submit to a search, his eyes still dead with pain. The holster he wore strapped about his thick waist was already empty; a detective was tagging the gun. Curly awakened suddenly, colored, and opened his mouth in anger. Then he shrugged and handed over his slim revolver. Neither Grant nor his son, it soon appeared, had a second weapon in his clothes. Then Kit Horne—

Ellery said: "No."

The old man cocked an inquisitive eye at him. Ellery jerked his thumb slightly toward the girl and shook his head. The Inspector stared, then shrugged.

"Uh—you, don't bother Miss Horne now. We'll attend to her later."

The two detectives nodded and marched off across the arena. Kit Horne did not move; she had not heard a word, but continued to study the zigzag design of the blanket in an expressionless absorption that was horrible.

The Inspector sighed and rubbed his hands together briskly. "Grant!" he said. The old showman turned his head with precision. "You and your son—get Miss Horne off to the side there, will you? This isn't going to be pleasant."

Grant drew a deep sobbing breath, his eyes fiery red, and touched Kit's pale bare arm. "Kit," he muttered. "Kit."

She looked at him in surprise.

"Kit. Come off here a minute, Kit."

She looked down again at the blanket.

Grant nudged his son. Curly rubbed his eyes for an instant, wearily, and then they lifted the girl bodily and swung her around. Terror gleamed there, the impulse to cry out; it drained swiftly away and she went limp. They half-carried her across the arena.

The Inspector sighed. "Takes it hard, doesn't she? Well, El, let's get to work. I want a long look-see at that body."

He motioned to several detectives, and they came forward to form a solid wall of official flesh around the corpse. Ellery stood within the ring, and Inspector Queen. The Inspector braced his spare little shoulders, took a last stimulative pinch of snuff, and then squatted on the tanbark. He removed the blanket with steady fingers.

．　　．　　．　　．　　．　　．　　．

There was something ironic in that dusty, bloody, once gorgeous costume. The dead man was dressed in black, a shiny romantic black. But the gloss of romance had been destroyed by Horne's descent to mortal earth, and it was now the rusty black of death. On his twisted, queerly dispersed legs were high-heeled boots of black leather which came well up to his knees, adorned with fancy stitching. Silvery spurs protruded from the boot-heels of the quiet feet. His tucked-in trousers were of black corduroy. Although his bandana was black, his shirt was of pure white sateen—a startling contrast. The shirt-sleeves were drawn in above the elbows and gripped tightly by black garters, while on his wrists he wore a pair of exquisitely fashioned black leather cuffs, embroidered in white stitching and studded with small silver ornaments, the much-coveted *conchas* of the cowboy-on-parade. Around his waist there was a snug-fitting black trouser belt; and swathing his torso and hips an ornate pistol belt, quite wide and looped for the insertion of cartridges. There were two holsters of beautiful black leather, one resting on the thigh below each hip. And both were empty.

These were the routine items to be duly noted. The Queens looked at each other, and then returned their attention to the body in a search for more interesting details.

Horne's outfit, so resplendent and brave, had been torn and dirtied by the steel-shod hooves of the horses. Rents in the white shirt revealed gashed hoof-wounds on the skin beneath. Neat, small, clean as a marker, there was a bullethole in the left side, a trench which obviously had ploughed through the heart. It had bled remarkably little, that wound; the satin edges of the hole were merely stuck to the skin beneath by pasty gore. The graunt old face was taut in death; the white head seemed curiously sunken on one side, behind the ear; and they noted with a sudden repulsion that some horse's wildly flying hoof had kicked the entire side of the man's head in. But the features were quite unmarked, except for dust and splatters of blood. The body lay in an impossible position—impossible, that is to say, for a living creature; it was evident that bones had been broken by the crushing weight of the trampling beasts.

Ellery, a little pale, straightened up and looked around. He lit a cigaret with slightly trembling fingers.

"Good thorough job," muttered the Inspector.

"I find it difficult," murmured Ellery, "to be anything but religious at the present moment."

"Hey? What's that?"

"Oh, don't mind me," cried Ellery. "I've never become accustomed to these bloody exhibits. . . . Dad, do you believe in miracles?"

"What the devil you talkin' about?" said the old man. He began to unbuckle from Horne's body the trouser belt, which was clasped snugly about the waist at the first hole; and then he struggled to detach the heavy pistol belt.

Ellery pointed to the dead face. "Miracle the first. His face wasn't touched, although those terrible hooves pounded all about him."

"What of it?"

"Oh, God!" groaned Ellery. "What of it? the man says. Nothing of it. That's exactly the point! If there was anything of it, it wouldn't be a miracle, would it?"

The Inspector disdained to reply to such obvious nonsense.

"Miracle the second." And Ellery blew smoke jerkily. "Look at his right hand."

The old man obediently, if somewhat wearily, complied. The right arm seemed to be broken in two places; but the right hand was healthily brown, and there was not a scratch on it. Gripped in the tight clutch of the fingers was the long-barreled revolver they had seen Horne flourish only a few moments before.

"Well?"

"That's not even a miracle; it's downright act of Providence. He fell, he was probably dead before he struck the ground, forty-one horses stepped all over him—and, by heaven, his hand doesn't drop the gun!"

The Inspector nursed his lower lip. He looked bewildered. "Well, but what *of* it? You don't think there's something—"

"No, no," said Ellery impatiently. "There can't be anything human about the causes of these phenomena. There's a surfeit of eye-witnesses for *that*. No, that's why I call these things miracles; they were accomplished by no human agency. Hence divine. Hence something to get a headache over. . . . Oh, hell, I'm going potty. Where's his Stetson?"

He broke through the ring of men and looked around. Then he brightened and stepped briskly across the dirt to a spot some eight feet off, where a high broad-brimmed hat lay ignominiously in the dust. He stooped, picked it up, and returned to his father.

"That's the hat, all right," said the Inspector. "Knocked off his head when he fell and, I s'pose, kicked away by some horse."

They examined it together. Its once noble crown was crushed in, like the head it had adorned; it was a black Stetson of smooth, marvelously soft felt with a very wide brim flaring at the edges. Around the crown there was a fine belt of braided black leather. Inside, in letters of gold, were stamped the initials *B H*.

Ellery laid the Stetson gently beside the crushed body.

The Inspector was peering intently at the dead man's two belts; Ellery watched him with some amusement. The pistol belt with its attached holsters was enormously long and heavy, since it was designed to go twice about the body of its wearer. Like the rest of Horne's showy gear it was elaborately adorned with silver *conchas* and gold nails, and its cartridge holders gleamed. A silver monogram bore a scrolled *B H*. Although the belt was soft and pliable and quite obviously kept perfect by loving fingers, it was quite obviously also of great age.

"Had this a long time, the poor coot," muttered the Inspector.

"I suppose," sighed Ellery, "it's like taking care of your precious books when you're a bibliophile. Have you the remotest notion how many hours I've put in oiling the calf bindings of my Falconers?"

They examined the trouser belt. It was in a perfect state of preservation, though very old; so old that the vertical creases—there were two, one crossing the second, the other the third buckle hole—had from long use worn the leather thin; so old, indeed, that the belt might have girdled the waist of a Pony Express rider. And as in the case of the pistol belt, this belt too displayed Horne's initials in silver.

"The man," murmured Ellery as he relinquished the belt to his father, "was an antiquarian of the Occident, by the beards of the *Academie!* Why, that's a museum piece!"

The Inspector, accustomed to his son's flights of fancy, spoke softly to one of the detectives near by, and the man nodded and made off. The detective returned with Grant, who seemed to have pulled himself together. He carried himself with unnatural stiffness, as if braced to withstand another blow.

"Mr. Grant," said the Inspector sharply, "I'm going to start this investigation the right way—details first; we'll get to the big things later. This looks like a long job."

Grant said hoarsely: "Anything ya say."

The Inspector nodded in a curt way and knelt once more by the body. Lightly his fingers moved over the broken clay, and inside of three minutes he had collected a small heap of miscellaneous articles from the dead man's clothes. There was a small wallet; it contained some thirty dollars in bills. The Inspector passed it to Grant.

"This Horne's?"

Grant's head jerked. "Yeah. Yeah. I—hell—I gave it to him for 'is last . . . birthday."

"Yes, yes," said the Inspector hastily, and retrieved the wallet, which had slipped from the rodeo owner's fingers. A handkerchief; a single key with a wooden tag attached bearing the words "Hotel Barclay"; a packet of brown cigaret-papers and a little sack of cheap tobacco; a number of long matches; a checkbook. . . .

Grant nodded dumbly at all the exhibits. The Inspector examined the check-book thoughtfully. "What was the name of his New York bank?"

"Seaboard. Seaboard National. He opened an account only a week'r so ago," muttered Grant.

"How d'ye know?" said the Inspector quickly.

"He asked me to rec'mend one when he got to Noo Yawk. I sent 'im over to m'own bank."

The old man replaced the check-book; its blank checks bore, plainly enough, the name of the Seaboard National Bank & Trust Company. According to its last stub-entry there was a balance of something over five hundred dollars.

"Find anything here," demanded the Inspector, "that oughtn't to be here, Mr. Grant?"

Grant's bloodshot eyes swept over the pile of small possessions. "No."

"Anything missing?"

"I wouldn't know."

"Hmmm. How about his duds? These things what he always wears? Look all right to you?"

The stocky man's hands clenched into fists. "Do I have to *look* at him again?" he shouted in a strangled voice. "Why the hell do ya torture me this way?"

The man's grief seemed genuine enough. So the Inspector said in a gentle voice: "Pull yourself together, man. We've got to check over everything; there's often a clue on the body. Don't you want to help us find your friend's murderer?"

"God, yes!"

Grant stepped forward and forced his eyes downward. And

his eyes swept from the horizontal boots to the gruesome con-
cavity of the poor mangled head. He was silent for a long time.
Then he threw back his thick shoulders and said harshly: "All
there; nothin' missing. That's his reg'lar movie outfit. Every
shaver from here to 'Frisco knew this rig-out in the days he was
makin' pitchers."

"Fine! All—"

"Interrogation," said Ellery. "Mr. Grant, did I hear you say
nothing is missing?"

Grant's head screwed around with unnatural slowness; his
eyes met Ellery's boldly, but there was something puzzled and—
yes, fearful—in their muddy depths. He drawled: "That's what I
said, Mr. Queen."

"Well, sighed Ellery, as his father squinted at him with a sudden alertness, "I suppose it isn't really your fault. You're upset,
and perhaps your faculty of observation isn't functioning as well
as it should. But the point is: there *is* something missing."

Grant turned abruptly back to look the body over again.
The Inspector seemed troubled. And Grant shook his head and
shrugged with a weary bafflement.

"Well, well," snapped the Inspector to his son, "what's the
mystery? What's missing?"

But Ellery, with a glint in his eye, was already stooping over
the body. Very carefully indeed he pried open the dead fingers of
the corpse's right hand, and stood up with Buck Horne's revolver
in his hand.

·   ·   ·   ·   ·   ·   ·

It was a beautiful weapon. To the Inspector, whose acquain-
tanceship with firearms was an intimate affair of a lifetime's
duration, the piece Ellery studied so attentively was a heavenly

sample of the old-fashioned gunsmith's art. He saw at once that it was not a modern arm. Not only the slightly antiquated design, but the softly rubbed-metal look of it, told of great age.

"Colt .45," he muttered. "Single action. Look at that barrel!"

The barrel was eight inches long, a slim tube of death. It was delicately chased in a scroll design, as was the cylinder. Ellery hefted the weapon thoughtfully; it was very heavy.

Wild Bill Grant seemed to have some difficulty in speaking. He moistened his lips twice before he could find his voice. "Yeah, it's a reg'lar cannon," he rumbled. "But a beauty. Ole Buck—Buck was partic'lar about the hang of his guns."

"The hang?" said Ellery with interrogative eyebrows.

"Liked 'em hefty an' liked 'em true. The balance, I'm talkin' about."

"Oh, I see. Well, this relic must weigh well over two pounds. Lord, what a hole it must make!"

He broke open the weapon; there were cartridges in all the chambers except one.

"Blanks?" he asked his father.

The Inspector extracted one of the bullets and examined it. Then he removed the others. "Yep."

Ellery carefully returned them to their chambers and snapped the cylinder back into place.

"This revolver was Horne's, I suppose," he asked Grant, "and not your property? I mean, it isn't one of the rodeo weapons?"

"Buck's," growled Grant. "Prime fav'rite with him. Had it—an' the pistol belt—fer twenty-odd years."

"Hmmm," said Ellery absently; he was absorbed in a study of the barrel. That the gun had been used a great deal was evident; it barrel was rubbed smooth at the tip, as was the peak of the sight. He transferred his attention to the butt. It was the most curious feature of the weapon. Both sides were inlaid with ivory—single pieces which had been carved in a steer's-head design, the center of which in each case was an oval, elaborately monogrammed *H.* The ivory inlays were worn and yellow with age, except for a narrow portion on the right sight of the butt; as Ellery held the revolver in his left hand, this patch of lighter ivory came between the tips of his curled fingers and the heel of his hand. He stared long and hard at it. Then he twirled the revolver thoughtfully and handed the gun to his father.

"You might include this piece of artillery with the other suspected weapons, dad," he said. "Just as a matter of precaution. You can never tell what these ballistic johnnies will dig up."

The Inspector grunted, took the revolver, gazed at it gloomily for a moment, and then turned it over to a detective with a nod. It was at this moment that there was movement at the eastern gate, and the detectives now on guard opened the big doors to admit a number of men.

.　　.　　.　　.　　.　　.　　.

Heading the little procession was a gigantic individual in plainclothes, with a face that seemed composed of overlapping plates of steel, and a thunderous step that outraged the tanbark. This Goliath was Sergeant Velie, Inspector Queen's favorite assistant; a man of few words and mighty, if mentally uninspired, deeds.

He bestowed a professional glance at the corpse, eyed the vast amphitheatre above his head with its thousands of buzzing, weary occupants, and rubbed his mastadonic jaw.

"Hot stuff, Chief." His voice was the voice of a bull-fiddle. "Exits?"

"Ah, Thomas," said the Inspector with a relieved smile. "Another one of these rush-hour murders. Relieve the police at the exits and station our own men. Send the officers back to their regular posts or duties."

"Nobody out?"

"Not a living soul 'til I give the word."

Sergeant Velie barged awesomely away.

"Hagstrom. Flint. Ritter. Johnson, Piggott. Stand by."

Five men of his own squad, who had accompanied Velie, nodded. There was professional joy in their eyes as they saw the magnitude of the task before them.

"Where's that rodeo doctor?" said the Inspector crisply.

The shabby rugged old man with the earnest eyes stepped forward. "I'm the rodeo medic," he said slowly. "Hancock is my name."

"Good! Come here, Doc."

The physician moved nearer the body.

"Now tell me all you know about this business."

"All I know?" Dr. Hancock seemed slightly alarmed.

"I mean—you examined him a few seconds after he fell, didn't you? What's the verdict?"

Dr. Hancock stared soberly at the crumpled figure on the floor. "There's not much to tell. When I ran over here, he was already dead. . . . Dead! Only today I examined him and found him in perfectly good condition."

"Died instantly?"

"I should say so."

"Dead before he hit the ground, hey?"

"Why—yes, I believe so."

"Then he didn't feel those horses steppin' all over him," said the Inspector, groping for his snuff-box. "That's a consolation! How many bullet wounds?"

Dr. Hancock blinked. "You must remember that mine was a cursory examination. . . . One wound. Directly through the heart in a leftward direction."

"Hmm. You familiar with gunshot wounds?"

"Ought to be," said the rodeo doctor grimly. "I'm an old Western myself."

"Well, what's the calibre of the bullet in his pumper, Doc?"

Dr. Hancock did not reply for a moment. He looked directly into the Inspector's eyes. "Now, that's a curious thing, sir. Very curious. I haven't probed—I know you'll want your Medical Examiner's physician to do that—but I'd swear from the size of the hole that he was shot with a .22 or .25 calibre!"

"A .22—" began Wild Bill Grant harshly, and stopped.

The Inspector's bright little eyes swept from physician to showman. "Well," he said suspiciously. "And what's so remarkable about that?"

"The .22 and .25, Inspector," replied Dr. Hancock with a little quiver of his lips, "are *not* Western weapons. Surely you know that?"

"Really?" said Ellery unexpectedly.

Grant's eyes were glowing with a joyful light. "I tell you," he cried, "there ain't a pea-shooter in my armory, Inspector! An' not a boy or girl in my show totes one!"

"Pea-shooters, hey?" said the Inspector genially.

"That's what they are—pea-shooters!"

"But," continued the Inspector in a dry voice, "because your people don't carry .22's, Mr. Grant, as a usual thing, doesn't say that one of 'em didn't carry a .22 tonight. Wasn't usual at all, tonight's business. No, sir. Besides, you know as well as I do that there are a number of big models that use .22 ammunition." He shook his head sadly. "And then the Lord knows how easy it is to buy a rod these days. No, Mr. Grant, I'm afraid we can't clear the slate of your bunch just on *that* account. . . . That's all, Dr. Hancock?"

"That's all," replied the physician in a small voice.

"Thanks. My own man, Doc Prouty, will be here soon. I don't think we'll need you any more, Dr. Hancock. Suppose you join that crew of—of. . . . Geronimo, is this New York or isn't it?—of cowboys over there!"

Dr. Hancock humbly retreated, clutching his little bag, the earnest light still in his eyes.

.   .   .   .

The body, being cold and rapidly stiffening clay, was left where it was, to the mercy of twenty thousand pairs of resentful eyes. Of Tony Mars, standing by in utter quietude, masticating a cigar so shredded and pulpy that little bits of it stuck brownly and wetly to his thin lips, the Inspector demanded information.

"Where the devil can we go for a heart-to-heart talk, Tony? Time's come to ask some questions, and I don't feel like doing it in front of half the population of Brooklyn and Manhattan. Where's the nearest cubbyhole?"

"I'll show you," said Mars tightly, and began to march off.

"Just a minute. Thomas! Where's Thomas?"

Sergeant Velie, who had the uncanny faculty of seeming to be in two places at the same time, materialized at the Inspector's side.

"Come along, Thomas. You guerrillas," snapped the Inspector to his five stalwarts, "you stick around here. Mr. Grant, you join us. Piggott, get that angel-haired cowboy—Curly Grant—and Miss Horne from among that gang over there."

Mars led the way to one of the small exits on the south wall of the oval; the Inspector clucked something, and the detective on duty opened the door. They emerged into a vast underground chamber with tiny rooms branching off, and it was to one of these that Mars went, the group at his heels. It proved to be a minor office, perhaps of a watchman or a time-keeper.

"Ellery, shut that door," growled the Inspector. "Thomas, no one's to get in here." He appropriated one of the two chairs in the room, sat down, inhaled snuff, smoothed his neat gray trousers, and waved his hand at Kit Horne, who was clutching the back of a chair. She was not dazed now; some emetic Curly Grant had applied to her shock had brought it out of her; but she was extremely quiet and, it seemed to Ellery, watchful. "Sit down, sit down, Miss Horne," said the Inspector in a kindly tone. "You must be tired." She sat down. "Now, Mr. Grant, let's get together," went on the old man more crisply. "We're alone, we're all friends here, and you can speak your mind. Any suggestions?"

"No savvy," said Grant tonelessly.

"Any idea who might have killed your friend?"

"No. Buck—" his voice trembled, "Buck was just a big kid, Inspect'r. Best-natured critter you ever saw. Didn't have an enemy in the world, I'll swear. Ev'ry-body knew him liked him—loved him."

"How about Woody?" said Kit Horne in a low, dangerous tone. Her eyes remained unwaveringly on Grant's florid face.

Something troubled came into the showman's eyes. "Oh, Woody," he said. "He—"

"Who's Woody?" demanded the Inspector.

"My reg'lar top-rider. Star of the show until—until Buck joined the outfit, Inspect'r."

"Jealousy, eh?" said the Inspector with a sparkle in his eye, as he glanced slyly at Kit. "Sorehead, I'll bet. Well, what's the story? Must be a story, or Miss Horne wouldn't have said what she did."

"Woody," said Ellery thoughtfully. "That isn't by an odd chance the chap with one arm?"

"Yeah," said Grant. "Why?"

"No reason," murmured Ellery. "I just didn't know."

"Well, there's no story," replied Grant wearily. "As you say, there might 'a' been some peeve on Woody's part, Inspect'r. Maybe some bad feelin' between him an' Buck. . . . Woody's got only one arm, so he's made capital of it. Doesn't hinder him none from ridin' an' shootin', an' he's sort o' proud of himself. When Buck came along. . . . I tole Woody this was only temp'rary, this business of Buck's bein' with the show. Yeah, maybe he resented Buck's buttin' in, Inspect'r, but I'd swear he wouldn't do nothin' so damn foolish as murder."

"That remains to be seen. Anybody else got a suggestion? You—the curly lad."

Curly said in a sort of despair: "Inspector, I wish to God I— we could help you. But this is just—hell, it ain't human! None of the people in our wickiup could possibly've—"

"Hope not, son," said the Inspector gloomily, in the tone of one who quaffs hope merely to quench despair. "You, Miss Horne?"

"Except for Woody," she replied stonily, "I don't know of a living soul who might have desired Buck's death."

"That's hard lines on Woody, Kit," began old Grant with a frown.

"It will be hard lines on whoever did it, Bill," said Kit in a conversational tone. They all looked at her quickly; but her eyes stared at the floor. There was an uncomfortable pause.

"S'pose," said the Inspector, clearing his throat, "s'pose you tell us how Buck Horne came to be with your show, Mr. Grant. We've got to start somewhere. What was he doin' with a circus outfit?"

"Circus outfit?" repeated Grant. "I—Oh. Buck's been out of the public eye fer nine-ten years. 'Ceptin' fer a spell maybe three-four years back, when he made one pitcher in a come-back try. Pitcher flopped, an' he took it passable hard. Went back to 'is ranch in Wyoming."

"Took it hard?"

Grant cracked his big knuckles. "I tell ya he was heartbroken! He was gettin' along in years, but he was a stubborn cuss an' wouldn't admit he was licked. Then the talkies came in an' he perked up again. Tole me on one o' my stopovers at the ranch that he was good as ever—wanted another crack at the movies. I tried to talk 'im out of it, but he says: 'Bill,' he says, 'I'm goin' loco out here, all alone. Kit, she's busy in Hollywood. . . .' Well, I says: 'Right, Buck. I'll pitch in, help much as I can.' So I helped—helped kill 'im," said Grant bitterly.

"And this stunt here, at the rodeo, was a build-up?"

"I had to do *somethin'*."

"You mean there wasn't much chance?"

Grant cracked his knuckles again. "At first I thought he didn't stand a show. But this last week—I dunno. He caught on. Papers took 'im up—Grand Ole Man o' the Movies business; that kind o' bunk. . . ."

"I beg your pardon," said Ellery, "for interrupting, but was this scheme for Horne's re-entry into motion pictures based on an actual connection with a producer?"

"You mean was it more'n a pipe-dream?" muttered Grant.

"Well—No producer—they wouldn't touch him with a ten-foot pole. But—well, I was goin' to help put up the ante. We'd form our own comp'ny. . . ."

"You alone?" demanded the Inspector.

Tony Mars said quietly: "I was considering it, too. And Hunter—Julian Hunter."

"Oho!" said the Inspector. "Hunter, the night-club bird—this Gay woman's husband we met tonight. Well, well." His little eyes twinkled frostily. "And now will somebody please tell me how it happens that Horne's best friend, and you, Tony, and Hunter were willing to put up the jack for Horne—and yet *his own daughter didn't put up a cent?*"

Grant swallowed hard, and his face settled into dusty bench lines. Curly made an impatient little gesture, and instantly relaxed. Kit sat very straight had been sitting very straight for long minutes. There were tears in her eyes—not weak tears, but tears of pure rage and chagrin.

"Bill Grant," she choked, "do you mean to stand there and say there *wasn't* a producer? Why, you yourself told me—"

The Queens said nothing; the Inspector, having some experience in this business of letting unexpected little dramas play themselves out, watched with bright inquisitiveness.

Grant mumbled: "Kit, Kit, I'm awful sorry. But it wasn't my fault; it was Buck himself made me say that. He didn't want yore money risked; said to tell you there was a producer so you wouldn't insist on puttin' up the cash. Business proposition, it was to him; plain business. Said if he couldn't int'rest hard-headed business men in his come-back he'd duck out altogether."

"You might add, pop," said Curly suddenly, "that Buck didn't know *yore* mazuma was in it, either!"

"Here, here," murmured the Inspector. "Regular fairytale, this is. We're getting more tangled up every minute. What is this?"

Grant shot a hard look at his son. "You, Curly, keep yore damn mouth shut when yo're not asked." Curly blushed and muttered: "Yes, pop." Grant waved his beefy right hand. "He's spilled it. All right, Buck didn't know my dough was in it. Wouldn't hear of it. Just wanted me to be his manager. We even signed a contract. That's why I had to go out an' bluff—make a stab at gettin' Mars here to come in with us. But on the sly I tole Mars I'd stand the whole business. That's what I was meanin' to do from the start, anyway."

"Do you think Horne suspected your real intention?"

Grant muttered: "Hard to say. He's always been a hard hombre to fool. These last couple o' days, he's acted kind o' funny. Mebbe he caught on. All his life he shied away from anything that—well, smacked o' charity, 'specially from his friends."

Kit rose suddenly and went up to Grant, standing very close. They looked into each other's eyes, and Kit said simply: "I'm sorry, Bill," and returned to her chair. Nobody said anything for some time.

"All of which goes to prove," said Ellery cheerfully in the silence, "that murder is the most effective cathartic for vocal indigestion. Miss Horne, whom will it be necessary to notify of your foster-father's death?"

She murmured: "No one."

Ellery's head shot round, his eyes fastening on Grant. But Grant only nodded, heavily.

"You mean except for yourself he had no family?"

"Not a single living relative, Mr. Queen."

Ellery frowned. "Well, perhaps you don't know, Miss Horne. But you must know, Mr. Grant. Is that true?"

"Right as rain. Except fer Kit, Buck was alone in the world. Left an orphan at six—brought up by an uncle who owned the ranch next to my father's in Wyoming. My ole man an' Buck's uncle used the same range fer their stock." Grant's voice was agony. "I—I never thought ole Buck's cashin' in his checks would get me this way. But hell. . . . His uncle kicked in, an' that was the end. Buck was the last of the Homes—one o' the oldest families in the Northwest."

During this exposition Mr. Ellery Queen's features might have been observed changing expression with the lightning facility of a chameleon changing color; why Grant's explanation should have disturbed him was obscure. But disturbed he was, although after a moment he made an effort and erased all emotion from his face. The Inspector studied him with a faint puzzlement; the old man kept quite still now, content to see what esoteric idea might be buzzing about in his son's brain, if indeed there was anything to be seen. But Ellery's shoulders twitched, and a small grin lit on his lips.

"How many riders did you announce as following Horne on that last sad processional of his, Mr. Grant?" he murmured.

The showman started out of a reverie. "Hey? Riders? Forty."

"But there were forty-one, you know."

"Forty. I ought to know. I pay 'em."

At this Inspector Queen's eyes narrowed. "When you said forty in the arena a while ago," he snapped, "you were speaking in round numbers, weren't you?"

Grant flushed darkly. "Round numbers nothin'. What is this? I said forty, an' I meant forty—not forty-one or thirty-nine or a hundred an' sixty!"

The Queens regarded each other with sparkling eyes. Then the old man scowled. "You—uh—you couldn't have made a mistake in counting, could you, son?"

"I was really an excellent mathematician in school," said Ellery, "and I don't think the problem of counting to forty-one would have taxed my numerative ability. On the other had, *est giebt Menschen die gar nicht irren, weil sie sich nichts Vemünftiges vorsetzen,* or words to that effect. However, since I've always posed as a rational animal. . . . Suppose we put this little problem to the test."

He strode toward the door.

"Where you going?" demanded the Inspector, as the others stared.

"Like all martyrs—into the arena."

"But what the dickens for?"

"To count the noses of the survivors."

.   .   .   .

They trooped back, through the little door by which they had entered the subterranean chamber, into the full glare of the *Colosseum's* tabernacle. There was a distinct quality of weariness in the mass noises now; detectives yawned all about; and the group of cowboys and cowgirls in the arena itself sprawled on the tanbark in varying attitudes of dejection and indifference.

"Now then," said Ellery briskly as they trotted toward the group, "suppose you count 'em yourself, Mr. Grant. Perhaps *I'm* crazy."

Grant growled something under his breath and, glaring at his costumed employees, strode about among them counting audibly. Most of them were sitting, heads sunken on their breasts; the old showman walked through a mushroom forest of large soft hats.

Then he came back, and all the amazement and bewilderment and pain which had struggled for mastery in his features since Buck Horne had crashed dead to the floor of the arena had vanished. His formidable jaw waved below grim lips like a banner. "I'll be a double-distilled son of a horse-whippin' so-an'-so if there ain't forty-one, the way Mr. Queen said!" he bellowed to the Inspector.

"You count that ugly little runt, Boone?" asked the old man quickly.

"Dan'l? No. He wasn't among 'em. There's forty-one without Dan'l." Brown faces had lifted now; they were staring at him curiously. He whirled about, and somehow without theatricalism his right arm perched on his right hip, holding his coat back and displaying his empty holster; he seemed himself to realize that the holster was empty, for he dropped his arm on the instant, scowling. Then he roared: "You mangy waddies! The gals too! Up on yer hin' legs an' let me get a good look at yore ugly maps!"

There was a moment of stunned silence, and then Ellery's grin faded. It really seemed for a moment that Mr. Wild Bill Grant of Wyoming and environs would have a small-sized revolution on his hands. One immense cowboy—Mr. Shorty Downs, an ordinarily jovial gentleman—took a long step forward and growled: "Would ya mind sayin' that again, Mr. Grant? I don't think I heard jest right the first time." And he doubled a fist like a bludgeon.

Grant glared into his eyes. "Shorty, you close yore trap an' pay attention! The rest o' you—stand up! There's one too many among ya, an' I'm on the warpath till I find the dirty murderer!"

They fell silent at that, the growls dying away; very quickly they got to their feet, men and women, and looked casually around at each other. Grant plunged into their midst, muttering to himself: "Hawes. Halliwell. Jones. Ramsey. Miller. Bluege. Annie. Stryker. Mendoza. Lu. . . . *Ah!*"

In the thick of the group he came to rest for an instant, after a single explosive sight. And then his cruel arm shot out and clamped powerfully about the shoulder of a man in cowboy costume.

He came swiftly out, dragging his captive as he might have dragged a trussed calf. The man was pale and drawn, with thin features shadowed in the purples and browns of dissipation—not at all a specimen of the Great Outdoors. He was wincing with the agony of Grant's grip, but there was something scornful in his very intelligent little eyes.

Wild Bill dumped him without ceremony into the dirt before Inspector Queen, and stood spread-legged over him, spitting and grumbling like a grizzly bear.

"This here one!" he roared when he had at last found his voice. "Inspect'r, this maverick's not a member of *my* show!"

5: GENTLEMAN OF THE PRESS

THE CAPTIVE picked himself out of the dirt, brushed specks of detritus from his glittering costume very carefully, and then poked Wild Bill Grant expertly in the pit of the stomach. Wild Bill said: *"Ouf!"* very loudly and doubled up in pain. Curly sprang forward like a spring released and aimed a hard brown first at the man's mouth. The man ducked, grinned without humor, and stepped behind the Inspector. A free-for-all was averted only by the intervention of Sergeant Velie, who clamped Curly's arms negligently behind the straight young back and gripped the captive's neck in his other hand without effort, so that they glared at each other across the Sergeant's impossible chest like two children. There was, as might have been expected, a surge of cowboys toward them.

The Inspector said in a snarl: "Back, the pack of you, or I'll run you all in." They stopped. "Now, Thomas, quit gagging this feller. I want him alive, not dead." Obediently Sergeant Velie released his hold on both men. They shook themselves rather sheepishly. Ellery, who for reasons of his own was watching Grant, saw his leathery complexion assume a saffron tinge that was like the hue of death.

The captive produced a cigaret and lighted it coolly. "And

that, Mister Tarzan," he said in a high-pitched, gatling-gun voice to the silent showman, "will teach you to keep your dirty hands off a poor hard-working member of the Fourth Estate."

Grant growled low in his throat.

"Stop it!" said the Inspector sharply. "All right, you. The fire-works are over. Talk, and make it simple."

The man puffed at his cigaret for a moment. He was slight, blond, and ageless. His eyes were tired.

"Well?" rapped the Inspector.

"I'm trying to think of simple words," drawled the man.

The Inspector smiled a thin smile. "Aha," he said, "a Broadway wisecracker. I thought I recognized the breed in spite of the scenery. Are you goin' to talk, or do I have to haul you down to Headquarters?"

"Horrors, no," grinned the man. "I'll talk, teacher—only spare the rod—or is the rod the hose in this case? Introducing God's gift to Fraudway, Mrs. Lyons's little boy Teddy—muck-raker, round-the-towner, the world's most famous tab columnist, and repository of more dirty secrets than you, and you, and you could shake a stick at."

Sergeant Velie made a sound like a disgusted bison. Something distinctly uncomplimentary left his hard lips and agitated the air.

"Ted Lyons," said the Inspector thoughtfully. "Well, well. Stepped right into a juicy little bump-off, didn't you? Now—"

"Of course," said Lyons jauntily, pulling up his gorgeous jeans with an exaggerated vigor, "now that we've properly met, Inspector, I'll toddle along. You've had your fun, our friend Mr. Buffalo Wild Bill Grant's had his exercise and a jab in the belly, and little Teddy has to dash downtown to the cruel newspaper mag-nut and report the biggest story of the year. So little Teddy—"

"Little Teddy owes us a few explanations, Little Teddy does," smiled the Inspector. Then his mood changed and he snapped: "Spit it out, Lyons. I haven't got all night to waste on you! What the devil are you doing here all dressed up like Jesse James?"

"Ah," said Lyons, "li'l Inspector's going to be nassy, eh? Listen here, old boy, know who I am? I'm Ted Lyons, and your whole damn bunch of Keystone Koppers couldn't stop me if I started walking out!"

The Inspector's eyebrows became arches, and he looked at Sergeant Velie. Sergeant Velie took one stride toward Lyons. . . . Lyons looked around. The little drama was being played to a magnificent audience of twenty thousand persons.

"All right, pardner," he said gravely, his head hanging. "I'll talk, pardner. I'll tell all. I killed Buck Horne with my little pop-gun, I did. I snuck up behind him, pardner, and I said: 'Buck, you mis'able c'yote, I'll fan yore hide for yuh! I said. . . .'"

They were too aghast at this monstrous creature's bad taste to protest. All except Ellery, for he had seen the look in Kit Horne's eyes; and he stepped forward and murmured: "You're a particularly annoying specimen of a pediculus, Lyons, and all that; I wonder if even you realize what a louse you are. Don't you know that Buck Horne's daughter is listening to every filthy word you're saying?"

"Ah, Sir Galahad," said Lyons rapidly; he was backing up, and his eyes were bright and dangerous. "Boloney, you, whoever you are. I'm getting out of here, and any flatfoot who thinks he's going to stop me—"

The rest was drowned in a rising tide of fury. Grant and his son, Sergeant Velie, Tony Mars, and half a dozen of the cowboys near by lunged at Lyons. He grinned wolfishly and his hand flashed up with an ugly, tiny weapon—a snub-nosed and incredibly small automatic pistol. The rush stopped abruptly.

"Are the big he-men yellow?" he chattered, his eyes flashing about. Sergeant Velie leaped forward like a catapult and smashed the automatic out of Lyons's hand. "Damn fool trick," he said unemotionally, picking it up out of the dirt. "Might hurt someone with that thing."

Lyons was pale.

"No guts anyway."

To their amazement the man began to laugh. "All right, all right," he chuckled. "Teddy gives up. But I tell you my paper—"

"Give me that rod, Thomas," said the Inspector evenly. The Sergeant handed it over. The Inspector pulled out the magazine, looked into the tiring chamber. Not one cartridge was missing.

"A .25," murmured the old man, and his eyes narrowed. "But it's not been fired, and it doesn't smell—" He sniffed the muzzle for a moment. "Bad for you, Lyons. Now talk, or as God is my judge, I'll see that you go up the river for pulling a gun on an officer!"

Lyons shrugged and lighted another cigaret. "Sorry. Apologize. I had a couple of snifters. Nothing to get screwy about, Inspector. I did it as a publicity stunt." His tired eyes were half-closed.

"How'd you get in here?"

"I rented a cowboy rig from a theatrical costumer on 45th Street. Got here half an hour before show time. Gate-keeper passed me through—must have thought I was with the show. I scouted around, got to the stable, picked me out a plug, joined the others in the big Ben Hur scene, and—here I am."

"You are, of course, the worst sort of exhibitionist," murmured Ellery, "but I fail to see what even your ego would gain from such a pointless and stupid procedure. Merely to join the troupe—"

"Nerts," said Lyons. "I'm over my schoolboy thrill days. I've got a cameraman planted in one of the boxes. I was going to get near Horne on some excuse or other, and have my box-man snap the two of us. Good break for me and the paper if I'd been able to pull it off. But, damn the luck, somebody bumped the old guy off before I could say 'Alexander Woollcott'!"

There was a little silence.

"Very brilliant, of course," said Ellery coldly. "Just how close to Buck Horne were you riding, Lyons?"

"Not so close, smart guy," said Lyons, "not so close."

"How close?"

"I was at the tail end of that bunch of ridin' fools."

The Inspector conferred with Sergeant Velie aside for a moment. "In which box is this cameraman of yours, Lyons?"

The columnist pointed negligently to a loge only a few feet away from the one in which the Mars party had been sitting. Sergeant Velie lumbered off. He returned in a moment with a very scared and loose-lipped young man carrying a small Graflex camera. Without words this man was searched camera and all. Nothing incriminating was found; and he was sent back to his place.

The Inspector was thoughtfully regarding the newspaperman. "Lyons, there's something smelly about this. Did you have a tip-off on what was going to happen?"

Lyons groaned. "Jeeze, I wish I'd had! I wish I'd had!"

"You mixed with the other members of the show, didn't you? Before you all rode out?"

"Not me. Wasn't taking a chance on being spotted."

"What were you doing?"

"Oh, just hanging around."

"Notice anything suspicious—anything that might help us?"

"Not a bloomin' thing, old chappie!"

"Where'd you get that .25 automatic you flashed a minute ago?"

"Don't worry, Commissioner. I've got a permit to go heeled."

"Where'd you get it?"

"Santa Claus sent it. Bought it, of course! What the hell—you don't think *I* pulled this job?"

"Tag that gat, Thomas," said the Inspector calmly. "And take those other hunks of hardware from him. Christmas, he's a walkin' arsenal!"

In the fancy holsters of Lyons's masquerade costume were two long-barreled revolvers. These the Sergeant gently removed; whereupon, handing them to an assistant, he went over Mr. Theodore Lyons's clothes and body with an impersonal vigor and thoroughness that brought groans to the victim's lips.

"Nothin' else, Inspector," said Velie.

"Where'd you get these guns?" demanded the Inspector.

"From the armory downstairs. I saw all the other chumps taking 'em, so I did too. . . . Hell, Chief, I didn't shoot 'em off at all!"

The Inspector examined them. "Blanks. I suppose you got the ammunition down there, too? All right, Thomas, escort this piece of prime scum out of the *Colosseum*. But mind—be sure nobody slips anything to him on the way out."

"I mind," said the Sergeant jovially; and, linking Lyons's arm in his, he marched the columnist to one of the small exits before that garrulous exponent of *The Lowdown*—the notorious name of his countrywide-syndicated column—could utter another word. The two men disappeared.

6: THE FACT REMAINS—

THE COLD corpse was lifted by horny silent hands and carried
to one of the innumerable small rooms beneath the amphitheatre. The Queens, Kit Horne, and the Grants retired once more
to the timekeeper's office.

"While we're waiting for Doc Prouty," growled the Inspector,
"—and as usual he's late!—suppose we dig a little deeper into
what happened today."

The stiff mask which for an hour had settled over Kit Horne's
features cracked and broke. "It's high time!" she cried passion-
ately. "Let's have action, Inspector, for God's sake!"

"My dear," said the old man gently, "you've got to have patience. You don't realize what we're up against. You all assure me
that Horne had no enemies—there's no lead there—and we've
got twenty thousand suspects on our hands. Nobody's running
away. I want you to tell me—"

"Anything, Inspector, I'll tell anything. This horrible—"

"Yes, yes, my dear, I know. I'm sure you will. How was your
father acting today? Did he seem worried or disturbed about
anything?"

She made a brave effort; with lowered lids, in a steady voice, she related the scene she had broken up between Woody and Horne.

"He seemed all right, Inspector. I was nervous for him, asked him if the doctor had examined him—"

"Oh, yes, I believe you said he'd been ill for some time," murmured Ellery.

"Yes. He's been—well, out of sorts physically for a couple of years now," explained Kit dully. "The doctors said it was just age. He was sixty-five." Her voice broke. "He's led a very strenuous life, and at his age there was bound to be a let-down. I didn't want him to go back to work at all. But he insisted it would do him good, tone him up. Today I asked him if the rodeo doctor had examined him, and he said yes, this morning, and everything was all right."

"But he didn't seem worried about anything?" asked the Inspector.

"No. I mean. . . . I don't really know. He wasn't *upset,* although there did seem to be something on his mind."

"You've no idea what it was, I suppose?"

Her eyes met his fiercely. "I wish I did!"

The Inspector turned to the showman. "How about you, Mr. Grant? Any idea what Horne might have had on his mind?"

"Hell, no. Nothin' important 'less he smelled a rat on that movie business. Kit, you must be imaginin' things—"

"Well, well," said the Inspector hastily, "let's not quarrel about it. Miss Horne, what happened today?"

"I—I was out late last night and didn't wake up until mid-morning. Buck and I—we've—we'd adjoining rooms at the Barclay, on West Forty-fourth Street. That's where the rest of the troupe are stopping, too. I knocked on Buck's door; he opened it and kissed me good morning. He was quite cheerful. Said he'd been up for hours—he was used to getting up with the sun, of course; he said he'd had a walk in Central Park, had had breakfast. . . . I had a snack sent up and Buck joined me in a cup of coffee. At about two o'clock we walked over to the *Colosseum* for the rehearsal."

"Oh, so you had a dress rehearsal, eh, Mr. Grant?"

"Yeah. Fancy duds an' all. 'Ceptin' Buck—didn't want to bother gettin' rigged out. We went through the routine a last time to get everything straight."

"I watched for a while," said Kit, "and then wandered off—"

"Pardon," said Ellery with a frown. "Mr. Grant, did you attend the rehearsal?"

"Shore."

"Everything go off strictly as scheduled?"

Grant stared. "Shore! Buck was kind o' nervous seemed to me. Tole me he was tickled pink at the prospect of performin' before an audience again."

Ellery sucked his lip. "What was the routine?"

"Nothin' much. Gallop around the arena—what you saw tonight when it happened, then Buck was to do a few simple ridin' tricks all by himself—flashy, but easy; then an exhibition of shootin'. Afterwards a little ropin'—"

"Nothing strenuous? He wasn't required to rope steers and throw them, for example, or ride a bucking horse?"

The Inspector regarded his son with a mildly disturbed air. But Ellery seemed to be wading through a mass of clogging and contradictory thoughts; as usual when he was excited, or in the throes of intangible composition, he took his shining *pince-nez* glasses from his nose and with absent energy began to polish the lenses.

"No," said Grant. "Nothin' like that—I wouldn't let 'im. Yeah, he did a couple of loops on a longhorn in rehearsal, but no real bulldoggin', nothin' dangerous."

"He wanted to, though?" persisted Ellery.

"Buck always wanted to do everythin'," replied Grant wearily. "Couldn't get it through his thick head that he was an ole man. An', by thunder, he could do it, too! I almost had to rassle him when we were makin' up the routine."

"Hmm," said Ellery, He replaced his glasses on his nose. "How very interesting." Kit and Curly stared at him in astonishment; in Kit's eyes there was a dawning glimmer of hope, and a flush came to her brown cheeks while her breath quickened. "You say, Mr. Grant, that Horne was scheduled to give an exhibition of marksmanship?"

"Yeah, an' he did, too, at rehearsal. He was a real sharpshooter, Buck was," replied Grant in a tight voice. "There's an old sayin' out West—a cowboy is a man with guts an' a horse. It don't take into account his ability to throw lead. Nowadays the boys are just punchers; in the ole days. . . ." He shook himself savagely. "Many a time I've seen Buck, with one of his ole long-barreled Colts, put six slugs into the heart of a two-inch target at a hundred feet! An' on split-second notice, too. Wasn't anything he couldn't do with a gun. Why, the show he was goin' to put on tonight was real fancy, Mr. Queen! Riddle targets plumb center while at full gallop on that starfaced roan stallion o' Kit's, clip coins thrown in the air—"

"I'm convinced," said Ellery with a smile. "I take it Buck Horne was something special in marksmen. Very well. Now, did anything unusual happen at today's rehearsal? Anything go wrong? Any little thing?"

Grant shook his head. "Went off like clockwork."

"Were all your riders present?"

"Every one."

Ellery shook his head impatiently—as if in anger with himself. He murmured: "Thank you," and stepped back, considering the tip of his cigaret with absent and lambent eyes.

"How about after rehearsal?" demanded the Inspector.

"Well," said Kit, "I told you about how I found Buck and Woody arguing in the stables. I didn't see him again—after I left his dressing-room, I mean—until just before I quit the building. Then I stopped into Mr. Grant's office. It was just after I'd left—Curly." There was a pained something in her voice, and Curly blushed to the roots of his hair and began to kick at the floor. He stopped when the Inspector looked at him casually. "I found Buck there, with Bill—with Mr. Grant."

"That right?" asked the Inspector, cocking an expressionless eye at the showman.

"That's right, Inspector."

"Go on, Miss Horne."

She shrugged helplessly. "But there's nothing more to tell. Buck was making out a check. I said hello and left the *Colosseum*—"

"Time," said Ellery pleasantly; he was interested again. "What was the purpose of this check, Mr. Grant?"

"Nothin' special. Buck asked me if I could cash a twenty-five dollar check fer him, an' I said yes. So he made it out an' I gave him the money."

"Indeed," said Ellery without inflection. "And what did you do with this check? Have you got it on you, Mr. Grant?"

"Why, no," drawled Grant. "I stepped out a minute m'self a

little later an' stopped in at my bank—the Seaboard National. So I deposited it."

"Innocent enough," agreed Ellery, and retired.

The Inspector gave him a sharp look, then turned back to Grant. "Was that the last you saw of him?"

"No. I was comin' back from the bank, just in the entrance to the buildin' here, when I bumped into Buck again. Had his hat an' coat on. 'Where ya bound?' I asked 'im. 'Hotel,' he says. 'Want to rest up fer t'night.' An' that's all. Never had another word with 'im. He come in late tonight, kind of excited, I thought, waved 'is hand at me as he rushed fer his dressin' room. There was hardly enough time fer him to change 'is duds an' get into the arena."

The Queens looked at each other. "That might be important," muttered the Inspector. "Got in late, did he? What time was it when he said he was going to the Barclay?"

"Round about four o'clock."

"Hmm. Did you see Buck again after you left the building, Miss Horne?"

"Yes. When I left I went straight back to the hotel. Buck came in about a half-hour or so later, and said he was going to take a nap. I changed my things and—and went downstairs. And—"

Curly Grant spoke for the first time. "From that time on," he said belligerently, "Miss Horne was with me. I met her in the lobby, and we went out for the rest o' the afternoon."

"Yes," said Kit in a whisper.

"And when you got back?" asked the Inspector.

"Buck was already gone; he'd left a note for me on my night-table. So I changed into my evening things and taxied to the *Colosseum*. I didn't see him again until," her voice quavered, "until he rode into the arena."

"Oh, so you were late, too?" said the Inspector slowly.

"What do you mean?"

The old man smiled and waved a deprecating hand. "Nothing at all, my dear, nothing at all!" He took a pinch of snuff and sneezed with violence. "Only—Mr. Grant *(k'choo!)* Mr. Grant said your father was late, so that means you must have been later still. You see? Very simple!"

Curly took a step forward. "Look here," he growled, "I don't cotton to that remark a-tall. I tell you Miss Horne was with me—"

"Ah, so you were late, too, young man?"

Grant looked from Kit to his son, with quick stony eyes. Curly set his jaw. "No, I wasn't. I left Kit when we passed the *Colosseum;* she said I'd better not take her to the hotel—"

The Inspector rose. "I understand. All right, Miss Horne. You, too, Mr. Grant—"

There was a reverberating knock on the door.

"Well?" snapped Inspector Queen. The door was kicked open; a cadaverous Machiavelli scowled in at them. His jowls were black and he wore an iron derby; between his teeth there was a foul-smelling sample of some misguided cigar-maker's art He carried a black kit.

"Here I am," he announced. "Where's the stiff?"

"Uh—that's all, Miss Horne, Mr. Grant. Thank you," said the Inspector hastily, and bundled the Grants and the girl out of the room. Sergeant Velie detached himself from a shadow of the wall outside and joined them quietly. "Back to the arena, Thomas!" shouted the Inspector, and Velie nodded.

"Now, you lazy son of an African witch-doctor," snarled the

old man to the black-jowled newcomer, "what in time d'ye mean by holding us up two hours on a homicide? By the——"

"And so on," said Machiavelli with a sour grin. "The old song-and-dance. Well, where's the stiff, you old pirate?"

"All right, Sam, all right. He's next door, gettin' stiffer."

"Just a moment, Dr. Prouty," said Ellery, as the newcomer turned to go. The *deus ex machina* who presided over the post-mortems of half New York City's murdered population stopped. Ellery put his arm on Dr. Prouty's shoulder and said something very earnestly. The police physician nodded, gripped his fulminating cigar more firmly, and hastened out.

The Queens were left alone.

· · · · · · ·

Father and son regarded each other gloomily.

"Well?" said the Inspector.

"A very deep well, I must say," sighed Ellery. "We return to criminal investigation in the best Queen manner—nothing less than suspects by the carload. You remember that damned Field case? A theatre full of potential murderers!* The French murder? A department store jammed with shoppers.** Old lady Doorn's queer demise? Just a hospital packed with doctors, nurses, patients, and neurotics.*** And now a sports arena. Our next murderer," he said dreamily, "will undoubtedly choose the Yankee Stadium as the scene of his crime, and then we'll have to call out the Jersey reserves to help us sift a crowd of 70,000!"

"Stop babbling," said the Inspector irritably. "That's what's got me worried, blast it all. We can't keep twenty thousand people under wraps forever. Lucky the Commissioner's out of town,

* "The Roman Hat Mystery"
** "The French Powder Mystery"
*** "The Dutch Shoe Mystery"

or I'd have him on my neck for bottling up half of New York this way. I'm sort of glad Henry Sampson's away, too."

"Nevertheless, despite commissioners and district attorneys," said Ellery inflexibly, "it must be done."

"What did you say to Prouty?"

"I told your estimable Examiner's physician to dig the bullet out of Horne's body."

"Ginger, that can wait! That rodeo medic—what's 's-name—said it was a .22 or .25, didn't he?"

"Let's be a little more scientific, Inspector dear. I'm very curious about that little messenger of death. Until we find out the story of that bullet, you mustn't permit a single member of the audience—or anyone else, for that matter—to get out of the building."

"Don't intend to," said the Inspector shortly, and after that they were silent.

Ellery began to hum a sad little tune.

"El what do you think?"

The tune stopped. "I'm thinking of poor Djuna, sitting in that box with the horrible lady from Hollywood, and Tommy Black."

"Cripes!" cried the Inspector. "I clean forgot about Djuna!"

"Don't fret," said Ellery dryly, "he's having the time of his life. His gods are smiling broadly tonight. The point is: what were you saying?"

"What d'ye make of this case?"

Ellery puffed thoughtfully at the low white ceiling.

"Strangely enough, a good deal."

The Inspector's mouth popped open; but a wordy catastrophe was averted by the opening of the door and the reappearance of Dr. Prouty, *sans* coat and hat, his shirt-sleeves rolled up to his elbows and his right hand displaying with something like gloomy triumph a very bloody little object wrapped in gauze.

.   .   .   .

The Inspector snatched it from Dr. Prouty's hand without ceremony, heedless of the red smear it communicated to his fingers. Ellery came forward quickly.

"Ha!" said the old man, examining the object intently. "A .25—automatic, all right. That rodeo doctor was right. Pretty good condition, eh, son?"

The conical slug exhibited an almost virgin shape. It was a tiny thing, remarkably harmless in appearance, and the blood coating seemed nothing more sinister than red paint.

"Went in pretty clean," growled Dr. Prouty, chewing his cigar with energy. "Smack through the pumper. Nice hole, too. Didn't even crack a rib on the way in; just glanced off."

Ellery turned the bullet over his fingers, his eyes far away.

"Anything else of interest?" demanded the Inspector glumly.

"Nothing much. Four snapped ribs, *sternum* smashed, arms and legs broken in several places, skull kicked in—you saw all that, I suppose—nothing that wouldn't be accounted for by the trampling of the horses that Sergeant of yours was telling me about on my way in."

"No other wound of any kind—I mean knife or gun?"

"Nope."

"Death instantaneous?"

"He was deader'n an iced mackerel when he hit the ground."

"You say," said Ellery slowly, "that the bullet left a clean hole, Doctor. Clean enough to give evidence of the angle of entry?"

"I was coming to that," mumbled Dr. Prouty. "You betcha. That piece of lead entered his body from the right—that is, going toward the left—on a downward line, making an angle of thirty degrees with the floor."

"Downward line!" cried the Inspector; he stared, and then began to hop up and down on one leg. "Fine. Fine! Sam, you're a honey, a life-saver—best old scoundrel that ever played poker. Downward line, hey? Thirty degrees, hey? By God, El, now we *have* got an excuse for holding that mob up there! The lowest tier is at least ten feet from the floor of the arena, where Horne was when he was shot. And even in a sitting or crouching position the murderer would be three-four feet higher than that. . . . Thirteen-fourteen feet. Audience, hey? Oh, this is great!"

Dr. Prouty, unruffled by this professional admiration, sat down, scrawled some hieroglyphics on a printed slip, and handed it to the Inspector. "For the Public Welfare gang. They'll be here any minute now to cart the stiff away. Want an autopsy?"

"Think it's necessary?"

"No."

"Then hold one," said the Inspector grimly. "I'm taking no chances."

"All right, all right, you old fuss-budget," said Dr. Prouty indifferently.

"And," said Ellery, "pay particular attention to the contents of his stomach, Doctor."

"Stomach?" echoed the Inspector blankly.

"Stomach," said Ellery.

"Right," growled Dr. Prouty, and strolled out.

The Inspector turned to Ellery, and saw that Ellery was still gazing with rapt and ardent eyes at the bloody bullet.

"Well, what's the matter now?" demanded the old man.

Ellery regarded his father sadly. "When was the last time you visited the movies, you incorrigible old realist?"

The Inspector started. "What's that got to do with it?"

"You remember a few months ago we went to that neighborhood theatre at Djuna's solicitation and saw what the management so ingeniously called a 'double-feature'?"

"Well?"

"What was the—ah—lesser of the two attractions, so to speak?"

"Some Western trash—Sa-a-ay! Kit Horne was in that picture, El!"

"Indeed she was." Ellery gazed intently at the bullet in his hand. "And do you remember the scene in that great cinema epic in which the beauteous heroine, galumphing down the hillside on—yes, it was *Rawhide,* by thunder the same horse!—plucked her six-shooter from her holster and—"

"And shot the strands of the rope through, the rope the villain was hanging the hero with?" cried the Inspector excitedly.

"And did that very thing."

The Inspector grew glum. "That must have been a movie trick. Easy enough to fake it. They do all sorts of things out there."

"Perhaps. But you'll recall that the camera snapped the scene from *behind* Miss Horne; she was distinctly visible all the time, as were the revolver in her hand and the rope she was shooting at. Nevertheless, I grant the possibility of a trick—"

"Darned decent of you. What of it, anyway?"

"I wonder, now. . . . Kit Horne was brought up—from childhood, mind—on a ranch in those great interstices—I beg your pardon, open spaces. Her guardian, the redoubtable Buck, was an expert marksman. Impossible to believe, under the circumstances, that Buck wouldn't have schooled her in marksmanship as well as those other desperate accomplishments of hers. Hmm. . . . And that young Lochinvar of ours—Curly, who comes out of the West all shiny and curly and heroic. Did you notice the facility with which he popped little glass balls out of existence by means of his trusty cannon? Yes, yes! And as for his sire, the great impresario of horse spectacles—where did I hear that he'd been one of the most famous United States Marshals of the last century, fighting desperadoes and redskins in the Indian Territory?"

"What the dickens you driving at?" groaned the Inspector, and then his eyes grew very round. "By ginger, El! Come to think of it—the box where we sat, Mars's box—must have been pretty well in the line of fire! Downward angle of thirty degrees, Sam makes it. . . . Cripes, yes! That would just about place it in the audience somewhere, rotten as I am in arithmetic. Shot through the left side into the heart as his horse rounded the turn—tightens it, son, tightens it!" He stopped suddenly, and grew very thoughtful.

Ellery surveyed his father through narrowed lids, juggling the little painted bullet carelessly. "What a beautiful crime this is," he murmured. "What finesse, what daring, what superb coolness in the execution. . . ."

"What I can't see, though," muttered the Inspector, unheeding, as he began to chew a strand of his mustache, "is how anyone could have shot so close. We didn't hear—"

"What is required? One death. What is utilized? One bullet. Short, precise, mechanical—very sweet, altogether. Eh?" Ellery smiled dryly as his father began to exhibit unmistakable signs of interest. "Ah, but there's a complication. The target is a living, swaying figure on the back of a galloping horse. Never still for an instant. Ever think how difficult it must be to hit a fast-moving target? Nevertheless, our murderer disdains to fire more than once. His single shot does the trick very thoroughly. Very thoroughly indeed." He rose and began to prowl up and down. "The fact remains, *Herr Inspektor,* and this is what my rambling remarks have been circuitously leading up to—the fact remains that whoever killed Buck Horne either was possessed of the luck of the devil, or else . . . was a quite extraordinary marksman!"

7: 45 GUNS

JULIAN HUNTER, summoned peremptorily from the Mars box, appeared in the doorway before Sergeant Velie's granite figure. The pouches beneath his eyes were more batrachian than ever; his pink cheeks were pinker and his expression more wooden, if that were possible, than before.

"Come in, Mr. Hunter," said the Inspector shortly. "Take a chair."

The pouches sank, and keen pupils glittered for an instant. "No, thank you," said Hunter. "I'll stand."

"Suit yourself. How well did you know Horne?"

"Ah," said Hunter. "The inquisition. My dear Inspector, aren't you being a little absurd?"

"What—Say!"

The night-club owner waved a manicured hand. "It's apparent that you consider me a potential suspect for the murder of that—uh—dashing old gentleman who came a cropper out there. It's too silly, you know."

"Rats. Come out of it, Hunter. That tack won't get you anywhere," said the Inspector sharply. "Now please answer my questions, and don't waste our time—we've a big job on our hands and I can't stand here arguing with you. Well, well?"

Hunter shrugged. "Didn't know him well at all."

"That doesn't mean anything. How *long* did you know him?"

"Precisely one week."

"Hmm. You met him when he hit town on this rodeo business?"

"That's it, Inspector."

"Through whom?"

"Tony, Tony Mars."

"Under what circumstances?"

"Tony brought him to one of my night-clubs—"

"Club Mara?"

"Yes."

"That's the only time you saw him? Before tonight, I mean?"

Hunter lighted a cigaret with steady fingers. "Mmm. Can't say, really." He blew smoke indolently. "It's possible Horne visited the *Club Mara* after that. I can't be sure."

The Inspector stared at him. "You're lying, of course."

Thick red surged into the pink cheeks, very slowly. "What the devil do you mean?"

The old man clucked. *"Tchk!* I beg your pardon, Mr. Hunter. No offense meant. I was just speculatin' out loud." Ellery, in his corner, smiled skeptically. "Y'see, I know you're in a deal with Tony—were in a deal, I should say, to finance Horne's comeback to the screen. I thought you'd surely have had a couple of meetings—"

"Oh," said Hunter, with a long quiet breath. "Yes, certainly. Very natural thought. No, I told the truth, Inspector. And it's not true that I was 'in a deal,' as you say, to furnish financial support for Horne's venture. Mars, Grant—they mentioned it to me. I was merely considering the proposal. A little out of my line, you see."

The Inspector performed the sacred rite of inhaling a pinch of snuff. "You were waiting, I suppose, to see what sort of reception Horne would get in this rodeo appearance of his?"

"Yes, yes! That's it exactly."

"Well! Nothing incriminating there, eh, Mr. Hunter?" The Inspector smiled and returned the old brown snuffbox to his pocket.

The room was quite still. A little pulse in Hunter's throat began to hammer suddenly, and the vein in his left temple. He said rather thickly: "If you're really thinking. . . . Why, Inspector, I was in the same box with you all evening! How could I possibly—?"

"Of courrrse," said the Inspector soothingly. "Of course, Mr. Hunter. Don't upset yourself. These little chin-chins—just a matter of form. Now you go back to the Mars box and wait."

"Wait? I can't—Can't I—?"

The Inspector spread thin deprecating hands. "We're servants of the law, you know, Mr. Hunter. I'm sorry, but you'll have to wait."

Hunter inhaled deeply. "Hmm. Yes. I see that," he said, and turned to go, sucking on his cigaret.

"By the way," drawled Ellery from his corner, "do you know Miss Horne well, Mr. Hunter—Kit Horne?"

"Oh, Miss Horne. No, can't say I do. I've met her on one or two occasions—once in Hollywood, I think, through Mrs. Hunter—I should say Miss Gay, my wife . . . but that's all."

He waited, as if expecting another question. It did not come, so after a moment he bowed slightly and left the office.

The Queens regarded each other with cryptic smiles.

"Why the silk gloves, Inspector?" asked Ellery. "I've never known you to handle a witness so softly before!"

"Don't know," murmured the old man. "A hunch, I guess. That bird knows something, and before I'm through with him I'll find out what." He stuck his head out of the doorway. "Thomas! Get that actress—the gaga Gay woman!" He turned back, smiling broadly. "Yes, and by the way, why the question about Kit Horne, eh?"

"Don't know, sire. Just a hunch, I guess." And Ellery grinned back until the willow-scent-silk figure of Mara Gay made a bowery frame out of the prosaic doorway.

·   ·   ·   ·   ·   ·   ·

The lady swept in like an elongated shadow of Portia, sat down with the sublimely indifferent dignity of the Virgin Queen, and glared at the Inspector with Medusa's venomousness. "Well," she sniffed, tossing her coiffured head, "this is *really* too much! *Really* too ridiculously much!"

"What's too much?" said the Inspector absently. "Oh, Miss Gay! Now, don't take that tone, please. I want—"

"*You* want!" snarled the Orchid of Hollywood. "And please don't 'please' me, Inspector What's-Your-Name! I'll take any tone I choose, *understand* that! Now"—she continued without pausing for breath as the Inspector chopped off a mildly astonished protest—"please *explain* what you mean by this vile, this outrageous *treatment!* Keeping me cooped up in that *awful* place for *hours,* not even letting me go to—go to the *ladies' room!* No, don't interrupt me. Do you realize that this is bad *publicity* for me? Not that I look down on publicity; it has its uses, but—"

"Sweet uses," murmured Ellery, garbling his Shakespeare.

"What? It has its uses, but this—this is *vile!* Those reporters, they've been telephoning their *papers* ever since this *happened.* Tomorrow I'll find myself *plastered* all over the country, mixed up in a—my God—a *murder!* My press agent will *love* it, but then he's such a *barbarian!* I tell you unless you let me get out of here at once—*at once,* understand?—I'll phone my attorney and—and—"

She paused, gulping.

"And fiddlesticks," snapped the Inspector. "Now pay attention. What do you know about this blasted business?"

The stare that had withered motion picture magnates burned harmlessly against the hide of the Inspector, who was made of asbestos. So she took from her evening-bag a diamond-studded lipstick and pursed her lips very provocatively. "Nothing," she murmured, "*dear* Inspector." Ellery grinned, and the Inspector blushed with fury.

"Don't give me *that!*" he barked. "When did you meet Buck Horne?"

"The horse-opera person? Let me see." She considered. "Last week."

"Not in Hollywood?"

"Inspector Queen! He left the screen ten *years* ago!"

"Oh. You were a babe in arms at that time, I s'pose," said the Inspector sourly. "Well, where *did* you meet Horne?"

"At the *Club Mara,* my husband's little place, you know."

Her husband's little place was a vast one-sixth the size of the *Colosseum,* with more marble and gilt in it than Broadway's most awesome motion picture palace.

"Who else was present when you met him?"

"Julian—my husband; that Grant person, Curly's father; and Tony Mars."

"You know Miss Horne for a long time?"

"That horsy little squirt?" She sniffed contemptuously. "She's been *presented* to me on the Coast."

"Presented to *you*, hey?" muttered the Inspector. "She would be—to you. All right, Miss Gay, that's all. I'm busy."

She gasped in sheer horror at this frightful implication of *lese majeste*. "Why, you old—"

Sergeant Velie gripped her arm delicately between forefinger and thumb and urged her out of the chair and the room.

·　　·　　·　　·　　·　　·　　·

Ellery sprang to his feet. "Are you quite finished with this mumbo-jumbo?"

"Hell, no. I want to see—"

"You," said Ellery firmly, "want to see none other than Major Kirby, god of the newsreel cameras."

"Kirby? But what the deuce for?"

"It seems to me that what we require more than anything else at the moment is someone on intimate terms with firearms—if you can imagine such a situation."

The Inspector granted. "You want a firearms expert, so you pick a movie man, hey? That's logic."

"The Major, I've been told," said Ellery, "is not only a crack pistoleer but is also something of an authority on something or other—I deduced firearms. That on the admittedly dubious word of Tony Mars—which you would recall if you'd thought about Kirby's visit to the box before the fracas. Well, send for him, and we'll find out soon enough how dependable Mars's information is."

Sergeant Velie was duly dispatched for the Major.

"But what do you want an expert for?" frowned the Inspector.

Ellery sighed. "Father, dear father, what's the matter with your wits tonight? We've a bullet, haven't we?"

The Inspector was distinctly annoyed. "Sometimes, my

son. . . . Don't you think I know enough about the mechan-
ics of my own job to have an expert look over the bullet,
and compare it with others? But what's the rush? Why the
dickens—"

"Look here—We've got to examine those forty-five shoot-
ing-irons immediately—not just some time, but at once, dad!"

"What forty-five guns?"

"Well, I suppose there are forty-five of them," said Ellery impatiently. "I noticed that the group of riders following Horne
seemed consistently to be wearing single holsters which means
a revolver per rider. That's forty. Then there are Ted Lyons's
three—the .25 automatic and the two .45's from the rodeo armory which he appropriated. Forty-three. Wild Bill Grant's and
Horne's own—forty-five. But why argue? Don't you see, dad,
we've got to *know?*"

The Inspector's irritation vanished. "You're right. And the
sooner the better. . . . Well, Hesse?"

One of his squad, a solid Scandinavian, charged in, his little
red eyes excited. "Chief, there's a *riot* upstairs! The boys got all
they can do to hold those people! They want to go home."

"So do I," growled the Inspector. "You pass the word around,
Hesse, to the uniformed men to use their billies, by God, if
they have to. Not a single soul goes out of this place until he's
searched to the bone."

Hesse's eyes widened. "Search twenty thousand people?" he
gasped.

"It's a tall order, I know," said the Inspector glumly. "But it
looks as if we've got to do it. Now, Hesse, you tell Ritter. . . ."

He walked out into the corridor with the detective, enumer-
ating the commands necessary to begin the task of searching to

the skin the population of a small city. This was the good Inspector's private meat; he began to look almost happy.

"Take all night," said the Inspector when he returned, "and I s'pose I'll be on the carpet tomorrow, but what the devil! Got to be done. . . . Oh, come in, Major!"

.   .   .   .

Major Kirby, looking tired, nevertheless contrived also to look curious. He snapped a glance at Ellery.

"Still grinding?"

Kirby shook his head. "Stopped long ago. Good grief, when the home office finds out how much film we've used there'll be war! Lucky I had plenty of stock with me. Well, sir, what can I do for you? Your Sergeant here tells me you wanted me especially."

"Not I," said the Inspector. "My son. Spill it, El."

"It all depends," said Ellery abruptly, "on you, Major. This evening we were informed that during the War you had achieved a reputation for being a crack pistol shot. Is that true?"

The Major's small black eyes turned to small black stones. "And just what," he said crisply, "do you mean by that?"

Ellery stared, and then burst into laughter. "Heavens, I'm not pumping you, man, as a murder suspect! I'm really interested for an entirely different reason. Is it true or isn't it?"

Kirby's expression wavered; then he smiled slightly. "I suppose it is. I won a few medals."

"And I was also told that you're something of a firearms expert. Is that true, too?"

"I've made a study of ballistics, Mr. Queen. More a hobby than a profession. I shouldn't care to call myself an expert—"

"Thy modesty's a candle to thy merit," laughed Ellery. "How would you like to engage in a little experting for me?"

Major Kirby stroked his mustache nervously. "Happy to oblige, of course," he murmured, "but I've a duty to my company, you know. That film we shot—"

"Nonsense! We'll arrange all that. You've a lieutenant of some sort in your crew upstairs, haven't you?"

"Yes. My chief cameraman will do. Name of Hall."

"Excellent! Suppose—"

"I'll have to talk to Hall first. We've made something of a scoop here tonight, Mr. Queen, with these pictures, and speed is our byword in this business." He became thoughtful. "Tell you what. I'll drop everything if you'll let my men go at once. Film they've ground out will be developed, printed, cut, and assembled with sound for distribution to Broadway theaters by morning. *Must* get it out. It's a go?"

"It's a go," said the Inspector unexpectedly, "but you and your men will have to go through the formality of a search, Major, before we release you."

The Major cooled. "Is that necessary?"

"I should hope to tell you!"

Kirby shrugged. "Very well. Anything for some action. All right, Mr. Queen, I'm with you."

The Inspector said genially to Sergeant Velie: "Thomas, there's a special job for you. Go upstairs, search Major Kirby and his crew, and every bit of equipment."

The Major seemed startled. "I say, now—"

"Just form, Major, just form," said the Inspector affably. "Go on now, the two of you. I've work of my own."

· · · · · ·

In twenty minutes the job was done. Sergeant Velie, than whom there was no more thorough disrespecter of persons on the metropolitan force, himself supervised a search which included Major Kirby's slender body, Major Kirby's natty clothes, Major Kirby's resentful and jeering crew of cameramen and sound engineers, Major Kirby's cameras, Major Kirby's ohms and watts and rheostats (in a manner of speaking)—in a word, everything connected with Major Kirby and his unit, down to the last coil of cable, was picked over, scrutinized felt, pinched, pressed, eviscerated, anatomized, dismembered, and divellicated.

The result was a complete absence of discovery. There was nothing on that platform, nor anything on the persons of the men on the platform and the apparatus on the platform, which even remotely resembled an automatic. Whereupon, under special escort, the group of newsreel men was packed out of the building, armed with a hastily scribbled message from Major Kirby to the editor of his newsreel company.

The Major was the last to be pawed over. Found pure, he was passed directly out of the building by a side exit into Ellery's arms. Ellery was waiting on the sidewalk with a huge police bag at his knee which contained forty-five pieces of assorted lethal hardware and some hundreds of cartridges.

The Inspector saw them off. "You'll shoot whatever you find in the way of artillery down to us at Headquarters?" asked Ellery soberly.

"You bet."

The old man stood gazing thoughtfully after their departing cab. Then he rather grimly went back into the *Colosseum*, to supervise the bodily search of twenty thousand persons.

8: A MATTER OF BALLISTICS

THE TAXICAB roared downtown. The bag nestled comfortably at Ellery's feet, and he nudged it every once in a while with his toe as if to reassure himself that it was there. What his thoughts were was masked by the darkness of the cab and punctuated by the orange period made by the tip of his cigaret; but the Major's thoughts were shining clear, despite the darkness.

For not long after the machine swung into Eighth Avenue, headed downtown, he said in a light tone: "I'm pretty lucky tonight, come to think of it."

Ellery made a polite noise.

The Major's little laugh put froth on the thunder of the exhaust. "I usually carry an automatic—habit I haven't been able to shake off since the War."

"But tonight you didn't."

"But tonight I didn't. That's right." Kirby was silent for a moment. "Don't know what made me leave it home. Premonition?"

"You recall what Emerson had to say about intuition in his *Persian Poetry!*"

"Eh? No, I'm afraid not."

Ellery sighed. "It doesn't matter, really."

Neither man spoke again until the cab pulled up before the dark fortress on Centre Street which was Police Headquarters.

．　　　．　　　．　　　．　　　．　　　．　　　．

With admirable foresight, Ellery had preceded their journey with a telephone call, so that they found a tall gangling gentleman of professorish mould, wearing horn-rimmed spectacles, awaiting them in the lobby downstairs. He was dressed in rusty brown, he wore a silly-looking hat two sizes too large for his cranium, and he had the lined dry face and the lantern-jaw of Father Prohibition.

This amazing creature nodded benevolently to Ellery and uncoiled his length from a bench like a snake. "Well, sir," he said in a cavernous roar, "what are you doing here at this time of night? I thought the Queen clan retired early."

"Haven't you heard?"

"Heard what?"

"We've had a little murder at the *Colosseum* tonight. That's why I called you. Sorry to get you out of bed at one in the morning, Lieutenant, but—"

"Poker game," said the tall man dryly.

"Then there's no harm done. Lieutenant, I want you to meet a brother-ballisticker—Major Kirby. Lieutenant Kenneth Knowles, Major, ballistics expert of the Department."

The two experts eyed each other and shook hands.

"Let's amble over to your office," said Ellery impatiently. "God, this bag weighs tons! There's work to be done."

They repaired to Room 114, on the door of which was printed the words: *Bureau of Ballistics.* Lieutenant Knowles ushered them through a neat office lined with filing cabinets into a laboratory.

"Now, gentlemen," said Ellery briskly, setting the bag down and opening it, "the problem is simple enough. I've asked Major Kirby, Lieutenant, to sit in on this because he's something of a ballistics fiend himself, and two authoritative noodles are always better than one."

The Lieutenant's spectacles gleamed with professional interest as he saw the tumbled heap of short arms in the bag. "Glad to have the Major, of course. But what—"

"Now I," said Ellery, "know absolutely nothing about firearms. I don't know a—a Luger from a howitzer. I want scientific information. First take a look at this bullet." He produced the red-coated pellet which Dr. Prouty had dug out of the dead man's torso. "The Inspector says it's from a .25. I want to be sure."

The little Major and the tall Lieutenant bent over the tiny slug. "He's right," said Knowles instantly. "That's from a .25 automatic pistol. Eh, Major?"

"No doubt about it. Looks like the Remington cartridge," murmured Major Kirby. "Hmm! So this is what killed Horne, eh?"'

"I presume so. At least, that's what the Assistant Medical Examiner excavated from his heart." Ellery frowned. "What can you gentlemen tell me about this bullet?"

Both men laughed. "Here!" chuckled Lieutenant Knowles. "We're not magicians. Can't tell much from a slug without putting it under the 'scope. Lucky at that, Mr. Queen—what do you say, Major? Ever see a discharged bullet in such prime condition for microscopic examination?"

"It's not much banged up, I'll admit," muttered Kirby, turning it over carefully in his fingers.

"You see," began the police expert in his best classroom bass, "it's not always true that an expert can 'fingerprint' a discharged bullet, as they say. By that I mean it isn't always possible, due to the condition of the bullet, to get a satisfactory picture of the marks. I've had bullets so damn smashed and battered—"

"Yes, yes," said Ellery quickly, "but give me a picture of this thing—a virgin picture, I mean. What's it look like, undischarged?"

"Can't see that that will help you," said the Lieutenant, surprised.

"Perhaps Mr. Queen doesn't know whether it will help or not," suggested Major Kirby with a smile. "Why, the .25 automatic with the proper ammunition—this bullet, for instance—is loaded with fifty grains, and is metal-incased. It's lead inside, of course, and it's contained in a jacket of cupro-nickel. Velocity at, say, twenty-five feet would be—let's see—seven hundred and fifty foot-seconds; energy is sixty-two footpounds. . . ."

"Enough," said Ellery weakly. "I can see that's not the right tack. Let's try it another way. Will this bullet—this .25 calibre bullet, mind you—fit anything but a .25 automatic pistol?"

"No," said both men at once.

"Well—how about the .22 revolver?" said Ellery feebly. "That's an even smaller arm, of course. Wouldn't the .25—"

Lieutenant Knowles went away. When he returned he was carrying three cartridges. "Better clear this up right now," he said. "There are very small .22's, of course, and they use .22 ammunition, which in that case is the so-called '.22 short.' Here's one of 'em." He displayed a cartridge incredibly tiny—it seemed little more than a half-inch long, and was very slender. "You couldn't fire this baby out of a .25 automatic. Now take a look at this one." He held up a cartridge which, while its circumference was identical with that of the tiny bullet, seemed twice as long. "This is what's called the '.22 long rifle,'" explained Lieutenant

Knowles. "It's a .22, all right, but it's made to fit much bigger weapons. The reason for that is that lots of people who want .22 bullet results also want .38 gun 'feel.' The weapons in which this .22 long rifle ammunition fits are big fellows—big as .38's, and bigger. But now take a look at this." He exhibited the third cartridge. It was thicker than the .22 short, and shorter than the .22 long. "This is the brother of this little bullet Doc probed out of the stiff. It's a .25 calibre automatic. It's the only bullet, far as I know, which will fit a .25 automatic pistol. Right, Major?"

"I think so."

"All of which means," groaned Ellery, "that I've lugged my arm off for nothing." He kicked the police bag full of weapons with viciousness. "In other words, the Horne bullet must have been shot from a .25 automatic—is that right? Couldn't have been shot from any other type or size of arm?"

"Now you've got it," said the Lieutenant with a grin, and he dug his right hand inside his coat. It whipped out with a blue-shining little pistol, flat as Tommy Black's hips, and so small that it nestled quite comfortably in the palm of Knowles's large hand. "Only four and a half inches long," he said with a smacking of his lips, "two-inch barrel, weighs thirteen ounces, magazine holds six husky little cartridges—slide lock safety, grip safety—why, this little Colt's a beauty! Always carry one. Want a look at it? Your murderer carried one just like it, Mr. Queen!"

Ellery reached for it eagerly. "Uuuump!" said the Lieutenant with a grin. "Wait 'til I pull the teeth out of my pet. Fellow like you's liable to plug me in the *kishkes*." He pulled out the magazine, dumped the six cartridges into his hand, and removed the seventh cartridge from the firing chamber. Then he replaced the magazine and handed the weapon to Ellery.

"Ah," said Ellery, and hefted the pistol cautiously. It felt a little heavier than he had expected it to, but it was still feath-er-light in comparison with the official revolvers he had been accustomed to seeing and, on occasion, handling. It snuggled in his palm very cosily. "I wonder why," he muttered half to him-self, "our man used this in preference to a bigger and more effec-tive weapon?"

Unexpectedly, the Major chuckled. "More effective? I say, Mr. Queen, you don't realize what that little jigger you're hold-ing is capable of. You could shoot right through a two-inch board with this thing at a very respectable distance!"

"Let alone soft human flesh," muttered Ellery. "So that's it. Not effectiveness. Then convenience. Small. . . ." He returned the pistol to the police expert and gazed raptly at his *pince-nez*. "Well!" He returned the glasses to his nose. "One question more before we dig into this bag. How long would it take to empty the magazine, firing at top speed?"

"I've done it in two and a half seconds, and it was a rusty old stop-watch at that," boomed Lieutenant Knowles.

"Two and a half seconds!" Ellery whistled, and momentarily grew thoughtful again. "Then we find the trail of our old friend the expert marksman again. One shot sufficed, eh. . . . Very well, gentlemen. Let's see what Santa Claus has brought us."

He squatted on the floor and began tossing revolvers out of the bag. The Lieutenant and the Major watched him in silence. And when the bag was empty Ellery looked up at them, and they looked down at him, and none of the three said a word for some minutes.

Then simultaneously they looked at the floor. Ellery had sep-arated automatics from revolvers. And in the pile of revolvers there were forty-four long-barreled weapons, and in the "pile" of automatics there was no pile at all, for only one weapon lay there—a lonely little exhibit. Ellery scanned the tag attached to the trigger-guard. It read: *Ted Lyons.*

Still in silence he scrabbled through the pile of cartridges. And he found no .25 calibre automatic bullets at all.

"Well, well," he said softly as he rose. "Not much grist in the mill. Apparently our friend the mongering newspaperman was the only occupant of the arena proper who carried a weapon capable of having fired the bullet which killed Horne. I suppose there's nothing to do but test Lyon's automatic."

.   .   .   .

Ellery strolled about, humming a mournful tune, as Lieutenant Knowles, assisted by Major Kirby, prepared to test the single suspect weapon. The Lieutenant busied himself setting up a peculiar-looking target of unknown substance on the firing-range; then he and the Major retired to a far corner of the room, conferring earnestly as Knowles examined the seven cartridges in Ted Lyons's pistol.

"Not blanks." Then the Lieutenant said: "I'm a rotten shot, Major. Want to pot that target?"

"Don't mind," replied Kirby, and taking up a position some twenty feet from the target pointed the small weapon and almost negligently squeezed the trigger. A continuous, deafening report raised by the echoes in the little laboratory made Ellery jump. By the time Ellery came to his senses the little man was smiling, some acrid-smelling smoke was drifting off, and the target looked like Swiss cheese.

"Nice work, Major," said Knowles admiringly. "Sprayed 'em in a circle, eh? That will give us a number of specimens. Let's get busy."

He strode back from the target, juggling half a dozen spent

bullets which were swathed in black greasy coats. He looked at them keenly when he got to the table. "Let's test these babies."

He removed his coat, waved Ellery into a chair, and then occupied himself with a very simple business. There was a familiar instrument on the work-table which had some curiously unfamiliar features. It seemed to be an unusual type of microscope.

"Companion 'scope," he explained. "Got a double comparison eye-piece, as you can see. You know this dingus, Major?"

Kirby nodded. "Quite well. I used one for some time in the army, and I've one at home for my own amusement."

Ellery watched the two men anxiously. The blood-coated bullet Lieutenant Knowles bathed in a solution, and then rubbed gently dry. It emerged quite clean; it was leaden in color. He studied it under the microscope for some time; and then he raised his head and motioned Major Kirby to the eye-piece.

"Beautiful markings!" exclaimed the Major, looking up. "It certainly won't be any trouble matching those marks to a comparison specimen, Lieutenant!"

"Maybe not. Now let's see how these bullets you just fired stack up," said Knowles briskly; and he busied himself again with the microscope. The fatal bullet remained where it was; but the six shot into the target a few moments before succeeded each other in slow order. There was much to-do with screws and careful turnings of the new specimens; both men conferred frequently, and the Major checked each of the Lieutenant's findings. And at the end they nodded with solemn certainty, and Knowles turned to Ellery with an air of finality.

"There's nothing certain but death and taxes, they say! Well, here's one thing sure, Mr. Queen—the bullet that killed your man *didn't* come from this fellow Lyons's automatic. Don't even have to use the universal molecular. The marks haven't anything in common."

Ellery digested this for a moment, then got to his feet and began to pace the floor. "Hmm. Nice to find *one* example of fixation in a wavering world. By the way, I suppose you're both absolutely sure?"

"No question about it, Mr. Queen," said Major Kirby earnestly. "When we can arrive at a conclusion at all, you may be sure it's the right one. This matter of checking fired bullets is now pretty much of an exact science. You see, all modern arms are rifled—I suppose you know what that means. The inside of the barrel is—well, you might almost describe it as etched spirally. The .25 automatic's barrel has six grooves and six lands in a left-hand twist—it sounds complicated, but it's really very simple. There's a spiral, or twist, which runs from end to end of the barrel inside, cut into the metal; the depressions made by the cutting are called the grooves, the raised spirals of metal *left* by the cutting are called the lands. Six of each, as I say. Now there are always minute differences in lands which are visible under the microscope. Naturally, when the bullet on firing passes through the barrel, it spins through the grooves, and the marks of the lands are left on the bullet. . . ."

"I see. And by putting two bullets under the microscope you can see if the markings are similar or dissimilar?"

"That's right," said the Lieutenant. "You focus the two specimens until they merge into one—or seem to; you see the left side of each slap against the other; then it's easy to see if all the markings match, or if they don't."

"And these don't?"

"And these don't."

Whatever Ellery in the helplessness of the moment was about

to say was choked back by an unexpected interruption. A tall, burly individual hurried into the laboratory, carrying a small bag.

"Ah, Ritter!" said Ellery eagerly. "More guns?"

The detective dumped the bag on the work-table. "From the Inspector, Mr. Queen. Sent 'em down with me—on the run. Found 'em, he said to tell you, on people from the audience."

And he disappeared.

Ellery opened the bag with shaking fingers. "Jerusalem, a ten-strike!" he cried, taking out the weapons. "Look at these—at least a dozen automatics!"

There were, to be exact, fourteen automatics. Of the fourteen—each was tagged with its bearer's name and address—four were of .25 calibre, the small four-and-a-half-inch weapons with which they were concerned. There were three revolvers in the batch as well; but to these they paid no attention.

Major Kirby and Lieutenant Knowles retired to the firing-range again, and for some time the resonant reports thundered through the office as they shot bullets into the target. They returned with four tagged bullets, each from one of the .25 automatics in the batch Ritter had brought from the *Colosseum*. These went under the lens of the comparison microscope one by one, and for some time there were no sounds but the intakes of breath in the laboratory.

And at the conclusion of the tests Ellery did not even have to ask the verdict. It was clear from the two experts' scowls that not one of the four bullets examined matched the bullet which had killed Buck Horne.

There was a note at the bottom of the bag. It said:

"El: Some popguns found on the mob. Sending 'em all along, though it's a cinch we want only .25's. Not half-through with this crowd. Would you believe so many birds here tonight came heeled? More later—if I find them."

It was signed by Inspector Queen.

"Lieutenant, will you stick around?" asked Ellery with desperate calm as he regarded the litter of weapons.

"You mean there'll be more? All right; I guess I can scare up a poker game with some of the boys. Good night, Major; it's been a pleasure. Give me a ring one of these days; I've got a private collection of firearms I'd like to show you some time."

"You have?" cried Kirby. "I've got a little collection of my own, you know! What's your oldest arm?"

"An 1840—"

Ellery grasped the Major's elbow. "Come along, now, Major," he said soothingly. "You may play with the nice Lieutenant some other time. At the moment urgent business calls us back to the *Colosseum*."

9: NOTHING

IT WAS past three when Ellery and the Major returned to the *Colosseum*—past three of one of the darkest nights Ellery could recall.

"There's no moon, so we can't yodel that ancient rallying call: 'There's blood on the moon!'" Ellery remarked as they pushed by a detective he knew. "Give me good old darkness every time as the proper setting for a murder."

"It's light enough in here," said Major Kirby dryly.

It was light enough, to be sure, to illuminate a very odd scene. The spectacle of unrestrained mass anger can be terrible; but there is nothing quite so depressing as the spectacle of mass resentment held in check by authority. The auditorium of the *Colosseum* was thunderous with silent rage. Few faces did not glare sullenly; and those that were meek were horribly tired. If this was the most stupendous reconnaissance in the history of modern policing, it was also the most disagreeable. If looks could kill, there would have been two hundred officers and plainclothesmen stretched out stark and cold on the floors.

As it was, the search of the twenty thousand proceeded quietly, rapidly—and fruitlessly.

Ellery and Major Kirby found Inspector Queen—fatigued

but imperturbable—presiding like Napoleon over the forces of investigation from a small table which had been set throne-like in the center of the arena. Reports came to him in an unending stream. At the innumerable exits detectives passed members of the audience from hand to hand until the exhausted and harried citizen found himself, somewhat dazed, on the sidewalk outside the building. Matrons summoned hastily from nearby precincts pawed over the women. Occasionally a man would be singled out of line, searched more thoroughly, and finally turned back to the arena under escort. Once the object of this special attention was a woman. These ephemeral celebrities were promptly brought up before the Inspector, who questioned them and had them more thoroughly searched. It was from this small but select group that the artillery which Detective Ritter had brought downtown to Headquarters had come; they were "suspicious characters," members of the underworld in good standing, with whose face every detective and officer of the police force was thoroughly familiar.

"Amazing," remarked the Major as they waited for the Inspector to conclude his interrogation of a brawny creature with sleepy eyes, "how many kinds of people a representative crowd like this will turn up."

"How many kinds of crooks," murmured Ellery, "and heaven alone knows how many kinds of murderers. . . . 'Lo, dad! We're back."

The Inspector rose quickly. "Well," he said with soft eagerness, "did you find anything?"

"Did *you?*"

The old man shrugged. "Nothing. Plenty of rodmen here tonight. Whole town's here, by damn. But—" He waved his hands helplessly. "There's another pile of guns waiting for examination. Is Knowles waiting downtown?"

"Yes. Any .25 automatics in the bunch?"

"One or two."

"Send them down to Knowles; he has the bullet and he's prepared to work all night if necessary."

"I'll wait until we've cleaned out this crew. Well, son, well! I asked you if you found anything!"

"Will you excuse me, Major?" murmured Ellery, turning to the silent companion.

"Certainly."

"You might be good enough to stand by," said Ellery. "It's possible we may need you—"

"Glad to help." Kirby turned on his heel and walked off.

"Nothing doing, dad," said Ellery in a rapid undertone. "Knowles and Kirby made it clear that only a .25 automatic could have fired the bullet. But not one of these cowboys had a .25; forty-four of the forty-five weapons were .44's, .45's, and .38's. The forty-fifth was the automatic Velie took from Ted Lyons. But comparison tests showed that it hadn't fired the fatal shot."

"So," grunted the old man.

"Another interesting fact Knowles dug out for me before I left h.q. With the exception of Wild Bill's revolver and the three guns Lyons had on him, all the guns taken from the rodeo crowd had been fired just once a piece—presumably therefore during that single fusillade at the moment Horne toppled from the saddle."

"All loaded with blanks?"

"Yes. Of course, there's the theoretical possibility that the single cartridge missing in each instance might have been a lethal bullet rather than a blank, but that doesn't help us because none of them is a .25. Grant's revolver has three cartridges missing; that corresponds with the number of signal-shots he fired from the center of the arena before the murder, as I remember it; and here, too, there's no possibility that his gun fired the fatal shot, because his is a .45. As for Lyons, neither his own automatic nor the two large-calibre guns he swiped from the armory had been fired at all—Have you examined the armory?"

"Yep," said the Inspector gloomily. "Nothing doing."

"Not a single .25 automatic?"

"Not one."

"Well, but good Lord!" cried Ellery in an exasperated tone, "this is ridiculous. That automatic *must* be here somewhere. It can't have got away. The place has been kept tighter than a drum-head since the instant of the murder."

"Maybe we'll turn it up in the crowd before we're through."

Ellery sucked a fingernail; then he rubbed his forehead wearily. "No. I don't believe that will happen. Too easy. There's something remarkably queer—and, yes, remarkably clever, too—about this, dad. I have the distinct feeling. . . ." He blinked suddenly, and then began to polish the lenses of his *pince-nez*. "Hmm. There's a thought. . . . You're staying on here, of course?" he said abruptly.

"Sure. Why?"

"Because I'm not! I've just remembered. There's something I must do."

"Must do?"

"Yes. Must have a peep at Buck Horne's room in the Barclay."

"Oh." The old man seemed disappointed. "I've been leaving that. Have to do it, of course. I've sent Johnson up to watch the place. But there's nothing special—"

"Indeed, there's something very special up there," replied Ellery grimly, "and I intend to see it before the hour's up."

The Inspector studied him for a moment, and then shrugged.

"All right. But make it snappy. Maybe I'll be through with the mob by the time you get back. Want Thomas to go alone?"

"No—Yes, come to think of it! And. . . . before I go. Dad, I want Kit Horne with me, too."

"The girl? She hasn't been searched yet."

"Then attend to it."

"And the rest of 'em in the Mars box, too. *Including* Mars," said the Inspector; and they quickly crossed to the southeastern part of the oval. The brave gaiety of hours before was quite washed out of them; the occupants of the Mars box for the most part sat in a rubbled silence, in attitudes of tired dejection. The only calm person there was the irrepressible Djuna; and he was calm because he was fast asleep in his chair.

The Inspector said: "I'm sorry, folks, but you can't go yet. Miss Horne—"

There were welts under her eyes. "Yes?" she said dully.

"Would you mind coming down here?"

They roused themselves at that; and in Mara Gay's eyes there seemed to be a kindling fire.

"And Mr. Grant, too—you, Curly," said Ellery pleasantly.

Wild Bill and his son, both in the box, stared and regarded Ellery hopefully. Then Curly sprang to his feet, vaulted the rail, and held up his arms for Kit. She followed him without effort, her skirts describing a graceful parabola as she dropped to the tanbark; she landed with a little thump in Curly's arms, and remained there for the fraction of a second. Young Lochinvar seemed loath to relinquish his fragrant armful; her hair tickled his nostrils and made them oscillate like tendrils in a breeze. But Kit disengaged herself gently and said to the Inspector: "Whatever it is—I'm ready."

"It's nothing much, Miss Horne. I'm just sending you back

to your hotel. But before you go—to keep the records straight, y'know; somebody might have slipped it to you without your knowing—you'll have to be searched like the rest."

She flared up suddenly. "You think *I*. . . ." Then she smiled and shook her head. "Of course. Anything."

They moved in a group toward one of the small exits. At a signal from the Inspector Sergeant Velie fell into step behind them, and an Amazonian matron who, from her physique, might have mothered every 200-pound policeman on the force.

In one of the small rooms below, the matron—duly admonished to be gentle if thorough—searched Kit; in an adjoining room Sergeant Velie performed a similar service for Curly. The young couple were out in a matter of minutes; form had been "satisfied"; nothing at all incriminating—let alone the .25 automatic pistol which persisted in remaining elusive—had been found on them.

The Inspector escorted them to the main entrance. There they paused, and Ellery whispered: "You're shipping the others off soon?"

"Yep. I'll have them frisked right away."

"Be very careful, dad, please! And—Really, you ought to send Djuna home. The poor tyke's had enough excitement for one evening. He'll be ill tomorrow."

"I'll send him home with Piggott or somebody."

"And—keep Grant here until I return."

"Grant, eh?" The Inspector nodded. "All right."

Their eyes met. "Well—good huntin'," said the Inspector.

"It's bound to be good," murmured Ellery. "Ah—by the way, you might release Major Kirby after another search. Just to be on the safe side, you know. I don't think we'll need him any more tonight, with Knowles holding down the fort at h.q."

"Sure, sure," muttered the old man absently. He took snuff with a marked degree of weariness in the gesture. "Y'know, there's been somethin' bothering me all night, son. What the dickens did you mean earlier tonight when you told Grant there was somethin' missing from Horne's body?"

Ellery threw back his head and gave an exhibition of silent mirth. "Lord, what an eternally surprising old coot you are, dad! Leave it to you to ask the right question at the right time."

"Quit stallin'," growled the Inspector. "What was it?"

Ellery stopped laughing and descended into a vast earthy calm. He tapped a cigaret slowly on his thumbnail. "It's really very clear. Did you notice the pistol belt Horne was wearing?"

"Yes?"

"How many holsters hung from the belt?"

"Why, one. . . . No, bedad, two!"

"Correct. Yet there was only one revolver on him; one holster then had no revolver. Query: Why does a man wear an old and treasured belt equipped with *two* holsters and still carry only *one* revolver? And that revolver also an old and treasured specimen?"

"There must be another one," said the Inspector with an expression of surprise. "That's right, by jiminy! Wouldn't be surprised if it was a mate to that fancy ivory-handled rod we found in his hand."

"I *know* it's a mate," murmured Ellery, and stepped abruptly out upon the sidewalk to rejoin Kit, Curly and Sergeant Velie.

The night air chilled the marrow. The Inspector watched them step to the curb. He watched a hawking taxicab dart up, and the four get in. He watched Ellery's lips, and watched the cab shoot down Eighth Avenue. He stood there watching, in fact, long after there was anything left to see.

10: THE SECOND GUN

Johnson, the detective inspector Queen had detailed to guard Buck Horne's room at the Hotel Barclay—a small, drab-looking, grizzled man with the air of the bona-fide shopkeeper and the eyes of a ferret—opened the door very wide and abruptly at Ellery's knock. He lost his tense expression at sight of Ellery, grinned, and fell back. They trooped in, and Sergeant Velie closed the door.

"Anything doin', Johnson?" rumbled the Sergeant.

"Nope. I was just thinking of taking off my shoes and havin' a nap when Mr. Queen broke up my beauty-sleep."

Kit went mechanically to a chintz-covered chair and sat down. She did not take off her gloves or coat. Curly, an overcoat over his Western clothes, dropped heavily on the bed. Neither spoke.

It was a large room, characterless in the typical hotel fashion, with a bed and two chairs and a dresser and a wardrobe and a night-table.

Ellery smiled at Sergeant Velie, said: "Make yourself comfortable, Miss Horne," stripped off his light overcoat, pitched his hat on the bed, and went to work.

Johnson and Velie watched him in a sort of boredom.

It was a matter of moments, so swiftly did he search. The wardrobe with Horne's clothes hanging neatly inside—city suits, an extra coat, two Stetson hats; the drawers of the dresser, which contained few and innocent articles; the drawer of the night-table. He straightened up thoughtfully; then regarded Kit with an apologetic grin.

"Mind if I go through your room, Miss Horne?"

Curly made a warlike movement. "Say, you, I don't like—"

"Curly," said Kit. "Not at all, Mr. Queen. Go right ahead. If I knew what you're looking for—"

"It's really not important," said Ellery quickly, going to the door of the communicating bathroom and opening it. Whatever he was mumbling was drowned in the closing of the door as he stepped through the bathroom into Kit's bedroom. He was back in three minutes, wearing a puzzled frown.

"It certainly should be. . . . Ah, the bed of course!" and he dropped to his knees beside Curly's startled legs and peered underneath the bed. Then he reached far under and pulled; emerging after a moment, flushed but triumphant, with a small flat theatrical-type trunk at the end of his arm.

This he dragged to the center of the floor and opened without ceremony. A moment's rummaging, and he straightened up with a savage gleam in his eye. He was holding in his right hand a revolver.

.   .   .   .

"Oh, *that!*" exclaimed Kit. "Why didn't you tell me you were looking for the other gun, Mr. Queen? I would have known—"

"So you *didn't* know," said Ellery slowly, looking at the weapon.

A faint wrinkle appeared between her candid brows. "Why,

no, I didn't. I didn't really notice in—in all the excitement. I took it for granted that he had both guns on him. But—"

"Was it his custom always to carry the two guns, Miss Horne?" Ellery asked dreamily.

"He didn't have a hard and fast rule about it," she said, her voice breaking a little. "He was notoriously careless, Buck was. Sometimes he took both, and sometimes he took one. I remember seeing both in that drawer of the trunk just two or three days ago. He must have taken only one with him tonight—last night. Oh, I'm so confused, so tired. . . ."

"Reasonable enough," agreed Ellery. "Relax, Miss Horne; it's been a hard few hours. . . . Doesn't it strike you as strange that while he took only one revolver of the pair with him, he still retained both holsters?"

She looked at him, startled; and then to his amazement began to laugh. "Mr. Queen!" she gasped; her laughter was tinged with hysteria. "I can see you don't know much about Western doodads. And you didn't examine the belt very carefully. Many, if not most, pistol belts have detachable holsters; but this one of—of Buck's was specially made. You can't *help* taking the two holsters along, you see; unless you leave the belt behind, too."

"Oh," said Ellery, flushing a little; and he bent his head to examine the revolver he had found.

It was an ivory-handled .45 single-action Colt, obviously and beyond question the twin of the revolver found clutched in the dead man's hand. Its long barrel was as delicately chased, and its cylinder, as the mate; and the cunning little patches of ivory in-laid on the sides of the butt were carved in a similar steer's-head design, sporting in the center of each an oval monogrammed *H*. The ivory inlays were worn and yellow, showing the same great age as those of the twin, except for one small patch on the left side of the butt; as Ellery held the revolver in his right hand, this portion of lighter ivory came between the tips of his curled fingers and the heel of his hand. The tip of the barrel and the upper edge of the sight were both rubbed smooth, as in the case of the first revolver.

"Seems as well-used and old as the other," muttered Ellery absently, and there was a glint in his eyes which was drowned out when he saw Sergeant Velie pounce forward and Curly's coiled figure spring from the bed.

Then he heard a wild sobbing. It was Kit—that Peerless Cowgirl of the Plains, Heroine of Countless Action Melodramas, Dauntless Daredevil of the West. . . . She was weeping with unashamed abandon, and her back heaved convulsively as she sobbed into her tear-dampened hands.

"Here, here, we can't have any of that," cried Ellery, tossing the revolver on the bed and darting forward. He was held back by a long hard arm attached to Curly's muscular shoulder; and even the Sergeant submitted to superior wisdom and stepped back. Curly took the little wet brown hands from the little wet brown face and whispered what must have been magical words in Kit's ears; for in a remarkably short time the heavings became less frequent, the sobs came more gently, and finally ceased altogether. Curly, frowning to conceal his pleasure, returned to his perch on the bed.

She sniffled three times and dabbed at her eyes with a handkerchief. "I'm—I'm so sorry. Wasn't that s-s-silly of me? Crying like a baby! I didn't realize how much I—" She tucked the handkerchief away and looked into Ellery's concerned eyes. "I'm quite all right now, Mr. Queen. I beg your pardon for making a scene."

"I—uh—" said Ellery fluently, and blushed. Then he picked up the revolver. "There's no doubt," he said with severity, "of the fact that this was Buck Horne's gun?"

She shook her head slowly. "Not the slightest."

"And it is, of course, the mate of the one we found in the arena?"

She looked unhappy. "I—I didn't notice which one he had, but I suppose it was—was the other."

"He had more than two revolvers?" snapped Ellery.

"Oh, no. I mean—"

"You're confused," said Ellery gently. "Do you know, Mr. Grant?"

"Shore do," growled Curly. "Why don't you leave the poor kid alone? That's one of Buck's two prize shooters. Had 'em twenty years or more. Pop's often tole me they were given to Buck by some ole Injun fighter—made up special for Buck, initials an' all. Some irons!" Enthusiasm leaped into his voice; he took the revolver from Ellery and hefted it appreciatively. "Feel the weight of that, Queen. Perfect, huh? No wonder Buck wouldn't part with 'em—used 'em all the time. He was a crack shot—you've heard *that*—an' he was finicky as Annie Oakley 'bout the hang of 'em. That's why he liked these so; they were plumb perfect in balance for 'is hands."

Johnson, from his corner, rolled his eyes eloquently and turned away with a faint groan. Sergeant Velie shuffled his primeval feet. Even Kit looked askance at the orator. But Ellery seemed extraordinarily interested.

"Go on," he murmured. "That's very curious."

"Go on?" Curly was surprised. "Ain't nothin' else to—"

"Isn't," said Kit mechanically; and they both colored. Ellery turned a humorous back upon them as he bent again over the revolver.

Employing a device which had served him in the past—a pencil wrapped in a silk handkerchief—he swabbed the interior of the eight-inch barrel thoroughly. The handkerchief emerged with nothing more suspicious than dust-specks, and remarkably few of these. But there was a generous oil-stain.

"Recently cleaned," he observed to no one in particular.

Kit nodded soberly. "That's not at all remarkable, Mr. Queen. Buck prized those weapons as if they were relics of his sainted mother. Cleaned them both nearly every day."

Ellery broke open the cylinder and peered into the cartridge chambers. The gun was not loaded. He rummaged in the trunk drawer again and found a box of cartridges. They were .45 calibre bullets—wicked-looking things almost two inches long. He hesitated, then returned the box of shells to the drawer; but the weapon he pocketed.

"Nothing else here, I think," he observed cheerfully. "Sergeant, you might go over the ground again to make sure I've missed no significant papers or things. But there *is* one thing more I'm going to do before I leave here, by Joe, and I intend doing that at once."

He smiled and went to the telephone on the night-table. "Is this the hotel operator? Connect me with the desk, please. . . . Night-clerk? Were you on duty yesterday evening? . . . Fine. Please come up to 841. This is—well, police business."

·   ·   ·   ·   ·   ·   ·

Sergeant Velie had just reported no luck in his ransacking of the room when there was a knock on the door, and Johnson opened it to reveal a badly frightened young man who wore the inevitable badge of servitude in his lapel, a carnation.

"Come in," said Ellery heartily. "You say you were on duty yesterday evening. At what time do you come on?"

"Uh—at seven, sir!"

"Ah, at seven! How very fortunate. You've heard the news, I take it?"

The young man visibly shrank. "Y-yes, sir. About Mr.—Mr. Horne. Frightful." He glanced fearfully at Kit out of the corner of his eye.

"Well, now," said Ellery expansively, "naturally we're interested in possible visitors to Mr. Horne's room during the past few days. Might give us a lead, you know. Were there any?"

Vanity being appealed to, the gentleman responded in the customary manner. He assumed a frowning air, scratched his forehead delicately with the tip of a womanish fingernail, and then the sun rose in his cheeks.

He exclaimed: "Yes, sir! Yes, I think. . . . There was someone night before last, sir!"

"At what time?" asked Ellery quietly. Kit was very still, hands folded in her lap, and Curly did not stir on the bed.

"Oh, about half-past ten, sir. I—"

"Please. One moment." Ellery turned to Kit. "What time did you say you returned to the Barclay night before last, Miss Horne?"

"Did I say? I don't think—I said I got in late and found Buck already asleep. That's true, Mr. Queen. I got in past midnight. I'd been out with Mr. Grant."

"Mr. *Curly* Grant?"

"Yes."

Mr. Curly Grant, who seemed to have something wrong with his throat, growled again.

"Go on, please," said Ellery to the clerk. "There was a visitor at ten-thirty. And?"

"Mr. Horne entered the lobby about nine o'clock, sir, got his key at the desk—that's how I know—and, I suppose, went upstairs. At ten-thirty a man stopped at the desk and asked for the number of Mr. Horne's room. A man—I think it was a man, sir."

"What d'ye mean—you *think* it was a man?" growled Sergeant Velie in his first oral contribution in some time. "Don't you know the facts of life yet? Can't you tell a man from a woman, or was there somethin' queer about the guy?"

The clerk exhibited terror again. "N-no, sir, I don't recollect anything but the—well, the vaguest kind of picture. You see, I was busy. . . ."

"Can't you recall anything of his appearance?" snapped Ellery.

"Oh, sir, he was sort of tall, I think, and big, and—"

"And?"

The clerk fell back against the door. "I can't remember, sir," he said feebly.

"Oh, botheration!" murmured Ellery. "Well! I suppose it can't be helped." Then hope glittered again in his eye. "Wasn't one of your colleagues at the desk with you who might have noticed this man?"

"No, sir, I'm afraid not. I was alone at the time behind the desk."

Sergeant Velie grumbled his disgust, and Ellery shrugged. "What else?"

"Why, I told him: 'Mr. Horne's in 841,' and he picked up the house phone and talked. I heard him mention Mr. Horne's first name in addressing him, and then I think he said: 'I'll be right up, Buck,' and he went away."

"First name? Hmm. That's interesting. Went upstairs? To this room?" Ellery gnawed his upper lip. "But of course you wouldn't know. Thank you. And please *don't* mention this to a soul, man. That's a command."

The clerk backed out precipitately.

Ellery nodded to Sergeant Velie and to Johnson. "Ah—Miss Horne, we'll leave you alone now. I hope I haven't given you too bad a time. But it's really been most helpful. Come along, boys."

"I'm stayin'," announced Curly defiantly.

"Please do, Curly," whispered Kit. "I—I don't feel like being alone. I don't want to sleep. . . ."

"I know, kid," he muttered, and patted her hand.

Ellery and the two detectives silently left the room.

"Now, Johnson," said Ellery with a snap, "don't disturb those love-birds in there, and mind you keep an eye on both doors. You'll have to park in the corridor all the rest of the night, I'm afraid. If there's any irregularity call the Inspector at the *Colosseum*. He'll send a relief soon."

And Ellery tucked his arm between the Sergeant's steer-like side and the Sergeant's bludgeon-like arm, and the two men marched off like half of the four Musketeers.

11: THE IMPOSSIBLE

IT SEEMED to Ellery that several years had elapsed since he and Djuna and the Inspector had so blithely taken seats in Tony Mars's box in anticipation of a naive evening. He paused to look at his watch as he and the Sergeant reentered the *Colosseum*. It was ten minutes past four.

"What on earth," he demanded of his silent companion, "would we do without Herr Einstein? It took the incomparable Teuton to make us realize how fragile Time really is—what an insecure place it holds in the scheme of things, *'Le moment où je parle est déja loin de moi. . . . '* I suppose you aren't acquainted with Boileau? The seventeenth century satirist, *'Le temps fuit, et nous traine avec soi—'*"

"How you talk," chuckled the Sergeant suddenly.

Ellery became silent with celerity.

They found—wonder of inestimable wonders!—the vast curving tiers of seats, which a few hours before had held twenty thousand, quite deserted. Except for the litter in the aisles, there was no sign of human occupancy. The fort had been evacuated—with trimmings—in something more than record time.

Except for the police, detectives, a few weary citizens, and the personnel of the rodeo, the *Colosseum* was empty.

"Wha'd you find?" croaked the Inspector, marble-gray with fatigue, as Ellery and the Sergeant entered the arena. Nevertheless he spoke with a certain eagerness.

"Nothing but this," said Ellery, and produced the second revolver of the Horne pair. The Inspector seized it.

"Empty," he muttered. "And it's the twin, all right. Why'd he leave it in his room?" Ellery patiently explained. "Ah, then that's out. Find anything else?"

"No papers or letters," reported the Sergeant.

"A visitor," reported Ellery; and repeated the testimony of the Barclay's night-clerk. The Inspector went into the expected convulsion at the clerk's deplorable lack of observation.

"Why, that visitor might have been Horne's killer!" he cried, scowling ferociously. "And that mugg—Didn't remember *anything* about him?"

"Tall and big," said the Sergeant.

"Huh!"

"And now," said Ellery, with a curious impatience, "tell me what's happened here."

The Inspector smiled bitterly. "Less than nothing. We've cleared the mob out, as you can see—got the last one on the street five minutes ago. And we *didn't* find the .25 automatic."

"You found no .25's at all?" exclaimed Ellery.

"A half-dozen or so. Most of them about an hour ago. I sent 'em down to Knowles at Headquarters. He called me up a few minutes ago."

"Yes, yes?"

"Not one of the .25's we found in the crowd tonight, he says, could have fired the bullet that killed Horne!"

"Not one?"

"Not one. The right automatic hasn't been found."

"Well, well," muttered Ellery, pacing up and down in the dirt. "A sweet state of affairs. I knew, I felt this would happen."

"You know what I'm goin' to do?" asked the Inspector presently, in plaintive tones.

"I can guess."

"I'm goin' to have the joint ransacked from top to bottom!"

Ellery clutched his throbbing temples. "The pleasure's entirely yours. This—this Tomb of Mausolus! Go on. Search. I'll wager one of Djuna's doughnuts to the contents of the Treasury that you don't find the gun."

"Don't talk nonsense!" snapped the Inspector. "It didn't get out of this building. We saw to that. It couldn't have walked away, could it? So it must be here somewhere."

Ellery waved his arm wearily. "I grant the full logic of the statement. But you won't find it."

.   .   .   .

It could not be said of the energetic little Inspector that he did not make valiant, even heroic, efforts. He swung into action by mobilizing his small army of investigators into squads. Sergeant Velie was detailed to captain the squad covering the arena itself. Detective Piggott headed the group in charge of searching the tiered bowl. Detective Hesse was deployed with five assistants to go through the dressing rooms, stable, anterooms, offices. Detective Ritter fell heir to the task of scouring corridors, ramps, areaways, cellars, storerooms, ash-cans, and whatever remained. It was a most thorough and workmanlike disposition of trained forces. The squads marched briskly away on their appointed errands. And Ellery stood helplessly by and cudgeled his aching brains.

The Inspector, fuming at the long delay necessitated by the

gigantic task before his men, set himself to clearing up a random detail or two which had hitherto escaped his attention. He summoned the two gatekeepers of the arena, the men stationed at the eastern and western main exits of the arena. Their testimony was brief and led precisely nowhere. Both men—old rodeo hands vouched for by Wild Bill Grant himself—swore that no one could have slipped by them into the arena without having been seen. And they had permitted no one inside who was not dressed in cowboy costume, except Dr. Hancock, the rodeo doctor, and Dan'l Boone. Ted Lyons having ridden in astride a horse, as a member of the troupe, they had not spotted him. But what was infinitely more important was that the two old gatekeepers stoutly asserted that no one had *left* the arena after the fatal shot by way of their doors.

Whereupon it seemed necessary to ascertain, if possible, if anyone might have slipped from the arena via one of the innumerable small doors dotting the concrete wall of the oval on the north and south. This was not easily determined; but the whole problem was swept aside by Ellery, who pointed out that the arena was the arena, they all knew precisely how many persons had been in the arena from the moment of Wild Bill Grant's entrance until after the murder, and that since everyone was still present and accounted for, no one could have escaped.

.   .   .   .

The search went on. The shock-drugged troupe of cowboys and cowgirls, still kept prisoner in the arena, were lined up in seated rows. The Inspector questioned them *en masse* and individually; he might have been addressing a group of stalagmites for all the information he elicited. They were all stolidly on the defensive; they sensed the Inspector's suspicion, and they closed their shells like the hardbacks they were—quiet, immobile, in a vague way dangerous.

"Now what I want to know from you people," roared the Inspector, "is if any of you noticed a particularly suspicious action when you were ridin' and whoopin' round the track just before the shot?"

No answer. They did not even turn their heads. Shorty Downs, that monster of muscle and tight skin, spat carefully past the Inspector; the brownish stream shot within twelve inches of the old man and landed with a little *spat!* on the tanbark. It seemed to be a signal of defiance; a ripple passed through the crowd, and glances grew darker and sharper.

"Won't talk, eh? Mr. Grant, come here a minute." The showman detached himself from the small group standing to one side, and dutifully trudged up to the Inspector. Ellery noted with a little start of surprise that Major Kirby was a member of the group; still present! The Major, he reflected, was a more inquisitive gentleman than he appeared.

"Well?" sighed Grant.

"*How* well?" retorted the Inspector.

"No savvy."

The old man waved his thin veined hand over the heads of the troupe. "How well d'ye know this bunch?"

Grant's features settled like plastic mud, and something cold took possession of them. "Well enough to know that not one of 'em would 'a' taken a pot-shot at ole Buck!"

"But that isn't answering my question."

"They're all ole hands—" began Grant icily; and then the ice melted away and was replaced by impenetrable steel. Something uneasy flickered in his hard eyes. "They're all ole hands," he repeated.

"Now, now, Mr. Grant, you wouldn't try to fool an old man, would you?" murmured the Inspector. "You began to say they're all old hands, and then you stopped. Why? Clear as daylight that you suddenly remembered they're all *not* old hands. Speak up!" he said sharply. "Who's the new man, or men?"

A faint sigh ran through the troupe, and there were black glances frankly directed at the Inspector. Grant stood very still for an instant, and then shrugged his heavy shoulders.

"Just rec'llected," he muttered. "Ain't nothin', Inspector. I *did* take on a new hand t'day—"

The man named Slim Hawes, who was squatting in the front row, growled something derisive and disgusted. Grant colored.

"Who?" demanded the Inspector.

Grant stepped up to the group. "You, Miller," he said tonelessly. "Come outa that."

The man with the purple-sided face rose from the center of the group, hesitated, and then shuffled out of line and shambled forward. The Inspector stared at him for a moment, and looked away. The hideous ravaged left cheek was revolting. He was plainly in a spasm of nervous fear; his lips trembled, showing the molasses-brown teeth, and he spat three times—long spears of tobacco juice—on his way forward. . . . Boone had evidently outfitted him; he no longer wore shabby clothes but was dressed in a shiny new outfit.

"I'm here," he mumbled, avoiding Grant's gaze.

The showman licked his lips. "Inspector, this is Benjy Miller. I took 'im on before sundown. But I tell ya—"

"I'll handle this. Well, Miller, what have you got to say for yourself?"

The man blinked. "Me? Say fer m'self? Why, noth-in'. I don't know nothin' 'bout poor ole Buck's passin', sir. Ter'ble thing to see, sir, all them hosses stompin' on poor Buck, an' me an ole bunkie o' Buck's—"

"Hmm! So you did know Horne, eh? Mr. Grant, how'd you come to take this man on so late?"

"He came to me from Buck himself, Inspector," said Grant doggedly. "Buck wanted me to do somethin' fer 'im. So I did."

"I been off the trail, sir," put in Miller eagerly. "Hard hit. Ain't had a job fer months. Struck Noo Yawk—hearin' Mr. Grant's rodeo was here—hopin' fer a job. Found out 'bout ole Buck's bein' with the show, an' seein' as he an' me was waddies together in the ole days, I looked 'im up. He—he staked me, Buck did, to a couple o' dollars, an' he sent me over here t'see Mr. Grant. That's all, sir; I can't figger it, sir. It's—"

The Inspector stared at the man's slightly drooling mouth for a moment, thoughtfully, and then said: "All right, Miller. Go on back."

Relief heaved through the ranks in visible waves. Miller stumbled hastily back to his place and sat down.

Then the Inspector said: "You, Woody, come here."

The one-armed man sat very still for an instant; then rose and clumped forward, his high heels striking hollow sounds from the tanbark. A short cigaret dangled from his thin lips, and his arrogant mahogany features were twisted into a sneer.

"Got round to me, huh?" he said mockingly. "Well, well! So One-Arm Woody's gonna be roped an' branded an' hogtied, huh? Mister, you ain't got nothin' on me!"

The old man smiled. "Why the speech, Woody? I haven't even asked you a question. But as long as you think I'm trying to guzzle you, I might's well ask 'em hot and heavy. Is it true that you and Horne had a run-in this afternoon—I mean yesterday afternoon, after rehearsal?"

"Shore it's true," snarled Woody. "That say I plugged 'im?"

"Of course not. But it doesn't say you didn't. You were sore because Horne was lappin' up some of your gravy, weren't you?"

"Sorer'n a cross-eyed bronc with the heaves," agreed Woody. "Dog-gone near plugged 'im on the spot, come to think of it."

"Humorous coot, aren't you?" murmured the Inspector. "How well did you know Horne?"

"Knew 'm from way back."

"Where were you in the bunch of horsemen following Horne, Woody?"

"Up front, on th' inside, ridin' with Curly Grant. Now listen close, Mister," said Woody with an ugly grin. "If yo're thinkin' I blew a hole through Buck Horne yo're way off yore feed. I bet there was most a thousan' people had their eyes on me when Horne was plugged. I was shootin' with the rest of the boys, wasn't I? I had my right arm h'isted in the air, didn't I? I ain't got no left arm, an' I was ridin' with my knees when I was shootin'—ain't that true? Horne was shot with a .25, an' I tote a .45—ain't that so? Back-track, Mister; yo're follerin' a blind trail."

·　　·　　·　　·　　·　　·　　·

Slowly the arena emptied. The troupe was separated into men and women; the women were taken downstairs and searched; the men were searched on the spot. No .25 automatic was found on any of them. Where upon they were watchfully escorted out of the building and packed off to their hotel.

The *Colosseum's* attendants were searched. No .25 automatic was found. They were sent home.

The other employees of Grant's rodeo—among whom was Boone, the lurching little bowlegs—were searched after the horses and the other animals had been attended to. No .25 automatic was found. They were shipped off after the others.

All outer doors were locked. With the exception of Mars, Grant, and Major Kirby, only the police remained in the *Colosseum*.

Ellery dawdled on the sidelines, nodding grimly to himself at each successive failure to turn up the missing automatic.

In silence they repaired to the upper floors at Mars's invitation. In the promoter's office they took seats, still silently; Mars went off on a raid of one of the refreshment booths and turned up with sandwiches and an urn of coffee. They chewed and gulped gratefully—and still without words. There seemed nothing to say.

After a while reports began to drift in. The first report was delivered by the slight, shy detective named Piggott.

He coughed apologetically. "Cleaned up the bowl, Chief."

"Look over all the litter?"

"Yes, Chief."

"Nothing?"

"Nothin'!"

"Take your men and go on home."

Piggott left in silence.

The second came five minutes later. This time it was Ritter, the burly member of the Inspector's squad.

"Halls, cellars, store-rooms, booths, stands, alleys," he droned. "Nothin' doin', Chief."

The Inspector waved him wearily away.

Hard on Ritter's heels trudged blond Hesse, the stolid—more stolid than ever.

"Went through the dressing rooms with a fine-comb, Inspector," he said mildly. "Every drawer, every damn corner. Also the

stables, horses' gear, animal pens, rooms, anterooms, offices. . . .
No luck."

"Did you search this room, Hesse?"

"Yes, Chief. Like all the others."

The Inspector grunted; and Tony Mars, his feet on his polished desk, did not even blink.

"All right, Hesse. . . . Ah, Thomas!"

Big Sergeant Velie tramped in, shaking the room; the iron
lines of his face sagged a little as if they had been subjected to
heat. He dropped into a chair and stared expressionlessly at his
superior.

"Well, well, Thomas?"

"We combed the arena," said Velie. "Every square inch, so
help me. We even used rakes, damn it! Dug down pretty deep,
just to make sure. . . . We didn't find the rod, Inspector."

"Hrrrumph," said the Inspector vaguely.

"But we did find *this*," said Velie, and dug a bludgeon forefinger into his vest pocket and brought out a small piece of battered
metal.

They all came to their feet at that, and crowded round the
desk.

"The shell!" cried the Inspector. "By God, that's a hot one—
found the shell and not the gun!" He grabbed it from the Sergeant's fingers and examined it avidly. It was a brassy-looking
piece of metal, crushed almost flat, and scarred and scraped as
if it had been kicked or stepped upon. Minute specks of black
dirt—the dirt from the arena floor—clung to it. "Where'd you
find this, Thomas?"

"In the arena. Sunk in the dirt about an inch, like it'd been
stepped on by somebody. About five yards from the track at

the—let's see—near the Mars box. . . . southeastern part of the arena."

"Hmm. Major, is this the jacket of a .25 calibre?"

Major Kirby glanced at the scrap of metal briefly. "No doubt about it."

"Near the southeastern end," muttered the Inspector. "By jinks, where does that get us? Nowhere!"

"Seems to me," said Grant, blinking, "it's mighty important where you found th' shell, Inspect'r."

"Yeah? It's so important it doesn't mean a consarned thing. How do we know the spot where the Sergeant found it was the spot where the murderer shot from?" The Inspector shook his head. "Look at it—crushed, kicked around. Sure, it might have come from somebody standin' in the arena; but it also might have been *thrown* from the audience, or dropped from one of the boxes at the lowest tier. No go, Grant; doesn't mean a thing."

"There," said Ellery with a little mutter in his throat, "I thoroughly agree with you. . . . Lord, this isn't credible!" They all turned to look at him. "A thirteen-ounce object four and a half inches long doesn't just vanish into thin air, you know. It *must* be here!"

·　·　·　·　·　·　·

But the fact remained that, despite a ruthless, careful, painstaking search by scores of men specially trained in the investigation of both probable and improbable hiding-places, the .25 automatic pistol which had killed Buck Horne was not to be found.

The fact stared them in the face with increasingly painful clarity. Everything had been gone over—literally everything; not only the superficial places but the tanbark track, the seats, all detachable flooring, all offices and filing cabinets and desks and safes, all aisles, horses' rigging, stables, the watering-troughs, the armory, the blacksmith shop, the forge, all booths, storerooms, packages and trunks, all nooks and crannies, passageways, ramps. . . . there was nothing that had not, it seemed, been exhaustively investigated. Even the sidewalks abutting the building had been gone over in the vague thought that the automatic might have been dropped out of a window.

"There's only one answer," said Tony Mars with a frown. "It went out on somebody who was here last night."

"Fiddlesticks!" snapped the Inspector. "I'll vouch for *that*. Every pocket, every package, every valise, every damn shred of every thunderin' soul who was in the place was gone over. That's out, Mr. Mars. No, it's still in the building some place. . . . Mars—for the Lord's sake don't laugh—you built this place yourself?"

"What? Sure."

"You—you didn't put in any secret passageways, or anything as crazy as that?" The Inspector blushed.

Mars chuckled grimly. "If you can find a hole in the solid concrete, Inspector, I'll crawl into it an' let you chuck stinkbombs at me. Show you the plans if you like."

"Never mind," said the Inspector hastily. "Just a sort of desperate notion—"

"All the same I'm goin' to bring out those blueprints." Mars went to his wall-safe—which had been thoroughly explored before—and produced roll after roll of architect's drawings. The Inspector was compelled to go over them. The others sat about and watched.

A half hour later, when Sergeant Velie had been dispatched on last-minute errands after suggestions by Mars as to possible hiding places (and had returned empty-handed), the Inspector shoved the plans back and dabbed at his brow with a shaking hand.

"That's enough for tonight. My God, what a head! What time is it, somebody?" Mars raised the dark blue shades; broad daylight streamed in through the windows. "Well, we'd better all get some sleep. I think—"

"Has it occurred to you," murmured Ellery from behind a barrage of fat smoke-rings, "that there are two detachable elements of the *Colosseum* which have not yet been searched?"

The Inspector started. "What d'ye mean?"

Ellery waved toward Tony Mars and Wild Bill Grant. "Don't take this personally, gentlemen. . . ."

"You mean Mars and Grant?" The Inspector laughed shortly. "Frisked long ago. I attended to that myself."

"You can frisk me again," said Grant coldly.

"Might be a good idea at that, old man. Thomas, do the honors. No offense meant, Tony." In silence Sargent Velie complied. Then he repeated the ritual on Tony Mars. The result was negative, as they all knew it would be.

"Good night," said Mars wearily. "I suppose you'll have the *Colosseum* padlocked, Inspector?"

"Until we find that gat."

"Well. . . . see you soon."

He left, closing the door slowly behind him.

The Major rose. "I think I'll be getting along," he said. "Anything more I can do, gentlemen?"

"Nothing, Major," said the Inspector. "Thanks a lot."

"I see," smiled Ellery, "that you decided to stay after all. Can't say I blame you, Major, under the circumstances. By the way, may I see you alone for a moment?"

Kirby stared. "Certainly."

Ellery went out into the corridor with him. "Look here, Major, you can be of great service to us," he said earnestly, "above and beyond what you've already done. Would your company be averse to lending a hand?"

"Naturally not—if it's news."

"Perhaps, perhaps not." Ellery shrugged. "At any rate, can you arrange a screening for me of the news-reel pictures your men took last night of the arena and bowl?"

"Oh! Of course. Say when."

"Well—ten o'clock this morning. I want a few hours' sleep. And I imagine you can use some yourself."

The little Major smiled. "Oh, I'm something of a night-owl. We'll be ready for you at ten, Mr. Queen." He smiled, shook Ellery's hand warmly, and walked with firm steps down the stairs.

Ellery returned to the office. At the door he bumped into Grant, who was coming out. The old showman muttered something which might have been farewell, and trudged off down the stairs.

Ellery dashed into Mars's office, startling his father in the act of buttoning his overcoat. "Quick, dad!" he cried. "Put someone on Grant!"

"On Grant? You mean, on Grant's tail?" The old man blinked. "What the devil for?"

"Don't ask now, dad, please! It's really important!"

The Inspector nodded at the Sergeant, and Velie disappeared. But he called the big man back. "Just a moment, Thomas. How thorough, El?"

"Everything! Details on every movement of Grant's—phone

tapped, correspondence intercepted and read, contents noted, every contact reported."

"You hear, Thomas? But take it easy. Don't put Grant wise to what's goin' on."

"Got you," said Velie, and disappeared for the second time.

The Queens were left alone in the huge building; the skeletal remains of their investigating force were waiting for them on the sidewalk before the *Colosseum*.

"Well," grumbled the Inspector, "I suppose you know what you're doing. The Lord knows *I* don't. What's the idea?"

"The vaguest. You've done the same about Kit Horne, too?"

"As you asked me. But I'll be blamed if I can figure out why."

Ellery struggled into his coat. "Who knows?" He adjusted his *pince-nez* firmly and hooked his arm in his father's. "Avaunt, Prospero! I tell you, the whole success of our case may depend on sticking closer to Wild Bill the Gorgeous Grant and Kit Horne than their own shadows!"

The Inspector grunted; he was accustomed to his son's crypticisms.

12: PRIVATE SCREENING

It is said in *Ecclesiastes* that the sleep of a laboring man is sweet; perhaps this points a stern moral to those who presume to labor with their brains rather than their muscles, for it is certain that after a prodigious effort of the cerebral cells the night before Mr. Ellery Queen crawled out of his bed of pain unrefreshed, ache-boned, cotton-mouthed, and already fifteen minutes late for his appointment with Major Kirby.

He gulped down two raw eggs, a steaming pannikin of coffee, an excited regurgitation of the preceding evening's events issuing from Djuna's chattering mouth, and then dashed downtown to Times Square.

The newsreel offices, adjunct of a large motion picture producing company, occupied the twelfth floor of a beehive building. Ellery emerged breathless from the elevator and found himself in the reception room just forty-five minutes late.

Major Kirby hurried out. "Mr. Queen! I thought something had happened to you. We're all set." The Major, remarkable man! exhibited no least sign of his all-night session; he was spruce, fresh, and his flat shaven cheeks were a healthy pink.

"Overslept," groaned Ellery. "How do you do it? By the way,

did you have any trouble with your editor, Major, over the excessive footage?"

Kirby chuckled. "Not a bit. He was tickled to death. We got the jump on every outfit in town. This way, Mr. Queen."

He conducted Ellery through a large, noisy chamber filled with lounging men. It was thick with cigaret smoke; its typewriters clacked like Chinese firecrackers; a large peculiar-looking ticker-like machine was being studied by a group; boys rushed in and out.

"Quite like a newspaper office," remarked Ellery as they pushed their way through.

"Worse," said the Major dryly; "it's a newsfilm office. And newsreel cameramen are just about one thousand percent more hard-boiled than newspaper reporters. This is a tough bunch; but they're mighty sweet lads on the pick-up!"

They went through a doorway down a rather depressing corridor lined with doors. Somewhere there was a deep whirr of machinery. Coatless men rushed by.

"Here we are," announced the Major. "One of our projection rooms. Use it for rushes. Come on in, Mr. Queen. Don't mind the smell, do you? It's the celluloid."

It was a bare-walled room with two rows of removable seats. In the rear wall several square orifices framed the snouts of motion picture projectors. The opposite wall was largely covered by a pure white screen.

"Sit down," said the Major in a cordial tone. "I'm ready when you are—"

"Would you mind holding up a bit? The Inspector left for Headquarters before I awoke this morning, but he left word that he would stop in here if he could break away."

"You're the boss." The Major sat down against the wall at a small table studded with buttons and lighted by a tiny powerful lamp. "Anything new?"

Ellery stretched his aching legs. "I'm afraid not," he replied ruefully. "You know, Major, we're face to face with an extremely metaphysical puzzle. Modern witchcraft! Problem: What happened to the automatic which fired the shot which killed Buck Horne? It can't have been slipped out of the *Colosseum,* and yet it isn't there. Apparently. Figure that one out."

"Sounds like something out of the *Arabian Nights,*" smiled the Major. "I'll admit it's a poser. But I agree with Mars—heavens, man, it's the only reasonable theory!—that somehow, in some way, the murderer managed to sneak the gun out of the building. Either personally or through an accomplice."

Ellery shook his head. "We're certain from indisputable testimony that not a living soul wriggled out of the place from the moment after the crime took place. And everybody thereafter—no exceptions, mind you—was thoroughly searched. No, Major, the answer is considerably more subtle than that. In fact," he frowned, "I wish it were as simple as you say. Because I'll have to confess I haven't the least notion of what's really happened to the hardware. . . . Ah, dad! Top o' the mornin'!"

Inspector Queen, looking smaller, thinner, and grayer than ever, appeared in the doorway of the projection room, flanked by Sergeant Velie and Detective Hesse. "Morning, Major. So you did get out of bed finally, did you?" He dropped wearily into one of the chairs, and waved his aides into others. "From the way you were tossing and groaning, you must've been havin' nightmares. . . . All right, Major. We're ready if you are."

Major Kirby twisted his head and yelled toward the largest orifice in the rear wall: "Joe!"

A bespectacled face popped into sight in the square window. "Yep, Major?"

"We're ready, Joe. Shoot 'er along."

Instantly the lights went out and they were left in a velvety, palpable darkness. There was a whirr and clacking roar of machinery from the operator's booth behind. Suddenly a title materialized on the screen, accompanied by a stock blare of dirge-like introductory music. The title read:

BUCK HORNE KILLED!

———

SENSATIONAL MURDER AT COLOSSEUM
N.Y.'S NEW SPORT ARENA!

The title flicked off, and another came on—a long passage:

EDITOR'S NOTE—These are the first pictures of the Horne shooting to reach the screen. These unique scenes of the events leading up to and following the shocking murder of Hollywood's best-beloved Western star are made possible through the enterprise of ——— News and the courtesy of the New York Police Department.

The title vanished, and the first view of the *Colosseum* the night before leaped onto the screen, accompanied by the newsreel announcer's voice.

"Here you see the vast crowd who packed the *Colosseum*," boomed the voice, as the scene slowly shifted from tier to tier of seats in the amphitheatre, "before the fatal shooting. The occasion was the grand opening at this world-famous sport arena in New York City of Wild Bill Grant's Rodeo. . . . Twenty thousand persons were enjoying the colorful spectacle of leaping horses, whooping cowboys—" The voice stopped and a burst of sound came from the amplifier as the cameras darted from one part of the arena to another, catching the sights and sounds of the preliminary events the Queens had witnessed the night before, including a brief glimpse of Curly Grant laughing and showing his teeth as he popped the little glass balls out of existence with careless shots from his long-barreled revolver. Suddenly there was a hush; the arena emptied; the camera swung and fixed on the huge western gate. Out pranced Wild Bill Grant on his horse; the camera followed him to the center of the oval. It caught his gallop, his sliding stop in a group of flying dirt-clods, his wave of the Western hat, his smile, the applause and stamping of feet, Grant's signal-shot toward the roof, and his bloodcurdling cowboy yell to gain silence. Then his opening bellow: "La-dees and Gentlemen, per-mit me to welcome you to the Grrrand Opening of Wild Bill Grrrant's Rrrrodeo! The Larrrgest Ag—" The roaring continued. Then the dramatic appearance of Buck Horne on his magnificent mount, *Rawhide*, the yelling entrance of the forty-one riders, the signal-shots, the swirl of the start of the gallop around the tanbark track. . . .

They leaned forward tensely as the events of the preceding evening recreated themselves with such startling faithfulness on the screen. . . . Someone sighed tremulously as there was a hasty glimpse of Buck Horne twisting sideways from his saddle at the instant of the thunderous fusillade—this was a long, indistinct volley—his fall, the wild confusion of milling horses and the screams of the spectators. . . . They sat silently as the camera leaped from long shots of personalities, of the Mars box, of the dismounted horsemen, of the rodeo doctor, and one of the blanketed body. . . .

When the lights flashed on again, no one moved for some time. Then the Major called in a low voice: "All right, Joe, that's all," and the spell was broken.

"Fast work, eh?" went on the Major with a grim smile. "That reel's in the State Theatre right now."

"Very enterprising," murmured Ellery absently. "By the way, how long does this run? It seemed to me longer than the usual newsreel episode."

"I should say it is. Naturally we've made this a special. Takes the same importance," chuckled Kirby, "as earthquakes and wars. Runs to just about a reel. About ten and a half minutes."

The Inspector stirred. "Nothing there we didn't get ourselves. I can't see, Ellery—"

Ellery, sunk in deep reverie, did not reply.

"Well, is there?"

"Eh? Oh, no, no. Perfectly right," sighed Ellery. He turned to Kirby. "You've been a trump, Major. I wonder if I could prevail upon you to spend some more of your company's money? Is it possible for you to wangle your apparatus so that we can get a still-photograph—close-up—of Horne at the instant the bullet entered his body?"

Kirby frowned. "Well. . . . It's not impossible. It will be considerably blurred, you know; blow-ups of film always are. Besides, this was a long shot—not focused for close-up. . . ."

"Nevertheless I want it most particularly. Be a good fellow."

"Anything you say, old man." Major Kirby rose and quietly left the projection room.

"These birds sure do work fast," rumbled Sergeant Velie.

"Ellery," said the Inspector, "what's this hocus-pocus for, anyway? I'm busy, drat it—"

"It's important."

.   .   .   .

And so they waited. Several men poked their heads in. Once a large fat gentleman with an autocratic air marched in, introduced himself as the editor of the newsreel company, and asked if Inspector Queen would like to "say a few words" about the shooting into the microphone—there was a studio a few steps down the corridor. . . . The Inspector shook his head.

"Sorry. I'd have to get the Commissioner's permission, and he's out of town. He doesn't like his officers making stabs at publicity."

"Oh, he doesn't?" said the large fat gentleman dryly. "I take it the regulation doesn't apply to himself? Say, I know that publicity hound! 'Scuse me, Inspector. Some other time, maybe, when His Nibs feels better. See you later." And he hurried like the White Rabbit out of the room.

They continued to wait. Ellery was deep in the waters of cogitation. Detective Hesse closed his eyes, folded his hands, rested his head on the back of the seat, and instantly fell asleep. He snored frankly. Sergeant Velie cocked an eye at his superior, decided he might chance it, and proceeded to snatch a few winks himself.

Outside there was bedlam. In the room quiet.

.   .   .   .

When Major Kirby returned, he was triumphantly waving a set of damp photographs, eight inches by ten. Sergeant Velie started, and opened his eyes. Detective Hesse snored on.

The Queens bent over the wet prints; eagerly, very eagerly.

"Did our best," said the Major apologetically. "I told you they would be out of focus. But we got the best magnification consistent with clarity."

There were ten photographs in a series, the difference between the positions of the subjects in the successive photographs being infinitesimal. That they had been enlarged from motion picture celluloid was apparent from the film-frame visible around the pictures. The prints were consistently blurred, covered with a sort of grayish lambency which was the result of distorted focus. Nevertheless, details were discernible.

They showed Buck Horne on *Rawhide* at the approximate time of the man's death, head-on to the camera, in a perfect frontal position—so that in the first picture the magnificent head of the animal stared directly into the lens, with the rider's body looming behind it and facing similarly into the camera. All the pictures were in a sort of middle focus, so that the entire body of the horse was visible. It was plain from the photograph that *Rawhide's* long-barreled body had been consistently parallel to the tanbark track during the entire time-period of the murder.

Five of the pictures revealed Horne an instant before his death. In this series the action was clear: in the first the victim had been sitting perfectly erect in the saddle, in the second he had begun to bend over in the saddle sideways to his left; in the third the leaning was more pronounced; and so on, until at the fifth his torso, still facing the camera, was leaning off the perpendicular to his left at an angle of thirty degrees. In comparison, *Rawhide* was in much the same position as in the first of the series; the horse's leaning to the left was microscopic. Three photographs revealed Horne at the instant of death, and two as he began to crumple in the saddle and slip toward the floor. In all the pictures his hat was on his head, his left arm was elevated in clutching the reins, and his right arm flourishing the revolver high above his head.

"If you'll recall the scene," muttered Ellery, intent on the damp prints, "he began to topple from the saddle just after *Rawhide* rounded the northeastern turn of the track. That accounts for his pronounced leaning toward the right—his left—in these pictures. Isn't that a sort of balance-compensation caused by centrifugal force, Major? Or am I being ridiculously unscientific again?"

They concentrated on the three photographs showing Horne at the very instant of death. Thanks to the victim's predilection for white satin shirts, it was possible to study the effect of the shot very closely. The first of the three pictures revealed a small black spot beneath the rider's crooked, elevated left arm, and a little toward the front at the level of the heart. The second revealed a slightly larger spot in the same place, and the third the largest of all—although the difference among the three was minute. These black spots were undoubtedly photographs of the bullet-hole.

On all the last five photographs the expression of the face was of shock, strain, distortion, lightning pain. Facing straight out toward the camera, as if its lens were the glaring eye of Death, he died again before their eyes.

Ellery looked up, and his eyes were veiled. "What a blind fool I've been," he said thoughtfully. "And how simple this problem was after all."

There was an astounded silence, and Major Kirby's jaw dropped an inch.

"Was?" cried the Inspector.

Ellery shrugged. "There are two things I don't know," he said with a sad smile, "two things of vast importance, by and by, which must be explained before the case is complete. But there's one thing I do know. Yes, there's one thing I do know, and there's no shadow of a question about its truth. . . ."

The Inspector clamped his lips shut, and glowered.

But Major Kirby said eagerly: "What's that? What's that, Mr. Queen?"

Ellery tapped the falling figure on the last photograph with an impersonal fingernail. "I know who killed this poor old exhibitionist!"

13: SOME VISITS OF IMPORTANCE

"You know who killed Horne!" gasped the inspector. "Well, for Christmas's sake, let's go get him!"

"But I don't know," said Ellery ruefully.

The Major and the old man stared at him. "*Blast* it!" cried the Inspector. "You getting smart again? What d'ye mean—you don't know? You just said you *do* know!"

"I give you my word," murmured Ellery, "I'm not pulling your leg, dad. It's precisely as I say: I do know, and yet I don't know. One of those things. You say: Let's get him. But I tell you in all truthfulness that if I walked out of this building this instant I shouldn't be able to lead you to the murderer. And yet I'm as positive I know who killed the poor fellow as—as old Jim Bludso was when he 'seen his duty.'"

The Inspector threw up his hands. "There you are, Major. That's what I've been putting up with all my life. A—a—"

"A sophist?" suggested Ellery sadly.

The old man glared. "When you get through speakin' in riddles, you'll find me downtown at h.q. 'Bye, Major. Thanks." And he stalked out in a huff, followed obediently by Sergeant Velie and a yawning Hesse.

"Poor dad," sighed Ellery. "He's always peeved at my little

circumlocutions. And yet, Major, for the life of me I couldn't make it clearer. This time I'm in dead earnest."

"But you said you *know*," began Kirby in a puzzled way.

"My dear Major, the fact that I know the superficial truth is—believe me—the least important feature of this ghastly business. I wish I knew the two things I *don't* know. There's the rub; I don't, and the Lord alone knows when I will, if ever."

The Major chuckled. "Well, it's too much for me. Now I've got to get back on the job. Remember—I'm at your service, Mr. Queen. Especially when you discover the answer to those two mysteries!"

"Always the newsgatherer, eh? May I have these prints?"

"Certainly."

.   .   .   .

Ellery strolled up Broadway, the prints in an envelope under his arm. His brow was like an old-fashioned washboard. He sucked at a cigaret which he had forgotten to light.

He came to himself with a start, searched for a streetsign, got his bearings, paused to light the cigaret, and then turned down a side street and walked rapidly toward Eighth Avenue. A hundred feet from the corner he stopped before a small building characterized by marble facing, deeply incised letters, and iron bars. The letters said: *Seaboard National Bank & Trust Company*. He went through the revolving door and sought the Manager.

"I'm investigating the Horne murder," he said pleasantly, flashing his special police card.

The Manager blinked nervously. "Oh! I see. I've been sort of expecting a call. Really, we know very little about Mr. Horne—"

"Enough for my purposes," smiled Ellery. "But I'm also interested in one of your other customers who's very much alive."

"Yes?" said the Manager blankly.

"William Grant—I presume that's the way he signs his checks."

"Grant! You mean the rodeo man? Wild Bill Grant?"

"That's right."

"Hmm," said the Manager, and rubbed his chin abrasively. "What is it you want to find out about Mr. Grant?"

"Horne made out a check in the amount of twenty-five dollars," explained Ellery patiently, "the afternoon of his murder. It was made out to Grant. I want to see that check."

"Oh," said the Manager again. "I—Did Grant deposit it?"

"Yes."

"One moment, please." The Manager rose and disappeared through the grilled door leading to the cashiers' cages, and returned after five minutes with an oblong of paper. "Here it is. Horne and Grant both being customers of ours, the voucher was merely canceled by the teller, photographed—we photograph all checks, you know—and kept on file for Mr. Horne's monthly statement."

"Yes, yes, I know all that," said Ellery briskly. "Let's have it."

He took the canceled check from the Manager and examined it. A moment's scrutiny, and he placed the check on the desk.

"Very good. Now may I have a peep at Horne's account-card?"

The Manager hesitated. "Well, matters like that are confidential, you know—"

"Police," said Ellery sternly, and the Manager bowed meekly and went off again, to return with a large stiff record-card.

"Mr. Horne was a customer of this bank for only a few days, you know," he said nervously. "There are only a few entries—"

Ellery looked over the card. There were five items noted. Four of them were small amounts—personal checks, apparently, for minor expenditures. But the fifth made Ellery whistle, and the Manager more nervous than before.

"Three thousand dollars!" exclaimed Ellery. "Why, he deposited only five thousand altogether in opening the account! Interesting, eh? I'd like to see that check and the teller who handled the transaction."

Both were forthcoming after a little delay.

The check proved to be made out to cash, signed properly and authentically by Horne—who, having surrendered his original given name to the mists of antiquity, always wrote "Buck" before his surname—and was also properly endorsed by Horne.

"Did Horne himself cash this check?" Ellery asked the teller.

"Oh, yes, sir. I handled it myself."

"Do you recall how he seemed while you were waiting on him? Was he preoccupied, jolly, nervous—what?"

The teller looked thoughtful. "Maybe it's my imagination, but I got the notion he was worried about something. And he seemed sort of absent-minded—hardly heard what I said, but just watched me putting the bills together in a desperate sort of way."

"Hmm. Did he ask for the amount in any specific fashion?"

"Yes, sir. He said for me to give him the three thousand in small bills. Nothing over a twenty."

"This was two days ago—the day before the murder?"

"Yes, sir. In the morning."

"I see. Thank you—both. Good day."

Ellery strode out of the bank with knit brows. He recalled now that only thirty dollars had been found on Horne's body, and no money at all in Horne's room at the Barclay. He hesitated a moment, and then went into a cigar-store to a telephone booth.

He got Police Headquarters on the wire and asked for Inspector Queen. The Inspector was not in. Evidently he had not yet reached Headquarters from the offices of the newsreel company.

Ellery went out, looked about, and then crossed Broadway. He found a telegraph office, and went in. He spent ten minutes in the composition of a long message addressed to Hollywood, California. The wire paid for, he sought a telephone booth in the telegraph office and once more called Spring 3100. This time he was successful.

"Dad? Ellery. Did you get a complete report on the contents of Buck Horne's dressing room at the *Colosseum?* . . . I'll hold on. . . . Yes? Well, was any cash found in Horne's room? . . . None at all, eh? Hmm. . . . No, nothing special. I've been meandering about. . . . I'll be downtown directly."

He hung up and went out, heading for the subway.

. . . .

Twenty minutes later he was seated in his father's office, drawling a recital of his discoveries at the bank.

The Inspector was extraordinarily interested. "Withdrew three grand two days ago, hey? Well, well. That's kind of hot, son." He grinned. "Do you realize that that was the same day he had his mysterious visitor at the hotel?"

"Perfectly. The sequence—if it is a sequence—seems to be about as follows. Horne visits his bank only a few days after he has made a deposit of five thousand dollars, and withdraws three thousand of it in small bills. That very night he has a mysterious visitor. And the next day he is murdered. . . ." He frowned. "Doesn't seem to fit, eh?"

"Not the murder part of it. But you can't tell," said the Inspector thoughtfully. "If—mind you, I say *if*—if you put the withdrawal of the three grand and the visitor together, you get something that looks almighty like blackmail. But then, if that's so, why the bump-off? Does a blackmailer kill his victim? Well, sometimes. Not most times, though—unless he'd sucked him dry. . . ." He shook his head impatiently. "It'll have to be looked into. I'm trying to trace his visitor, but it seems an impossible job. By the way, I got Sam Prouty's autopsy-report this morning."

Ellery started. "I'd forgotten completely about it! What did he say?"

"Nothing. Plain nothing," grumbled the Inspector. "Couldn't add a single item to what he told us on the scene."

"Oh, that!" said Ellery with a flirt of his hand. "I didn't mean *that*. The stomach, dad, the stomach—that's what I'm interested in. Didn't Prouty say?"

"He said," said the Inspector glumly. "Sure he said. He said Horne hadn't eaten for a good six hours before his death—maybe more."

Ellery blinked; then quickly he began to examine a fingernail. "Is that so?" he murmured. "Well, well"

"Well, what?"

"Eh? Oh, nothing, anything new?"

"Look at this." The Inspector rummaged through his desk and brought out a tabloid newspaper folded back, with something on the revealed page heavily ringed in red pencil. "Before I show you this. Doc also said there was no trace of poison in Horne's innards."

"Poison? Poison? Lord love that man! . . . What's that you've got?"

"Read what Santa Claus brought this morning."

"Lyons?" asked Ellery absently, extending a long arm.

"Yump," groaned the Inspector. "This Lyons bird is better

than a whole Homicide Squad. Sees all, knows all, hears all. I'd like to wring his blasted neck!"

Lyons's column of gossip and Broadway prattle was, as might have been expected, replete with tasty little items concerning the Horne murder. It spared no one, least of all the Inspector. The pertinent names loomed large in the column— Kit Horne, Wild Bill Grant, Tommy Black, Julian Hunter, Tony Mars, Mara Gay. . . . One item was rather amusing. "Detec-stiff Inspector Queen thought ye ed—the kid himself—might have bumped the Great Bucko just because ye ed had a little gat in his didies. Go rest, old man, go rest! You need one."

"Ah," said Ellery with a chuckle, "the well-known Bronx gesture. What's this?" His eyes narrowed. Near the foot of the column there was an innocent-seeming paragraph which took on the color of vitriol on closer examination.

"And what big-wig of the hardburly-girly clubs," Ted Lyons asked derisively, "who was present in the flash when some unknown gladiator popped off the w.k. Buck Horne at the *Colosseum* last p.m.—not only was all set to fi-Nance said flicker fav-Writ's return to the Silly Screen but is also 'secretly' the dark horse behind Cauliflower Row's latest White Hope?"

"Now I wonder," snapped the Inspector, "how the devil Lyons found *that* out."

"My amazement is rather more pointed," murmured Ellery. "I wonder if Tony Mars knows it. Hunter backing Black, eh? On the q.t. I see the possibilities. . . . Well, dad," he jumped to his feet, "I can't dawdle. Got to see Knowles," and he made for the door.

"Hold your horses a minute. What did you mean this morning when you said you knew who—"

"Fo'give me, pater," cried Ellery in haste, "I should never have opened my mouth. You'll find out; you'd think me a lunatic if I said any more now. See you later," and he hurried from the Inspector's office.

He made his way to Room 114; and there found Lieutenant Knowles busy with a collection of colored cards.

"Damned nuisance, this filing system," growled the ballistics expert without looking up, "but how it helps sometimes in court! Well, Mr. Queen, what's the good word? Any more artillery?"

"There's no relief from the war," laughed Ellery, and produced from his overcoat pocket the ivory-handled .45 calibre revolver he had found in Buck Horne's hotel room during the early hours.

"Say, haven't I seen that rod before?" asked Lieutenant Knowles sharply, taking up the weapon. Ellery shook his head. "Then it must be its twin brother. I've got one just like it in the batch that came over from the *Colosseum!*"

"You certainly have. And it *is* a twin. The two belonged to Horne, except that this fellow was left behind in his wardrobe trunk."

"She sure is one pip," said Knowles with appreciation. "These old babies sometimes are. Little old-fashioned in type and design, but it's like stamps. I'm an amateur stamp-collector, you know. The older they are the nicer they are. I've got—"

"I know, I know," said Ellery, wincing. "I've met philatelists before. What I want to know is—"

"Whether this could have fired the bullet that killed Horne?" Knowles shook his head. "I told you it could only be a .25, and an automatic to boot."

"Yes, yes, I know that." Ellery sat down on the expert's laboratory table. "Have you got the mate to this handy?"

"In the file, all tagged." The Lieutenant went to a large cabinet, pulled out a drawer, and came back with the first Horne revolver. "Now what do you want to know?"

"Pick up both revolvers," said Ellery queerly. "One in each hand, Lieutenant."

Rather wonderingly, the expert obeyed. "Now what?"

"Was it my imagination, or am I right in believing that one of these weapons is a trifle heavier than the others?"

"Knowles, old boy, you're always being asked the craziest questions!" said the Lieutenant with a burst of laughter. "Good God, Queen, is that all? Why so serious? Find out for you in a minute. As a matter of fact, one of 'em *does* feel a mite heftier than the other. But I'll make sure."

He dumped the revolvers one at a time on a scale. And he nodded. "Yes, *sir.* This baby with the tag is almost a full two ounces heavier than the other."

"Ah," said Ellery with satisfaction. "How very nice."

The expert squinted at him. "No question, I suppose, about the authentic ownership of the two revolvers? I mean—they both really belonged to Horne, didn't they?"

"Heavens, yes," said Ellery. "No question about that at all. Lieutenant, you'd be amazed if I told you what your scale has confirmed for me." Then he rubbed his palms together. "How beautifully it works out!" he sighed, and grinned. "You might tag that second one, Lieutenant, for filing and reference. We'll probably have to give 'em all back soon. Meanwhile hold on to them. By the way!" He began to scowl. "Do you think that tagged revolver was deliberately manufactured to be heavier than the other one? You know, they were both made at the same time—specially made for Horne."

"Quite likely," assented Lieutenant Knowles. "If Horne was a two-gun man—carrying 'em as he did in pairs—he probably wanted each one to fit the feel of his hand. Not necessarily so," he added hastily. "Might have been an accident in manufacture. Some of the oldest short arms weren't made any too carefully."

"I should say these were made very carefully," said Ellery. "Well, Lieutenant, thanks for a profitable ten minutes. See you some time."

And he quickly left the office of the Bureau of Ballistics. Outside in the corridor he stopped smiling, and for a moment polished the lenses of his *pince-nez* reflectively.

14: AGENDA

THE LOOSE and vasty association of crime investigators and criminal-hunters, when they foregather on some fantastic afternoon in the capital city of the Fifth Dimension, might do worse than adopt as their organization's war-cry that immortal device on the national aegis of Vraibleusia: viz., *Something will turn up.* It would look particularly nice in Old English on a field *or,* with an embellishment of *gules* for symbolism. Statistics are uncertain, but it is not fanciful to say that half the sleuths in this world are waiting for something to turn up, while the other half are busily nosing along the trail of something that has already turned up. In either event the spirit of the motto holds.

The waiting period, however, is not necessarily a period of inaction. On the contrary, it is a period of frenzied activity which is termed "waiting" only because it accomplishes nothing and arrives nowhere. The activity, then, is of a negative sort; meanwhile, the something that is to turn up is biding its time— perhaps the psychological moment. It is the genius of most detectives that in the midst of a frantic and useless motion they preserve a calm philosophy. It is the philosophy of fatalism. The activity is merely animal energy expended to satisfy the conventional requirements of duty.

Ellery Queen recognized the signs from afar, and settled down—having no conventional requirements of duty to satisfy—to wait in a Stoical serenity. The worthy Inspector, however, who drew the sum of $5,900 *per annum* from the City treasury for his services as a guardian of the peace, was compelled to go through the motions. One of the motivating forces was that bugaboo of all old-line policemen, the Commissioner. The Commissioner, who was drawn back from a sandy Florida gambol by the magnetic echoes of the Horne murder, vented his irritation on the Inspector—obviously the cause of his curtailed vacation; whereupon the Inspector was silent and pale before the Commissioner, and voluble and red before his Department. It was a trying time for all concerned.

The conventional things had been done. Buck Horne's movements for weeks before his murder had been checked and rechecked so many times that the Squad was growing just a bit weary writing out reports. "Might's well do one with a dozen carbons," groaned Ritter, who was a notorious malcontent; and not without justice, for the twelfth checking elicited no more than the first. The victim had passed his last few weeks on earth in a Matilda-Queen-of-Denmarkish innocence. All his correspondence was examined; it was meagre, blameless, and as dry as a squeezed lemon. His friends and acquaintances in the East were questioned; they told nothing of importance. The wires between Wyoming and New York, and between Hollywood and New York, sizzled with questions and answers; the total result of which was zero raised to the nth power.

There was no one, it seemed certain, under heaven and on earth who had the faintest motive for seeking Buck Horne's life—excepting One-Arm Woody, and he was eliminated because of his physical handicap.

The identity of the visitor to Horne's room at the Barclay on the night before Horne's murder continued to remain a mystery.

And the *Colosseum's* doors remained closed. Remained closed because of the weary insistence of Inspector Queen and the increasing irritation of Commissioner Welles. For the automatic which had fired the bullet which had in turn caused Buck Horne's heart to stop beating was still undiscovered, despite an almost daily gleaning of the *Colosseum*. And Wild Bill Grant tore his hair and raved and shouted maledictions for the benefit of the reporters, vowing that never again would he bring his rodeo to New York. The Inspector piously echoed this sentiment, and the Commissioner almost dislocated his shoulders shrugging when he heard about it.

One line of inquiry—in the fruitless repetition of examination and cross-examination and re-examination of those harassed citizens involved in the Horne investigation—seemed fertile. That was the matter of Buck Horne's finances. When questioned about this by the gentlemen of the press, the Inspector grew coy. He would not (or could not) say. Nevertheless, there was much mysterious activity on the part of Messrs. Ritter, Johnson, Hint, Hesse, and Piggott. The question was: What had happened to the three thousand dollars which the deceased had withdrawn from his account in small bills two days before his murder? No slightest trace of the money had been found.

It was a good question, but (it seemed) a very hard one to answer.

.   .   .   .

Ellery's waiting took the form of a sociable relaxation. Perhaps for the first time since his undergraduate days he began to cultivate the gay life. His long tails emerged from the mothballs and flirted whimsically about polished dance floors. The laundry bills showed heavy additions for stiff bosoms and wing collars. He began to totter into the Queens' West Eighty-seventh Street apartment in the small hours, slightly the worse for wear and vitriolic highballs. His sleep these nights was the profound coma of the physically exhausted, not unaided by the soporific effects of alcohol; and in the mornings he consumed pints of black coffee in a vain effort to scald the fuzz off his tongue. Djuna, a highly moral creature, complained in vain.

"It's all in the cause of science," Ellery groaned. "God, what martyrs we are sometimes!"

The inspector, who was attacking an egg at the moment, sniffed grouchily; and then examined his son with paternal anxiety.

"What the deuce are you accomplishing by this stepping out of nights?" he demanded. "You turning playboy on me?"

"To the last, no and yes," replied Ellery. "To the first—a good deal. I am coming to know my characters. What a drama this is, dad! Take the Hunters, for instance—"

"You take 'em," growled the Inspector. "*I* don't want 'em."

Nevertheless, it was a fact that Ellery had begun to cultivate his acquaintances of the Mars box. He spent much time with Kit Horne, who went through all the social motions with a mechanical smile while something distant and thoughtful glimmered in her soft eyes. In company with Kit, he attacked the nightclubs; more often than not with the Grants as members of the party; and more often than not the *Club Mara*. And there he was accorded the privilege of observing the regally emaciated Mara Gay—that Orchid of Hollywood—and Julian Hunter. He even met Tony Mars several times, and on two occasions found a group of representatives from the rodeo troupe hilariously engaged in consuming as much liquor as Julian Hunter's waiters could serve. There was a gloss about the days and nights during the period, an artificial sheen that covered something hard and unreal. Ellery lived, breathed, laughed, talked, and moved like a man in a dream.

Nevertheless, he did not permit reality to desert his senses altogether. It was impossible for him to spend every moment in the company of his new friends. So each morning found him at Police Headquarters reading the reports of the detectives detailed to survey the movements of Kit Horne and Wild Bill Grant—a survey, it will be recalled, dictated by him. In the case of Grant, he was irritated to find that the old Westerner was conducting himself in a vastly innocent manner. Whatever he had hoped to discover from placing a spy on Grant's movements, contacts, and telephone conversations, it was certain that the hope was thus far a vain one. Grant drank hard, kept his troupe in hand—not a simple task—hovered watchfully over his son and Kit, and for the rest pestered the Inspector and Commissioner Welles with demands for the reopening of his rodeo.

As for the reports on Kit, they showed more promise. The girl's faraway look, it turned out, had cold purpose behind it. An interesting incident was recorded one morning in the report of the detective assigned to watch her.

.   .   .   .

One night, several days after the murder, the operative had followed the girl from the Hotel Barclay to the *Club Mara*. Slim and brown in a white evening-gown, Kit had said coldly to the head waiter: "Is Mr. Hunter in?"

"Yes, Miss Horne. In his office. Shall I—?"

"No, thank you. I'll find it myself."

She had made her way along a row of private booths to the rear, where Hunter maintained his magnificent suite. The operative had checked his hat and coat, insisted upon a table near the rear, and ordered a highball. It was early, but the club was already crowded; Hunter's famous jazz orchestra was blaring away at a new Calloway tune with the approved African tempo and savagery; couples were closely entwined on the darkened dance-floor; there was sufficient noise and darkness to cover the detective's investigation.

He had risen quietly from his table and followed Kit Horne.

He saw her knock on the door marked: *Private. Mr. Hunter;* and after a moment observed the door open and Hunter's well-garbed figure silhouetted against the bright background of the office.

"Miss Horne!" he heard Hunter exclaim in cordial tones. "Come in, come in. Glad to see you. I—" and then the closing door shut off the rest.

The operative looked about. The nearest waiter was lost in darkness. He was not observed. He pressed his ear to the panel.

He could not hear words, just tones. Now this operative, a specialist, was a highly trained eavesdropper; it was his boast that he could interpret emotions even if the words he barely heard were blurred and indistinguishable. So that his report became a study in homespun psychology.

"It started sociably," went his report. "Miss H. from her voice was quiet, ready for anything; and she had made up her mind about something. J. H.'s voice boomed; I could hear he was friendly; but there was something queer, phoney, about it—he was slapping it on thick. I got the feeling they were sparring around for an opening. Then Miss H. got mad; her voice came through higher, tighter; she was slapping the words down like bricks. Laying the law down to Hunter about something. Hunter forgot to be friends; voice colder than ice; sneer came into it; words shot out fast, then slow, then fast again, as if the sneer was a cover-up for worry. She didn't get it, because she got madder. I thought for a minute there would be a real blow-up. I was just getting ready to break in when I heard them stop jawing. So I wiggled out of the way. A second later the door smashed open and Miss H. came running out. I saw her face clearly; she was white, her eyes were hot and angry, and her lips were pressed tight together. She was breathing fast. She passed right by me and did not see me. He stood in the doorway a minute or two, looking after her in the dark, when he could not see her. I could not see his face, but his hand on the door was tight, knuckles white. Then he went back into the office. Miss H. took a cab back to the Barclay and did not go out again last night."

The Inspector reached for one of his telephones. "Something at last," he snapped. "I'll find out what all this hocus-pocus is, by God! There's your sweet nice Western lassie for you!"

Ellery started out of a reverie and clamped his hand over the telephone. "Dad! No!"

The Inspector was startled. "What? What's this?"

"Please don't," said Ellery quickly. "You'll spoil everything. For heaven's sake, hold off. Wait. We can't afford—"

Inspector Queen leaned back, annoyed. "And what," he demanded, "is the holy use of putting a man on a hot trail and then when he finds out something, not doin' anything about it?"

"A little incoherent," grinned Ellery—who knew the battle was won, "but nevertheless a reasonable question. The answer is: that a possible relationship between Hunter and Kit Horne was not in my mind when I asked you to have the girl shadowed."

"Suppose it wasn't," said the Inspector sarcastically. "After all, you can't foresee *everything*. All right, now we find out there's somethin' up between Hunter and the girl. Why should we sit back and lose a chance, maybe, to get some new lead?"

"I'll tell you why, and I'm not underestimating the possible importance of this unexpected Kit-Hunter relationship," said Ellery. "There are two reasons. One is that you probably won't get a word out of either of them. The other is—and this is by far the more vital consideration—that it will give away our hole card."

"What hole card?"

"The fact that Kit Horne is being shadowed. You see," said Ellery patiently, "once that girl knows she is under incessant surveillance, we lose our—"

"What?"

Ellery shrugged. "What's the use of going into that? I admit the chances are all against anything coming out of it. But everything must be sacrificed to keep the way clear for that bare eventuality's coming to pass—and for us to be aware of it when it does come to pass."

"For a feller that went to college," grumbled the Inspector, "you sure do talk like a Kentucky mountaineer with the mumps!"

·   ·   ·   ·   ·   ·   ·

To add to the Inspector's irritation, a telegram was delivered to Ellery one morning at breakfast; a telegram which, under the circumstances, might have contained brilliantly illuminating information for all the old man knew; a telegram, in effect, which Ellery read quickly and without changing expression, and then flung into the healthy fire in the living room. The Inspector, whose pride was hurt, asked no questions; and although Ellery could not have been unconscious of his father's pique, he offered no explanations. Had the old man been aware that the wire bore a Hollywood, California, source-line, he might have decided to swallow his pride and demand enlightenment after all. As it was, it was not until the very end that he discovered the contents of the telegram.*

.   .   .   .

Ted Lyons continued to write sprightly tidbits about the celebrities involved in the Horne case.

Another complication arose at this time to add gray hairs to Tony Mars's head, swell Wild Bill Grant's profane vocabulary, and etch new lines on the face of Inspector Queen. The contract between Grant and Mars called for the rental of the *Colosseum* to Grant for a period of four weeks. Under the terms of the agreement, therefore, Grant was still entitled to the use of the premises for four weeks less one day—the day of the fatal opening. Yet three weeks had already elapsed, and the *Colosseum* was still kept barred by the police. There would have been no difficulty had not Tony Mars's other plans interfered. The stumbling block was the championship heavyweight prize-fight in which Tommy Black was the challenger. The articles had been signed months before, and the date set. The date had been so arranged that the fight was scheduled to take place in the *Colosseum* on the

---

* Mr. Queen has often been criticized by readers for his seemingly heartless lack of co-operation with the Inspector in cases which claimed their joint attention. A psychiatrist could probably discover the truth in short order. It is necessary only to refer the interested reader to *The Greek Coffin Mystery* for the simple explanation. It will be remembered that in that investigation, which in point of time was one of the earliest Mr. Queen engaged in, he was repeatedly outwitted by a very clever criminal. His experience of giving on several occasions what seemed to him the proper solution, and then finding he was completely wrong, made him vow never to talk about his reasoning until he was utterly convinced, beyond any doubt, that the reasoning was correct.—J. J. McC.

Friday night following the last performance of Wild Bill Grant's Rodeo. With the battle only a week off, Mars found himself in an uncomfortable position. Tickets had been printed long before; the champion's manager and cohorts were adamant; Grant would listen to no arguments but insisted on resuming his rodeo exhibition the instant the police ban was lifted from the *Colosseum*. . . . Powerful strings began to tug at Centre Street.

·   ·   ·   ·   ·   ·   ·

It was field day for the press; and Grand Marshal of the field was Ted Lyons. After squeezing every last drop of gossip from the Mars-Grant-Centre Street controversy, he turned his attention to Tommy Black.

The item that set the bomb appeared without warning in Lyons's column one morning. "Shades of Gentleman Jim and the Manassa Mauler! How times do change. . . . What prominent challenger for the Biff-Bang title in the mastodon class is training on a diet of jazz, orange-blossoms, and Orchids? And what's the matter with the Orch's better half—or laugh—who's being made an old cuck by said stumble-bum, as every wise guy on the Main Stem knows? Come, come, Rollo; your house is afire."

The first echo of the explosion reached Headquarters a half-hour after it rolled back from the cliffs of the downtown canyons. Julian Hunter, to the delight of an assembled and derisive staff, marched into the editorial offices of Lyons's tabloid, carefully placed his derby and stick on an idle typewriter, kicked in the door of Lyons's sanctum, took off his coat, and invited the columnist to put up the columnar hands. Lyons had made an impolite noise, in the creation of which he was a master, had pressed a button kept handy for just such emergencies, and Mr. Hunter soon after found himself outside the office, on the floor, propelled by a muscular gentleman who acted as the columnist's bravo. Mr. Hunter, retrieving his outer garments, had departed with murder in his eyes. And the next morning Lyons's column had continued the barrage of thinly camouflaged insinuations.

The second echo rolled back on the first night, the detonation being set off within the sacrosant precincts of the *Club Mara* itself.

·   ·   ·   ·   ·   ·   ·

The Inspector was aging. The case had drawn itself out to the most microscopic of vanishing points; Ellery was increasingly irritable and uncommunicative; the press was clamoring for action; there was an undercurrent of talk on Centre Street about a "shake-up, boys, a real shake-up!" Rather desperately the old man concentrated on Julian Hunter, now that Lyons was turning up delicious dirt and Hunter had lost his temper.

"I've told you all along," he muttered to Ellery that evening, "that Hunter knows more than he admitted. About the Horne business, I mean. Ellery, we've simply got to do something."

There was pity—and still reservation—in Ellery's eyes. "We must wait. There's nothing to be done. Time, dad. Only time will turn the trick."

"I'm goin' down to that bird's club tonight," snarled the Inspector, "and you're goin' with me."

"But what for?"

"I've been finding out things about Hunter, that's what for."

An hour before midnight found the Queens at the door of the *Club Mara*. Sergeant Velie's mountainous figure loomed dimly on the sidewalk across the street. The old man was cool enough, cooler than Ellery, who had a sick feeling in his stomach. They entered, and the Inspector asked for Hunter. There was some difficulty at first; the gentleman, it appeared, was not in evening dress. The gentleman, however (Ellery being properly attired) produced a gleaming little shield, and after that there was no trouble.

They found Hunter at a large table near the dance-floor, engaged in silent communion with a bottle of rye whisky. The man was pale as a goat, and taut; even the pouches beneath his eyes seemed to have shrunk and tightened. He kept looking at his glass, and a waiter kept mechanically refilling it.

He might have been thousands of miles away for all the attention his companions paid him. Sitting together, laughing, knees frankly touching, were the orchidaceous Mara and huge, black-browed Tommy Black. The pugilist's paws, covered with fur, pressed gently on the woman's dainty hands. They flirted openly before Hunter; neither, in fact, seemed aware of Hunter's existence. The fourth member of this singular party was Tony Mars, dressed in ill-fitting evening togs and worrying a cigar as if it were the Commissioner's hand.

The Inspector, with Ellery hovering uncomfortably in the background, came up to the table and said: "Good evening, folks," in a very friendly tone.

Mars started to rise; then he sank back again. Mara Gay cut a trilling laugh in half and stared at the little Inspector. "Why, look who's here!" she cried shrilly. She was a little drunk, and her eyes were strangely bright. In her extreme *decollete* the full thin sinuosity of her torso lay exposed. "And there's Sherlock Holmes! C'mon join us, Sherlock—an' you, too, Gran'pa. Whee!"

Julian Hunter put down his glass and said quietly: "Shut up, Mara."

Black doubled his fists and placed them before him on the cloth. His immense shoulders contracted a little.

"Hello, Inspector," said Mars thickly. "Cripes, I'm glad to see you! Been tryin' to buzz you all day. What's the matter with takin' the padlock off my place. . . ."

"Some other time, Tony," smiled the Inspector. "Ah—Hunter, I'd like to see you for a couple of minutes."

Hunter looked up, briefly, and looked down again. "Come around tomorrow."

"I think I'll be busy tomorrow," said the Inspector gently.

"Tough."

"I've been called that, too, Hunter. Will you take me somewhere where we can talk alone, or do you want me to spill it here?"

Hunter said icily: "You can do what you damned please."

Ellery took a quick step forward, and stopped when the Inspector thrust his little arm out. "All right, then I'll speak before your friends. I've been lookin' you up, Hunter. And I've found out some mighty interestin' things about you."

Hunter moved his head the merest bit. "Still barking up the murder tree?" he sneered. "Why don't you arrest me for killing Horne and be done with it?"

"Arrest you for killing Horne? Whatever made you think that? No, it isn't that, Hunter," said the Inspector dreamily. "It's something else again. It's that business of gambling."

"Of *what?*"

Inspector Queen took a pinch of snuff. "You're running a gambling joint upstairs, Hunter."

Hunter gripped the edge of the table and hauled himself to his feet. "Say that again?" he said in a strangled undertone.

"You've got one of the toniest layouts in the city upstairs. And one of the fanciest hunks of protection, too," said the Inspector amiably. "Oh, I know I'm risking my shield by saying it, but the fact is that your joint—I should say joints—are being protected by a bunch of divvying crooks in City Hall."

"Why, you stupid old fool," began Hunter thickly; his eyes were steaming and red.

"Not only that, but you're one of the big money boys behind the fight racket, Hunter. You engineered the Murphy-Tamara fake, you're workin' hand-in-glove with Pugliezi in the wrestling racket, and there's even talk that you've got Tony Mars under your thumb. Only I don't believe that; Mars is on the square. And then it's common talk that you've fixed the Harker-Black fight in a big way; Tony would never go for that. . . . Sit still, Black; your punch won't do you any good here."

The prizefighter did not remove his small black eyes from the Inspector's face. Mars sat very still.

"Why, you meddling little rat!" shouted Hunter, and stumbled forward with curling fingers. Mars rose quickly and pushed him back. Mara Gay sat pale and rigid, very sober now. And Tommy Black did not even blink. "Why, I'll have you kicked out of the Department. . . . you dried-up old baboon. . . . I'll throttle you like—"

Ellery pushed by his smiling father and said coldly: "I thought you were drunk, but now I know you're insane. Are you going to take that back, or do I have to thrash you?"

It was all very confusing and embarrassing. Waiters began running toward the table. The orchestra struck into a loud number with furious gusto. People craned. The noise mounted. Black rose and, taking Mara's arm, quietly walked her off into the crowd. For an instant Hunter's attention was diverted; a trickle of saliva crept down his chin; his eyes started wildly from his head and he lunged for Black, screaming: "And you, too, damn your soul! You b—" Mars clamped a hand over his mouth and pulled him down in the chair. . . .

Ellery found himself on the sidewalk beside his father, walking toward Broadway filled with a vast disgust for himself, the world, and everything in it. Curiously enough, the Inspector was still smiling. Sergeant Velie fell silently into step with them.

"Hear the riot, Thomas?" chuckled the old man.

"Riot!"

"Darn near. Society!" The old man snorted derisively. "Blue blood! Scratch 'em all, all these crooks, and you'll find just plain stink underneath. Hunter. . . . bah!"

"Find out anything?" asked the Sergeant, scowling.

"No. But that bird's tied up in this business somewhere, I'd stake my life on it."

Ellery groaned. "You've gone about it in exactly the wrong way if you expect to get anything out of him."

"Says you," jeered the Inspector. "Fat lot you know about *that* sort of thing. I tell you, I've ripped the hide off him. Sure, he was soused. But you mark your daddy's words. It won't be long before he forgets there ever was such a thing as caution. We'll know the whole story soon, El; mark my words, mark my words!"

Whether the Inspector was a lucky prophet or a shrewd psychologist, the fact remained that the period of gestation was drawing to its close.

Spurred on by malice, perhaps, Hunter manipulated strings too insistent to be denied. Things began to happen.

And two of the things that happened crowded each other in the happening. The first was that the very next morning Commissioner Welles ordered the ban on the *Colosseum* lifted.

The other was that the evening papers ran an announcement

to the following effect: On the coming Friday night Tommy Black would fight Heavyweight Champion Jack Harker for the title, as originally scheduled, at the *Colosseum*. And on Saturday, the next night—working, as Mars told the reporters, "faster than hell" to accomplish the feat of removing the ring, ringside seats, and other props of the fistic battle—Wild Bill Grant's Rodeo, "monster Western attraction which opened so tragically some three weeks ago," would have a second Grand Opening for the edification of the kiddies and the satiation of the curiosity-seekers.

15: GLADIATOR REX

"LADIES AND gentlemen of the radio audience here we are at ringside in the modern coliseum of sport arenas Tony Mars's *Colosseum* in New York City about to broadcast on this lovely Friday evening the Battle of the Grand I mean the Century ha ha. . . . this program is being broadcast through the courtesy of the ———— Broadcasting Company as you very well know on a nation-wide hook-up and is also linked to England, France and Germany. . . .

"It's almost time for the big scrap to begin let me see it will begin in exactly twelve minutes how's that for timing ha ha. . . . I suppose you can hear the noise out there *Deutschland* it looks like all New York and a good part of Chicago are here to view the most important event in fistic history. . . . The little ole *Colosseum* which has a seating capacity of twenty thousand is packed to the rafters who says boxing is on its last legs ha ha. . . . Yes, and you can't say that about the speculators either they had a field day today somebody in the row behind me just told me he paid one hundred smackers in good American do-re-mi for the privilege of seeing this fracas who says times are hard ha ha. . . .

"Well I hope the gentleman gets his money's worth tut tut I didn't mean that for seriously folks this looks like one humdinger of a scrap eight minutes to go you know this is the championship heavyweight battle between Tommy Black challenger and Champion Jack Harker for those of you who tuned in late being broadcast by courtesy of the ———— Broadcasting Company on an international network much excitement around here but can learn very little if anything ha ha. . . . Oh it's just two of the lads making love to each other no seriously folks it's the main preliminary going on hear that gong that's the bell for the thirteenth round of the scheduled fifteen-round bout between George Dickens the Georgia Black Boy and Battling Ben Riley of Boston and a good set-to it is too believe you me fast all the way with Riley having a shade the better of it excuse me a moment please can't see much of what's going on or hear either there's so much yelling you'd think this was the Democratic National Convention ha ha. . . .

"Ringside tonight is glittering with the nobility beg pardon the bluebloods you'd think this was opening night at the Metropolitan the ladies are out in all their glory and *lavallieres* is that the way you pronounce it Paree. . . . who's that I see why yes there's the lovely Mara Gay famous screen star the Orchid of Hollywood you know looking lovely as ever by the side of Julian Hunter the well-known society man and Broadway club-owner her husband at ringside. . . . Gorgeous Mara's rooting for Tommy Black tonight I'll bet he's a California boy you know. . . . and there's old Tony Mars himself right next to the Hunters old Tony Mars most famous sports promoter in this little old world who built this magnificent temple of sports you know. . . . and yes there's Wild Bill Grant the old-time fightin' deputy of the West with his son Curly and Miss Kit Horne the well-known Western movie star and. . . . excuse me a minute folks (Bill who's that tall young fellow next to Miss Horne fellow with the *pince-nez*

eyeglasses and the sharp face oh thanks) and there's Mr. Ellery
Queen of the Centre Street Queens looks like the police department is well represented tonight because I see good old Commissioner Welles on the other side of the ring talking to Chief
Inspector Klein and. . . .

"According to the official announcement after the boys
weighed in this afternoon Black tipped the scales at one nine-
ty-two and the champion weighed. . . ."

.   .   .   .

"They're coming into the ring hear that terrific uproar that's
the champ the good old champ himself Jack Harker coming into
the ring bundled up in his famous old striped bathrobe with his
manager Johnny Aldrich and his handlers Jack's looking fine tonight his face is deeply tanned and a little drawn trained up to
the minute he's freshly shaved you know that's a superstition of
his and yes there's Tommy Black there's Tommy Black coming
and what an ovation he's getting ladies and gentlemen of the radio audience what an ovation. . . . do you hear that thunder that's
just the crowd roaring for Tommy ha ha. . . . he's a popular boy
looks fit as a fiddle he's wearing a new black satin robe and his
bandaged hands look like two hunks of steel you know the bet-
ting has been funny on this fight at the last minute the odds on
the challenger to win came down and now I understand they're
quoting even money. . . . wait wait wait there's old Jim Steinke
ready to make an announcement. . . .

"Well folks it's all set the boys are in the center of the ring
taking their final instructions from the referee Henry Sumpter
old Henry the Eagle-Eye they call him you know yes they just
touched gloves. . . . both boys look confident. . . . Tommy looks
especially so even though he's scowling he looks more and more

like the old Mauler every day you know he even weaves in the famous Dempsey style and he packs a punch they say almost as hard as—

"There'sthegongthesecondsareoutoftheringTommycome-soutfirstfightinghardhe'slikeaflashthereitgoesleftt'thejawright-totheheartandcoverup. . . . nothing important or serious Jack's smiling they're dancing around the champ hasn't struck a blow yet they're feeling each other out Tommy makes another lunge. . . . Therehegoeslikelightninglikelightning. . . . two lefts to the chin like a pile driver Jack made a face at those they hurt although he seems all right. . . . wow what a fighter that Tommy Black is the champ still hasn't landed a blow. . . . therehegoeswitha*terrifi-c*righttoTommy'shead which would have meant curtains had it landed. . . . but it didn't Tommy's head just wasn't there and. . . .

"*Ooooo!* Wait a minute wait a minute there's. . . . *Ooooo!* ladies and gentlemen Tommy Black just landed eight straight lefts in a row to the Champ's chin and topped it off with a vicious short right hook to Jack's jaw on the button on the button Jack's grog-gy his knees are buckling. . . . he's covering up he's hanging on. . . . the referee is trying to separate the two boys Tommy is will-ing enough he looks like a killer now but the champ's hanging on like a leech. . . . they're apart they're sparring Tommy's teeth are showing in a snarling grin he won't stop he rushes in cool and murderous and there. . . . *Yes!* another left and a right and a left and a right and a left and. . . .

"*Jack'sdownhe'sdown!* . . . two three four five six seven he's try-ing to get up eight ni. . . . he's up in a crouch dancing away Tom-my's after him the referee Henry Sumpter is following closely and. . . .

"*OOOF* the champ's down again hear that terrific noise that's the crowd they're going crazy. . . . five six seven eight nine. . . .

TEN! He'soutandthere'sanewheavyweightchampionofthe-
worldtheworld. . . . ladies and gentlemen a new heavyweight
champion is crowned in the most sensational one-round knock-
out in the history of the ring and. . . .

*"Tommy Tommy boy come here and say a few words into the mi-
crophone! TOMMY!"*

·   ·   ·   ·   ·   ·   ·

It was an auspicious beginning for a new round of events.
They improved as they succeeded each other. Ellery, to whom
the brutality of the prize-ring meant little except a faintly dis-
gusting exhibition of savagery, had kept his attention more on
his companions than upon the gladiators in the ring. And so
he alone of the hundreds pressed closely around the ring saw
the bitter scowl of Julian Hunter, the cold calculating glint in
Tony Mars's eye, and the ecstatic and hoydenish frenzy on the
beautiful face of Mara Gay when the champion lay twitching on
the canvas and Tommy Black, indeed murderous and cool—as
the garrulous announcer had pronounced him—danced up and
down in a neutral corner, never taking his tigrish eyes off his
opponent's prone body.

He hung around. There was something to hang around for.
With his genius for capitalizing a situation, Tony Mars immediately after the first clamor died down, announced that he was
"throwin' a big party" for the successful fighter at the *Club Mara*
that very night. Perhaps the fact that a threatened double-cross,
in which for the benefit of the gamblers Tommy Black was to
throw the fight to the champion, had been averted, moved Mars
to this lavish display, for he was a notoriously careful man where
money was concerned, although generous at impulsive moments;
at any rate, it was to be open house. Representatives of press as-

sociations, well-known sporting editors, promoters, the Grants, Kit Horne, the entire rodeo troupe (who had been present in the wildly excited flesh at the battle)—all were invited.

Midnight found the *Club Mara* in the grip of a strange ecstasy. The doors were closed. The immense room was festooned with flowers and trophies of the prize-ring. Mars, cold and cordial as of old, presided. Liquor flowed freely. At the central table, like a muscular Silenus, sat Tommy Black, smiling, unruffled, unmarked, in evening clothes that were moulded like plaster to his big body.

Ellery wandered about quietly. He sought Wild Bill Grant, and could not find him. A word with Mars on the side elicited the information that Grant had politely declined; he was tired and had the next night's opening to think about. But Curly was present, and Kit Horne—a most unenthusiastic and bright-eyed young woman, smiling when smiled to, talking when talked to, and for the most part watching Julian Hunter as if he were a monstrous curiosity who both repelled and fascinated.

The room roared with noise—the popping of corks, the banging of glasses, the shouting of people. The hilarity centered about Black, and was led by Mara Gay, who looked ethereally beautiful in her scanty gown. She was magnificently drunk—more drunk with admiration of Black, his success, his physique, his animal magnetism—than with liquor. The forty members of Grant's troupe, amazed at the freedom with which wine and whisky flowed, made merry and drank, grateful for these favors. Drank until one would say the human stomach could hold no more. But except for heightened mahogany complexions and slightly slurred tongues, they showed few effects. Woody, prominent with his one arm, stood on his chair and bellowed: "Le's give 'em *The Cowboy's Lament,* boys!" And after that the night was rent with hoarse and raucous sounds that were intended to convey certain sad sentiments in song. Dan'l Boone, overcome by the tragedy of it all, sank to the floor and wept bitter tears. The newspapermen for the most part drank silently.

Ellery continued to wander about.

In the small hours the party broke up into small groups. Ellery saw Kit, very sober, rise with a queer little gesture of impatience, say something to Curly, and then make for the cloakroom. Curly meekly followed. Ellery did not see them again.

Black, freed from the compulsion of training, ignored the protests of his manager, a small fat perspiring man, and imbibed freely of excellent champagne. It was amazing how so little wine went so quickly to the head of the athlete. In ten minutes he was royally drunk. By this time he had ceased to be the lion of the evening, for the excellent reason that none of his admirers remembered any event older than a half-hour. Tommy Black's manager, apparently despairing of keeping his champion sober, had tucked a small black bottle under his arm and retired to a corner to get quietly drunk by himself.

So Ellery went over to Black's table and sat down. Mars was there, steadily drinking. All about them swirled the mad noise.

"Look who's here," growled Black, fixing Ellery with a wavering and ferocious glare. "Li'l policeman. Tell your ol' man he better watch his gab, boy, better watch it. But Tommy Black don't hold no hard feelings. Have drink, boy, have drink."

Ellery smiled. "I've guzzled my quota, thanks. Well, how does it feel to be champion of the world?"

"Good!" roared Black enthusiastically. "Damn goo', boy! Hey!" he bellowed. The bellow was drowned in the greater thunder of hilarity. "Aw hell, can' talk here. C'mon over som'res, you, an' I'll tell you the story of m'life."

"Delighted," said Ellery amiably. He looked around. Hunter and Mara Gay had disappeared somewhere. He thought he knew where. "Let's amble over to one of those alcoves, Tommy, and you can tell me all about the trials and vicissitudes of your rise to fame. Want to come, Mr. Mars?"

"I'll come," said Mars dully. Except for a certain hesitancy in his voice he might have been sober.

The three men made their way laboriously through the crowd to the left wall, where stood rows of booths intended for private parties. Ellery adroitly steered his companions toward a certain one. When they sat down he was sure he had been right. There were familiar voices from the next booth.

Black began: "Tell y'. M'ol' man was a tinsmith in Pas'dena an' m'ol' lady—" And then, very abruptly, he stopped. His name had been mentioned in the adjoining cubicle. "Who in hell—?" he began to shout, and stopped again. This time his eyes narrowed and he sat very quietly, most of the liquorish color draining from his cheeks.

Mars sat up tensely. Ellery did not move a muscle; experimenting scientists must preserve their equanimity.

"Yes, and I'll say it again, damn your soul!" came the low voice of Julian Hunter. "You and this Black gorilla. Making a laughing-stock of me. When I married you, you common chippie, I elevated you—d'ye understand? I'm not going to have you drag my name through the muck of the tabloids just because you get a hankering for gorilla meat—d'ye understand? Lyons hinted you were having an affair with Black; and, by God, I believe the filthy scoundrel!"

"It's a lie," shrieked Mara Gay. "Julian, I swear—I tell you I *didn't!* He's just been nice to me. . . ."

"I admire your conception of 'nice,'" said Hunter coldly.

"Julian, don't *look* at me that way! Why, *I* wouldn't. . . . I wouldn't *dream*—"

"You're lying, Mara," said Hunter without emotion. "You're lying to me about Black, as you've lied to me for years about others. You're nothing but a dirty, common—"

Black's big fists doubled on the cloth before him, and his dark skin became stony with passion.

Ellery grew rigid; and yes, calculating, too. The even unhurried voice of Julian Hunter went on, cutting down the actress's pleas, ignoring her mounting hysteria, excoriating and reviling her in words that burned in the hazy air. But it was what he said. . . .

"I've got more on you, Mara, than just being unfaithful to me with every brute who's got hair on his chest," said Hunter quietly. "A lot more. Oh, I'll admit that exploitation of your weakness for men wouldn't hurt you much; the publicity would probably help that fine, sensitive artist's 'career' of yours—"

"Go to hell!" she screamed.

"—but there's something else about you, my dear, that not even your reputation for cinema wickedness could outlive. If I should. . . . Well, suppose I went out into the middle of the floor this moment and announced to the reporters out there that Mara Gay, the Orchid of Hollywood, is nothing but a plain d—"

"For God's sake, *stop!*" she screeched. And then Tommy Black, without so much as a muscular tightening of his body as warning of his intention, flashed out of his chair and sprang to the next booth.

Ellery and Mars scrambled to their feet and dashed after him, putting restraining hands on his taut arms. He shook them off without bothering even to look around; so savagely that Mars staggered backward and fell, hurting his head on the floor, and Ellery was flung, stunned, against a pillar.

In a haze he saw the prizefighter, crouched as in the ring, the cloth of his black evening coat stretched like mail across his wide back, grasp Hunter by the throat, yank him out of his chair, shake him as he would have shaken a child, and then set the man down softly. Mara Gay, white-faced, had her mouth open, paralyzed, unable even to scream. Hunter seemed dazed.

And then Black's immense right fist swished up and struck Hunter on the point of the chin. Hunter fell to the floor without a sound.

Perhaps it was the spark which was required to set the tinder aflame. The next thing Ellery knew the *Club Mara* was a bellowing bedlam, a nightmare of whirling, staggering, fighting figures, of flying crockery and hurtling chairs.

In the confusion he managed to slip away, capture his coat from a frightened cloakroom girl, and gain the sweet fresh air.

His nose was wrinkled as if a bad odor lingered in his nostrils. And his eyes were very thoughtful.

16: IOU

". . . . And scored his second kayo of the evening, this time his distinguished opponent being the Great Kazoo himself, Julian Hunter. What fun! There were magnums of champagne. . . ."

Mr. Ellery Queen read Ted Lyons's column through in silence at the breakfast table the next morning. Although Ellery could not remember having seen the tabloid columnist at the *Club Mara* the previous evening, Lyons's latest eruption in *The Lowdown* was presumptive evidence that he had been present. He described in snatches the hilarity, the cast of characters, and the dramatic highlights of the evening. He gave the stars their due, and did not neglect to comment on the subtier phases of the piece. Ellery himself was mentioned as "one of the victims of the new champ's muckety-amuck." And then Ellery's eyes narrowed. For at the end of the piece there was a startling insinuation—startling even when one considered the electrical source.

What hold, demanded Lyons in not so many words, had Hunter over his famous wife, Mara Gay—a hold not by any stretch of the imagination connubial? "The 'sipers will tell you (if you aren't hep already) that this precious pair lead a cat-and-dog life, with hubby putting on the dog and wifey meowing like the

queen of tabbies herself." Was it just domestic infelicity which
made Mara so nervous and highstrung, her eyes so alternately
brilliant and dull? demanded Lyons. "There's TNT in that little
nest, folksies; and does hubby know it? And does wifey know
what it would do to her career if it came out in the wash? Yes, he
and she does or do!"

Ellery dropped the paper and helped himself to more coffee.
"Well, what do you think of it?" asked the Inspector.

"I've been stupid," said Ellery. "Lyons, of course, like all ro-
dents, has keen eyes. The woman is a drug addict."

"Should 'a' known," grumbled the old man. "That dame's always looked queer to me. Gives you the willies. Cokey, hey? So
that's what Hunter was threatening her with last night!—What
are you' grinning about?"

"Grinning? I'm grimacing. Over the possibilities."

"What possibilities? Oh, you mean her being on the hop! Say,
I've got some news for you."

"News?"

"It'll *be* news in the late morning editions. I got a tip from
Tony this morning over the phone. Know what's happening?"

"I haven't the faintest notion. For heaven's sake, what is it?"

The Inspector rather deliberately took his morning's first ration of snuff. When he had sneezed the prescribed three times
and vigorously wiped his little nose, he said: "Last-minute decision. Wild Bill Grant's show has a new trouper."

"You mean for the reopening tonight?"

"Yep. . . . Guess who it is."

"I'm the world's poorest guesser."

"Kit Horne."

"No!" Ellery stared. "She's really joining the rodeo troupe?"

"That's what Tony Mars told me over the phone. He says it's

a new build-up—cash in on the murder publicity and all that. I don't believe that."

"Nor do I," said Ellery with a frown.

"I think," smiled the Inspector, "that the poor kid's got a—what d'ye call it?—revenge complex. Why the devil else should she want to join a rodeo when she's a movie star in her own right? I tell you, it's plain as the nose on your face. I bet this gets her into trouble over her movie contract."

"If I judge the young woman correctly," said Ellery, "a mere contract won't stand in her way. So. . . ."

"And then again, maybe it's because of this Grant boy," said the old man. "I'd say there was more than a professional bond between those two. Because—"

The doorbell rang. Djuna ran into the foyer. When he reappeared it was to usher into the Queen's living room Kit Horne herself.

Ellery sprang to his feet. "My dear Miss Horne!" he exclaimed. "This *is* a surprise. Come on in and join us in a cup of coffee."

"No, thank you," she said in a low voice. "Good morning, Inspector. I've dropped in for just a moment. I—there's something I want to. . . . well, tell you."

"Now, isn't that nice," said the Inspector heartily, setting a chair for her. She dropped into it limply. Ellery offered her a cigaret and she declined it. He lighted one himself and stood by the window, smoking. One glance into the street below assured him that the detective set to follow the girl was on duty; the man was leaning against an iron fence across the street. "What is it, my dear?"

"It's a queer story." She twisted her gloves in a knot. She was nervous; her eyes were shadowed by huge violet arcs and there was a drawn look about her. "It has to do with Buck."

"With Mr. Horne, hey?" said the Inspector sympathetically. "Well, well, we can certainly use every scrap of information, Miss Horne. Just what is it?" and his small bright eyes examined her very keenly indeed. Ellery smoked quietly by the window. Djuna, who knew his place, had disappeared—notwithstanding his first worshipping glance—into the culinary regions.

"Frankly," she began, fumbling with her gloves, "I—I don't know how to begin. It's so very difficult." Then her hands stilled and she looked up at the Inspector fearlessly. "Perhaps I'm creating a tempest in a teapot. But to me it seems—well, important, if not significant."

"Yes, Miss Horne?"

"It concerns—Julian Hunter." She paused.

"Ah."

"Not long ago I went to see him—to the *Club Mara,* alone."

"Yes, my dear?" said the Inspector.

"It was at his own request. I—"

"He telephoned you, sent you a note?" said the Inspector sharply, envisioning carelessness on the part of his operative.

"No." She seemed surprised at the purposelessness of the question. "He managed to get me aside one evening at the *Club* and asked me to call the next night, alone. He wouldn't say what for. Of course, I went."

"And?"

"I saw him in his private office. At first he was very polite. Then his mask came off. He told me a terrible thing. You know he runs a gambling house, Inspector?"

"Indeed?" said the Inspector. "What's that to do with it?"

"Well, it seems that about a week before—before Buck died, just after we came East and Tony Mars introduced us to Hunter, Buck visited the gambling house Hunter runs—above the *Club Mara*. Buck played."

"Poker? Craps?"

"Faro. And he lost a lot of money."

"I see," said the Inspector softly. "You know, we've been checking up on your foster-father's finances, Miss Horne. Not here. I mean in Wyoming. And we found that he had withdrawn every cent he had—before he came to New York."

"You didn't tell me that," said Ellery sharply, from the window.

"You didn't ask me, my son. How much did Horne lose, Miss Horne?"

"Forty-two thousand dollars."

Both men whistled. "That's a heap of money," murmured Inspector Queen. "Too much money, in fact."

"What do you mean?" snapped Ellery.

"He had only eleven thousand and some-odd in his Cheyenne bank altogether, Ellery."

"He withdrew it all?"

"Every cent. Except for his ranch property, that was all he had in the world. Not much, hey? . . . So, Miss Horne, he lost over forty thousand dollars! I think I see what's coming."

"Yes," she said, and lowered her eyes. "He didn't lose it all in one session. I think Hunter said he lost it over a period of four days. And he gave Hunter IOU's."

"He didn't give Hunter any cash at all?" frowned the Inspector.

"Hunter said no."

"That's funny! But he must have bought chips?"

Kit shrugged. "A few hundred dollars' worth, said Hunter. Hunter told me he gave Buck credit for the rest. It seems, according to Hunter, that Buck pleaded temporary poverty."

"Hmm. There's something screwy somewhere," muttered the Inspector. "Horne came to New York with eleven grand, deposited five in a bank, withdrew three a few days later—what the deuce happened to all his money if he didn't give Hunter any cash? That visitor, eh, son?"

Ellery was silently contemplating his cigaret. Kit sat very still. The Inspector took a turn about the room.

"And what did Mr. Hunter want from you?" asked the old man abruptly.

"Hunter said now that Buck was dead and he could never collect on the IOU's, that *I* should pay him the amount of the debt!"

"Why, the dirty crook," murmured the Inspector. "You told him to go plumb, I suppose?"

"I certainly did." She raised her head again, and her eyes flashed blue-gray lightning momentarily; "I'm afraid I lost my temper. I didn't even believe him, and I demanded to see the IOU's. So he brought them out of his safe and showed them to me. Oh, they were genuine enough! And when I said that Hunter must be running his game crookedly, that Buck would never have lost that much at his own old game, faro, if the game was on the square, he grew angry and began to threaten me."

"Threaten you? How?"

"He said he'd make me pay."

"How did he propose to do that?"

She shrugged. "I don't know."

"And then you walked out on him?"

She said with spirit: "Not before I told him what I thought of him! And I left with a promise to pay Buck's debt."

"You did?" The Inspector was shocked. "But, my dear girl, you didn't have to—"

"A debt," she said, "is a debt. But I play poker myself, Inspector, and I had a little card up my sleeve. I said: 'Mr. Hunter, I'll hold myself personally responsible for discharging my foster-father's indebtedness to you.' He became very nice to me at once. 'But not,' I went on, 'until Buck's murder is cleared up and it's demonstrated that you're in no way involved.' And with that I flounced out."

The Inspector coughed. "A tall order, Miss Horne. Are you financially able to keep that promise? It seems like a lot of money."

Kit sighed. "It *is* a lot of money. I'd never be able to do it if not for—for Buck's insurance. He's carried a large policy for many years—a hundred thousand dollars. And since I'm the sole beneficiary. . . ."

"I wonder if Hunter knew—" the Inspector began to mutter.

"He had no unusual expenses—aside from the gambling—since your arrival in New York?" asked Ellery.

"I'm sure he didn't."

"Hmm." Ellery stood bent in thought; suddenly he threw back his shoulders. "Oh, come now," he said cheerfully, "these things will undoubtedly explain themselves when we know all the truth. Let's change the subject. I hear you're joining Grant's show, Miss Horne. Sudden decision?"

"Oh, that." Her little brown chin hardened. "Not entirely. I think it's been in the back of my mind ever since the night Buck was shot. But I'm not really taking Buck's place as an attraction, Mr. Queen; I didn't want the thing announced at all, but for some reason Mr. Grant insisted on it, and he was supported by Mr. Mars. I'm just being one of the troupe."

"May I ask what you hope to accomplish?" asked Ellery gently.

She rose and began to pull on her gloves. "Mr. Queen," she snapped, "I shall never stop looking for Buck's murderer. I know it sounds melodramatic, but that's the way I feel about it."

"Ah, then I take it you believe the murderer of Horne is dangling about the fringes of the rodeo and the *Colosseum* crowd?"

"It would seem so, wouldn't it?" she said with a grim little smile. "And now I must be going." She walked toward the foyer. "Oh yes!" she said suddenly, coming to a stop in the foyer archway. "It almost slipped my mind. The troupe are having a little celebration this afternoon shortly before the opening tonight. I think you ought to be there, Mr. Queen."

"Celebration?" Ellery was genuinely surprised. "Isn't that in—ah—slightly bad taste?"

"You see," she sighed, "it's a very special occasion. Today's Curly's thirtieth birthday, and according to some legacy from his mother he comes into a good deal of money. Curly didn't want any fuss made under the circumstances, but Wild Bill asked me if it would be all right, and of course I said yes. I don't want to be a spoil-sport, especially where—Curly's concerned."

Ellery coughed. "In that case I'll be very happy to come. At the *Colosseum*?"

"Yes. They're rigging up some tables and things in the arena. I'll expect you, then."

She offered her hand, man-fashion, and he took it with a reassuring smile. Then she shook hands with the Inspector, grinned frankly, and left the apartment. They watched her run lightly down the stairs.

"Nice filly," said the Inspector as he closed the door.

·   ·   ·   ·   ·   ·   ·

The Inspector had his coat on and was about to leave for Centre Street when the doorbell rang again. Djuna ran to answer it.

"Now who the deuce could that be?" grumbled the Inspector. Ellery, who was at the window watching the operative swing briskly into action as Kit Horne strode off down the street toward Broadway, turned quickly.

Major Kirby stood smiling in the foyer archway.

"Ah, come in, Major!" said Ellery.

"Always seem to have the knack of coming places at the wrong time," said the Major. He was glittering in freshly pressed clothes, he carried a jaunty stick, his velour was perfectly brushed, and there was a gardenia in his lapel. "Sorry, Inspector—I see you're ready to go out. I shan't be a minute."

"That's all right," said the Inspector. "Have a cigar?"

"No, thanks." Major Kirby seated himself and carefully hitched his trousers up. "Met Miss Horne on the stairs as I was coming up. Little social visit, eh? . . . Just dropped in to see if I could be of further service, you know. I've sort of fallen into the habit of co-operating with the police, and damn it if it isn't a pleasant feeling!"

"For people with milk-fed consciences," grinned Ellery.

"I'm officiating at the *Colosseum* again tonight," said Kirby. "My old job presiding over the news cameras. I wanted to find out if you and Inspector Queen had anything special in mind for me."

"Special?" The Inspector frowned. "What d'ye mean?"

"Oh, I don't know. It will be sort of—funny, going over the same routine as a month ago."

"You think somethin's going to happen?" snapped the Inspector. "We're having men all over the place, but—"

"Oh, no, no, really. I've nothing like that in my noodle. But I can film special things, you know, in case—"

The Inspector looked puzzled. Ellery smiled and murmured: "Decent of you, Major. But I'm sure tonight's will be all good clean wholesome fun. At any rate, I'll see you at the arena this evening."

"Sure enough." The Major rose, adjusted his cravat, sniffed his gardenia, and shook hands. On the way out he patted Djuna's head. He was still smiling when the door closed upon his neat little figure.

"Now what the devil," growled the Inspector, "did *that* mean?"

Ellery chuckled and slipped into an armchair before the early fire. *"Que diable alloit-il faire dans cette galère,* eh?" The Inspector snorted. "You're the most suspicious doyen! Always smelling the blood of an Englishman and ferociously growling fe, fi, fo, fum! Go on down to your Bastille. The man was just being friendly."

"Nosey, I call it," asserted the Inspector with a snap of his jaws, and slammed the door on his way out.

17: CELEBRATION

LATE AFTERNOON found Mr. Ellery Queen leaning against the concrete wall rimming the oval arena of the *Colosseum,* speculating on the cursoriness of human grief. Anguish dulls; memories dim; it is only the scene that remains the same, an uncomfortable and silent reminder of what was and what is as opposed to what might have been. There, not twenty feet away, was the very spot on the tanbark where a man's contorted limbs had sprawled in their last earthly obeisance short weeks before. Now quick men in serving togs pounded over the place bearing platters of food.

"Out, damned spot," he sighed, and strolled over to the assembling group.

A long table had been set up on the dirt core of the oval, constructed out of wooden horses and boards covered with cloths. The table gleamed with silverware and glassware; there was a profusion of salads and *hors d'oeuvres* and crystalline hams. . . . He looked around. Nowhere was there the faintest sign of the scene of the night before. The ring, the ringside seats, were gone; as were the lowered overhead arcs and the electrical equipment of the newspapermen and the broadcasting people.

The caterers concluded their preparations; Wild Bill Grant appeared with his arm about his son's broad shoulders.

"Everybody here?" roared Grant.

The troupe, already dressed in their regalia for the evening performance, applauded vigorously.

"Then set an' fall to!" roared Grant. "Here's one cook-wagon gives you more'n slumgullion 'n' hash!" And he followed his own advice by dropping into the chair at the head of the long table and attacking the sugarbrown carcass of a ham.

Curly sat down at his father's right, Kit to the left. Ellery was a few seats farther along the table on Kit's side. Tony Mars sat across the table from Ellery. Next to Curly there was a tall ruddy old gentleman who parked a small Stetson and a lawyer's brief-case beneath his chair.

The troupe fell to, as directed. A product of the effete East, Ellery marvelled at their appetites. Food began to disappear with alarming speed. There was a constant chatter of chaffing and broad commentary from full mouths and powerfully champing jaws. Only the head of the table fell silent.

And gradually a pall settled over the table, and the clamor of the troupe grew less. Perhaps it was Wild Bill's own depressed and moody air, or Kit's grim quiet presence, although she did her best to be sociable. But as the food disappeared, so did the talk; until with the last scrap there was a booming silence over which one might have said the ghost of Buck Horne gloomily presided.

Grant threw down his napkin and rose. His bowed legs shook a little, and his heavy face was a deep brown-red. "Folks!" he shouted, with an attempt at geniality. "You all know the reason fer this barbecue. Today my son Curly is thirty years old." There was a mild cheer. "Now that he's a man, (laughter) he comes into his own. His mother, bless 'er soul, who's dead an' buried these nineteen years, made out her last will an' testament 'fore she passed on, an' in that will she made provision fer our son. She directed that when he got to the age of thutty he was to receive ten thousand dollars. He's thutty today, an' he gets it. Mr. Comerford, who's been the fam'ly lawyer since the French 'n' Injun Wars, seems like, come all the way from Cheyenne to make the legacy legal, like, an' pay his respects; though the Lord knows he didn't tote any *money* from the West, what with gangsters an'—an' all. I got only one more thing to say." He stopped, and after their polite grins at his feeble attempts at humor, there was a strained and expectant silence; and suddenly a ripple that had no movement and was the more horrible for that flashed down the long table and left staring eyes behind. "I got only one more thing to say," Grant repeated, and his voice faltered. "I only wish to the good God my ole pardner Buck Horne was—was here."

He sat down, and frowned at the cloth.

Kit sat rigid, staring at Curly across the table.

The tall old Westerner rose, stooped for his briefcase, and then straightened up. He fumbled with the catch. "I've got here," he announced, "the sum of ten thousand dollars in cash, done up in one-thousand-dollar bills." He got the brief-case open, dipped his hand inside, and it emerged with a neat stack of yellow-backs held together by a rubber-band. "Curly my boy, I consider it a great privilege to be the instrument of carrying out your dear mother's last wishes. Use the money wisely and well, as she wished you to."

Curly rose and took the sheaf of bills rather mechanically. "Mr. Comerford, thanks. An' you, pop. I—Hell, I don't know *what* to say!" and he sat down abruptly.

They chuckled and chortled over that, and the spell was broken.

But only for a moment. Wild Bill Grant said: "You boys an' gals better take a last look at yore gear. We don't want no slip-ups t'night," and quietly nodded to the chief caterer. Chairs were instantly scuffed back, cowboys wandered off, the caterer's men-attacked the dishes. . . .

It was all as simple and uneventful as that. And yet Ellery felt, and saw reflected from the honest brown faces about him, the same feeling, the intangible presence of something unearthly which might have been the efflorescence of a ghost and was merely a manifestation of mass consciousness. Superstitious, impressionable, the group of alien men and women shuffled off, headed by the saturnine One-Arm Woody, bound for their dressing rooms, whispering of portents and dire things in the air. Many repaired to the stables to seek solace in their horses, or to go over their gear, while others felt furtively for their good-luck pieces.

The tables were whisked away and all traces of the festivities, such as they had been, were removed, so that soon not a crumb remained in the arena. A gang of workmen flocked into the amphitheatre through the various entrances above and began to put the finishing touches on the preparations for the evening's performance.

Ellery stood quietly by himself, off at one side, watching.

Only ten feet away Grant was attempting to talk cheerfully to his son and Kit. Kit was pale, but smiling. And Curly was unnaturally silent. The old lawyer beamed on them from the side. Grant continued to be cheerful. . . . And then in the midst of a sentence that famous old Indian fighter and United States Marshal stopped, grew white, gulped hard and noisily, and, muttering something, half-ran across the arena to the exit which led most directly to his office.

Curly and Kit were stunned, and Comerford rubbed his face foolishly.

Ellery came alert as a dog to the point. Something had happened. But what? He strove—so imperfect is unprepared and innocent observation—to recall Grant's precise position at the instant he had ceased talking; and the best he could recall was that the showman had stared over Curly's shoulder at that peculiar instant, had stared at the eastern main gateway from the arena, the gateway through which the troupe had shuffled a few moments before.

It was almost, Ellery reflected minutes later as he stood a lone and slender figure of puzzlement among Tony Mars's busy workmen, it was almost as if Grant had seen a strange face in the dark gateway.

18: DEATH RIDES AGAIN

BYRON HAS said somewhere that history "with all her volumes vast hath but *one* page." It is a more polite way of saying that history has a habit of repeating herself. Perhaps the ancients had something of this in mind when they created the Muse of history in the form of a woman.

It occurred to Mr. Ellery Queen on that Saturday night as he and the Inspector sat in the self-same box with the self-same people—excepting one—watching much the same performance, that history is not only a repetitious jade, but a malicious one to boot. One expects, knowing the universality of human nature, that the records of human achievement in succeeding eras shall exhibit more or less of the same character. What one does not expect, however, is plaster-of-Paris fidelity.

And that, it seems, was precisely what history was about on the evening of the reopening of Wild Bill Grant's Rodeo. . . . a little improvement upon the usual performance.

The fact that the scene was the same was an important contributing circumstance; the *Colosseum* was jammed with a curious, unruly crowd. The fact that, with the exception of Kit Horne, the occupants of the Mars box were the same who had occupied it a month before, aided the illusion not a little. The fact that Major Kirby stood with his crew on a platform erected in exactly the same spot as before, and made exactly the same preparations, was surely not untoward, though worthy of remark. The fact that the same whooping, charging horsemen and horsewomen amused the audience of thousands before the grand announcement was merely a matter of routine, as was Curly's exhibition of marksmanship with the catapult and the little glass balls. The fact that the troupe disappeared, and that Wild Bill Grant galloped in and, taking up a central position in the arena, discharged his revolver in the air for attention and bellowed an announcement—this began to color the atmosphere and work on strained nerves.

But the great fact was that there was no warning, no slightest sign of what was to happen. And here again history repeated herself.

.   .   .   .

The police themselves contributed to the tragedy of complete duplication. The arms which had been confiscated after the murder of Buck Horne had perforce been returned. The very same revolvers therefore were in the hands of the very same supernumeraries when the play began its second performance. Only Buck Horne's twin ivory-handled .45's had not come back to the scene, for these had been turned over to Kit Horne on her insistent demand and packed away in her trunk at the Barclay. And, of course, Ted Lyons's automatic was absent, as was Ted Lyons; the journalistic gentleman's reputation for ubiquitousness had for once destroyed itself. The police and Wild Bill Grant saw to that.

The feeling was strongest in the Mars box. Tony Mars was even more nervous than he had been a month before, and he chewed his cold cigar even more savagely. Mara Gay was as sparkling, as brilliant, as quicksilverish as ever; her eyes were pin-points; and again she whispered to the bulky athlete at her side, now champion heavyweight of the world. And it seemed strange that Julian Hunter should sit in the same seat at the rear of the box, alone, sardonic, watching his wife and Tommy Black. . . . quite as if he had never been punched into insensibility by those punishing fists, or had never accused his wife of unfaithfulness with the brute who sat whispering to her before his cupped eyes.

And there it was! Grant's signal shot, the wide swing of the eastern gate by the old special and—not Buck Horne this time, but One-Arm Woody, the rodeo veteran, charged out on a dappled horse. . . . even at that distance exultantly triumphant. Followed by Curly Grant and Kit Horne—riding *Rawhide,* that tragic Pegasus—and the rest of the thundering herd. And there was the Roman roar of the crowd as the riders swept around the tanbark track to the accompaniment of blaring music and sharp gun-fire reports of horses' hooves. And then they halted on the south side of the oval, Woody only a few yards from the Mars box, the others in twos on restless mounts strung out behind, toward the far western turn. Wild Bill's second announcement! There was the faintly derisive shout of Woody, sitting his horse like a mutilated warrior, and the last sharp signal from Grant's long-barreled revolver. Then Woody's sinewy right arm dipped, came up with a weapon, shot toward the roof, dipped down again to his holster as in salute. . . . and the seething ripple of sinuous motion through forty-one riders—Woody and the forty at his back, many feet behind. And Woody's horse leaped forward as he shouted the long-drawn out *Yoooooow!* of the wide range, and an instant later the cavalcade shot forward in furious motion.

Woody galloped round the eastern turn of the oval, going like the wind.

The troupe flashed up to the tanbark below the Mars box.

The cameras ground.

The crowd clamored.

The Queens sat silent in the grip of a terrifying premonition. There was no reason for it, and yet the best reason in the world. It was unexpected, and yet it was inevitable.

To the utter and devastating stupefaction of the twenty thousand people in the bowl, flesh turned to stone, hearts suspended, eyes staring like marbles. . . . in the midst of the answering crash of the volley from the raised revolvers of the troupe as they thundered past the Mars box, Woody—directly across the arena—jerked convulsively, crumpled in his saddle, and tumbled like a sawdust man to the tanbark to be ground under the horses' hooves on almost precisely the spot where Buck Horne had fallen dead a month before!

19: IBID

MUCH LATER, when it was all over and the miasma of mental nausea had lifted a little, Ellery Queen was to confess that, taking everything into account, that was the most trying moment of his professional career. It was made doubly trying by the fact that weeks before he had professed—cryptically through some subtle necessity—to know who had killed the first victim of that astounding criminal whose weapon vanished as if by magic and whose very figure seemed cloaked in invisibility.

Recriminations came naturally to shocked minds. It was, for instance, surely in the mind of Major Kirby. And it was certainly uppermost in Inspector Queen's outraged thoughts. "If you knew," the Inspector's distended and astonished eyes might have been saying in that first instant when the Queens sat paralyzed and stared from the swirling horses to each other, "why didn't you come out with it at that time and prevent this second murder?"

There was no answer that Ellery felt he might at that precise moment put into words. And yet he knew in his heart that the murder of Woody had been unforeseeable, unavoidable; there was nothing he could have done to prevent this supplementary letting of blood; and there was every reason in the world for his compulsion to preserve silence. . . . now more than ever before.

These things hurtled through his brain, and he tasted a little of the self-constituted martyr's bitterness. And the cool tenant of every sensitive brain—that little impersonal observer who sits in Gautama serenity in an inner recess among the turbulent gray cells—told him simply: "Wait. This man's death is not upon your head. Wait."

.   .   .   .

An hour later the same group that had surrounded the dead body of Buck Horne a month before surrounded the dead body of the one-armed rider—mangled, crushed, bloody, his limbs all askew and mercifully concealed beneath a blanket.

Police, detectives, were holding the crowd in check.

The arena was strictly guarded.

Major Kirby's men, under the little man's direction, were feverishly grinding away at the scene.

The troupe moved restlessly about. Their horses under the charge of Boone were placidly drinking at the watering troughs.

No one said anything; Kit Horne stood by in a coma of bewilderment; the Grants were still and pale; Tony Mars was on the verge of hysteria; in the Mars box Hunter and Champion Black peered intently over the rail into the arena.

.   .   .   .

Dr. Samuel Prouty, Assistant Medical Examiner of New York County, rose from his knees and flipped the blanket back over the dead man. "Shot in the heart, Inspector."

"Same place?" asked the Inspector hoarsely, who looked as if he were living through the horrible episodes of a preposterous nightmare.

"As the other one? Pretty much." Dr. Prouty closed his bag. "Bullet nipped through the fleshy part at the bottom of the stump of his left arm and lodged in the heart. If he'd had a whole arm he'd probably be alive this minute. As it was, he almost escaped. An inch higher, and the slug might have lodged in the stump."

"One shot?" asked the old man tremulously. He seemed suddenly to have remembered Ellery's peroration on the marksmanship of the murderer.

"One shot," said Dr. Prouty.

.   .   .   .

The routine things were done. Forearmed by unhappy experience, Inspector Queen took every precaution against the possible escape of the criminal and the disappearance of the weapon.

"I suppose it's a .25 calibre again?"

Dr. Prouty probed for the bullet. He brought it out soon enough—a well-preserved little slug covered with blood. It was unquestionably the bullet of a .25 automatic pistol.

"What about the angle, Sam?" muttered the Inspector.

Dr. Prouty grinned mirthlessly. "Damn remarkable, I call it. Just about the same as the angle the Horne bullet made."

The riders were segregated and their arms collected. They were searched. Everyone was searched. Sergeant Velie combed the arena again, and again found the shell—a battered shell, obviously again kicked about by human and equine feet, and in a spot yards from where the first shell had been found.

But the .25 automatic remained merely a fantastic notion.

Lieutenant Knowles, the police ballistics expert, was on the scene this time. Once more the ghastly and tedious business of searching twenty thousand people was begun. Some .25's— so repetitive was the event!—were again turned up. In a long chamber off the arena Knowles set up a makeshift laboratory. He pressed Major Kirby into service, and the two men spent long minutes firing into an improvised target made of absorbent cotton loosely rolled. With the aid of the microscope the Lieutenant had brought with him, comparisons were made between bullets of the .25 calibre automatics found, and the bullet from the dead man's body. . . . The search continued. Inspector Queen, in a fine roaring rage, was everywhere at once.

The Commissioner of Police himself made an appearance, and an official close to the Mayor.

Everything was done. Nothing was accomplished.

When it was all over, only one thing seemed certain besides the fact that murder had been committed.

·　　·　　·　　·　　·　　·　　·

Lieutenant Knowles, weary and slouching, appeared with his report, Major Kirby striding silently at his side.

"You've examined all the guns?" snapped the Inspector.

"Yes, Inspector. The automatic that was fired at your dead man isn't here."

The Inspector was silent. It was so incredible that words were superfluous.

"But there's one thing I can state positively, although I'll check up with my universal when I get back to the laboratory," continued Lieutenant Knowles. "Major Kirby thoroughly agrees. The bullet that killed Woody shows the same identifying marks as the bullet that killed Horne."

"You mean they both were fired from the same automatic?" asked the Commissioner.

"Right, sir. No doubt about it at all."

And Ellery Queen stood by and gnawed at the fingernail of

his right forefinger, deep in thought and unwilling shame. No one paid the least attention to him.

· · · · · · ·

The ghastly comedy played on. Gradually the crowd was weeded out, sent away. The arena was finecombed. The bowl, the offices, the stables, the whole maze of the *Colosseum* was gone over with eyes and fingers quickened by official censure.

And the automatic remained missing. It seemed that there was nothing to do but confess complete mystification and failure. . . .

And then while the Commissioner, the Mayor's representative, the Inspector, Lieutenant Knowles, and Major Kirby stood eying one another in the curiously strained manner of men who are afraid to face an unpleasant truth, Curly Grant furnished a diversion—a radical diversion, since it was so far the only event of significance in the period of Woody's murder which was not the duplication of a kindred event in the Horne murder.

Curly appeared in the eastern gateway, wild-eyed, disheveled, and loped like a mustang across the tan-bark track to his father, who was standing alone in the arena contemplating his boots. They all turned sharply, sensing something wrong.

They heard very clearly what Curly Grant had to say. It was said in a voice choked with bewilderment, resentment, and anger.

"*Pop! The money's gone!*"

Wild Bill Grant looked up slowly. "What? What's that you're sayin', son? The—"

"The money! The ten thousand! I put it in a cash box in my dressin' room this afternoon, an' now it's gone!"

20: THE GREEN BOX

CURLY GRANT's dressing room was little more than a closet. It contained table, mirror, wardrobe, and chair. On the table there was an ordinary green metal box. The box was open, and the box was empty.

The Inspector was perhaps sharper than usual. Before leaving the arena he had been called aside by the Commissioner and the Mayor's representative. They had "chatted" for some time. Then the two officials had stamped off. The incident had left Inspector Queen acutely irritable.

"You say you put the dough in this box?" he snarled.

Curly nodded shortly. "It was handed to me by Mr. Comerford, pop's lawyer, this afternoon at the jamboree in the arena. S'pose you heard about that. Afterward I came in here, put the money in this box, an' locked the box. The box was in the drawer here. When I just came in here I found the drawer open, an' the box just like you see it."

"When was the last time you saw the box with the money actually in it, Grant?" rasped the old man.

"When I stowed 'er away this afternoon."

"Were you in here before the performance tonight?"

"No. Didn't have to be. Was dressed fer the show this afternoon."

"Didn't you lock your door?"

Curly's jaw hardened. "No. Never do, by thunder! I know these folks. They're friends o' mine. Wouldn't pull a dirty trick like that on me."

"You're in New York now," said the Inspector dryly, "and not everybody who floats around this dump is a friend of yours. My God, anybody who leaves ten grand lyin' around behind an unlocked door deserves to lose it!" He snatched the box from the table and carefully examined it.

Now Mr. Ellery Queen had until this moment presented the appearance of a slightly astonished codfish. The murder, the vain search for the automatic, and now the theft of Curly Grant's legacy—particularly the theft of Curly Grant's legacy—had left him completely dumfounded, with his mouth witlessly open, as if his brain had received a severe shock; as if, in fact, some jeweled theory had been jarred out of its nice precision by a totally unexpected event.

But habit and a certain resource of resiliency came to his rescue, and a more rational light shone from his eyes. He stepped forward and blinked at the ravished box over his father's shoulder.

It was in effect nothing more than an ordinary little cashbox. Its lid opened upward, double-hinged at the back. But instead of the usual eye-and-flap on the front, this box had two sets of eyes and flaps, and one was on each of the short sides of the box. When the lid was lowered, the flaps fitted over the eyes on the body of the box, and locks could be slipped through the eyes, thus furnishing double protection—a lock on each side.

Now each eye of Curly Grant's box held the ring of a lock, and the locks in both instances were still shut and untouched. The box had been forced open by a much cruder method than breaking the locks. The thief had grasped the locks and twisted them until the strain upon the metal eyes had told and the eyes themselves had given way. The eyes lay on the table, twisted rings still entwined with the closed locks. In each case the eyes had been turned toward the back of the box, as was clear from the convolutions of the twisted metal.

The Inspector put the box down and said grimly to Sergeant Velie: "These dressing rooms were searched for the rod before, Thomas, weren't they?"

"Right, Inspector."

"Well, have the boys go over them again—not for a rod but for the swag. Didn't find ten grand on anybody searched tonight, did you?"

Velie grunted. "Not much."

"Well, by God, nobody can tell me that dough'll disappear like the .25, Thomas.' Raid those dressing rooms!"

Sergeant Velie silently departed. Ellery leaned against the wardrobe, deep in thought, his confusion and stupefaction superseded by a new and apparently invigorating line of thought.

"Yo're wastin' yore time," said Curly defiantly. "You won't find no ten thousand of *my* dollars in these rooms, not by a long shot!"

The Inspector did not reply. And so they waited. Kit sat in the only chair, elbows on her knees, chin cupped in her hands, and stared expressionlessly at the floor.

And then, of course, Sergeant Velie barged triumphantly into the room, a mammoth in the doorway, and flipped something across the room to the table. It landed with a little thud.

They looked at it, startled. It was a sheaf of yellow-backed bills held together by a rubber-band.

"Ha!" exclaimed the Inspector with sour satisfaction. "There's *one* mystery solved, anyway! Where'd you find it, Thomas?"

"In one of the dressing rooms along here."

"Come along," said the Inspector; and dumbly they followed him, astonishment in the eyes of all except Ellery.

.　　.　　.　　.　　.　　.　　.

Sergeant Velie paused by an open door.

"Here she is," he said. "This room." He pointed to a small table, its drawer open and cluttered with unimportant odds and ends of masculine character. "Found it in that unlocked drawer. Right on top. Damn crook didn't even take the trouble to hide the loot," growled Velie.

"Hmm," said the Inspector. "Whose room is this, Grant?"

Curly chuckled hoarsely, to the Queens' amazement, and even Wild Bill uttered a short ugly laugh. As for Kit, she shook her head with weary resignation.

"Ain't found a crook at all," drawled Curly. "You've lost one."

"Lost one? What the deuce d'ye mean by that?"

"This room belonged to One-Arm Woody!"

.　　.　　.　　.　　.　　.　　.

"Woody!" exclaimed the Inspector. "So that's the ticket. One-armed wonder stole the dough and was knocked off before he could get away with it. Now isn't that queer? I don't see. . . . Murder and robbery just couldn't have had anything to do with each other! God, what a mess!" He groaned and shook his head. "Here, Grant, you're sure these are the same bills that lawyer gave your son this afternoon?"

The old showman took the sheaf and counted the bills. There were ten. "Look the same. I couldn't say for sure. Comerford didn't bring the money with him from Cheyenne. I had it in trust, an' Mars gave me the cash—saved me the trouble o' goin' to the bank. I gave 'im a check on m'own bank."

"Thomas, get Tony Mars."

The Sergeant returned with the haggard promoter very shortly. Mars examined the bills. "Tell you in a minute," he muttered. "I always keep a raft of cash in my safe upstairs, an' I've got the serial numbers somewhere on me. . . ." He fished in his wallet. "Here it is! Check 'em, Bill." He read the numbers slowly aloud. And Grant nodded with each number.

"Fine!" said the Inspector. "I mean—terrible. It's more of a mess than ever. Here's your money, Mr. Curly Grant; and for the love of heaven hang on to it, will you?"

. . . .

In the small hours, with dawn a hair's-breadth away, the Queens—that normally affectionate father and son—were back in their Eighty-seventh Street apartment. Djuna was fast asleep and they did not disturb him. The old man pottered into the kitchen and brewed some coffee. They drank it in silence. Then Ellery paced the livingroom rug, and the Inspector with ashen face sat before the fire; and for long hours they remained that way—long after the sun was up and there was a stir of morning traffic in the street below.

A blank wall at the end of a dark alley. . . . Every living soul in the *Colosseum* had been searched; every square inch had been gone over. And with no result. The automatic had not been found, as if after exploding the cartridge which had buried itself in Woody's body the wielder of the weapon, like Merlin, had caused it to vanish by merely wishing it away.

And so the Inspector sat, and Ellery pounded up and down, and there seemed nothing to say.

But gradually a look of relief spread over Ellery's drawn features as normal intelligence recovered from the shock; and once he even intoned a vague quotation as he chuckled to himself.

Then Djuna appeared and bundled them both off to bed.

21: ON THE SCREEN

ELLERY AWOKE to the accompaniment of a vigorous shaking.

"Git up!" shouted Djuna in his ear. "There's a feller here."

Ellery blinked the drowse out of his eyes and groped for his dressing gown.

The visitor proved to be a brash young man bearing a large manila envelope. "From Major Kirby, Mr. Queen," he said. "Just printed 'em, he said to tell you."

He tossed the envelope on the table and left, whistling.

Ellery tore open the brown packet. Inside were a dozen damp, curly photographic prints. They depicted the last earthly moments of the late unlamented One-Arm Woody.

"Ah," said Ellery with satisfaction. "That Major chap's a prince, Djuna, simply priceless. He anticipates your every wish. Hmm." He examined the series of infinitesimally differing photographs with scrupulous attention. . . . It was amazing how faithfully these pictures coincided with those earlier pictures of Buck Horne's demise. Except for the figure of Woody himself, with its distinguishing characteristic of the left-arm stump, these might be the same photographs the Queens had examined in the Major's projection room a month before.

Again the camera had caught horse and rider at the instant of the bullet's impact. Again the horse's brawny length was parallel to the track, and again the series showed Woody leaning to the left as his horse crept by micrometric degrees around the northeastern turn of the oval.

"Nothing *wünderlich* there," muttered Ellery to himself. "An exact duplication of conditions. Naturally the phenomena would repeat themselves. Horsemen obey natural laws—I hope." He spent some time studying the key photograph—that in which, clearly, Woody had died. In the head-on view of the photograph, the one-armed rider's body was leaning a sharp thirty degrees off the perpendicular toward the southern side of the arena. Quite as Buck Horne's had leaned. Due to the mottled pattern of Woody's ponyskin vest and the obtrusion of his left-arm stump, it was difficult to make out the bullet hole. But from the expression on the man's face it was quite apparent in which picture he had died.

Ellery put the photographs thoughtfully away in his secretary, and went about the mechanical business of consuming Djuna's breakfast.

"When did the Inspector leave?" he mumbled out of a mouthful of shirred egg.

"Long time ago," asserted Djuna. "Say, when you goin' to turn'm up?"

"Turn whom up?"

"The murd'rer! . . . Goes around murd'rin' people," said Djuna darkly. "Seems to me he ought to fry."

"Fry?"

"In th' electric chair! You goin' to let him git away with it?"

"Am I God?" demanded Ellery. "Djuna, you place the weight

of a fearful responsibility on my frail shoulders. And yet I think—no, I know—that the race is quite run. Well, the coffee, old son. Did dad say he'd pop in at the projection room this afternoon?"

. . . .

Early afternoon found Ellery seated in the projection room of Major Kirby's newsreel offices by the side of a stoop-shouldered Inspector with circled eyes and at least half a dozen newly etched wrinkles. Major Kirby had disappeared for a moment.

"Maybe we'll see something in these newsreel shots they took last night," grunted the Inspector out of a vast discouragement.

"The .25 hasn't been found?"

The old man stared at the white screen. "I tell you it's just not possible. . . . No."

"I'll admit that's the prime poser now," murmured Ellery. "It has a simple explanation. I'm convinced of it. Apparently everything humanly possible has been done, and still. . . . Did Dr. Prouty confirm his hasty diagnosis about the angle of the Woody bullet?"

"This mornin'. As he said. Downward angle, practically like the Horne bullet."

Major Kirby came in smiling. "Ready, gentlemen?"

The Inspector nodded sourly.

"Shoot, Joe." And the Major seated himself by Ellery.

The room darkened at once and sounds came out of the amplifier near the screen. On the screen flashed the newsreel insignia of the Major's company, and then the first tide announcing the second murder in four weeks at the *Colosseum* "under exactly the same circumstances."

They watched in silence. The scenes and sounds flowed on. They saw Grant, heard his announcement, saw the opening of the eastern gate, the entrance of Woody and the troupe, the short dash around the track, the halt, heard Grant's further announcement and signal, Woody's answering shot, saw the beginning of the charge. . . . It was all very clear and very dull. Not even the sight of Woody falling to the track, of the trampling confusion of horses stamping over the body, of the wild scenes that followed, aroused them from their lethargy.

And when it was all over and the lights flashed on again, they sat wearily contemplating the blank screen.

"Well," said the Inspector with a groan, "that turned out a frost! Might have known. Sorry, Major, to've bothered you. I guess we'll just have to resign ourselves. . . ."

But there was something profoundly agitated in Ellery's eyes of a sudden. He turned sharply to Kirby. "Was it my imagination, Major, or is this film longer than the one you ran for us after the Horne affair?"

"Eh?" The Major stared. "Oh! Much longer, Mr. Queen. At least twice as long."

"How's that?"

"Well, you see, when we sat in here a month ago and took a look at the Horne scenes, you were seeing the fully prepared theatre version of the newsreel. That is, fully cut, edited, titled, assembled, and so on. But this is just a working print. Uncut."

Ellery sat up straighter. "Would you mind elucidating? I'm not quite sure I grasp the niceties of the difference."

"What the deuce has that to do with it?" demanded the Inspector in an aggrieved tone. "Suppose we did—"

"Please, dad. Eh, Major?"

"Why," said the Major, "when we shoot a scene we film practically everything that happens. That consumes a lot of celluloid—much more than we could possibly confine within the limits of a newsreel, which of course contains perhaps six or eight different subjects in the same reel. So when the film is developed and dried here, our cutter gets busy. He's the fellow who goes over the film frame by frame and cuts out whatever he thinks unnecessary or less necessary than the rest. Snips the superfluous footage away, you see. Then he takes what's left—the meat of the film—and assembles them in a short, snappy, episodic film version of what took place."

Ellery blinked at the white screen. "And that means," he said in a curiously unstable voice, "that what we saw in the Horne reel in this room didn't represent *everything* your crew photographed on the night of the Horne murder?"

"Why, certainly not," said the Major, surprised.

"Oh, Lord!" groaned Ellery, seizing his head. "That's what comes of being unscientific. By heaven, this almost converts me to rule by technologists. There we may suppose such elementary mechanical knowledge as the function and routine of a film-cutter will be common. . . . Dad, do you realize—! Major, what in the name of Moses happens to the excess film that your cutter clips off the original celluloid?"

"Well," said Major Kirby, with a puzzled frown, "I can't see what—The old saw is that it's left on the cutting-room floor. Actually, we save it. There are miles and miles of that cut stuff stowed away in our library. We—"

"Enough, enough!" shouted Ellery, springing to his feet. "What an ignoramus. . . . Major, I want to see those deleted scenes!"

"Easy," said the Major. "You'll have to give us a little time, though. Cement the scenes together. They'll be jerky. . . ."

"We'll wait all night if necessary," said Ellery grimly.

.   .   .   .

But it was necessary to wait in the projection room little more than an hour. The Inspector, who had left divers tasks dangling at Headquarters, spent most of the hour on the telephone. Ellery spent the hour in consuming cigarets and enforcing a severe patience upon his leaping pulses. Then the Major returned, signaled to the operator, and the tiny theatre darkened for the second time.

There was no sound this time. The scenes were, as the Major had predicted, jerky and quite without continuity. But the Queens watched this extraordinary film as if it represented the high-water mark of the cinema art.

It was most confusing at first, as if some madman had assembled the scenes, the lack of continuity an echo of his own disordered brain. A few glimpses of the pandemonium in the bowl . . . these recurred frequently, showing scurrying thousands in the audience, distant shots of police attempting to preserve order, craning necks, staring eyes, unrhythmic mass movements of the audience which seemed inspired by a demented director whose aim was a nightmarish chaos in the handling of enormous numbers of supernumeraries. There was a long scene which showed the deleted details of Curly Grant's dexterity with his revolver. Then, unexpectedly, a long shot of the Mars box—apparently taken with a telescopic lens, for the figures were quite distinct. Ellery and the Inspector saw themselves sitting quietly; and Djuna, and Kit Horne, and Mara Gay and Tommy Black, and Tony Mars, and at the rear Julian Hunter. This was before the death of Horne, and the scene was placid. . . . They returned to this scene a little later, and found themselves watching themselves apparently only a moment before the fatal shot. Tony Mars had just risen, perhaps in excitement, and for a second or two the seated figure of Julian Hunter was blotted out. Then Mars moved, and

Hunter was still there, quietly seated. . . . Some of the scenes were "atmospheric"—apparently scrapped by the cutter because of their relative unimportance. One of these showed bow-legged Hank Boone, that illustrious son of the plains, scuttling after the restive horses just after the murder; Boone led them one by one to the trough where, under the spell of water, they magically quieted; one horse was balky and refused to drink; he furnished a diversion, rearing and bucking with fine abandon. He was a magnificent old stallion with intelligent eyes; Boone slapped his flanks smartly with a quirt and a cowboy pushed into the field of the camera and snatched the whip from Boone's hand, patting the horse and quieting him in short order, whereupon a detective clumped into the scene and ordered the cowboy—from his gestures—curtly back into the group; and Boone, staggering a little, continued his task. . . . There was one startling shot of Wild Bill Grant, half his body caught by the camera at the time of the murder; perhaps a moment or so later, for he was urging his mount furiously from the center of the arena across the dirt to the track upon which the rearing, milling horses ground the fallen man's body to mash. . . . There were several flashes of "persons of prominence" who had prevailed upon the newsreel company on the plea of "unfortunate and ill-advised publicity" to delete those portions of the reel which revealed their faces. And much to-do about the later stages of the investigation:

The Queens sat in the projection room for almost three-quarters of an hour; and when the lights came on suddenly and the screen went blank, neither they nor the Major had anything to say. Ellery's inspiration, it appeared, had proved barren. And the Inspector, who considered an hour of his precious time had been cruelly wasted, rose and jabbed such an inordinate ration of snuff up his nostrils that he was seized by a fit of sneezing which brought crimson to his face and tears to his eyes.

"*Tchu!*" he exploded in a last blast, and wiped his nose viciously. Then he glared at Ellery. "And that's that. Ellery, I'm going."

Ellery's eyes were closed, and his long lean legs reached comfortably under the seat in front of him.

"I'm going, I said," repeated the Inspector huffily.

"I heard you the first time, honorable ancestor," said Ellery in a clear voice, and he opened his eyes. Then he rose slowly and shook himself like a man coming out of a dream. His father and the Major stared at him.

He began to smile, and he put his hand out to Kirby. "Do you know what you've done today, Major?"

Kirby took the hand bewilderedly. "What *I've* done?"

"You've restored my faith in the movies. What's today? Sunday? There's a day for restoration of faith! Almost makes you believe in old Jahweh, the Mosaic God. No, that would make it *Shabboth*, wouldn't it? I believe I'm all mixed up. Small wonder!" And he grinned broadly, pumping the astonished Major's hand up and down like an ansa. "Major, good day and a benediction upon the head of whoever invented the cinema. May he be thrice blessed. . . . Dad, don't stand gawping! There's work to do. And *such* work!"

22: THE VANISHING AMERICAN

"Where are we going?" gasped the Inspector as Ellery hustled him across Broadway, westbound.

"The *Colosseum.* . . . No. by Jove, it's like a fairytale. . . . Now I *know!*"

But the Inspector was too occupied matching his little hopping steps to Ellery's hungry stride to ask what his son knew.

The *Colosseum,* closed on two counts—Sunday and the police ban—seemed lively enough despite the handicaps. Guarded by detectives who were under strict orders, there was nevertheless no *ukase* against accessibility; the Queens learned at once that most of the troupe were in the building somewhere, and that Grant himself had come in not an hour before. Ellery steered the Inspector toward the nether regions.

Then they visited the great amphitheatre. It was empty.

They made a round of the dressing rooms. Members in good standing were present and accounted for, for the most part dawdling, smoking, and making conversation.

Ellery Queen found Mr. Hank (Dan'l) Boone in a dressing room cloudy with smoke and redolent of whisky.

"Boone!" cried Ellery from the doorway. "Want to see you."

"Huh?" croaked the little cowboy; and wearily swung about.

"Oh. Th'—th' sheriff, b'jinks. C-come on in, sheriff. Have li'l snifter?"

"Go on along, Dan'l," growled one of the cowboys. "An' don't be drunker'n ya have to."

So Boone tottered obediently to his feet and waddled to the door. "Sheriff, I'm yore man," he said with gravity. "'Portant?"

"Might be," smiled Ellery. "Come along, Boone. I've a number of nice bright questions to ask you."

Boone wagged his head and staggered along by Ellery's side. The Inspector stood waiting for them at a turn of the corridor.

"How well," asked Ellery quietly, "do you recall the night Buck Horne was shot?"

"My Gawd!" exclaimed Boone. "You startin' *that* all over ag'in? Mister, I'll never forget it long's I live!"

"Oh, one month suits me perfectly. Now you remember Inspector Queen ordered you to take care of the horses after Horne was shot—in the arena, I mean?"

"Shore do." Boone was wary now, and his little blood-flecked eyes flickered from Ellery to the Inspector and back again. He seemed strangely uneasy.

"Do you recall exactly what happened?"

Boone wiped his unsteady chin with vague fingers. "Seems like I do," he muttered. "Took the horses to water, an'—an'—"

"And what?"

"Why, jes' took the hosses to water."

"Oh, no," smiled Ellery. "There was something more than that."

"Was there?" Boone scraped his jaw. "Now ain't that a— Saaay! Shore, shore! One o' the hosses—piebald stallion, 'twas— got ornery, the critter! Wouldn't dip 'is muzzle. I had to whack him one acrost th' flanks."

"Ah. And what happened then?"

"One o' the waddies, he run up an' took the whup away from me."

"Why?"

"Musta been a mite pie-eyed," mumbled Boone. "Never oughten to whup a hoss, Mister. An' that was a danged fine animal—*Injun*, 'twas. Buck Horne's ole trick movie hoss. Miller, he—"

"Oh, Miller was the cowboy who took the quirt away from you?"

"Yeah, Benjy Miller. New hand—feller with the gosh-awful burn on 'is whiskers. He was ridin' *Injun* that night. Buck was up on Kit Horne's *Rawhide*. Felt sorrier'n a cock-eyed cow in pasture with two crops o' clover to nibble at an' not a way o' tellin' which was the sweeter-lookin'. Mister," mourned Boone, "I never done that before, whuppin' a good hoss. . . ."

"Yes, yes," said Ellery absently. "You were upset. Be kind to animals, and all that. Are the rodeo horses always kept in the stables in this building?"

"Hey? Naw. Stables here 're fer the show. Keep the hosses in th' buildin' jest b'fore, durin', an' after the show fer shoein', rabbin' down, an' so on," said Boone. "After th' shows we take 'em over to that big liv'ry stable on Tenth Avenoo for beddin' down."

"I see. By the way, where's Miller? Have you seen him today?"

"He's aroun' some'eres. See'm on'y a couple hours ago. I—"

"Fine, old timer. Thanks a lot. Come along, dad," and Ellery hastened off with the Inspector, leaving Dan'l Boone staring wordlessly after them.

.   .   .   .

A number of members of the troupe had seen and spoken to Miller that day, it turned out, but the man was not to be found. He had actually come into the *Colosseum* with a group of the others, but after a time had dropped out of sight.

The Queens repaired to Wild Bill Grant's office above, and found the showman in scowling contemplation of his feet on the desk. He looked at them sourly when they came in.

"Well," he growled, "what the hell's eatin' you now?"

"The hunger for a little information, Mr. Grant," said Ellery affably. "Have you seen that man Miller in the last few minutes?"

Grant started, then sank back and sucked at a cigar. "Who?"

"Miller. Benjy Miller. Chap with the scarred face."

"Oh, *him*." Grant stretched his thick arms slowly. "Saw him aroun' t'day," he said with indifference. "Why?"

"Have you any idea where he is *now?*" asked Ellery.

Grant lost his air of indifference. He swung his feet to the floor, and frowned heavily. "What's the big idea? Why all this sudden int'rest in my troupe, Mr. Queen?"

"Only in Miller, I assure you," smiled Ellery. "Well, well, sir, where is he?"

Grant hesitated. His eyes shifted. "Don't know," he said finally.

Ellery glanced at his father, who began to show signs of interest. "Do you know," murmured Ellery, settling back comfortably in a chair and crossing his legs, "I've been intending to ask you something for a long time now. But it slipped my mind until a few minutes ago. Mr. Grant, how well did Miller know Buck Horne?"

"Well? Well?" growled Grant. "How the tin-horn devil should *I* know? Never saw the critter b'fore in my whole life. Buck recommended him, an' that's all I c'n tellya."

"How do you know Buck recommended him? On Miller's say-so?"

Grant broke into a savage chuckle. "Hell, no. I'm no pilgrim, man. He give me a note from Buck, that's how I know."

The Inspector started. "A note from Horne!" he shrieked. "Why in the name of a merciful God didn't you tell us that a month ago? Why, you said—"

"Tell you?" Grant bunched his chaparral brows. "Ya didn't ask. I said he come from Buck, an' I tole no lie. Didn't ask for no note, did ya? I—"

"Well, well," murmured Ellery hastily, "let's not wrangle over it. Have you that note about anywhere, Mr. Grant?"

"In m'duds somewhere," said Grant, beginning to poke about in his pockets. "I know I—Here 'tis! There, read that," he growled, tossing a crumpled sheet of paper across his desk, "an' see if I put anythin' over on you."

They read the note. It was written in blotty ink on a piece of Hotel Barclay stationery, in a wide windy scrawl. It ran:

"Dear Bill:

"This is Benjy Miller, an old friend. Needs a job badly—had hard luck in the Southwest somewhere, I guess. Drifted into town and hunted me up. So give him a job, will you? He's a smart hand with a rope, right enough, and a good rider.

"I'm staking him to a few dollars, but what he really needs is a job. Hasn't got a horse, so let him use one of mine, *Injun,* my old Hollywood standby. I'm using Kit's for luck. Thanks—

Buck."

"That Horne's fist, Grant?" demanded the Inspector suspiciously.

"Sure is."

"You'd swear to it?"

"I'll let *you* swear to it," said Grant coldly; and, rising, he went to a filing cabinet and returned with a legal document. It proved to be a contract between Grant and Horne. At the bottom of the last sheet were the signatures of the parties. The Inspector compared the scrawled "Buck Horne" of the contract with the handwriting of the note.

He returned the contract without speaking.

"On the level?" asked Ellery.

The Inspector nodded.

"So you don't know where Miller is now, eh, Mr. Grant?" said Ellery pleasantly.

Grant rose and kicked his chair. *"Hell's fire!"* he shouted. "What d'ye think I am to my employees—a wet-nurse? How th' hell should I know where he is?"

"Tut, tut," murmured Ellery. "Such temper." And he rose and strolled from the room. The Inspector remained for a moment to converse with Mr. Wild Bill Grant. Whatever it was he said, it must have given him satisfaction, for when he came out he was actually—for the first time in days—grinning; and from the room Ellery could hear Mr. Wild Bill Grant engaged in kicking Tony Mars's furniture.

·   ·   ·   ·   ·   ·   ·

They questioned the detectives on duty. Had any of them seen a cowboy with a badly burned face leaving the *Colosseum?* One man, it seemed, had. Two hours or so before, Miller had quit the building. The detective had not noticed which way he had gone.

The Queens departed post-haste for the Hotel Barclay, the troupe's headquarters.

Miller was not there. No one could be found who had seen him enter the hotel that afternoon.

By this time the Inspector was alarmed, and Ellery too showed signs of uneasiness.

"It begins to look," muttered the Inspector as they stood helplessly in the lobby, "as if—"

Ellery was whistling nervously to himself. "Yes, yes, I know. As if Miller's slipped through our fingers. Strange, very strange. I'm afraid—Tell you what! What are you going to do now, dad?"

"I'm going back to h.q.," said the Inspector grimly, "and start the ball rolling. I'll find Miller and sweat him if it's the last thing I do. Why the deuce should he take it on the lam if he's just one of the boys?"

"Not so fast. Because a man drops out of sight for three hours isn't justification for calling the hounds out. He may have dropped into a speakeasy, or a movie. Well, do what you think best, dad. I think I'll stay here. . . . No, I'm going back to the *Colosseum*."

.   .   .   .

At six o'clock, in the fading light, the Queens met again at the *Colosseum*.

"Dad, what are you doing here?" exclaimed Ellery.

"Same thing you're doing."

"But I'm fiddling around. . . . Have any luck?"

"Well," said the Inspector cautiously, "it looks as if we've struck something."

"No!"

"Miller's gone."

"Definitely?"

"Looks that way right now. I've had the detail cover all his known hangouts since he hit the city—aren't many. The whole troupe's accounted for, except Miller. And none of 'em knows where he is. Last seen around two or three o'clock, leaving the building. Then he dropped out of sight."

"Did he take anything with him?"

"Didn't have much to take except the clothes on his back. It's on the teletype now. Being watched for. We've spread the alarm. Oh, we'll get him."

Ellery opened his mouth, and closed it again without saying anything.

"I've been digging into Mr. Miller's history a little," said the Inspector. "And d'ye know what I found?"

"What?" asked Ellery, startled.

"Nothing, that's what. A blind trail. Can't find out a darned thing about the guy. He's a mystery. Well, he won't be much longer. I think we're on the right track now." He chuckled. "Miller! And Grant's tied up in it somewhere, mark my words."

"I've got all I can do to mark my own," said Ellery. Then he grinned quizzically. "How about the downward direction of the bullets that killed your two dead men?"

The Inspector's chuckle died, and again he looked unhappy. "Oh, that," he said. "That sticks in my craw, I'll admit. . . ." He threw his hands up in despair. "We'll cross that bridge when we come to it. I'm going back to Centre Street."

23: THE MIRACLE

ELLERY CONTINUED to wander about the *Colosseum*. In his wanderings, which were for the moment aimless—being devoted merely to the expenditure of animal energy while his brain was busy with a Brobdingnagian mental jigsaw—he chanced across the large metallic gentleman of few words who was Inspector Queen's right hand. Sergeant Velie in his stubborn way was engaged in mining. He was attempting to dig nuggets of fact out of what was obviously a salted mine. The facts he unearthed were no facts at all, but fancies. If there were facts beneath the terrain, they were extraordinarily well hidden.

Wild Bill Grant's troupe of performers sat about with solemn countenances, nodding submissively at every word.

"Trained seals!" mumbled Velie at last, without changing expression. "Got no minds of your own. Can't you talk without having to get the okay from your boss? Where's this rat Miller, you bunch of bow-legged, four-flushin' blowhards from the West?"

Their eyes began to flash.

Ellery, intrigued, paused to watch the performance.

There was a premonitory sigh, like the faint grumbling of

a volcano in the labor-pains of eruption. Sergeant Velie smiled coldly and continued to address them.

He derided their lingo. He questioned the legitimacy of their birth, and the chastity of their mothers by inference. He sneered at their morals. He laughed outright at their horses. He called them "stinking sheep-herders," than which there was no more awful accusation. He assailed their code of honor. He even introduced a faint note of doubt concerning their manhood, in the case of the males, and their femininity in the case of the women.

In the pandemonium that ensued, Ellery discovered—among other things—that Sergeant Velie was in his turn a particularly evil-smelling type of coyote, that he was plumb full of rattlesnake juice, that he was the double-distilled son of a pediculous half-breed and a female goat, that he was a poisoner of water-holes, that his heart was full of cactus thorns and his mouth as dry as alkali, that he was slicker than cowlick and lower than a snake's belly, and finally that he deserved no less protean fate than to be "staked out"—a peculiarly Western form of amusement in which the salient features were the removal of the victim's eyelids, the pegging of one's wrists and legs to the ground, and the deposit of one's residuary carcass, face to the glaring sun, upon an enormous anthill.

Ellery listened with a delighted smile.

He also learned, among the more blasphemous accusations that rattled about the Sergeant's unmoved head, that they had not known Benjy Miller well, that he had been an "onfriendly cuss," that they cared nothing for Benjy Miller, and that Sergeant Velie and Benjy Miller might, singly or en double, go to hell.

Ellery sighed and moved on up the corridor.

·   ·   ·   ·   ·   ·   ·

He prowled about quietly until, with the aid of judicious inquiries, he found the vanished Miller's dressing room. It was like all the others, a mere hole in the wall equipped with a table, mirror, chair, and wardrobe. He sat down in the chair, placed his cigaret case conveniently on the table, lighted a pill, and devoted himself to thought.

Six cigarets later he muttered: "I begin to see. Yes. . . . Would be consistent with a special psychology in the case of. . . ." He sucked his lip. "But those searches. . . ."

He sprang to his feet, crushed the cigaret out on the floor, and went to the door. He looked about. Ten feet away a tall cowboy was stumping along, talking to himself in an angry undertone.

"Hi, there!" cried Ellery.

The cowboy slued his head about and squinted sourly. It was the gentleman known as Downs.

"Huh?"

"I say, old man," said Ellery, "did that fellow Miller occupy this dressing room by himself?"

Downs drawled: "Hell, no. Who'd ya think he is—Wild Bill hisself? Dan'l Boone divvied this room with 'im."

Ellery blinked. "Ah, Boone. That little chap seems to be a child of destiny. Would you mind getting him for me, like a good fellow?"

"Run yer own errands," suggested Downs, and stamped off.

"Surly brute," muttered Ellery, and went off in search of Boone. He found the little man communing with himself in an otherwise empty room, seated dolorously on the floor, short legs doubled under him in an Indian-chief attitude, and rocking slowly back and forth with the unconscious rhythm of a graybeard before the Wailing Wall. In his hand there were the fragments of what seemed to have been a stone arrowhead.

"Allus said," he was groaning to himself aloud, "that damn palomino scrounchin' on my Injun arrowhead started this jamboree. . . . Hey?" He looked up, a dazed little owl.

Ellery darted in, yanked little Boone to his feet, and hurried him back along the corridor to the room he had been thinking in.

"Whut—whut—" spluttered Boone.

Ellery plumped him in the lone chair and leveled a long forefinger at his shrinking figure. "Miller was your roommate, wasn't he?"

"Huh? Shore, shore, Mr. Queen!"

"You saw him today, didn't you, Boone?"

"Huh? Shore. Didn't I tell ya—" Boone's eyes were round as mescal buttons, and he opened and shut his mouth like a goldfish.

Ellery smacked his lips with satisfaction. "Did Miller go into this room today?"

"Shore, Mr. Queen!"

"Alone?"

"Reckon!"

Ellery began to whistle a difficult tune from *Lakmé*, the intricacies of which absorbed his attention for some time. Meanwhile he was gazing about the room speculatively. Still whistling, he went to the table and jerked open the drawer. There was a clutter of odds and ends inside, none of which seemed to interest him after a casual inspection. Boone watched in bewilderment.

Ellery went to the wardrobe and opened the door. Its interior was hung with various colorful garments, all of them from their small size the property of Boone. But Ellery, poking about among them, turned up one costume which from its large dimensions must have been worn by the vanished Miller for the rodeo performances. "Didn't even take his duds away," muttered Ellery, feeling through the pockets of the jeans.

"Weren't his'n," said Boone eagerly. "B'longed to th' show."

Ellery stiffened; he had felt something hard in one of the pockets. A look of remarkable intelligence came over his face, and then vanished as he wheeled sharply, ordered Boone to remain where he was, and ran to the door.

"Sergeant!" he shouted. "Sergeant Velie!" The name echoed down the corridor.

The good Sergeant popped out of one of the dressing rooms, tense and alert. "Yeah?" he cried. "What's up, Mr. Queen?" and he lumbered swiftly up the corridor. Heads poked out of rooms; Ellery drew Velie quickly into the Boone-Miller cubicle and shut the door.

Velie looked from the stricken figure of Boone to the open wardrobe. "What's the trouble?"

"Did you search this room last night, Sergeant?" asked Ellery softly.

"Sure."

"The wardrobe, the clothes inside?"

"Sure."

"Did you search it again this afternoon?"

A pucker appeared between Velie's eyes. "No. Meant to later. Didn't get round to it."

Ellery went silently to the wardrobe and brought out the jeans he had been feeling a few moments before. He held it high. "Did you look through these last night, Sergeant?"

Velie's eyes flickered. "No. Weren't here last night."

"Miller was wearin' them jeans last night!" cried Boone suddenly.

"Ah," said Ellery, lowering his arm. "Then that accounts for it very satisfactorily. Who searched Miller himself, Sergeant?"

"I did. And the rest o' the gang, too." The Sergeant's reptilian eyes were narrowed. "Why?"

"You didn't find anything on Miller?" persisted Ellery gently.

"No!"

"Don't take such a belligerent tone, Sergeant," murmured Ellery. "I'm completely satisfied that you're a competent searcher. If you didn't find anything on Miller last night, it's because there wasn't anything to find. Excellent! Then it was brought into this room today, and placed in Miller's discarded jeans."

"*What* was put in Miller's pants?" growled Velie.

Calmly, with the certainty of omniscience, Ellery wrapped a handkerchief about his right hand and slipped his hand into the pocket. But he did not withdraw it at once. He said sharply: "Who's been inside the *Colosseum* today, Sergeant, besides the rank and file, and Grant?"

Velie licked his lips. "Grant's son. Kit Horne. I think I saw Mars and Black, the pug."

"Not Hunter or Mara Gay?"

"No."

Ellery drew his hand out of the pocket of Miller's jeans.

·   ·   ·   ·   ·   ·   ·

Whereupon a veritable miracle occurred. For his hand emerged holding a very tangible little piece of reality—an object for which he, Sergeant Velie, Inspector Queen, and the assembled detective strength of the New York City Police Department had been searching for weeks. It was something moreover which had not been found in Boone's room until this moment for the remarkably simple reason that it had not been in Boone's room during previous searches. Obviously, then, it had been brought to Boone's room and Miller's jeans *after* the last thorough search.

And the last thorough search, on the authority of Sergeant Velie, had been conducted the night before, directly after the murder of Woody.

That much, at least, was clear.

Dan'l Boone uttered a gasping little cry. And Sergeant Velie stiffened.

Ellery's hand lightly held a small, flat, innocent-looking little .25 automatic pistol.

24: THE VERDICT

"WELL, I'LL—BE—DAMNED," breathed Sergeant Velie gustily. "What the hoppin' hell do you know about that!"

"Let's not be too sanguine," said Ellery, gazing almost with fondness at the little weapon. "There's a mathematical possibility that this isn't the right one. On the other hand. . . ." He fell silent, and began with scrupulous care to swathe the automatic in the folds of his handkerchief. Then he dropped it into his pocket.

"Now, boys," he said genially, and his eyes glinted in the direction of the silent Boone, "I want one thing understood at once."

"Yeah?" whispered Boone, licking his lips. Sergeant Velie said nothing.

"Boone, old horse-nurse," said Ellery, "do you value your carcass?"

"Huh?"

Ellery crossed the floor and placed his hand on the little cowboy's shoulder. "Can you keep your mouth very tightly shut?"

"I—uh—guess so, Mr. Queen."

"Let's see you try."

Boone goggled, and his mouth slowly closed.

"Excellent for a beginning," said Ellery crisply, and there was no mirth in his eyes. "Boone, I give you my word. If you so much as breathe a solitary syllable about this—about our finding this automatic—I swear I'll see you behind bars. Do you understand?"

Boone licked his lips again. "Got ya, Mr. Queen."

"Good." Ellery straightened. "You may go back to the others now." Boone rose and wobbled to the door.

"Remember what I said, Boone," said Ellery . . .

The little cowboy nodded once, and disappeared.

"I don't have to warn you, Sergeant," went on Ellery quickly, "that I don't want this to get about."

Velie looked hurt.

"To *anyone*."

"Not the Inspector, either?"

"No, no." Ellery frowned. "I think that's best. Let me do the talking. This little affair is entirely between you and me. I'm certain Boone will keep quiet. . . . By the way, what was the procedure today with visitors to the *Colosseum?* They weren't searched on their way in, were they?"

"Only on the way out."

"I see. Yes, of course. Very convenient, I must say." Ellery poked his elbow affectionately into Sergeant Velie's laminated ribs and marched, humming, from the dressing room.

.   .   .   .

He made his way quickly to Grant's office. The old showman was still there, staring at the wall in the falling gloom.

He looked up. "Huh. Back again, hey?"

"Back in the approved frontal position," chuckled Ellery. "Sorry to intrude. May I use your telephone?"

"Go ahead."

Ellery consulted a directory, then called a number. "Connect me with Major Kirby, please. . . . Major? Ellery Queen again. . . . No, no more previews, Major. . . . Ha, ha—yes! . . . Uh—Major, are you very busy? . . . I see. Then perhaps you can make it. I should very much like to have you meet me in the lobby of Police Headquarters in half an hour. . . . Good of you. Hop on it!"

Ellery hung up, faintly smiling. Wild. Bill Grant's chair creaked a little.

Ellery said: "Thanks, Mr. Grant," with the utmost cheerfulness, and left the office.

. . . .

A half-hour later he confronted two silent men in the laboratory of the Bureau of Ballistics at Police Headquarters. Major Kirby was breathing hard, as from a brisk walk. Lieutenant Knowles looked inquisitive.

"Glad you made it," said Ellery to the Major. "Not really necessary, I suppose, but you've been in on this from the beginning and I didn't want to be hoggish. It's really due you, this climactic part of the fun." He took from his pocket the object wrapped in his handkerchief. Very carefully he undid the folds.

"The .25!" cried Major Kirby, with a sharp intake of breath.

"*A* .25," corrected Ellery gently. "The purpose of this conclave, gentlemen, is to establish whether we are justified in using the definite rather than the indefinite article."

"I'll be blasted," grinned Lieutenant Knowles. "Where'd you find it?"

"In a most unlikely place, Lieutenant," chuckled Ellery. "Don't be afraid to handle it. I've already had it tested for fingerprints and there aren't any." He shrugged. "Proceed, *mes amis.* Test for bore-marks. End this really unbearable suspense." And he himself breathed rather more quickly than seemed necessary.

Lieutenant Knowles picked up the weapon, hefted it thoughtfully, and then withdrew the magazine. There was no necessity for excessive care; this little Colt arm was equipped with a "safety disconnecter" which automatically broke all connection between the trigger and sear upon withdrawal of the magazine. The magazine was empty. And there was no cartridge in the chamber. He looked up inquiringly.

"Yes," murmured Ellery, "unloaded when I found it. Teeth pulled. Not really important, you know."

Lieutenant Knowles loaded the automatic, adjusted his target, pulled the trigger without fanfare while Ellery dodged the falling shells spewing out of the ejector, and removed the exploded slugs from the testing target. Each bullet was imbedded in a blackish wad of burnt powder and grease.

Knowles selected one after some scrutiny of the seven he had discharged and, going to his laboratory table, carefully cleaned it. Then he went to a file and after some exploration returned with two bullets.

"From Horne and Woody," he remarked; and sat down before his comparison microscope. "I established, you know, with the help of the Major, that both were shot from the same gun. So I can use either of these for comparison. Well, we'll find out soon enough."

Major Kirby moved nearer the table.

Lieutenant Knowles set one of the bullets from the file on a stage of the microscope, and the bullet he had just selected from those discharged in the laboratory on the second of the twin stages. He began to fuss with his instrument. Satisfied that he had jockeyed the bullets into the same focus, he manipulated a wheel which caused the images to move together and merge.

When he had completed this operation, he was peering through the eyepiece of the microscope at a single image. The image was that of a whole bullet; actually, it was composed of the two left sides of the bullets, so juxtaposed that they seemed to form a whole.

He peered intently, then raised his head and beckoned the Major. Kirby eagerly looked through the eye piece.

Ellery watched them with, an anxious expression on his face.

"Well, see for yourself," said Major Kirby at last, raising his head; and Ellery took his place at the instrument.

He saw the bullet greatly magnified, and was surprised to note the wealth, of detail brought out by the 'scope. It was like examining Tycho through a powerful astronomical telescope. There were actually valleys, hills, craters—it was like a lunar landscape. But the really astonishing feature of the exhibit was the similitude of the two sides of the image. Crater for crater, valley for valley, hill for hill, the two sides seemed identical. If there were infinitesimal differences caused by the minute variations of bullet-contour or firing conditions, they were not perceptible to his eye.

He straightened up. "So that's the gun, eh?" he said slowly.

"Pretty sure of it," said Lieutenant Knowles. "In fact, I'm positive. Be a terrific coincidence if two bullets from different barrels showed such similarity. Impossible!"

"Why not try the universal?" suggested Major Kirby.

"I'm going to. Universal molecular 'scope," explained Knowles to Ellery, "will prove or disprove it beyond doubt. Equipped with vernier—facilities for microscopic measurement. Be a minute."

He removed one bullet from the stage of the comparison microscope and placed it on the stage of another instrument. Studying the grooves through the eyepiece, he calculated the angle of pitch—the angle the grooves made with the bullet's axis—and set down his result in degrees and minutes. He measured the depth of the valleys, which, were scratches. He used a micrometer to determine the distance between various marks on the bullet. . . . When he was quite finished with the first slug, he laid it aside, put his notations conveniently before him, and repeated the entire process with the second.

It took very much longer than a minute. It took longer than an hour. And Ellery, impatient of this meticulous cautiousness of science, walked about smoking, muttering to himself, and thinking with such absorption that he was quite startled to hear himself addressed by Major Kirby.

He came to, and found the two experts smiling at him.

"Success," said Major Kirby quietly. "There's no ballistics expert in the world who could deny the facts, Mr. Queen—now. This automatic you found fired the bullets which killed Horne and Woody."

Ellery stared at them in silence for an instant. Then he heaved a long sigh. "Journey's end," he said at last. "Or should I say—penultimate stop on our itinerary. Well, gentlemen. . . ." He strode swiftly to the table and picked up the automatic. He studied it fondly for a moment, and then put it without expression into his pocket. Lieutenant Knowles looked faintly startled.

"I have," said Ellery calmly, "a most unorthodox request to make of you gentlemen. It's of the utmost importance that no one—literally no one—learns the results of your little experiment."

Lieutenant Knowles cleared his throat. "Hrrrrm! I don't know—I've my duty to the Department, Mr. Queen. You mean—"

"I mean that not only don't I want anyone at all to know that this weapon fired the shots which killed Woody and Horne," said Ellery, "but I don't even want the fact that the gun has been *found* to leak out. Do you understand, Lieutenant?"

The expert rubbed his jaw. "Well, I suppose you're the doctor. You've pulled off some funny ones around here in the past. I've got to keep my records straight, though. . . ."

"Oh, keep your records, by all means," said Ellery quickly. "Ah—and you, Major?"

"You may depend upon me to keep my mouth shut, of course," said Major Kirby.

"It's a pleasure to work with you, Major," smiled Ellery; and he went quickly from the laboratory.

CHALLENGE
TO THE READER

And so once more I come to what might be termed the "seventh-inning stretch" of my novels. Time out, ladies and gentlemen.

I ask in a variation of a theme I have harped on now for four years: Who killed the two horsemen in the arena of the Colosseum?

You don't know? Ah, but really you should. The whole story is now before you: clues galore, I give you my word; and when put together in the proper order and the inevitable deductions drawn, they point resolutely to the one and only possible criminal.

It is a point of honor with me to adhere to the Code. The Code of play-fair-with-the-reader-give-him-all-the-clues-and-withhold-nothing. I say all the clues are now in your possession. I repeat that they make an inescapable pattern of guilt.

Can you put the pieces of the pattern together and interpret what you see?

A word to the small army of well-intentioned hecklers who worry the life out of the author each time he blithely lays down a challenge. The contents of the telegram which in the story I send to Hollywood, and the contents of the reply thereto, are not necessary to your logical solution. As you shall see, a solution is possible without knowledge of either; they are merely confirmation of logical conclusions arrived at from analysis. So that actually you should be able to tell me *what my telegram said!*

—ELLERY QUEEN

25: BEFORE THE FACT

SUNDAY EVENINGS were usually restful ones in the Queen household. It was on Sunday evenings that the Inspector completely relaxed, and there was a tacit rule that at such times it was forbidden to talk shop, indulge in theories about crime, mull over real cases, read detective stories, or in other way profane the atmosphere.

So after dinner that evening Ellery shut himself up in the bedroom and very quietly took up the extension telephone. He called the number of the Hotel Barclay and asked for Miss Horne.

"Ellery Queen speaking. Yes. . . . What are you doing this evening, Miss Horne?"

She laughed a little. "Is this an invitation?"

"I might do worse," agreed Ellery. "May I have an unequivocal reply to the question before the House?"

"Well, sir," she said in a stern voice, "I'm full up."

"Which, translated, means—?"

"A gentleman has already requested my company for this evening."

"A gentleman with curly hair?"

"How smart you are, Mr. Queen! Yes, a gentleman with curly

hair. Although I'm afraid that didn't require much of a deduction." Then her voice broke a little. "Is it—is there anything in the wind? I'm so tired of waiting. . . . I mean, is it important for you to see me tonight, Mr. Queen?"

"It's important for me to see you any night," said Ellery gallantly. "But then I suppose it's futile and foolhardy for me to enter the lists when a young man with such divinely spiracled hair and such facility with firearms is the other contestant. No, my dear, it isn't really important. Some other time."

"Oh," she said, and was silent for a moment. "You see, Curly's taking me to the movies this evening. He loves 'em. And I—oh, I've been so lonesome since. . . . you know."

"I really do," said Ellery gently. "Wild Bill going with you?"

"He's more tactful than *that*," she laughed. "He's dining with Mars tonight and some other promoters. Has some new scheme up his sleeve. Poor Bill! I really don't know—"

"I'm certainly playing in luck tonight," said Ellery ruefully; and after a moment hung up.

He stood quite still in the bedroom, thoughtfully polishing the sparkling panes of his *pince-nez*. Then he began to move about.

Five minutes later he appeared in the living room, fully clad for the street.

"Where you going?" demanded the Inspector, looking up from the comic section of the Sunday newspaper.

"For a stroll," said Ellery lightly. "Need a little exercise. Getting a bit convex about the abdomen, I think. I'll be back soon."

Inspector Queen sniffed at this obvious evasion and returned to his funny-sheet. Ellery rumpled Djuna's hair in passing and very quickly disappeared.

· · · · · · · ·

It was an hour before he returned. He was flushed and a little nervous. He went into the bedroom, emerged a moment later without his overcoat, and dropped into an armchair beside the Inspector. He stared into the fire.

The Inspector put the science page down. "Had a nice walk?"

"Oh, lovely."

Inspector Queen stretched his slippered feet nearer the fire, sniffed snuff, and remarked without turning his head: "I'll be jiggered if I know what to think about this case, son. I'm really—"

"No talkin' about cases," said Djuna, aghast, from his monkey's perch atop a chair.

"Point well taken," said Ellery. "Thank you, Djuna."

"Point is," muttered the Inspector, "I'm buffaloed. By God, I wish—What d'ye know, son?"

Ellery tossed his butt into the fire and peacefully folded his hands on his stomach. "Everything," he said.

"What's that?" said the Inspector blankly.

"I said I know everything."

"Oh." The Inspector relaxed. "Another one of your jokes. 'Course, you *always* know everything about everything. You're one of God's Four Hundred, you are. Isn't a subject on which you aren't an expert—like these book detectives—see all, know all. . . . bah!"

"I know everything," said Ellery gently, "about the Horne-Woody case."

The Inspector ceased grumbling on the instant. He sat very still. Then he began to pluck at his mustache. "You—you really mean that?"

"Cross my heart and hope to die of imbecility. The case is finished. Complete. Ain't no more. Doggone, we're done, pardner. . . . The truth is," said Ellery with a sigh, "that you'll be shocked by the beautiful simplicity of it."

Inspector Queen eyed his son for some time. There was no mockery on Ellery's sharp features. And there *was* an air of tension, of excitement sternly repressed, about him that began insistently to stir the Inspector's own blood. Despite himself, his eyes began to shine.

"Well," he said abruptly, "when's the pay-off?"

"Any time you prefer," said Ellery slowly. "Now, if you like. I'm growing positively weary of mystery. I'd like to get this off my—conscience."

"Then let's go and stop gabbling," said the Inspector; and he made for the bedroom.

Silently Ellery followed, and watched the old man slip off his slippers and pull on his shoes.

He himself put on his overcoat in more leisurely fashion. His eyes were glowing.

"Where we bound?" grunted the Inspector, going to the closet for his hat and overcoat.

"Hotel Barclay."

The Inspector started. Ellery adjusted his scarf tenderly.

"What part of the Hotel Barclay?"

"One of the rooms."

"Oh! Thanks."

They left the apartment and strode down Eighty-seventh Street toward Broadway.

At the corner of Broadway they waited for the traffic light to change to green. The Inspector's hands were jammed in his pockets. "By the way," he said with sarcasm, "if it isn't too much to ask—what the devil are we supposed to do in one of those rooms at the hotel?"

"Search it. You see," murmured Ellery, "there's one thing we overlooked."

"Overlooked searching the Barclay?" said the Inspector sharply. "What are you talkin' about?"

"Oh, I'll admit there seemed no purpose in it at the time. We went over Horne's room, and Woody's room, and all that. . . . But—" He consulted his watch. It was a few minutes past midnight. "Hmm. I really think we should have reinforcements, dad. Velie, say. Good man, Velie. One moment, and I'll buzz him." He hurried his father across the street and darted into a drug store, emerging five minutes later with a smile. "He'll be there waiting for us. Come on, old Grumbles."

The Inspector went on.

Fifteen minutes later they marched across the lobby of the Hotel Barclay. It was rather crowded. In the elevator Ellery said: "Third, please." At the third floor they left the elevator, and Ellery, taking his father's arm, proceeded along a long corridor and paused before a certain door. Out of a shadow stepped Sergeant Velie. None of the three said anything.

Ellery raised his hand and knocked softly. There was a little murmur from behind the door, and then a hand fumbled, with the knob. An instant later the door swung open, revealing the face—the dour and for the moment startled face—of Wild Bill Grant.

26: THE FACT

THE THREE men walked silently into grant's room, and after a moment of hesitation Grant closed the door behind them.

Staring at them from two chairs were Curly Grant and Kit Horne, both of them white-faced.

"Well?" growled Grant. "What's it this time?"

There was a black bottle on the table, and three moist glasses.

"Having a bit of a night-cap, I note," said Ellery pleasantly. "Well, it's a little embarrassing, to tell the truth. But the Inspector had a notion, you see, and I couldn't dissuade him." He grinned shamelessly, and the Inspector scowled so hard he added a new wrinkle to his forehead. "Because, you see, the Inspector wants to search your room."

The Inspector reddened. Sergeant Velie edged nearer the bulky figure of the showman.

"Search my room?" repeated Grant hoarsely, with a puzzled look. "What th' devil for?"

"Go ahead, Thomas," said the Inspector in a weary voice; and without emotion the Sergeant went to work. Grant doubled his big brown fists and for an instant seemed inclined to protest physically against the intrusion; then he shrugged and stood still.

"I shan't forget this, Inspect'r," he said slowly.

Curly sprang to his feet and shoved Velie roughly aside before that worthy could open the top drawer of the bureau. "Lay off that!" he snapped, and strode forward to scowl into the Inspector's face. "What the hell is this—Russia or somethin'? Where's yore warrant? What right've ya got to come into a man's room—?"

Wild Bill took his arm gently and propelled him half-way across the room. "Keep yore shirt on, Curly," he said. "Go on, you. Search yore head off an' be damned to you."

Sergeant Velie blinked in an interested way at Curly, caught the Inspector's nod, and went back to the bureau.

Curly flung himself down by Kit's side like a rebuked child. Kit said nothing at all, merely stared at Ellery in a shocked way.

Ellery polished his *pince-nez* with rather more vigor than usual.

Sergeant Velie was thorough, if disrespectful. He went through' the bureau like an impatient thief. Drawer after drawer which, opened, lay virginly neat before his eyes, was slammed shut in a state of chaos. Then he turned his attention to a wardrobe trunk. The devastation traveled. He attacked the bed. He left it a shambles.

And meanwhile the Grants, and Kit, and the Queens were silent spectators.

The closet. . . . The Sergeant pulled open the door, rasped his horny palms together, and sprang forward at the clothing. Suit after suit turned shapeless under his pressing, squeezing, slapping hands. Nothing. . . . He squatted and tackled the shoes.

When he rose, there was something pained about his expression; and he glanced at Ellery once with the faintest perturbation. That gentleman continued to polish his glasses, but his eyes were noticeably sharper and he edged the slightest bit closer to Grant.

Sergeant Velie groped about the shelf. His hand encountered a large round white box. He pulled it down and ripped off the lid. A wide-brimmed, dun-colored Stetson, apparently brand-new, lay majestically revealed. He picked up the Stetson. . . . and started.

Then he came slowly out of the closet, carrying the box, and laid it on the table before the Inspector. He glanced briefly and queerly at Ellery.

Lying peacefully in the box, on the bottom beneath where the Stetson had rested, there was a flat, dull, tiny weapon—a .25 calibre automatic pistol.

. . . .

Grant's body quivered, and the color drained from his rocky face, leaving it the hue and consistency of earth-stained marble. Kit uttered a choking little cry, and then pressed her hand quickly to her mouth, her eyes fixed with horror on the old Westerner. Curly sat turned to stone, unbelieving, stupefied.

The Inspector stared at the weapon for a split-second, then snatched it out of the box, dropped it into his pocket, and with remarkable swiftness reached into his hip-pocket and brought out a .38 Colt police revolver. This he permitted to droop negligently from his fingers.

"Well," he said calmly. "What have you got to say for yourself, Grant?"

Grant stared unseeing at the revolver. "What—My God, man, I—" He braced himself and drew a deep unsteady breath. His eyes were the eyes of a dead man.

"Didn't you tell me," said the Inspector softly, "that you don't own a .25 automatic, Grant?"

"I don't," said Grant in a slow, confused way.

"Oh, you deny that this little feller," the Inspector tapped his pocket, "is yours?"

"Ain't mine," said Grant lifelessly. "I never saw it before."

Curly got uncertainly to his feet, eyes fixed on his father; and he swayed a little from side to side. Sergeant Velie quietly pushed him back into his chair, and stood over him.

Before any of them realized what was happening, Kit uttered a strangled cry, as appalling as the snarl of a tigress, and sprang from her chair directly at Grant. Her fingers clawed for his throat. He did not move, made no effort to defend himself. Ellery leaped between them and cried: "Miss Horne! For heaven's sake, none of that!"

She retreated, drawn up stiffly, a look of unspeakable loathing on her brown face.

And she said: "I'll kill you if it's the last thing I do, you two-faced Judas," very quietly.

Grant quivered again.

"Thomas," said the Inspector with a little crackle in his tone, "I'll take care of these people. Take that bean-shooter out of my pocket and beat it down to h.q. Get Knowles. Have him test it. We're waiting here. . . . None of you," he said sharply, as Sergeant Velie obeyed, "make one funny move. Grant, sit down. Miss Horne, you too. And you, young feller, stay where you are." The muzzle of the police revolver described a tiny arc.

Ellery sighed.

·　　·　　·　　·　　·　　·　　·

After a century the telephone bell rang in the room. Both Grants and Kit started convulsively.

"Sit still, all of you," said the Inspector gently. "Ellery, take that call. Must be from Knowles, or Thomas."

Ellery went to the telephone. He listened blankly for several moments, and then hung up.

"Well?" demanded the Inspector without taking his eyes from Grant's hands.'

Grant did not move a muscle. Almost in agony his eyes were fixed on Ellery's lips. It was quite like the scene in a courtroom, when the jury has filed in and the prisoner sits staring at the lips of the foreman for the verdict which will mean life or death.

Ellery muttered: "The Sergeant reports it's the same automatic that killed Horne and Woody."

Kit shuddered. Her eyes were wild with a feral emotion, and confused too, like the eyes of an animal blinded by sudden light and taut with the consciousness of danger.

"Put out your hands, Grant," said the Inspector sharply. "I arrest you for the murder of Buck Horne and One-Arm Woody. And it's my duty to warn you that anything you say may be used against you. . . ."

27: THE HEEL OF ACHILLES

ELLERY QUEEN, *Gent.*, was never an enthusiastic patron of the journalistic art. He read newspapers as infrequently as possible; the conservative ones bored him, he liked to say, and the lurid ones sickened him.

Nevertheless Monday morning found him on the sidewalk before Police Headquarters purchasing copies of four different morning sheets from a newsboy who accepted his coins with suspicious fingers.

But since there was no necessity for explaining this sudden change of habit to the newsboy, Ellery merely nodded and hurried into the big gray building.

He found Inspector Queen shouting in his battery of telephones. To this accompaniment he read the journals he had bought. The story of the capture of Wild Bill Grant was, of course this morning's *piece de resistance*. The showman's lined features stared at him from the front pages of the two tabloids, and less generously from the front pages of the two full-size papers. The banners variously described Grant as "fiend," "pal-killer," "Western bad man," and "rodeo promoter."

Curiously enough, Ellery read nothing beyond the headlines

and prefatory paragraphs. Then he flung the papers aside, folded his hands pacifically, and regarded his father.

"Well, what's happened this morning?" he asked cheerfully.

"Plenty. Grant's mum—won't talk, won't say yes or no," snapped the Inspector. "But we'll break *that* down. The point is, we've got the gat. Knowles says there's no question about the automatic from Grant's room having been used in the two murders." The Inspector paused, and something thoughtful came into his sharp eyes. "Funny," he said slowly, "but it seemed to me Knowles was keepin' something back. Knowles!" He shrugged. "Must be my imagination. The man's a jewel. When do I get some explanations, darn you? The Commissioner's been camping on my wire all morning."

"Don't tell me that gentleman's interested in *reasons*," murmured Ellery. "He's been howling for results, hasn't he? Well, you've given him results, haven't you? You've delivered a murderer, F.O.B. New York, evidence clear—haven't you? What more does he want?"

"Still," said the Inspector, "he's human enough to want to know how and why. And, come to think of it," he added, eying Ellery suspiciously, "I'm a little curious myself. How's it happen Grant leaves that gat lyin' around loose that way? Pretty dumb for a slick killer, seems to me. Especially after the way he smuggled it out of the *Colosseum* twice under our noses. I think—"

"Don't," said Ellery. "Has Curly been around?"

"Hart at the Tombs called me up three times. The boy's been making a pest of himself. Seems old man Grant won't even see a lawyer—absolutely refuses. Can't figure it. The boy's frantic. And Kit—"

"Yes, what about Kit?" asked Ellery with sudden gravity.

The Inspector shrugged. "She's been here to see me already this morning. Wants Grant prosecuted to the limit."

"Very natural," murmured Ellery, and seemed to find something distasteful in his cigaret.

.   .   .   .

Ellery hung about Police Headquarters all day. He wore an air of expectancy, and looked quickly up at the door every time a member of the Homicide Squad appeared to report to the Inspector. He smoked innumerable cigarets, and several times made telephone calls from a public booth in the main lobby downstairs.

He refused with a smile on three separate occasions during the afternoon to offer an explanation of the solution. He shook his head at District Attorney Sampson, three newspapermen from syndicates, and the Commissioner himself. At no time did he quite lose his head-cocked, waiting air.

But nothing out of the ordinary happened all day.

At six he and the Inspector left Headquarters and took the subway uptown.

At six-thirty they were sitting at a silent repast, and it was apparent that neither had his usually robust appetite.

At seven the doorbell rang and Ellery sprang to his feet. The visitor was Kit Horne—pale, distrait, very nervous.

"Come in," said Ellery gently. "And sit down, Miss Horne. I'm glad you decided to come."

"I—I scarcely know what to do or think," she said in a low voice, as she slowly sat down in the armchair. "I don't know where to turn. I'm completely—completely. . . ."

"Don't blame you," said the Inspector sympathetically. "It's hard finding out the real streak in a man who's seemed to be a friend. If I were you, though, I wouldn't let this interfere with my feelings in—well, in other people."

"You mean Curly?" She shook her head. "Impossible. Oh, it's not his fault, but—"

The doorbell rang again, and Djuna jumped into the foyer. A moment later the tall figure of Curly Grant appeared in the doorway.

"What did you want me—?" he began; and saw Kit. They stared at each other wordlessly. Then she colored and half-rose. The man looked miserable, hung his head.

"No," said Ellery in a fierce whisper, and she looked at him, startled. "I want you here. I want you here *particularly*. Don't take it out on poor Curly. Please sit down, Miss Horne."

She sat down.

Djuna, coached in advance, appeared with a tray. The awkward moment was bridged by the cheerful clink of ice and glasses; as if by tacit consent the talk turned to light things, and in ten minutes Ellery had them faintly smiling.

. . . .

But as the minutes passed, lengthening into an hour, and then two hours, the talk languished; and even the Inspector began to grow restless. Ellery was in a fever. He was everywhere at once, speaking quickly, smiling, frowning, smoking, offering cigarets—quite as unlike the normal Ellery as it would be possible to conceive. Despite—perhaps because of—all his efforts, the gloom deepened. Each passing moment now seemed a year. Until finally even Ellery ceased his valiant efforts to disseminate cheer, and no one said anything at all.

It was precisely at nine o'clock that the doorbell rang for the third time.

Without warning. It came in the midst of a heavy silence. It twitched the Inspector's mustache, shocked Kit and Curly into rigidity, and raised Ellery from his chair like a yanked rope.

"No, Djuna," he said quietly to the boy, who as usual had made for the door. "I'll go myself. Excuse me," and he darted into the foyer.

They heard the opening of the door. They heard a man's deep tones. And they heard Ellery say, in a voice steady and dangerous: "Ah, come in, come in. I've been expecting you."

Ellery loomed in the archway from the foyer, his face white as his linen. An instant later a tall man—taller than Ellery—appeared beside him on the sill.

There was an eternal moment, such a moment as life meets infrequently on the normal stream of time. Time for that moment gathered its energies and leaped, exploding, into the brain.

They all stared at the man in the archway, and the man in the archway stared back at them.

It was the man of the frightfully burnt cheek, the ill-clothed shambling Westerner who had vanished so mysteriously from the *Colosseum* the day before. . . . Benjy Miller. Under the brown skin of his unmutilated right cheek there was a deathlike pallor that matched the pallor of his worn knuckles as he clutched the jamb.

"Miller," said the Inspector in bewilderment. "Miller," and rose uncertainly from his chair.

Kit Horne gave vent to a formless choking sound that brought all eyes upon her. She was staring at Miller. The man in the doorway met her eyes for a brief instant, and then looked away, taking a quick step into the room. Kit bit her lip, looked from side to side, drew in her breath spasmodically, eyes filled with a terror that was beyond quelling.

"But what th' devil—?" muttered Curly in an astonished way.

Ellery said in a barely audible voice: "Tell them."

Miller paused a yard from the archway, his big hands clenched tightly. He licked his lips and said: "Inspector Queen, I killed—I killed—"

"What!" shouted the Inspector, springing to his feet. He flashed a furious look at Ellery. "You—What d'ye mean? *You* killed Buck Horne and Woody?"

Curly Grant swore softly to himself.

Miller's fists unclenched, and clenched again.

Kit began quietly to sob.

And Ellery said: "He killed Woody, but he did *not* kill Buck Horne!"

The Inspector pounded the table in his fury. "By God, I'll have the truth now if I go crazy tryin' to get it! What's all this foolishness? What d'ye mean—Miller killed Woody but didn't kill Horne? The same gat was used!"

"And the same hand used it," said Ellery wearily. "But Miller *couldn't* have killed Buck Horne. You see, MILLER *IS* BUCK HORNE!"

POSTLUDE: SPECTRUM ANALYSIS

"In fine," said Ellery Queen, "the non-essential colors vanished from our imaginary color-wheel, leaving—what? An iris of unmistakable spectrum-lines which clearly told the whole story."

"Your obscure metaphor," I said with some irritation, "leaves me rather more than cold. I'll confess it's still a deep, dark puzzle to my feeble brain. I know all the facts now, but I'll be hanged if I can make any sense out of them."

Ellery smiled. It was weeks after the solution of the Horne case; the reverberations had echoed off into the limbo of all forgotten crimes; the amazing and pitiful *denouement* was a thing of merely professional interest. For some reason which I could not fathom little was printed by the avid press that was comprehensible. Buck Horne had committed two murders in a remarkably clever manner; why, and a good deal of how, remained a mystery. And then there was the matter of the detective work which had led to the solution; nothing appeared in the papers concerning this, either, and I had been unable to find out why.

"What is it," murmured Ellery, "that mystifies you?"

"The whole blasted business! But particularly how you solved the problem. And I might add," I continued with some malice, "if you ever did solve those two minor problems you were in the dark about. For instance, what really did happen to the automatic in both crimes?"

Ellery chuckled and puffed away at his cigaret. "Oh, come now, J. J., surely you know me better than to accuse me at *this* stage in my career of faulty craftsmanship. Of course, I knew the essential answer—the interchange of personalities—only a few hours after the first body was found. . . ."

"What!"

"Oh, yes. It was really the result of an elementary series of deductions, and I'm astounded at the blindness of the people who worked with me." He sighed. "Poor dad! He's an excellent policeman, but he has no vision, no imagination. You need imagination in this business." Then he shrugged and settled back comfortably. Djuna came in with an urn of coffee, and a platter of excellent brioches. "Suppose I begin," said Ellery, "at the beginning.

"You see, despite the presence of thousands of persons at the scene of the crime, any one of whom might have been the criminal—and despite the unique and puzzling circumstances of the crime itself, I'm talking about the 'Horne' murder now—there were six facts which stood out prominently—"

"*Six* facts?" I said. "That seems like a lot of facts, Ellery."

"Yes, this case provided me with a plethora of clues, J.J. As I say, these six facts stood out prominently during the first night's investigation as significant clues. Two of them—one physical, the other psychological—combined to tell me something that I alone knew from the very inception of the investigation. Suppose I take them up in order, drawing the inferences as I go— inferences which brick by brick built up the only possible theory that covered all the facts."

He stared into the fire with a quizzical half-smile on his lips. "First," he murmured, "the trouser belt around the dead man's waist. Amazing thing, J.J. It told such a clear story! There were five buckle-holes, the second and third of which were characterized by deep ridges in the leather running vertically across the holes—ridges left, patently, by repeated bucklings at those holes. Now Kit Horne—poor kid!—had told me that Buck had been in failing health for some time in the recent past, and in fact had lost weight. Mark that!

"Loss of weight—buckling-marks on the belt. Interesting juxtaposition of facts, eh? The significance struck me immediately. What did Horne's recent loss of weight mean in relation to the *two* buckle-ridges on the belt? Surely this: In normal times Horne had obviously buckled his belt at the *second* hole, as evidenced by the welt across the second hole; when later he began to lose weight he was constrained to buckle his belt at the *third* hole—that is, drawing his belt tighter as his girth lessened. Yet what did we find on the night of the murder of, presumably, Buck Horne? That the victim was wearing the belt, which fitted snugly, buckled at the *first* hole!"

He paused to ignite a fresh cigaret, and again—as I had so many times in the past—I reflected on the remarkable keenness of his perceptions. Such an unimportant little detail! I believe I remarked something to this effect.

"Hmm," he said, drawing his brows together, "it's perfectly true that the business of the buckle-holes was trivial. And not only trivial in appearance, but trivial in significance. It was just an indication. It didn't prove anything. But it showed the way.

"Now I've just demonstrated that Horne normally buckled his trouser belt at the second hole, and later as he lost weight at the third hole; yet the man whose dead body we found was wearing the belt buckled at the first hole. This was an unaccustumed position, for the simple reason that the *only* ridges or welts were across the second and third holes; in other words there was no ridge at all across the first hole, where the dead man had actually buckled the belt. But here was a puzzling set of facts. How was I to explain the phenomenon that Horne, who habitually buckled at the second notch, and then for some time was forced to tighten his belt to the third notch, suddenly on the night of his murder buckled at the first notch—that is, *loosened his belt to the extent of two full notches?* Well, what usually makes a man loosen his belt? A heavy meal, you say—eh?"

"That was in my mind," I confessed, "although I can't see a man dining so heartily before a strenuous performance; or even if he did, dining so heartily that he would have to let out his belt two notches."

"I agree. But the logical possibility existed. So I took the logical step. I asked Dr. Prouty, who was to perform the autopsy, to ascertain the contents of the corpse's stomach. In due course he reported that the corpse's stomach was quite empty; apparently, he said, the victim had not taken food for six hours or so before his death. So that was out as a possible explanation for the sudden switch to the first buckle-hole.

"What remained? Only one thing; deny it if you can: I was forced to the conclusion that the belt which the dead man wore that night *didn't belong to him.* Ah, but it *was* Buck Horne's belt: it was monogrammed with his initials, and Grant—his closest friend—testified to Horne's ownership. But see where this leads us! For if the belt did not belong to the man who was wearing it, but did belong to Buck Horne, then Buck Horne was not the man who was wearing it. But the man who was wearing it was the dead man. Then *the dead man was not Buck Horne!* What could be simpler, J.J.?"

"And that gave you the whole story?" I muttered. "It sounds horribly weak and unconvincing, somehow."

"Weak, no," Ellery smiled. "Unconvincing, yes. For the excellent reason that the human mind refuses to accept large explanations from small facts. Yet isn't most of our progress in science the result of insignificant observations, brought about by this very process of induction? I'll admit that at the moment I wasn't free from the mental cowardice of the herd. The conclusion seemed incredible. I shied away from it. I didn't believe it. It flew in the face of the normal. Yet what other explanation could there be?"

Ellery stared thoughtfully into the fire. "And then there was something else to strengthen the doubt. The dead man had had contact—although it must have been fleeting, for the testimony ran that 'Horne' had dashed into the *Colosseum* late—with the rodeo troupe. And after the death of the rider presumed to be Horne, Kit—Horne's foster-daughter, mind—had actually seen the victim's face when she lifted the blanket from the dead body; as had Grant, Horne's lifelong friend. And the face itself had not been mutilated, J.J.—only the skull and body. These facts seemed to render my conclusion that the dead man wasn't Horne even less convincing. But I didn't discard my conclusion, as perhaps another might have been tempted to do under the circumstances. On the contrary, I said to myself: 'Well, unconvincing or not, the point is that *if* the dead man *isn't* Horne, as my first deduction indicates, then the dead man certainly bears a most remarkable resemblance to Horne in face and figure.' Inescapable inference, J.J., if you accept my first premise. At any rate, I wasn't satisfied, not mentally easy at all. I looked about for confirmation of my conclusion. I found it almost at once, and that brings me to the second of the half-dozen clues I mentioned."

"Something that confirms the conclusion that the dead man wasn't Horne?" I said blankly. "For the life of me—"

"Don't gamble your life so carelessly, J.J.," chuckled Ellery. "It's so incredibly simple. It revolved about the ivory-handled revolver found in the dead man's right hand—*right* hand, re-member—the twin of which I found in Horne's hotel room later.

"Now both weapons had been used by Horne for many years; Kit said they were her foster-father's favorite weapons, and so did Grant and Curly. Again no question of ownership, please note; the initials on the butts, and both Kit's and Grant's instant acceptance. So the guns were Horne's; of that much I could be sure.

"What were the new indications? The first gun was found still clutched in the dead man's hand—right hand—even after his fall from the horse. I myself had seen him draw this weapon from his right holster and wave it with his right hand as he set the horse to galloping around the oval; and the newsreel con-firmed these observations. But when I examined the revolver itself I noticed an extremely odd thing." He wagged his head lightly. "Follow carefully. The handle, or butt, or grip—whatever the technical term is—was inlaid with ivory on both flat surfac-es, and the ivory was yellow and worn with age and use, *except for a narrow portion on the right side of the butt.* As I held the gun in my *left* hand, this patch of. lighter ivory came between the tips of my curled fingers and the heel of my hand. Later that night I held the twin in my *right* hand and noticed that, although the ivory inlays were just as worn and yellow as in the first gun, there was again one portion comparatively fresh-looking—this time on the *left* side of the butt between the tips of my coiled fingers and the heel of my hand. What did all this mean? That the second gun—the one from the hotel room—was the gun Buck Horne had habitually gripped in his *right* hand, for when I held it in my *right* hand the strip of unworn ivory came on the left side of the butt, where it should come in a right-hand grip. The other gun, the first one, which the dead man had been clutching in his *right* hand, was obviously the weapon gripped by Horne for many years in his *left* hand, for the unworn strip of ivory came on the right side, where it should come in a left-hand grip." He drew a deep breath. "In other words, to reduce it to its simplest form, Buck Horne, who used twin guns, always gripped one in his right hand and the other in his left, never changing, for if he had used them indiscriminately for either hand there would be no unworn patches at all. Remember this.

"Further, Horne was undoubtedly an ambidextrous marksman; that is, he fired—judging from the identically worn muzzles, sights, and butts—equally *often* with either hand; and inferentially, then, equally well. This habit of Buck's using a specific weapon for each of his two hands was later confirmed by a small point; I had Lieutenant Knowles weigh the two guns and found that one was some two ounces lighter than the other. Apparently then each was perfectly balanced to the strength, grip, and 'feel' of the particular hand in which he habitually held it.

"Now then, to return to the important discrepancy. The murdered man was gripping with his *right* hand the weapon Buck Horne always gripped with his *left*. It struck me immediately that Horne would never have wielded that gun with the wrong hand. And—"

"But suppose," I objected, "that by accident he had taken the left-hand gun with him that night to the *Colosseum?*"

"It wouldn't have made a particle of difference to my deductions. By every dictate of habit, weight, feel, he would have recognized it the instant he picked it up as his left-hand gun, would have automatically placed it in his left holster, and would have performed with it gripped in his left hand. Remember, there was no compulsion for him to use his right hand that night while he fired blank cartridges into the air; he was merely holding the reins with his left, or waving his hat at one point; either hand would have served for the normal little activities it was called upon to engage in.

"So! Since the dead man had gripped Horne's left-hand, gun with his right hand, had even used the right holster, when Horne would have gripped the weapon in his left hand and used the left holster—here was startling confirmation that it wasn't Buck Horne at all who was murdered that night!"

He paused to sip some coffee. How simple—as he said—it was when he explained it!

"I now," continued Ellery serenely, "had two perfectly interlocking, or complementary, reasons for questioning the identity of the victim; and while either one, alone, might have formed the basis for no more than a strong presumption, the combination of both removed all doubt from my mind. The dead man was not Buck Horne. Squirm as much as I might at the odd conclusion, I was compelled to accept it.

"But since it was not Buck Horne's body which had tumbled to the tanbark that night, I said to myself: In the name of a merciful God, whose body *was* it? Well, as I've already suggested, it was obviously the body of someone whose physique, with the scarcely perceptible exception of a larger waist-line, was similar to Horne's; someone who looked amazingly like Horne in features, who could ride and shoot expertly, and who probably could approximate the timbre of Buck's voice. As for this last point, I might say here that the voice did not play an important role that night; for the supposed Buck Horne arrived late for the performance; merely *waved* a greeting to Grant, as Grant himself related, went at once to his dressing room, and appeared shortly thereafter on the field astride *Rawhide*. Probably then he never actually spoke to anyone at all; or if he did, it was a monosyllable."

"So far," I agreed, "it's clear, Ellery. But, as I said, some things stick in my craw. For instance, I know from having read the newspapers the actual identity of the man who was murdered in that first crime; but how the dickens could you have worked it out so early in the case?"

"There," murmured Ellery, snuggling more deeply into the armchair, "you touch on a sore spot. I didn't know. I didn't know *exactly*. But I knew generally enough to advance my theory to a solution. Let me go on, and you'll see.

"I naturally asked myself: Who could this man—this dead man—be who so closely resembled Buck Horne in face and figure? My instinctive thought was a twin brother; but Miss Horne and Grant both asserted that Buck had no blood-kin of any kind alive. Then in mulling over Horne's background the answer came to me in a flash. It was a perfect development of the man's history, a perfect and indeed inevitable explanation of the resemblance between Buck Horne, ex-movie star, and an unknown man. For Buck had been an actor who specialized in outdoor roles, roles that called for all sorts of strenuous activity and at times even feats of acrobatics—as anyone who has seen Western movie heroes leap from windows into saddles, hurtle horses over cliffs—the usual folderol—knows. But what do motion picture companies resort to when their stars cannot perform these daredevil stunts—or, more pertinently, how do producers avert the physical hazards, the risks to life and limb, to a Western star—after all valuable property? It's a common practice with which everyone today is familiar through the so-called 'fan' magazines and newspaper exploitation. *They use doubles.*"

I gasped, and Ellery chuckled again. "Shut your mouth, J.J.—you look disagreeably like a fish out of water. . . . What on earth strikes you as so amazing about that? It was a perfectly logical line of reasoning. It matched the facts superbly. Producers use doubles for more reckless feats of daring; these doubles are selected primarily for two qualifications. First, in physique they must resemble the stars they impersonate. Second, they must be able not only to accomplish the feats of which the stars are capable, but to do even more, since it's they who perform the really perilous stunts. In a Western-star situation, the double would undoubtedly be a good horseman, a roper, perhaps even a marksman. Now, facial resemblance is not absolutely essential in most cases, for the particular shots of action can be so filmed that the double's face is not caught by the camera; but there are notable instances of doubles who can not only do what the stars can do, but who look amazingly like the stars as well. . . . Yes, the more I thought about it the more positive I was that the man murdered in the arena was Buck Horne's old movie double. As a matter of confirmation I wired a confidential source in Los Angeles to find out from the studio whether there had been such a double. I received a reply a few days later; I had been right.* There had been such a double, but the studio had not been in touch with him since Buck's last picture some three or four years before and had no idea where the man might be found. The man's name, which the wire supplied, was obviously a screen name, and of no

---

* Mr. Queen emphasizes this point once more. The inspiration to wire Hollywood was a direct result of his thinking; so that he was justified in his Challenge in stating that the wires were confirmatory, not essential.—J. J. McC.

use to me. But even had I not checked with Hollywood I should have been morally certain that the theory of a movie double was the correct solution of the victim's identity."

I threw up my hands.

"Shall I stop?" asked Ellery.

"Lord, no! I'm just genuflecting to the god of reason. If you stop now I'll brain you. Go on, for heaven's sake."

He looked embarrassed. "I *shall* stop," he said sternly, "if you spout any more bilgewater like that. . . . Where was I? Yes! The next question was inevitable: Why had Buck Horne secretly re-engaged his old-time double to take his place in the rodeo performance without mentioning it to either Grant or Kit?—for their stupefaction and grief at sight of Horne's supposedly dead body could not have been anything but genuine. Well, there are two *innocent* reasons conceivable: one, that Buck had become suddenly ill, or worse; that he did not wish to disappoint his audience, and furthermore was too proud to confess his condition to Kit, to his best friend Grant, or to Mars the promoter; or two, that his performance included some feat or feats which Buck was unable to perform. But Buck had not become suddenly ill; he had been examined by the rodeo doctor the day of the performance and pronounced fit, according to Kit Horne and the doctor himself. Had he possibly taken ill *between* the doctor's examination and the performance itself? This would mean that he would have had to arrange for the deception on the spur of the moment, very shortly before the performance. Yet everything indicated that the deception was planned *not* the day of the performance, but the day *before*. For one thing, he had had a mysterious visitor to his hotel room the previous night. For another, he had withdrawn from his bank the previous day most of his balance. It seemed fairly clear that he had, then, called in his double the night before the opening, and turned over to this man one of the twin guns *plus* a payment for the man's services—all of the three thousand dollars which Horne withdrew that very day, or part. His clothes, too, in all probability—remember Grant said that at the last rehearsal before the opening Buck had performed not in costume, despite the fact that all the others were in costume. . . . The fact that everything was planned at least a day *in advance of* the doctor's examination eliminated the theory that the double had been engaged because Horne was taken ill *after* the examination."

"Sounds reasonable," I muttered.

"*Is* reasonable. Now, as for Buck's routine during the show being too difficult for him—just as untenable. The last rehearsal was held the afternoon of the opening and it was unquestionably Horne himself who performed. Why do I say that Horne himself was at the rehearsal, not the double? Well, he had actually spoken to many intimates that afternoon: Woody, Grant, Kit— who no matter how remarkable the double's resemblance would not have been deceived in any prolonged *tête-a- tête conversation*. For another, he had actually written out a check, before Grant's eyes, immediately after the rehearsal, Grant cashing it for him; and I found that the check had been passed through the bank. The signature, *ipso facto,* then, was genuine; from all these things it was apparent that it must have been Horne himself who went through the rehearsal. But since a rehearsal is a duplicate of the real thing, and since Horne went through the rehearsal without a hitch, as Grant and Curly both testified, then obviously there was nothing in the performance beyond Horne's capacity.

"Now, if Buck hadn't taken ill suddenly, and there was nothing in his rodeo routine which he could not, or was afraid to, do—why had he summoned his old movie double out of the past and paid the man to substitute for him? Even aside from that—why, when his double was murdered, didn't Horne come forward and reveal himself, offering an explanation and his services to the police? If he were innocent of implication in the crime, he would feel dutybound to come forward.

"Two explanations came to mind for Horne's not coming forward—providing he were innocent. The first is that he had an enemy of whose intentions he was aware in advance, that he hired the double to take his place, knowing that an attempt would be made on his life and thereby offering up the double as a sort of sacrifice; that after the murder he refrained from coming forward to insure his continued safety, since as long as Horne's enemy believed Horne dead, Horne was secure. But in this case, wouldn't Horne have managed to notify his own closest kin, Kit, or his best friend, secretly? This was one of the reasons that prompted me to insist upon Grant's and Kit's being watched every moment, their letters intercepted and read, and their phones tapped. But nothing came of it—no message from Horne, as far as could humanly be discovered. The apparent failure of Horne to get in touch with his foster-daughter or friend made me discard the theory of a voluntary disappearance because of a known enemy; and suggested the only other possible theory of innocence that would account for Horne's disappearance and the death of a man taken to be Horne. That was that on the eve of the opening Horne had been kidnaped by his enemy or enemies, that Horne's place had been *taken* by the double for some purpose unknown; that the double was murdered, either by his own gang or a friend of Horne's who had somehow discovered the deception. But this was such a loose and unsatisfactory theory, there was so little to bolster it—no communication from the kidnapers, for example, no apparent motive (for if it was to extort money from

Horne's daughter or friends wouldn't there have been a communication?)—that, although I could not definitely discard the theory as impossible, it was so weak that I could justifiably drop it to work on a more promising tack. At the same time, it was the vague possibility of the truth of this theory or the other that kept me from disclosing what I knew about the dead man; had I done so prematurely, without a definite decision as to the facts, I realized that I might be wrong and might bring about the death of Horne. I could not, of course, foresee the murder of Woody."

He was silent for a long moment, and from his frown I could see that the entire Woody incident was distasteful to him. I knew how incensed he always became at the blithe practice of detective-story writers who permitted their detectives to sit by being suave and witty while characters fell dead all about them.

He sighed. "At that stage, then, I raised the pertinent question: Since innocent explanations of Horne's disappearance and the murder of his double were barren, was it possible that Horne himself had killed the double that night? And now I come to the four other major clues which were apparent to me the first night of the investigation. They not only narrowed the field of possibilities but placed upon the murderer two definite qualifications which Horne, if he were the murderer, had to satisfy.

"The first two concerned the topography of the *Colosseum* amphitheatre, and the nature of the death wound. The arena is the lowest part of the bowl, naturally; even the first tier of seats, the boxes, are higher by ten feet than the floor of the arena. Now the bullet in both murders had penetrated the victims' torsos, according to Dr. Prouty, on a distinctly downward fine. On the surface this would indicate that the shots in both instances were fired from above—that is to say, from the seats, the audience. But while this, was accepted as verity by everyone concerned, I saw that there was one question which had to be settled be-

fore we could say with positiveness that the murderer had shot
from above. And that was: What was the exact position of the
victim's body at the instant the bullet pierced his flesh? For the
conclusion that the shot came from *above* would be correct *only*
if the victim's torso at the instant of the bullet's entry were in a
normally erect position; that is, normally at right angles to the
floor—erect on the horse's back; that is, not slumped forward
obliquely or tiled obliquely backward or sideways."

I knit my brows. "Hold on; that's a little hard to follow."

"Here. I'll illustrate. Djuna, be a good child and get me some
paper and pencil." Djuna, who had been sitting wide-eyed and
still during the whole colloquy, jumped up and eagerly supplied
the requested articles. Ellery scrawled quickly on the paper for
some time. Then he looked, up. "It's impossible, as I say, to determine the angle of fire until one knows the exact position of
the body at the time of the bullet's entry. The specific cases will
clarify the point. Enlargements of the film which showed the
position of both victims' torsos at the instant of impact revealed
that both were leaning *sideways* from the saddle to the right at
angles of about thirty degrees from the vertical. (It's left from
the standpoint of the victims, but right from the standpoint of
the observer, or camera; I'll call it right consistently to avoid confusion.) Now follow these diagrams."

I rose and went to his chair. He had drawn four little pictures, which looked like this:

"The first diagram," he said, "shows the victim's torso in the normal erect position, as Dr. Prouty visualized it. The little arrow over the figure's heart represents the bullet's course in the body; Prouty said it was a downward line making a thirty-degree angle with the floor. Diagram two shows the figure still in the same position; that is, if the torso was precisely at right angles to the horse's back; with the extension of the arrow in a dotted line to make clearer the angle of fire. The line is definitely downward, as you see, and seems to support the conclusion that the bullet was fired from above. Well, that conclusion would be correct *if* the victim had been erect in the saddle, as the drawing shows him. But the victim *wasn't* erect in the saddle; according to the film enlargement he was leaning to the right at an angle of thirty degrees, as the third diagram shows!

"In diagram three, then, we bend the figure to the right, as it actually was; retaining, as we must, the bullet course in the body. For, once the bullet is in the body, whether we look at the body on the floor, sitting up, bent backwards, or leaning sideways, the bullet course will always be the same in relation to the torso; if the torso swings, the bullet course swings with it; they are unchangeable elements in relation to themselves. . . . And in diagram four we extend the line of direction from the bullet as it is lodged in the right-ward-leaning torso, and what do we find? That the line of direction, the course of the bullet, is virtually *parallel* to the floor! In other words, with the double's torso and Woody's torso (for both were approximately the same) leaning at an angle of thirty degrees to the right, the bullet wound shows a *horizontal*, not a downward, direction! Showing that the shot was fired not from above, but from virtually a level!"

I nodded. "And, of course, the reason Prouty said it was a downward angle of thirty degrees was that he assumed the men were riding straight as statues in the saddle. It was the thirty-degree angle of lean, so to speak, that caused the thirty-degree angle of bullet course."

"Rather complexly put," laughed Ellery, "but substantially correct. Now, when I knew this, I automatically ruled out two classes of suspects—and what a sweeping elimination *that* was! One, all those who sat in the audience, including even the first tier of seats, the boxes; for the floor of the boxes were ten feet from the floor of the arena, and anyone sitting in a box would therefore be some thirteen feet or more from the floor of the arena. A shot from this height directed at a man leaning thirty degrees sideways from a horse would have caused an even more pronounced downward angle, penetrating at more than sixty degrees, if you care for mathematics; it would have looked superficially as if the victim had been shot from the roof! And group-elimination two—the men working on the newsreel platform in the arena itself, the platform also being elevated ten feet from the level of the arena. Anyone shooting from this height would be shooting for one thing head-on rather than from the right—the head-on views of the camera prove that; and moreover the line again would be more than thirty degrees downward.

"But the line of entry was parallel to the floor, as I've shown. Then the murderer, in order to have been able to shoot a horseman in the breast on a line parallel to the floor, must himself have been a horseman! Do you follow that?"

"I'm not an idiot," I retorted.

He grinned. "Don't be so sensitive. I'm not quite sure it's immediately understandable. Yet it's a clear-cut deduction. Had the murderer been standing on the floor of the arena, the course of the bullet would have shown a slight *upward* direction. Had the murderer been in the audience the course of the bullet would have shown a sharp *downward* direction. So for the bullet to enter the victim's body on a perfectly straight line the murderer must, as I've said, be at the same height from the floor as the victim, and shooting on a straight line, too. But since the victim was a horseman, the murderer must have been a horseman, too, shooting with his pistol raised to the level of his own heart.

"The only logical suspects, then, I saw at once, were the horsemen in the arena, the troupe of riders following the victim in each instance. There was one other person on horseback besides the troupe: Wild Bill Grant. But Grant couldn't possibly have fired the shots; both times he was in the exact center of the arena at the time of the murder. The camera snapped the victims head-on, which meant that the shots, which pierced the victims' bodies from the right, must have been fired from the specific direction of the Mars box, nearly at right angles to the victims. But Grant was virtually facing the victims, like the cameras. Grant, then, couldn't have fired the shots. But the entire troupe was directly under the Mars box at the instant the shots were fired; this checked with my deduction about a horseman having been the murderer. From the standpoints of direction and angle of entry I could now make the positive assertion."

"I see that, all right," I said, "but what I can't understand is why you permitted twenty thousand innocent people to go through the embarrassment and annoyance of being detained and searched for the weapon, when you knew perfectly well not one of them could be the murderer."

Ellery squinted quizzically at the flames. "There you go, J.J., falling into the common error of confusing definitions. The carrier of the weapon wasn't necessarily the murderer. There are such creatures as accomplices, you know. It would have been relatively simple, in the confusion following both murders, for one of the suspect horsemen to have thrown the weapon to some spectator in the audience—over the rail above his head. And, of course, it was imperative that we find the murder weapon. *Ergo,* the heroic measure.

"Now, if the murderer was one of the riders in the arena, then Horne—on the hypothesis that he was the murderer—must have been acting as a member of the troupe! Now how could he have been? Simply enough. I said to myself: Naturally he isn't Buck Horne now, but someone else. He's made up, disguised. Not at all a difficult task for an ex-actor. What did Horne look like? I knew he had white hair. Obviously, then, if he wanted to disguise himself, he would dye his hair. Then by a change of costume, slight alterations of posture, walk, voice, he could easily have deceived people who had known him as Buck Horne only superficially. And then, too, observe the cleverness of his psychological action in assuming a hideous scar. A mutilation like that catches *all* the attention, for one thing, and tends to make people neglect the other features; and then too, as I saw myself, people's tendency is to *avoid* looking at a mutilated face for fear of giving offense to the unfortunate afflicted. I rather applaud Horne's shrewdness there."

"Hold on," I snapped. "I think I can charge you with a serious blunder; I hope you didn't neglect to do it wilfully. If you were so sure Horne was acting as a member of the troupe, why didn't you line 'em up and give 'em the once-over—eh?"

"Reasonable question," agreed Ellery. "But the answer is also reasonable. I didn't line up the troupe and attempt to uncover the impostor because it was evident that Horne was playing some sort of game. It isn't often that you'll find a murderer willing to hang about the scene of his crime. Why was Horne doing it? Why, if he wanted to commit murder, did he choose this complicated and perilous method? A dark street, a shot, a quick getaway—it would have been very easy for him to have killed his victim in the usual way. But he chose the hard way: why? I meant to find out. I wanted to give him enough rope to hang himself. Actually, he *had* to wait. There was something he still had to do, which was to kill Woody. I'll explain that in a moment.

"In addition," continued Ellery with a little frown, "there were a number of factors which challenged my curiosity and, I suppose, my intellect. Aside from motive, which was a complete mystery to me—what the devil had happened to the automatic? That was a real poser. And then, too, without a complete case— if I unmasked Horne and he stubbornly refused to talk—we should probably not have been able to secure a conviction.

"So I delayed exposing Horne, never anticipating—having no earthly reason for anticipating—another murder." He sighed. "I spent some uncomfortable moments over that, J. J. At the same time, in the most innocent way I could contrive, I began to hang around the troupe—trying to spot Horne without arousing his suspicions. Well, I was unsuccessful. They were a clannish group, and I could get nothing out of them. The man's personality was submerged in the larger personality of the troupe. I cultivated Kit Horne socially in the vain hope that Horne might communicate with her.

"But after the murder of Woody—immediately after, the next day—one of the troupe disappeared. A man who had called himself Benjy Miller. A man moreover who had been given employment on the eye of the original performance a month before on the *written recommendation* of Horne himself! A man who superficially, at least, if you discarded the color of his hair and his scar, might have been Horne. A man who—and this proved to be the clincher, as I shall demonstrate in a moment—had been 'authorized' by Horne in the letter of introduction to ride Horne's own favorite horse, *Injun;* despite the fact that there was no really sound reason for 'Horne' not to have ridden his favorite mount himself on the opening night. From these facts I could not doubt that the vanished Miller was in reality Buck Horne; and therefore Buck Horne satisfied the first qualification of my murderer: he was in the arena on horseback in the case of both crimes." I sighed.

"The second qualification of the criminal was deducible from the fifth and sixth of my major half-dozen clues. The fifth was something I was conscious of as a spectator, and it was confirmed by the newsreel sound pictures taken by Major Kirby's unit, and by Lieutenant Knowles's report. After Grant signaled the beginning of the ride I recalled but one volley of shots from the guns of the charging horsemen behind the supposed Horne. Only a few seconds elapsed between the riders' volley and the fall of the dead man to the tanbark—so few that there was not time for more than that single very slightly ragged fusillade, and then the horses and men became a milling mob, preventing further shooting. There could be no question about the fact that only one volley had been fired: in proof we found that each of the revolvers of the troupe proper had been shot off just once.

"Now the sixth and last fact was that each of these revolvers, as well as Horne's and Grant's and that mad chap Ted Lyons's, could not have fired the fatal shot; Lieutenant Knowles said undeniably that only a .25 calibre automatic pistol could have fired the fatal shot, and all but one of the weapons collected from the troupe were of .38 calibre and over. And ballistics tests proved that the exception, Lyons's .25, could not have been the murder weapon.

"What did these two facts, juxtaposed, signify? Well, fundamentally enough, if the murderer was one of the troupe and yet the examined guns of the troupe couldn't have fired the fatal shot, then the murderer had used a weapon which we had *not* examined. But how is this possible? you ask. You say: These people were thoroughly searched and the murder weapon not found. I answer: The murderer hid the weapon somewhere. Let me leave that for a moment; the immediate point is that use a .25 automatic he did, and since there was only *one* fusillade, he must have used it *at the time the guns of the troupe went off.* In other words, the murderer carried a second weapon, loaded with lethal bullets, and had discharged it at the same time he fired the blank-filled revolver. *Used, then, both hands in shooting.* Was this, I asked, an indication that the murderer was ambidextrous?"

"I'm not quite sure," I objected, "that you were justified in assuming the murderer shot both weapons off at the same time. It was a ragged fusillade, didn't you say?"

"Yes. But remember that the hands of the troupe were raised—they were shooting their blanks at the roof. I reasoned that the murderer would have been constrained not to make himself conspicuous; he would have had to shoot his blank at the roof with the others, as we know he did. But since after the single fusillade there were no other shots, I was justified in assuming that his other hand had held the lethal weapon and fired it at approximately the same time.

"But to return to this very curious little question of ambidexterity. Was it possible? Certainly, although not necessarily. But since it was possible, the trail again led back to Buck Horne, who for years had used *twin* guns. A two-gun man is, as far as shooting is concerned, ambidextrous. Buck was not only the logical suspect on other counts, then, but satisfied the qualifications of the murderer on two new counts. Not only was he a two-gun man, but he was a remarkable marksman also—testimony. The man who fired the fatal shots was a remarkable marksman—had disdained to fire more than once when, in fact, it would have been simple for him to have fired the entire magazine of the automatic before the echoes of the fusillade had died away. Check again.

"But how had he rid himself of that second weapon so cleverly that the most minute search failed to turn it up? The disappearance of the weapon was the most baffling feature of both crimes." He paused. "I was to penetrate to the secret only after the one-armed braggart, Woody, died."

"That's certainly been puzzling me," I said eagerly. "Far as I know, not one word of explanation has been written in the newspaper accounts. How the deuce did he do it? Or didn't you discover it before the end?"

"I knew the answer the day after Woody died," he replied grimly. "Let me go back for a moment. It was apparent that both murders had been committed by the same culprit; the circumstances were identical and the extraordinary disappearance of the weapon, despite another exhaustive search, indicated that the same method had been used to dispose of the weapon in the second murder as the first. The very vanishment of the weapon in the Woody murder was reasonable proof that we were dealing with the same murderer.

"Now, why had Horne killed Woody, the top-rider, before disappearing? The fact that the men were more or less professional rivals surely was too feeble to explain the act; as a matter of fact Woody had more motive—on the surface—to kill Horne than Horne had to kill Woody, for it was Woody who was the aggrieved, since Horne had appropriated what Woody considered his own spotlight. No, there was only one probable explanation: somehow Woody had discovered Horne's deception, and guessed that it was Horne who had committed the first crime. Had he confronted 'Miller' with his knowledge that Miller was really Horne, Horne would have had to kill Woody to save his own skin."

"It's all very well to theorize on possibilities," I said smartly, "but I thought you work only on demonstrable proof."

"I make that effort," murmured Ellery. "And I believe I can provide a confirmation of this theory that will convince even you, you skeptical money-changer. Where's the confirmation? In the ten thousand dollars that, having been stolen from Curly Grant's green box, was almost immediately after found in Woody's room."

"How does that confirm it?" I demanded, puzzled.

"In this way. An examination of the rifled box indicated that *Woody hadn't stolen that money.* Ah, a tall conclusion, I hear you say. Not at all. The two locks of the box had been twisted until the eye-hinges had snapped off. Both had been twisted in the *same* direction; specifically, toward the back of the box. There was a hinge on each side, remember; none at the front. Do you see now?"

"No," I said in all honesty.

"It's so reasonable," said Ellery plaintively. "By habit a man will twist consistently in one direction and with the same hand, the hand he favors, particularly if the twisting requires muscle. If he has two hasps to twist, he will twist the one on the right side first with his right hand (if he is right-handed), and then turn the box around and twist the left-hand hasp. By turning the box around he automatically puts himself again in a position to twist toward the right with the right hand. In such case the twists in the strained metal would appear in *opposite* directions rather than the same direction, as we found in the case of the Grant box. But we're talking now of normal people with two hands who favor one of the hands, as most people do. Consider Woody; he had only one hand altogether! He certainly would twist the right-hand hasp first, and then turn the box around to twist the left-hand hasp, in which case the twistings would appear in opposite directions. But the twistings actually appeared in the *same* direction. So the hasps were not twisted by Woody. Therefore Woody didn't steal the money.

"Had Woody been the thief, moreover, would he have hidden the loot in an unlocked drawer of his own dressing-room table, to be found by even the most casual search? The fact that the cash was openly left in an unlocked drawer of a table in Woody's room proves that, if he put it there himself, he did not know the money was stolen; if he did not put it there himself, then he knew nothing of the theft at all and the money was planted in his drawer to make him appear the thief.

"But to return to the rifled box. The fact that the hasps were twisted in the same direction rather than in opposite directions tends to show that the two hasps were twisted *simultaneously*— that is, the thief grasped each hasp in one hand and twisted both toward the back of the box in the same operation. Ah, but what have we here? Two strong hands, it appears! This was metal— granted, weak poor metal, but metal nevertheless; it would take strength to twist one of the hasps with even a favored, or stronger, hand; yet here the thief had exerted equal strength with *both* hands. Indication? Certainly of an ambidextrous thief. Yes, yes, I know," he continued hastily, checking the objection on my lips, "I know you're going to say it's not a foolproof conclusion. Perhaps not. All I call it is an indication, and that you can't deny.

If the thief was ambidextrous, and the murderer, Buck Horne, was ambidextrous—certainly a remarkable coincidence, eh? I was completely justified in theorizing that it was Horne who had stolen Curly Grant's money.

"But why the deuce should Horne, or Miller, or whatever you choose to call him, have stolen Curly's money—the money of his best friend's son? Desperation? Dire need? Cupidity overwhelming friendship? But see; if Horne stole that money how does it transpire that the money turns up the same day in Woody's room? Horne, then, whatever the explanation was, didn't steal the money out of cupidity; I think it is simple to reconstruct the situation. Woody having discovered Horne's identity as Miller in some way—perhaps by penetrating his disguise—confronted Horne with his knowledge. What would a man like Woody do in such a case?"

"Demand blackmail, of course—hush money," I muttered.

"Quite so. He had to appease Woody until he was able to silence him forever. He seized the opportunity presented by Grant's settlement of Curly's legacy. He stole the money, gave it to Woody—who, having no time to suspect it was Curly's, no reason to hide it—put it away in his dressing-table drawer. Horne knew that by the time the theft was discovered Woody would be dead, the money would be found, returned to Curly, and no one—except Woody, naturally!—would suffer. How clever Horne was! Had he paid Woody off with his own money, Horne could never have retrieved that money later even if it was found in Woody's drawer; as Miller he would have had no claim to it. But by using Curly's money temporarily he held on to his own wad, and Curly got his back. . . . Everything fits for Buck Horne as the criminal. He satisfies all the qualifications logically as well as plausibly."

"He was running a fearful risk, though," I said, shivering. "What could he have done had he been recognized as Horne?"

"It's hard to say," replied Ellery thoughtfully. "Yet the risk was not so great as you think. Aside from Woody only two persons, really, might recognize him because they knew him so well. Kit and Wild Bill Grant. Even Kit had been seeing her foster-father very infrequently of late years, as she told me herself. But if she did by chance penetrate the Miller disguise, Horne was sure he could depend on her loyal silence. The same was undoubtedly true of Grant, who had been Horne's closest friend from their boyhood days. All along I suspected that Grant became aware of the truth not long after the first murder; the man was a nervous wreck. The afternoon of Woody's murder he seemed to catch sight of someone, and he turned pale as a ghost; I've no doubt he saw Miller's face there—a reminder that Miller was Horne."

Ellery lit another cigaret and puffed slowly at it. "It was this very friendship with Grant—on which Horne relied—that provided the trap to draw Horne back after his disappearance in the Miller identity. I knew that only one thing would bring him back; danger that Grant, his best friend, or Kit, whom he considered his daughter, would be accused of his own crimes." He paused. "I suppose it was a wretched trick, but I couldn't help myself. I chose Grant as living bait for self-evident reasons, knowing that the old-timer's prime virtue of loyalty to a friend would not permit Horne to let that friend suffer for crimes of which he was innocent. But how to frame Grant so that he might be arrested? The only thing that would force a quick arrest would be concrete evidence—obviously the best evidence in any case is the weapon found in possession, presumably, of a suspect. The fact that Grant couldn't have committed the crime for pure reasons of position I knew would make no difference; apparently no one else had analyzed correctly the matters of direction and angle of entry. And I knew that action would be swift after Grant's arrest.

"At any rate, I had to find that automatic. I did find it—by accident, you say? Perhaps not quite by accident. Look at it this way. Why had Miller disappeared at all? Well, his crimes were committed, he was through, he now had to look out for his future safety. But Miller was not Miller; Miller was really Buck Horne; Miller was a name and an identity manufactured for a temporary and specific purpose. Poor dad—he wondered why he could find no trace of this Benjy gentleman's past! There wasn't any. So I put myself in Horne's place. If *Miller* disappeared, for whom would the police search? Obviously, for *Miller.* The thing to do, then, was to *disappear as Miller,* and immediately discard the Miller disguise and identity forever. The police would then look for Miller forever without the slightest success. But if he was going to put the police on an eternally false trail in an eternal search for a nonexistent person, it would not hurt—would help, in fact—to have the police believe that the vanished Miller was the murderer of Buck Horne and Woody. The weapon plus the disappearance would be enough for the police. So I figured that Miller, or Horne, had left that weapon somewhere to be found by the police *after his disappearance.* Where could he leave it? In one of two places: his hotel room, or the dressing room he had occupied in the *Colosseum.* I chose the dressing room first and, sure enough, there was the automatic.

"Having found it, that very night I myself—don't look at me that way, stranger!—I myself planted the automatic in Grant's room, first making sure that he would be out for the evening. You know the rest. I steered the Inspector there, we found the weapon, Grant was arrested, the papers obligingly broadcast the news for me—and Horne showed up, per schedule, to keep his friend, as he thought, from being convicted of the crimes. Showed up, incidentally, with the Miller disguise on, I suppose, to prove that he *had* been Miller. And that," said Ellery with a wry smile, "spells finis. Pretty, eh?"

Djuna refilled the coffee cups, and we drank in silence for some time. "Very pretty," I said after a while. "Very pretty indeed. But not complete. You still haven't solved the mystery of how Horne secreted the weapon so beautifully in the first place."

Ellery started from a reverie. "Oh, that!" he said with a little deprecatory wave of his hand. "After putting it off to the last, I quite forgot to clear it up. Interesting, of course. But again mere child's play." I grunted. "Oh, yes, J.J., it was very simple—once you knew. It's always the simplest mystery that appears to be the deepest. Our old friend Chesterton employs the psychology of the simple mystery so very cleverly! It seems a shame—Father Brown couldn't have been here" He laughed, and wriggled in his chair. "Well, what was the problem? The problem was: Where had that automatic been all the time after the first murder, and second murder, too? What had Miller, or Horne, done with it to have made it apparently vanish so that not even an exhaustive search by scores of detectives turned it up?

"In Major Kirby's projection room the second time—after the Woody affair, you know—I discovered that the first newsreel scenes of the Horne murder did not constitute *all* the film shot at the *Colosseum* that night, but was a shortened version for theatre distribution.

"When the Major ran the deleted scenes for me, we saw things we could not have seen except on the night of the murder, and then of course we were incapable physically and emotionally of panoramic observation. In one scene after the murder the camera caught that bibulous little cowboy, Boone, leading the string of riderless horses to water, at one end of the arena. One horse was balky, refused to drink. Boone, rather drunker than usual, committed the unforgivable sin of lashing the animal; and lo! into the field of the lens rushed a cowboy, snatched the whip from Boone, and at once soothed the balky horse. I learned from Boone that this angry, horse-calming gentleman from the wide open spaces was none other than our friend Miller! And the horse? The horse was a canny chunk of precious old meat named *Injun*. And who was *Injun? Injun* was Buck Horne's animal! Do you get the implications? Well, for one thing Miller's ability to quiet an irate beast who belonged to Horne confirmed the theory that Miller was Horne. For another, the odd reaction of the horse, his *refusal* to drink when all the other animals quite eagerly lapped up the water, gave me an equally odd thought, which was fed by the fact that 'Miller' had leaped across the arena and prevented Boone from—what, J.J.?"

"From lashing the horse," I said.

"No. *From forcing the horse to drink.*" Ellery chuckled as I gaped. "The automatic, remember, had not been found anywhere in the bowl. The premises from roof to cellar had been ransacked, all the humans searched to the point of nausea. Even the horses' rigging had been scrupulously gone over. Yet there was *one* thing, strange as it sounds, which had *not* been searched." He paused. "*The horses themselves.*" He paused again.

I tortured my brain. "I'm afraid," I confessed at last, "I don't get you."

He waved a cheerful hand. "Because it's ridiculous, eh? Yet examine it. Was it possible that the automatic had been hidden, not *on* a horse, but in a horse?"

I stared incredulously.

"Yes," he said with a broad grin, "you've guessed it. I remembered that *Injun* was not an ordinary animal. Oh, no. Boone—and Kit, too—had said that *Injun* was Buck's old *trick movie horse*. And there it was. *Injun*, by refusing to drink, as well as told me that at that very moment he had the pestiferously elusive automatic—a small weapon only four and a half inches long, mind, and flat to the bargain—*in his mouth*."

"Well, I'll be damned," I gasped.

"You may well be," murmured Ellery. "From that conclusion a reconstruction of events was simple. Horne, after shooting his double, had merely leaned forward and slipped the automatic into *Injun's* mouth. Oh, *Injun* knew who was on his back!—a little paint on the cheek, and dyed hair, wouldn't fool an old detective with such sharp senses as a horse. All Horne had to do, then, was wait until all the searching was over, knowing that *Injun* would keep the gun in his mouth and keep his mouth shut; and then, after the string of horses had been taken to the Tenth Avenue stables to be bedded down for the night, he retrieved the pistol from *Injun's* mouth. The ruse had been so successful that Horne had no hesitation in repeating the procedure in the second crime, using, of course, the same weapon."

"But wasn't there a fearful danger that *Injun* would get tired of keeping the gun in his mouth," I said, "and would drop it right on the scene of the crime? What a *debacle* that would have been!"

"I fancy not. If Horne had decided on that method of disposing of his weapon, he must have been certain there wouldn't be a slip-up. Which automatically makes you conclude that *Injun*, trained in tricks by Horne from colt-hood, must also have been taught to keep his mouth closed over whatever Horne slipped into it *until Horne himself ordered him to open it*. You can do it with dogs, you know; and horses are certainly just as intelligent, if not more so. . . . Incidentally, I now knew why Horne had, against all habit, employed a .25 calibre automatic as the murder weapon. He needed the tiniest weapon which would be fatal; a weapon which was least bulky, least weighty, considering its depository."

Ellery rose, stretched, and yawned. But I was sitting there by the fire still puzzled; and he looked down at me with a quizzical grin. "What's the matter, O Rain-in-the-Face?" he asked. "Something still bothering you?"

"Decidedly. Everything's been so dashed *mysterious* about this problem," I complained. "I mean—the papers ran just the barest details of the story, and nobody seems to know much about anything. I remember a few weeks ago when the story came out, after Horne shot himself—"

"In this very room," murmured Ellery lightly; but his eyes were pained. "*That* was a moment, my masters! Poor Djuna fainted. Don't think so much of blood and thunder now, do you, Djuna, old son?"

Djuna became a little pale about the jowls; he smiled in a sickly fashion and crept out of the room.

"What I meant to say," I went on, irritated, "is that I hunted through every darned sheet in the City and I couldn't find a solitary word about *motive.*"

"Ah, motive," said Ellery thoughtfully; and then very quickly he went to his secretary and stopped short, frowning down upon his desk set.

"Yes, motive," I repeated doggedly. "What the devil's all the secrecy about? Why did Horne kill this poor chap who'd been his movie double years back? There must be a reason. Man doesn't plan a complicated crime and forfeit his rightful identity forever just for fun. And I'm sure Horne was no maniac."

"Maniac? Oh, no, not a maniac." Ellery seemed to be having unusual difficulty in expressing himself. "Ah—you see, granted that he had to kill somebody, the question arose as to ways and means. Should he kill the double openly, and allow himself to be arrested, tried, and executed? Self-preservation, and a shrinking from the shame which would be heaped upon Kit's head, made him decide against this. Should he kill the double and commit suicide? The same reasons said no. So he took the intricate but really only way out, according to his lights. You might say—"

"I *do* say," I interrupted severely.

"—that it was silly for Horne so to have planned his crime that in working it out he lost his identity *as* Horne. But actually was it so silly? What was he losing—his money? He had taken practically all of it with him! His career? Ah, but that was just a pleasant fiction, he must have realized at the last; an old man for years he had stubbornly refused to bow to Time, chafing against the inevitable, and now at last he saw that there *was* no movie career in the offing, that he was a useless old husk, that Grant's proposed investment of money in Horne's comeback was merely a friendly gesture, nothing more. I repeat: What was he losing by dying as Buck Horne in—I might point out—a last blaze of publicity?"

"Yes, but what was he *gaining?*" I asked dryly.

"A good deal, from his point of view. He was gaining peace of mind, he was satisfying his peculiar code of honor, and he was making a sacrifice for the good of Kit. Kit told the Inspector and me that Horne was carrying a hundred thousand dollar insurance policy, of which she was the only beneficiary. Now mark this. He had contracted an enormous debt by his gambling losses at Hunter's place; forty-two thousand dollars! How was he to pay it? And yet pay it he must, according to his code. With his movie career blasted, with his personal wealth insufficient to cover the debt—unless he sold his ranch, and this I suppose he could not bring himself to do, desiring it to remain Kit's—how was he to pay Hunter? It was literally true that he was worth more dead than alive. So, by passing out of the picture as Horne, he made the hundred thousand available, liquid—available to pay off the gambling debt (he knew Kit well enough to foresee that she would take care of *that*), and the balance he knew would safeguard Kit's future. If you grant him the desire to accomplish these things and still live out the few remaining years of his life, even if anonymously, then surely it is apparent that Horne, as Horne, had to die—that in achieving the death of his double Horne had to go through the whole complicated plan of presumably dying himself."

"Yes, yes," I said impatiently, "that may all be very true, but you're evading the important point. You've wandered far, my lad! You said before: 'Granted that he had to kill somebody.' Well, I don't grant any such thing! That's what's bothering me. *Why* did he have to kill somebody? Specifically, why did he have to kill his double?"

"Oh, I imagine there was a reason," muttered Ellery, without turning.

"You *imagine?*" I cried. "Don't you *know?*"

Ellery faced about and I saw something very grave and determined in his eyes. "Yes, J.J., I do know. I didn't know until Horne himself told me. Told me and the Inspector. . . ."

"But I thought Miss Horne and the Grant fellow were here, too, that night," I said.

"Horne sent them away." He paused again. "And before he shot himself he told us."

"Does Grant know?" I asked abruptly. "Old man Grant?"

He tapped a cigaret on his thumbnail. "Grant knows."

I mumbled: "He sent the girl away. . . . Hmm. I suppose she meant everything to him, and he would do anything to protect her—his foster-daughter—her safety, her reputation. . . . If there had been something—well, doubtful, about her parentage and the double knew it and was threatening to tell Kit. . . . She's an orphan, didn't you say?"

Ellery was silent. For so long a time that I thought he had not heard me. Then he said, in a very sharp tone: "What did you think of the new Nobel award for literature, J.J.? It seems to me—"

But to my vague and gossipy conjectures he preserved a loud and stubborn silence.

A silence, appropriately enough, that was Buck Horne's epitaph.

DISCUSSION QUESTIONS

- At the moment of the "Challenge to the Reader," were you able to predict any part of the solution to the case?

- After learning the solution, were there any clues you realized you had missed?

- Did any aspects of the plot date the story? If so, which ones?

- Would the story be different if it were set in the present day? If so, how?

- What role did the setting play in the narrative?

- If you were one of the main characters, would you have acted differently at any point in the story?

- Did you identify with any of the characters? If so, who?

- What sort of detective is Ellery Queen? What qualities make him appealing to readers? What qualities make him an effective crime-solver?

- Did this novel remind you of anything else you've read? If so, what?

- If you've read other Ellery Queen novels, how does this compare with what you've read?

H.F. Heard, *A Taste for Honey*

Dolores Hitchens, *The Cat Saw Murder*
Introduced by Joyce Carol Oates

Dorothy B. Hughes, *Dread Journey*
Introduced by Sarah Weinman
Dorothy B. Hughes, *Ride the Pink Horse*
Introduced by Sara Paretsky
Dorothy B. Hughes, *The So Blue Marble*

W. Bolingbroke Johnson, *The Widening Stain*
Introduced by Nicholas A. Basbanes

Baynard Kendrick, *The Odor of Violets*

Frances and Richard Lockridge, *Death on the Aisle*

John P. Marquand, *Your Turn, Mr. Moto*
Introduced by Lawrence Block

Stuart Palmer, *The Puzzle of the Happy Hooligan*

Otto Penzler, ed., *Golden Age Detective Stories*

Ellery Queen, *The Chinese Orange Mystery*
Ellery Queen, *The Dutch Shoe Mystery*
Ellery Queen, *The Egyptian Cross Mystery*
Ellery Queen, *The Siamese Twin Mystery*

Patrick Quentin, *A Puzzle for Fools*

Clayton Rawson, *Death from a Top Hat*

Craig Rice, *Eight Faces at Three*
Introduced by Lisa Lutz
Craig Rice, *Home Sweet Homicide*

Mary Roberts Rinehart, *The Haunted Lady*
Mary Roberts Rinehart, *Miss Pinkerton*
Introduced by Carolyn Hart
Mary Roberts Rinehart, *The Red Lamp*
Mary Roberts Rinehart, *The Wall*

Joel Townsley Rogers, *The Red Right Hand*
Introduced by Joe R. Lansdale

Vincent Starrett, *The Great Hotel Murder*
Introduced by Lyndsay Faye

Cornell Woolrich, *The Bride Wore Black*
Introduced by Eddie Muller
Cornell Woolrich, *Waltz into Darkness*
Introduced by Wallace Stroby